ALONE

Praise for the works of E. J. Noyes

Ask, Tell

"This is a book with everything I love about top quality lesbian fiction: a fantastic romance between two wonderful women I can relate to, a location that really made me think again about something I thought I knew well, and brilliant pacing and scene-setting. I cannot recommend this novel highly enough."

- Rainbow Book Reviews

"Noyes totally blew my mind from the first sentence. I went in timidly, and I came away awaiting her next release with baited breath. I really love how Noyes is able to get below the surface of the DADT legislation. She really captures the longing, the heart-break, and especially the isolation that LGBTQ soldiers had to endure because the alternative was being deemed unfit to serve by their own government. I applaud Noyes for getting to the heart of the matter and giving a very important representation of what living and serving under this legislation truly meant for LGBTQ men and women of service."

- The Lesbian Review

"EJ Noyes was able to deliver on so many levels… This book is going to take you on a roller coaster ride of ups and downs that you won't expect but it's so unbelievably worth it."

- Les Rêveur Reviews

"Noyes clearly undertook a mammoth amount of research. I was totally engrossed. I'm not usually a reader of romance novels, but this one gripped me. The personal growth of the main character, the rich development of her fabulous best friend, Mitch, and the well-handled tension between Sabine and her love interest were all fantastic. This one definitely deserves five stars."

- ceLEStial books Reviews

Turbulence

"Wow… and when I say 'wow' I mean… WOW. After the author's debut novel *Ask, Tell* got to my list of best books of 2017, I was wondering if that was just a fluke. Fortunately for us lesfic readers, now it's confirmed: E.J. Noyes CAN write. Not only that, she can write different genres…Written in first person from Isabelle's point of view, the reader gets into her headspace with all her insecurities, struggles and character traits. Alongside Isabelle, we discover Audrey's personality, her life story and, most importantly, her feelings. Throughout the book, Ms. Noyes pushes us down a rollercoaster of emotions as we accompany Isabelle in her journey of self-discovery. In the process, we laugh, suffer and enjoy the ride."

- Gaby, goodreads

"This was hot, steamy, even a little emotional… and I loved every second of it. This book is in first person. I know some don't care for that, but it works for this book, really. Always being in Isabella's head, not knowing for sure what Audrey was thinking, gave me almost a little suspense. I just love the way Noyes writes. I know I am fan-girling out a bit here, but her books make me happy. All other romance fans, I easily recommend this. I just hope I don't have to wait too long for another Noyes book."

- Lex Kent, goodreads

"The entire story just flowed from the first page! E. J. Noyes did a superb job of bringing out Isabelle and Audrey's personalities, faults, erratic emotions and the burning passion they shared. The chemistry between both women was so palpable! I felt as though the writer drizzled every word she wrote with love, combustible desire and intense longing."

- The Lesbian Review

Gold

This is Noyes third book, and her writing just keeps getting better and better with each release. She gives us such amazing characters that are easy for anyone to relate to. And she makes them so endearing that you can't help but want them to overcome the past and move forward toward their happily ever after.

- The Lesbian Review

"This book is exactly the way I wish romance authors would get back to writing romance. This is what I want to read. If you are a Noyes fan, get this book. If you are a romance fan, get this book. I didn't even talk about the skiing… if you are a skiing fan, get this book."

- Lex Kent, goodreads

Pin's Reviews—"I love everything about it—the setting, the protagonists, sweet and convincing romance, a nice bunch of secondary characters, the skiing…The writing is excellent with great dialogue and pacing. There is some well-placed angst along with a really believable conflict. On top of all that, the ending (the entire last chapter) is truly great. I love when the author knows how to write a really satisfying ending."

- Pin, goodreads

Other Bella Books by E. J. Noyes

Ask, Tell
Turbulence
Gold
Ask Me Again

About the Author

E. J. Noyes lives in Australia with her wife, a needy cat, aloof chickens and too many horses. When not indulging in her love of reading and writing, E. J. argues with her hair and pretends to be good at clay target shooting.

ALONE

E. J. NOYES

BELLA
BOOKS
2019

First Bella Books Edition 2019

Editor: Cath Walker
Cover Designer: Judith Fellows

ISBN: 978-1-64247-047-5

Acknowledgments

This novel is a little different (good different, I promise!) and I'm so grateful to have had a bunch of awesome people who got what I was trying to say, and then told me when I wasn't saying it very well...

Christina, thank you for all your wonderful nuances, and your excitement. Barupies forever!

Thanks, Kate and Andy, for yet again giving me so much of your time and brainpower. Also, Kate, thanks for the gentle encouragement every time I said, "But it's just so *weird*!"

BFF Kate, even though you read two versions of this, cheered me on, and had really good and constructive ideas, I'm not thanking you until you read THAT BOOK. Oh and maybe that other book and its sequel. I believe we're at an impasse xx.

Ann, thanks for teaching me far more about the American taxation system than I ever thought I'd need to know.

Thank you to the Bella Crew, who are all heroes—complete with pinned-on capes, and undies on the outside.

Cath, I hope you know that it's only *less work* because of everything you've taught me. Best. Editor. Ever.

Pheebs...I'm trying so hard to think of some clever tie-in, like how being with you means I'm not alone, but I can't figure out the words. I'm sure you can imagine what I'm kinda trying to say. You're really great, I love you. Aren't you glad you married such a wordsmith?

CHAPTER ONE

My foot catches on the clothes hamper and I stumble forward, only just stopping myself before I hit the glass-enclosed shower.

"Fuck!"

The sound of my voice startles me. How long is it since I spoke aloud?

At least a few days?

Maybe a week?

I say it again, quieter this time. "Fuck." The word tastes strange, rolling around my mouth like something foul needing to be spat out. I want to try another word, a softer one to balance the expletive, and reach deep into my brain for something to say. Nobody will hear me, so it doesn't matter what I choose. I settle on my name. "Celeste." My voice catches on the second syllable. I try again and add my last name. "Celeste Thorne."

Studying my face in the bathroom mirror, I state as clearly as I can in a voice rusty with disuse, "I am twenty-nine years old. My birthday is January sixth. Today is day..." A glance at the calendar tacked up beside the mirror. "One thousand, one hundred and eighty-one. I am still a person." I lean closer, and the features staring back don't seem to belong to me. "I am still a person."

The more I stare, the more I think I look like a hosed-down watercolor painting. My face seems to melt, features sliding into each other until I see Mother...then my younger sister, Riley... my foster mothers and my adoptive mother. Teachers. Lovers. Friends. I see everyone except myself.

Have I gone crazy? Just a little? Probably. Anyone would. I exist in memories, both old and new. I exist with my false things.

The false things only began a few months ago. It's mostly voices, but sometimes I feel a phantom touch. Or I can smell Mother. My birth mother. Stale sweat, cigarette smoke, and the cloying smell of cheaply-cut meth and sour clothing that's been left in the washer too long or put on while still damp. The arrival of her stench panics me like nothing I've ever known and I have to smell myself—my armpits and hair and skin. I have to do it, even though I know it's not me because I always smell the same. Clean, like soap and shampoo and deodorant because I can't stand the thought of being anything like *her*. Grabbing a double handful of my shirt and inhaling the fresh, laundered scent helps to clear my olfactory hallucinations.

But I can't do anything to get rid of the other hallucinations.

Occasionally I have the sensation of a hand brushing lightly down my back. Other times, a bruising grip on my bicep that makes me desperate to jerk my arm away. Sometimes it's a single spoken word, or if I'm lucky I'll get a full sentence or two. And then they are gone. It's not me touching myself and it's not me talking to myself in my head. I hear *them* the way I hear birds outside, rain on the roof or the gurgle of coffee brewing.

Even though I know none of it's real, it doesn't stop it from happening. It can't be real, can it? No. The reality is that there's only me, and now after more than three years here, I'm not even sure I know who *me* is anymore.

The Controllers know. I told them right away and I dutifully record each of these "false things" in my daily logs. It's a natural reaction, they told me. A perfectly acceptable outcome—expected actually. My request for medication to make the false things go away was denied. I could almost hear their incredulous laughter behind the screen as the cursor blinked and blinked and blinked. Eventually, I had to ask them the question.

SE9311: It's not you, is it? You're not here playing the voices in my ear somehow? You're not doing something to make me think something is touching me?
Cont A: No. I assure you that nobody is there.

Nobody is there. Here. Except me.

I mark off another day on the calendar and swallow my dietary supplements with a handful of water from directly under the faucet, as I do every morning. I do everything I'm supposed to. I take my vitamins. I work out and eat a balanced diet. I don't drink. Much. It's important that my body remains strong for the duration of the study. They don't seem to care so much about my mind. But I guess that's the whole point.

The advertisement was small and plain, taped by an unknown person to the wall of the coffee shop I was planning to quit at the end of the month. I would have missed the sheet of paper if I hadn't been looking at the hot blonde sipping a macchiato underneath it. I set down the milk I was steaming, slipped out from behind the counter and murmuring an apology, leaned over the blonde to pull the flyer off the wall.

Subjects wanted for psychological study.
3 years minimum, 4 years maximum.
Attractive compensation.

"Who put this there?" I asked Brett, my slimy and overly-handsy boss. I could tell by the sound of the milk frothing that he was fucking up the latte I'd abandoned.

Brett shrugged and started pouring. "Some guy in a suit, this morning. Paid me fifty bucks. Did you restock the sugar like I asked?"

I shot a withering glance at his foam art. Even after eight years owning a café, he still couldn't make a damned foam fern. "Yes, all the dispensers. I'm taking a break. Right now."

"Jeee-sus, Thorne. Get your ass back here."

But I was already out the rear door, phone in hand. Standing against the wall near the dumpsters, shivering without my coat, I dialed. A professional voice answered almost immediately with a simple, "Hello, how may I assist you?" Nothing more, nothing to tell me who I'd called.

My words floated into cold air on visible breath. "Um, hi. I'm calling about an ad I saw? The psychological study?"

"Can you quote the reference for me please?"

"Reference?"

"At the bottom of the page, ma'am, there will be a reference code." Patient, encouraging.

I lifted the paper, skimming over it. On closer look I saw it in small lettering, plain as anything—Quote this reference. Heat warmed my cheeks. "Uh, S-E-forward slash-eight-three."

"Transferring you now."

Once I'd been assured that it wasn't a joke, and had answered a few basic questions, I was invited to come in for a proper interview the next day. Brett told me if I skipped work I shouldn't bother coming back. I handed over my apron, told him I'd come by Friday to pick up my paycheck, and walked out.

Now, years later, I can't remember what they asked at the interview. All I remember is an older guy in an expensive-looking suit telling me the study would require me to live in total isolation, secluded on a small compound in a remote place. I was to be without human contact and they would study the effects. Something about colonization of other planets—seeing how regular people cope on their own should something untoward happen to their fellow space travelers, and if they're able to maintain a fragment of sanity and self-awareness to stay alive. Sanctioned by the government. Full ethics approval according to the code. One hundred percent legal and above board.

I would also be responsible for maintaining the food and energy systems that they would be testing concurrently with the psychological study. Gotta make sure you can eat, drink, and stay warm on Venus while you're trying not to go crazy from loneliness, I guess. Or is that…stay cool on Venus?

I also clearly heard him say that the pay was one hundred thousand dollars per year for the three years minimum I would be required to complete. Once I made it to three years, I would then receive five hundred dollars for each additional day I stayed. If I made it the full four years I'd also earn a bonus, leaving me richer by the lovely round figure of half a million dollars. Even after setting aside almost a third of my payment for tax, it would leave me enough to buy a house, a car and get me set up to go back to college if I wanted. I'd leaned forward eagerly and asked where to sign.

The Suit had laughed and ushered me into another room for compatibility testing, followed by swaths of psychological assessments, personality mapping, physicals, and endless multiple-choice quizzes. I still don't know who is responsible for the experiment—the identity of the research institution was hidden behind layers of names and subterfuge, and in the documents I signed they are simply called, for all legal intents and purposes, "The Organization." While reading my contract, I learned an unnamed agency contracted The Organization to conduct the studies on their behalf. It *has* to be NASA. Maybe they'll let me be an astronaut when I'm done in here.

Being a test subject seemed simple enough, even enticing. I have no family, few friends, no girlfriend. The only women I slept with were the friends of friends or those I picked up in bars. Nobody would miss me. Except maybe my good friend, Heather. And Allison.

Allison. Sweet and kind, but fierce and opinionated. A casual but generous lover. My face in the mirror turns into hers. Why am I thinking of Allison now? On the morning I flew out to start this life, she left me a drunk voice mail, sent just after two a.m. Though I know there's no way the Controllers would let me listen to it, even if the message wasn't long gone, I'm suddenly desperate to hear the voice mail again. Screwing my eyes closed, I travel back through memories until I find it.

"A text? Celeste, you fucking bitch. Have some balls." A long, silent pause. "Call me." Then a sigh, and in her sigh, I hear everything. It's a weary exhalation as though she is having an epiphany in those few seconds. "Actually…don't."

Years ago, before I surrendered my phone to The Organization, I listened to the message over and over again. I memorized every rise and fall in the rhythm of those thirteen words. Unlucky thirteen. I became addicted to the sound of defeat in Alli's voice, as if she'd only just then realized that I wasn't really worth it. She wasn't the first person to reach that conclusion.

The face in the mirror becomes my own again.

I pull my long hair into a messy ponytail, dress and rush outside into the cold air for my morning jog. Three loops around the compound will take just over forty minutes, hopping over fallen logs and bounding across the creek. I keep my eyes on the ground, wary of things that want to trip me. A sprained or broken limb could be disastrous.

One hundred and eighty-one days ago when I chipped the corner of a tooth on a sneaky olive pit, Controller C instructed me to take a sleeping pill at a specified time. I woke up with a cotton ball taped to the crook of my elbow, a repaired tooth and no idea who fixed it. When I run my tongue over my molar, I feel the slightly rough edge of the filling. Must be hard to get a dentist and all the equipment needed for perfect dental work to wherever the hell I am. I imagine X-ray machines and the like for broken bones would be nearly impossible. I've lasted this long, and there's no way I'm leaving and missing out on that extra money and my bonus payment because of my own carelessness.

I slow to a walk. The inch of snow crunches underfoot and reminds me of winters when I lived in Wyoming, Illinois, Michigan, Washington, New York, Ohio, Iowa, Colorado, Vermont, and countless other places that have faded from my brain. Wrapping my arms tightly around my midsection, I walk to the far northern edge of my fenceless cage. The compound is unfenced for normality, they told me, because for some reason it's important that I feel I'm living a regular life. Regular. It's a laughable description.

But I don't laugh.

I stop and lean back against one of the poles topped by a security camera and can feel the cold hard stripe of the metal against my back, even through my hoodie. The cameras mounted on these poles around the compound face out, not in. I think it's for my security. Not my surveillance. If they wanted to, I'm sure they could swivel the cameras to watch me. Watch me running, collecting my monthly supply drop, polishing the solar panels or tending my garden in the greenhouse. Watch me losing my sanity a little bit at a time.

I brace my back and push away from the pole to cool off with one more lap at a walk. The compound is an uneven shape with zones that follow the dips and curves of the landscape rather than being perfect concentric circles. I follow the line of the green zone which starts where the trees grow denser into a real forest. The zone is clearly marked with metal signs every thirty feet or so, and I'm careful to stay a few feet away and in the white zone where it's safe.

Despite being told very clearly what would happen if I stepped past the invisible border into the green zone or beyond into the yellow and red, the first week I was here I tried it out. Why wouldn't I? There was nothing better to do. Whenever I think of crossing that line, my limbs tremble with the memory of the moment I went from white to green.

The hard pulse from the implant embedded in my left bicep was instantaneous. Sharp current through my muscles made them seize immediately and I fell to my hands and knees. Twitching, trying to crawl back to the white, I was too slow and the implant shocked me again. I lay groaning into the dirt, finally managing to drag myself to safety where I stayed for what felt like hours, unable to make myself move. I thought I'd peed myself but it was only the wet ground seeping through my jeans.

Since then I keep a respectful distance from the invisible barrier, not wanting to find out what would happen were I to go into the yellow. Green is not overly painful—sort of what I imagine being tasered would feel like—but it's not a sensation I want to inflict voluntarily on myself again.

Rubbing gloved hands over my face, I stroll toward Hug Tree and wrap my arms around its trunk. My hands meet my arms midway between wrist and elbow on the other side, and I cling to the smooth bark, pressing myself into it. The tree can't hug me but it relieves the tension in my muscles. It gives me pressure back against a body that has forgotten how to be held. If I close my eyes and try really hard, I can almost imagine I'm anywhere but here. I can pretend I'm in a nice home, being hugged by someone who really loves me.

"Nobody loves you, nobody wants to hug you, you're pathetic," Mother tells me. Her voice has a familiar biting sneer to it. "You're too fuckin' needy. Remember rule number one?"

I do, and I recite it in my head. *Never let you see how much I needed you and never let you see how much you could hurt me.*

CHAPTER TWO

Freshly showered and with a mug of sweet black tea in hand, I sign in to the computer system and send my logs from yesterday so they'll be ready for review before my daily session. There are still thirty minutes before one of the Controllers will come online for my check-in, plenty of time to eat before my "human" contact. I make and eat a simple breakfast of frozen hash browns and powdered scrambled eggs in the clean modern kitchen and waste time wandering aimlessly around the clean modern house.

Everything here is better than what I've left behind. The food is good and usually what I ask for. The dwelling is comfortable and well thought out—a hall connects my bedroom to an open plan living space and kitchen, with bathroom, computer room, and stairs down to the basement branching off along the long hallway. The house is full of high-tech appointments and appliances, and when I first arrived it still smelled of new construction and fresh paint.

I don't pay rent, I have no bills and my time is mostly my own. Most people would say that I want for nothing. Except the one thing I cannot have. No human contact, at all. No faces or voices, which means no voice or video calls. No movies. No television. No music with vocals. No books with author pictures on the back page.

A few months into my stay, I used the colored pencils and paper supplied by the Controllers to draw faces. Happy faces, sad faces, angry faces. I stuck them around the habitat and gave each one of them names and exciting backgrounds. We had conversations and shared our hopes and dreams and stories about our lives, until one night getting up to pee after too much beer, I caught sight of my mass of floating heads. In the dim moonlight they looked like the faces from that movie about that village of creepy demon kids. I flicked all the lights on as quickly as I could and threw my *friends* in the trash.

Yankee Doodle went to—stop. Day two of this repeat. Not so bad really. The repetitions started early on, like a radio constantly tuned to the most annoying station. My life is a series of uber-persistent earworms. I've had song lyrics, lines from books and movies, and things people said to me stuck in my head for hours, days, a week sometimes. Four or five months ago, I was stalled on two lines from a *Twilight* movie for eighteen days straight and contemplated running into the red zone to knock myself out, just for some reprieve.

I settle in the computer room with my second mug—coffee this time—and navigate to the logging interface to start my daily report by documenting what I've done so far this morning. How I feel. What I think. I'll come back and forth during the day to add things, but I never edit what I've already written. I don't like to look back.

The Organization's contact requirements aren't arduous. Every morning I must engage in an instant messaging "conversation" with a Controller. I have to give them daily text logs, something more than *Today I inflated the tires on the ATV and planted potatoes.* And once a week I'm obliged to record a video log—minimum and maximum time not specified—they just want to see me talking, probably so they can gauge something from my speech patterns and expressions.

Within today's text log, I begin a list of stuff that I miss, something I started early in my stay.

Things I miss:
-Lou's deep-dish pizza.
-Long flights of stairs, walking up and jogging down.
-Fresh milk.
-Walking down the street holding hands with someone.

The messaging system overrides what I'm working on, sliding down like a window shade, forcing me to interact. *Stuck a feather in his*—stop.

Today it's Controller B. Even after years of messaging with the four people behind the screen, I have no idea of who they are. Male. Female. Super sophisticated AI. They are nothing more than text on a monitor. They know everything about me but I know hardly anything about them except the little I've gleaned from those words. In the beginning I was afraid and obsequious. Now I'm casual and indifferent.

Cont B: Good morning. How are you feeling?

SE9311: Fine, thanks.

Cont B: You have a supply drop scheduled for tonight.

SE9311: Great, thanks. Did you get me new sunglasses?

Cont B: Three pairs. Try not to lose these.

I grin. Sometimes I order supplies just for the hell of it, but this time, I really did lose my sunglasses. It's completely ridiculous, because obviously there are only so many places they could be but despite a week of looking, I still can't find them.

SE9311: I'll try.

Cont B: Why haven't you recorded a video log this week?

SE9311: I have a pimple.

Cont B: No you don't. Nice try.

Of course they know I don't. There's a single camera in the corner of the computer room that they probably use to record me while I'm in here, but nowhere else inside, because they think being constantly watched would change my normal behavior. What's normal? I do yoga and dance and perform elaborate, silent sock-puppet theater. I walk around naked when I feel like it, which is quite frequently. I sing loudly and off-key. Looking up at the camera, I flash them an apologetic smile followed by a facetious salute.

SE9311: Caught me.

Cont B: It's been 6 days since your last video log. Please submit one by the end of tomorrow. Do you have anything else to report?

It doesn't seem like six days have passed since I last recorded myself talking about random things.

SE9311: Nothing to report, but one question - is Venus the planet hot or cold?

Cont B: Hot. Closer to the sun than Earth. Sun, Mercury, Venus, Earth, Mars…

Derp, of course.

SE9311: Thanks. Astronomy always confuses me.

Cont B: No problem. I'll talk to you on my next shift.

Talk is a relative term. I haven't *talked* to anyone since day zero, unless I count conversations with myself and the false things. And I don't. I stare at the list I started working on before Controller B arrived, pause and add three letters.

-Sex.

The cursor blinks…blinks…blinks, waiting for me to elaborate. After all these months this is the first time I've listed *sex* and I'm not entirely sure why I just typed that word. It's always surprised me but until this moment, I think I've missed the idea of sex rather than the actual act. But right now, I'm aware of a desperate ache, a longing so deep that I wonder if it'll ever go away. I blame thinking about Allison. Seeing those three letters unleashes something and I type frantically.

I miss fucking. I miss my mouth on breasts, teeth on nipples, fingers inside me stroking and pushing me over the edge. I miss waking up with a lover beside me. I miss the way women smell. I miss whispered confessions and desperate directives. I miss hair trailing over my skin. I miss the taste as she comes in my mouth, thick and hot.

Someone's going to have an interesting time reading over my logs from today. The words stir me further, building to a throb that threatens to grow and smother me. I can't write anything else because I'm suddenly overwhelmed with need. I leave without saving my log, and rush into my bedroom where I strip off my clothes. I'm already wet.

My gratification is fast and hard, nipple held tightly between thumb and forefinger for exquisite pain. I think of nothing but a faceless, voiceless woman straddling my face with her sex in my mouth and a hand grasping my hair. Middle finger stroking, stroking, sliding hard and fast until I climax in a sweaty, shivering mess. Coming down, softly playing that bundle of nerves, I feel the burn again and I push another climax through on the back of the first. The second is bigger, harder, yanking the cords of my muscles and lifting me from the bed, back arched, my cry loud and hoarse. I lie sweaty and trembling for a while and wait for my body to solidify.

"You always love it when I do that," Allison says in her bedroom voice.

I ignore her and put tentative fingers in my mouth, tasting what remains of my arousal. It's bitter, unsatisfying and nothing like the taste of a woman who has just come in my mouth.

* * *

Whenever we play games, Celeste One is hard to predict, sometimes good and sometimes bad. Celeste Two is a sneaky, underhanded bitch. Celeste Three just isn't very smart. I slide the tiles around the holder, rearrange my D and E, and glare at the empty seat opposite me. "I can't believe you took my spot, Two. I had the best word lined up." I stare at the board for a minute then align tiles in a subpar spot. DRESS. Double letter on the S. Eight. I add it to Celeste One's score and update the tally. A quick rummage in the bag for fresh tiles, set them in the holder without looking at them. Stand up, move to my left.

I talk to the empty seat on my right. "Don't let her get to you, One. That was still a great move you made." Three looks at her tiles, arranged in no real order, and sets CAT down on the board. Five points, no bonuses. Poor Three, she's almost twenty points behind One and fifty behind Two. Replacement tiles. The bag is nearly empty.

I move again to the seat on my left, staring across the table. "You snooze, you lose, One. And seriously, Three, that's the best you could do? Hopeless." Two's grin is sadistic, she loves to watch the others fail. Her tiles are lined up alphabetically and it takes her a while to form words, but when she does they are laid out for maximum effect.

The move comes to Two quickly and with perfect clarity. I lay an O next to the S that One set down and run the word OPENING down the board. Triple word on the O. I wrinkle my nose and count Two's score. Thirty for OPENING and six for SO. Not bad. After Two's move, One is sulking and doesn't want to play anymore. Three doesn't understand why One is upset.

I stand up and push all three chairs back under the table. Time to do some work. For the rest of the day, in preparation for my supply drop, I clean the fridge and deep freeze, rearrange my pantry stores and start transferring all my waste from the shed. It takes me an hour to line up everything I want taken away, recyclables mostly and stuff that doesn't burn well.

The rest of my waste goes to the pit where I throw a bonfire every few weeks, dutifully inviting everyone I know. Nobody ever attends. So rude. While my rubbish burns I sit on a log with a glass of wine or a beer and watch the flames. I pretend I'm at a party talking to girls and try to ignore the noxious fumes from burning the by-products of my sad existence.

Wind cuts through my jacket, and spits light snow onto me. The snow's been steady this season, nearly every day. I've always assumed I'm somewhere in the northeast quarter of the USA but I don't know enough about star-mapping to figure it out. I could be anywhere really. It's cold and snowy in winter, rains a little during mild springs and the summers are hot and wonderfully stormy. Flakes in my eyelashes blur my vision and with my head down, I push into the heated greenhouse. *Yankee Doodle*—stop. On my knees, I check what I've grown. Snip off unhealthy pieces of plants. Fertilize and water. My chard looks great, the leaves dark green and silky under my fingers. I'll have some for dinner.

Growing my own vegetables is part of my routine, along with tending to the as-yet-unproductive fruit trees, getting them established for the next candidates. The thought of another candidate moving in once I'm gone makes me feel strange. I'm the first person to live here, and I have a possessive attachment to this place that takes so much from me and gives nothing in return. It's very confusing.

"Celestial Celeste," Mother slurs in my ear.

"Go away."

"Digging in the dirt. Filthy little bitch. Why you doin' that?" The words sting as much as if she were actually standing beside me speaking them.

The muscles in my jaw tighten, making my teeth clench. "I need fresh food. I'm being paid to test their systems."

Mother snorts derisively.

The sound triggers a memory, and I can't help myself. I have to respond. "Remember when you threw away that box of crackers after you made me steal them and we didn't get to eat any? And then you slapped me for complaining that I was hungry? Do you remember that? I do."

I wait for her to retaliate, but she doesn't. Dredging up something she's done and throwing it in her face usually gets rid of her. As I tend to my plants, I imagine the way Mother looks, or rather the way I remember her. She might have been pretty once, I think. Some of my memories have warped over time.

Riley got all Mother's physical attributes, or those Mother had before meth and whatever else ruined them. Short with full breasts, curvy hips, straight blond hair. Typical feminine perfection. Even her nose was cute, like a little ski jump. My little sister also got Mother's predisposition to addiction. Physically—and I like to think mentally and emotionally too— I'm nothing like either of them. Except the color of my eyes, which are a blue so bright and intense I always think they look unnatural.

I've had four lovers tell me I look like an artist, whatever that means. Strong jaw, straight nose. Nondescript brunette hair that curls when there's moisture in the air. I'm tallish and lanky, small-breasted and wiry. Almost androgynous. I'd be more so if I could bear to cut my hair short, but I can't. Not since Mother hacked it off when I was five, and five and a half, and seven, and eight and three-quarters, because I had head lice. Lice treatments cost money. For Mother, it was a no-brainer.

After sparing me from the horror of physically resembling Mother, the universe still saw fit to give me some sort of *fuck you* and made me sound exactly like her. My voice is deep and gravelly, like I'm a lifelong three-pack-a-day smoker. Talking through closed doors to dealers and addicts, I was mistaken for her over and over again. Even sometimes now when I hear myself, I want to cringe.

The first few times she spoke to me here I thought it was me, speaking without realizing. So strange, because I haven't seen or heard her since I was twelve, but I carry her with me in a place I thought inaccessible. The voices trigger unwanted thoughts and feelings. In all my time here, I've managed to avoid becoming depressed or at least I think I have. I try not to be self-pitying because while the loneliness is hard it's also bearable.

The fact I'd remained fairly stable made me proud, like a warped sort of accomplishment. But the false things flipped everything on its head and now it's harder to suppress my distress. I can't pretend I'm not alone because the hallucinations are forcing me to acknowledge and participate in this sad version of my life, *Clockwork Orange* style.

My hand is still shaking from Mother's visit and when I cut the stems of chard, I accidentally nick the side of my forefinger. It's not deep but it bleeds freely from the straight-edged slice. I stick my finger in my mouth. It tastes like blood and dirt. Earthy and metallic. Not unpleasant.

My first aid is quick and perfunctory. I hold my clumsily dressed finger up to the webcam while I'm recording my weekly video log, as ordered by Controller B this morning. "I cut myself accidentally because Mother was talking to me." Even after my quick bouts of speaking aloud earlier, my voice still sounds odd, grating and harsh. I drop my hand to the desk, thumb playing over the rough bandage on my finger. I look around the room then back at the webcam.

"They're starting to bother me. I'm scared it's going to happen more and more often and I'm going to crack. They won't even have a fucking conversation with me. Just talk *at* me and leave. I'm still a little...not paranoid but...no, actually yeah I guess I'm paranoid that it's you guys somehow doing it. I know it can't be. I know it's not rational but I still feel like I want to look around for a speaker or something when I hear them." Because the reality that I have actually lost my mind is harder to accept than the Controllers playing a cruel trick on me.

For the first time ever, the intense scrutiny of the webcam makes me feel like I'm being judged. Interrogated. I look down at the keyboard. "I've been thinking about what's going to happen when I leave here. How I'm going to talk to people. Little things like that. Taking lovers and being around my friends. I'm worried I've forgotten how to be with people." Tears prickle. I rub the heel of my hands against my eyes. "Other than that, I've got nothing else to say. Situation normal." I stop the recording, send it through without watching it, and leave the computer room.

My bedroom is sparse but comfortable. Queen bed with a perfect mattress. Dark mahogany furniture to hold books and clothing. They allowed one personal item that wasn't a forbidden item. I chose a lambskin rug that was given to me by my maternal grandma the day I was born, just a few months before she died. It's been toted back and forth across the country and set on the bed or couch or floor space of every place I've ever slept. Every foster house, each shitty apartment I stayed in, I'd accidentally leave something behind—a toy, a piece of clothing, a piece of myself—but the lambskin somehow made it through. Here it sits atop the neatly made bed, the worn white wool contrasting with the navy blue comforter.

Navy blue. Riley's favorite color. Chewing the skin at the corner of my thumbnail, I leave my room and walk back to the computer. I open next month's requisition form and with one finger, type: New sheets and comforter, not navy blue please.

CHAPTER THREE

Sleep. Wake up. Run. I trip on a branch, half hidden by last night's snowfall, and crash onto my hands and knees. Nothing is broken but my palms are grazed, and I lift both stinging hands to my face to stare at tenacious dirt and small pieces of gravel embedded in my skin. I've had worse.

I ignore the pain and finish my laps, then head back around and up to where the dwelling is situated atop a very small hill. A small spear of morning light breaks through the gray sky and bounces off the windows. Now I have two sunrises—the reflected one in front of me and the real one behind. I play a game with myself, looking at one, then spinning around to find the other. Adult peek-a-boo. Can I catch one of them out? No.

Heather follows me over to the solar banks, talking the whole time. "Why do you like the sunrise so much, Celeste? Most people would rather be in bed. You've always been so weird about early mornings."

"Means I'm alive, Heather-Bear. Woke up to see another day." I keep my head down, eyes on my sneakers. "Why are you here? Did my sister tell you to come and see me?"

The only response is the sound of wind pushing through the trees. Riley probably did ask Heather to check on me. No... no she couldn't. Riley is dead. Heather is somewhere else, not here. I'm alone.

I sweep half an inch of accumulated snow from the bank of solar panels next to the greenhouse then check on the supplies I've been ignoring all morning. The trash I left in a neat pile is gone, replaced by a clump of cardboard and Styrofoam boxes strapped together and encased in a webbing sling. The bundle and concrete slab on which it sits are covered with a dusting of snow so light it looks like frost.

I scuff my shoes over the snow on the concrete. The drop can't have been here for long and as usual, I slept through the delivery. No tire tracks or marking of any kind in the snow to indicate how it got here. They either use the world's quietest helicopters or heavy-duty drones. Maybe strong men with pack animals.

I don't even know why I care how the supplies get here. Long ago, I concluded the delivery method was probably another part of the experiment, like testing the genetically engineered fruit trees and vegetables, and monitoring the prototype energy and waste removal systems. Everything here is a test, a dozen corporations muscling in to see how their own tech performs. I guess the people running the experiment on my slow mental degradation had to get the money to pay for it somehow.

Every time I feel a bit of my mind slipping away or feel lonely or sad, I remind myself that I'm going to help someone in the future if they're stuck on Mars. It's important I get it right, that I do my best. I might save lives. It's hard to remember exact details about the study, details that were the bare minimum to begin with. I learned early on, reading the contract and talking to the Controllers, that confidentiality is rule number one here.

"You and your goddamned secrets," Mother sneers.

"Go away, *Mother*."

She hawks and spits. "Little bitch. I fuckin' hate the way you call me that. Always thinkin' you're better than us."

I know she hates it, and that's why I do it. Riley always called her Ma and until I was about seven, I did too. Then I started taking notice of the adults asking—Where is your mother? Does your mother know about that bruise? Does your mother have any clean clothes for you? Is your mother coming to collect you? Has your mother given you anything for lunch?

Even at that age I could hear the distaste, the disbelief, the disgust, and the way that one word always sounded so accusatory. She was never a Mom or Mommy. She was barely a Ma. Mother fit her better than anything, and I made sure to always say the word the same way those adults said it. And I learned to keep out of her reach when I did.

I leave my supplies—they've already waited for hours, and nobody is going to steal anything—and head back inside to shower, eat, log, check in.

Cont A: Thank you for yesterday's logs.

SE9311: You're welcome.

Cont A: Can we discuss your text log?

SE9311: Absolutely.

I've never been a prude and masturbation is a frequent part of my logs. I wonder if Controller A will show any sort of interest or get flustered. Probably not. By now I know they aren't interested in the finer details, they only want to know how I'm *functioning*.

Cont A: Thank you. You've never indicated you miss anything sexual before. Why do you think you added it in now?

SE9311: Not sure.

No response. I know my two-word reply isn't enough for them, and I take a few moments to collect my thoughts, then keep typing.

SE9311: I was thinking about an old lover yesterday morning. Don't know exactly why, but that's my best guess.

Cont A: Did it stir a physical response?

SE9311: Yes.

Cont A: Did you masturbate?

SE9311: Yes. As noted.

Cont A: To climax?

SE9311: Is there any other reason for masturbating?

No response. I sigh.

SE9311: Yes. Twice. All my systems are working as intended.

Cont A: Thank you for the information. I trust you received the supply drop in good order.

SE9311: I haven't checked the contents but the drop is there. Thanks.

A question has been burning at the back of my mind for the past few weeks. I sit in the comfortable leather chair, fingers resting lightly on the keyboard. I like this keyboard. It's springy to type on. Comfortable under my fingertips. Plain black with no brand markings. Perhaps they'll let me take it when I leave, or tell me where I can get one of my own.

Cont A: You look pensive. Is everything all right, SE9311?

SE9311: Can I ask you something?

Cont A: Yes, of course.

The unspoken implication is that I may not get the answer I want, or even *get* an answer.

SE9311: My hallucinations. Are they happening when you'd expect or did I crack earlier than anyone else would?

The cursor blinks and blinks and blinks. I like to think they are deciding how much to share with me because they care about my feelings. The Controllers are impersonal but never impolite. I guess getting your test subject offside isn't a desirable outcome.

Cont A: Actually, the arrival of the hallucinations is later than what we'd anticipated.

I've never been precocious enough to be early for anything, and I'm surprised to hear I'm technically ahead of the curve on this one.

SE9311: Thanks.

Cont A: You're welcome. If there's nothing else, I'll leave you to it. Have an enjoyable day.

Now, as always, the day is pretty much mine to do whatever I want. I make a note in today's log about talking to Controller A and my surprise that I'm apparently doing okay with the whole *going crazy* thing. I cut an inch off my hair and give myself messy bangs, deciding it looks okay in a trying-too-hard-faux-hipster kind of way.

The sky has gone completely gray and snow has begun falling again, and I know from experience that the cardboard boxes of my supply drop are going to get soggy and break apart if I don't get to work. I remove the sling, place it in the storage shed ready to give back to them next month, and start transferring everything on my pull-along cart. Dragging it over rough ground soon has me sweating, and I have to unzip my coat and pull off my beanie. I could hook the cart to the ATV but the exercise makes me feel good and most importantly, takes up time.

I cart food, both perishables and non-perishables. Sort through toiletries and replacement first aid items like Band-Aids and ibuprofen. Unpack clothing. Find my new sunglasses—three pairs as promised—Oakley, Ray-Ban and one no-brand pair that is very Holly Golightly from *Breakfast at Tiffany's*. I slip those on and keep unpacking. Books. Light bulbs. Diesel for my backup power source. Fuel for the ATV. Ammunition. A new set of pretty light purple sheets and cover for my comforter.

There's something new and different in the dry ice, and the moment I realize what it is, my mouth waters. A big Lou Malnati's pizza box. The box tells me "Someone must really like you" and I wonder which Controller organized this treat. Which one of them really likes me? I tear open the box and yank out four different Chicago deep-dish pizzas. Then I cry but I don't know why.

After carefully stashing my pizzas in the chest freezer, I continue with my mindless back and forth. It takes an hour or so to finish unpacking everything else until the chest freezer is full of vacuum-sealed meat and frozen vegetables, and the pantry has enough canned and shelf-stable food to last me six months if I'm extravagant. I've never gone more than six weeks without a drop, but the fear they might forget me is always there and I've been squirreling supplies away this whole time.

As a reward for finishing my big chore, I choose an apple from the assortment in the fruit box, stretching my mouth as wide as I can to take a massive bite. The fresh fruit and vegetables only last a week or so after the supply drops, and then all I have left is canned or dehydrated or from the limited greenhouse range, leaving me to dream of delivery days and fresh things. I think of the lucky person after me who might use my genetically engineered fruit trees. My fingers are sticky with apple juice. I lick them and nibble the apple right down until only the barest amount of flesh is left around the core.

Celeste, throw that in the compost, not the—stop.

It's Celeste Three's turn at the Monopoly game we started last night. She rolls a seven and moves the boot forward. Go to Jail. I'm yet to find a game that Three is good at, and I've come to the conclusion that she's awful at everything, and honestly just not very smart. She's the awkward girl at parties who stands in corners and listens to people say mean things about her. She won't pay to get out of jail, and would rather try to roll her double or wait three turns. Three never rolls the double because she's just that bad. But I still like her.

Celeste One needs an eleven to get Free Parking and collect the cash in the middle. She rolls a ten, lands on New York Avenue and buys it. Now she has two of three orange properties. I'm not in the mood for Celeste Two's smug shit. Instead, I leave her to wait her turn, tip all the dry ice from the Styrofoam boxes into a bucket and carry it outside with my freshly boiled kettle.

"Are you going to make the fog, Cel?" Riley's voice is right against my ear, excited and childish. Her arrival always startles me—my sister has been dead for over five years.

"Yes."

"Just like the play Mrs. Larsen took us to."

I nod. "Mhmm. You were so scared, remember?"

Riley doesn't respond.

"Remember? You were so scared that you held my hand all the way home, then you slept in my bed."

No answer.

"Riley? Are you still there?"

I pour hot water over dry ice and watch a slow, thick fog rolling over the edge of the bucket and along the ground.

* * *

Controller A two days in a row. Slightly odd, but not unheard of. Maybe they are pulling double shifts. Maybe she's got a sick mom with medical bills. Maybe he has a mortgage, or a wife at home about to have a baby. Maybe they really like their job. Or me.

SE9311: Hi, sorry I'm late.

Cont A: That's quite all right. How are you? And happy birthday.

Shit, I'd totally forgotten today is my birthday. I'm now thirty years old. Am I supposed to feel different? Suddenly wiser? I don't, but I do feel like I should do something to celebrate. Maybe I'll bake myself a cake.

SE9311: I'm good. Thanks for the birthday wishes and the pizza in the supply drop, it's awesome! Could you please pass along my thanks to whoever organized it?

There's a long pause and I imagine it's because Controller A probably doesn't know how to respond. I've never been so effusive before, but they've never sent me authentic deep dish.

Cont A: You're welcome, and I'll be sure to do that. Do you have anything to report?

SE9311: Nothing, no.

Cont A: You look tired. Has there been a change to your sleep patterns?

I stare at my hands on the keyboard. Sleep is one of my unchanged routines. Every night I'm asleep by ten p.m. and awake each morning by six a.m. I don't even need an alarm clock.

SE9311: I don't think so. If I'm waking up during the night, I'm not aware of it.

Cont A: You're not becoming ill?

SE9311: I don't think so. I'll keep an eye on myself and be in touch.

Cont A: Please do. If there's nothing else, I'll leave you to continue your day.

Before I can respond, another message lands.

Cont A: Enjoy the pizza and your birthday, SE9311.

The messaging system closes down before I can respond. Controller A is probably still watching me from the camera mounted in the corner. I swivel to face it, give the camera a thumbs-up and a smile. Cheesy but I really am grateful.

I make a chocolate cake from scratch and slather it with thick, rich frosting, knowing even as I do it, I won't finish it. No candles. No gifts. No singing. I eat cake for lunch and dinner and breakfast the next morning, then throw the remainder in the trash. *Celeste, throw that in*—stop. I've had my cake and eaten it and now it's time to move on with my life. If it can be called that.

My birthday slips into another day, another week, a new month? Time means nothing to me. It moves in erratic stretches. Fast then slow. Elongated but also condensed. It goes in all directions. Time is not linear. I like it this way, and hope it stays when I go back to the real world.

Snow continues to fall nearly every day, and when I run, it flicks up against my legs and face. The slow part of the creek is frozen at the edges and soon the ground will be covered in a foot of snow and I'll have to run inside on my treadmill, staring out the window and wishing I was outside. I've never lived anywhere it didn't snow.

Heather's arm is looped through mine, pulling her tight against me, so she can share my heat. "You're not bothered?"

"Not at all." I push the crossing signal button. "Why would I be?" It's been threatening snow all afternoon. I look up, squinting into the twilight.

"I don't know, I guess I just thought you'd be pissed."

"After knowing me for all these years?" I smile down at my friend. "Me and Allison aren't dating and I don't have dibs on her, so she can sleep with whoever she wants."

Heather stretches on tiptoes to kiss my cheek. "You're so ridiculously zen, you should run a meditation center, Celeste. Then you could buy that farm you're always talking about. Maybe even run your zen clinic

from your farm." Heather looks up and holds her hand out, laughing.
"Finally! It's snowing. Now you'll shut up about it."

I stand outside, looking up at the gray sky until my neck cramps and I'm shivering. But nothing falls from the sky. I'm a few minutes late for my morning check-in but Controller D doesn't say anything about my tardiness. Even when I apologize.

SE9311: Hi, sorry.

Cont D: No problem. Just a heads-up, we've got a drop scheduled for tonight.

SE9311: Great, thanks.

Cont D: I trust there are no issues?

They seem unusually taciturn. No questions about yesterday's logs or how I'm *feeling*. Did Controller D have a fight with their significant other? Annoying coworker stole their lunch? Traffic snarls on their way to work? People have lives outside of this thing I'm in, and I have to make myself remember that, or I'll fall into the dark pit of my insular world and never be able to climb out.

SE9311: No. None.

Cont D: Thank you. Enjoy your day.

And then he…she…they are gone.

I hurry to get everything ready for the drop. Trash stacked, pantry, fridge and freezer cleaned. I make fresh pasta for dinner because I can and it will waste almost an hour of my day.

"You goddamned fuckin' show-off," Mother sneers.

Startled, I turn the handle of the pasta machine too quickly and my sheet of dough hits the counter and breaks off. Staring at the jagged edge of my otherwise perfect pasta I feel an uncharacteristic surge of anger, and the burn in my stomach frightens me.

I am many things. Impulsive. Sympathetic. Lonely. Generous. But I'm not usually angry. Anger has always felt like a pointless emotion for me, and many years ago I decided that where Mother was concerned, I would let it go lest I become consumed by rage. I close my eyes, inhaling the doughy scent on the counter until my nerves settle. Then I pull the pasta out of the rollers and start again.

Dreamless sleep. Dreamy awakening. Sleepwalk through my morning. By the time I'm done moving everything from the supply drop, it's almost noon but I still don't feel like I've woken fully. It's a clear day but still cold and windy, and the briskness makes my body sluggish and unresponsive. But I kind of like the feeling. It reminds me of nights so long ago at friends' houses talking and passing bottles and a joint around until the sun rose. That all stopped after Riley.

"Don't blame me, Cel. Not my fault I died. Blame Ma. She made me what I was," my sister insists. She laughs softly in my ear and her breath is warm against my skin. I leave her in the shed with the trolley and the webbing sling, and trudge back toward the warmth of the house.

The faint drone of a plane catches my attention. I look up and curl my fingers to make binoculars so I can track it across the sky. There're people in there, thousands of feet above me, but they are there. I'm not totally alone. The plane passes behind clouds and when it comes out again, I'm staring directly into the sun.

A branch cracks, the noise bouncing sharply off the trees and along uneven ground. I whirl toward the sound and about a hundred feet or so away, down in the red zone, spot color that shouldn't be there. Not white snow or the dull brown of tree trunks, but the bright tan of fur. Something's moving down there? I blink hard, trying to rid myself of the light spots that are dancing across my field of vision from accidentally looking at the sun through my hand-binoculars.

Maybe it's a wild dog. *B-I-N-G-O and Bingo*—stop.

"Could be a deer," Riley suggests. "Deer is tasty. What do they call it again? Why don't you get the gun?"

"Venison, and yeah it is but even if I manage to kill it cleanly, I don't know how to make deer steaks."

"With a knife, silly. Come on, go get the gun. It'll run up here and die once you shoot it. Fresh meat, Cel, and I'm so hungry… We haven't had any proper food for days."

The gun. I never used to shoot, but now I'm good with the rifle because I have nothing but time to practice. I should take up knitting. Or painting.

I race inside, grab the rifle and my hearing protection from the basement gun safe that's never locked and sprint back toward the sound. I hear it clearly, closer now, slow measured steps. I quickly slip on the earmuffs and drop into a firing position, aware of the instant cold damp on my jeans from kneeling in the snow. Hot breath clouds on every exhale.

Looking through the dense cluster of trees that comprise most of the yellow zone, I spot the flash of deep tan again. B-I-N-G-O. It's just like the practice targets. "I'm sorry, animal, I'm sorry," I murmur as I raise the rifle to my shoulder, sight and pull the trigger.

CHAPTER FOUR

A split second after the rifle discharges, an anguished scream penetrates my earmuffs. High-pitched. Distorted. It reaches a crescendo, drops then picks up again. I once heard that foxes sometimes sound like people screaming so it must be a fox, not a deer like I'd thought. Like Riley thought. Shit. Yuck. I don't want to eat a fox.

Considering I just shot him, it's unsurprising he's screaming. I'm very sorry, Mr. Fox. I pull the muffs from my ears, leave them looped around my neck then turn to walk away, hoping desperately he doesn't suffer for long.

The fox shouts expletives, loud and clear. No, animals don't swear. But…people do. The words are just a memory of someone I once heard who is angry at a ball game score, at someone who cut them off in traffic, at the woman who took the last carton of milk from the grocery store refrigerator. Then I hear what sounds like French or Italian or maybe Spanish? I don't speak another language. If I don't know the thing I'm hearing, does that mean it's not in my head? Does it mean it's really real? A real...*person?* No, it can't be. More curses, in English, then the expletives stop and another prolonged cry takes their place.

My heart pounds, every muscle in my body straining toward the sound. It's not real. It can't be real. What I see down the rifle scope tells me it is real. I think. A person is in the yellow zone. A person I seem to have just shot. I scrunch my eyes closed. It's not a person. It's just a visual hallucination from retinal damage caused by me staring at the sun earlier.

Mother's rank odor invades my nose. "Killing people now, eh?" she asks conversationally. "Shoulda given you more credit." A cackle. "Shoulda asked you to take care of a few people for me."

I stumble backward, scrabbling at a tree trunk to keep myself from falling. I wave frantically, trying to keep Mother from coming closer. "Go away, go away, GO AWAY!" My wild flailing does nothing except drive home the fact I've really lost it. Calm down, Celeste. Just relax. There's nobody here. Nobody. Except maybe the not-real-person just down the hill. I turn back and raise the rifle to take another look through the scope.

The person in the yellow zone is still there. They are wobbling. No, it's me that's wobbling, my hands trembling so much I'm afraid I might accidentally shoot the person again. I clear the rifle and take another look down the scope. It's still a person and no amount of staring or blinking changes the image.

I sling the rifle over my back and run, run, run. My skid right before the line of the green zone is as good as any game-winning slide across home plate. *There's no crying in baseball—* stop. I haven't watched that movie in ten years.

The words of the manual are burned into my brain. And my muscle memory. "...green and yellow...pulses at forty-five second intervals...red, your implant will render you unconscious and a member of the control team will return you to the white zone..."

The person is actually a woman wearing a large hiking backpack, lying on her side in the snow, legs squirming. Blood seeps through fingers splayed over her right thigh. Tan pants, not tan fur. Beneath her leg, the snow is tinged red.

I lean forward and glance left then right along the invisible line of the green zone boundary. "Hello?" Such a stupid thing to say. There's no answer. My palms and armpits are damp and cold, and my body lets out an unconscious shudder. Again, I call out, "Hello? Can you hear me?"

A groan is the response as, slowly, she twists to look at me. She's *looking* at me, right at me, and my body freezes under her scrutiny. Thankfully my mouth still works. "I'm sorry. I think I just shot you. I…you shouldn't be here."

Finally a weak, softly accented voice floats across the fifty-foot space. "You did shoot me. Goddammit. Why?" A *real* voice, and someone new. It's magnificent.

"I'm sorry. I'm sorry." I'm shaking so hard I think I might fall over. I drop to my knees, straining forward as far as I dare. "Is it bad? Are you okay?"

"I don't know. Why did you shoot me?" she asks again. She's really hung up on the *why*.

"I thought you were…not…you shouldn't be here. How'd you get here? You'll have to go. Right now."

"No, I can't move, I need help. Please. Can you help me?"

"I…you need to—" The second request for her to leave dies on my tongue. How the hell can she leave if she can't even move because of the bullet I just put in her leg? But what am I going to do with her? I have no idea, but I know I can't leave her out here for lions and tigers and bears. Oh my. I *think* she's in a spot where the cameras won't intersect. But maybe she's within their range and the Controllers can see her. See me. See us. I look around, expecting one of the Controllers to come out at any moment. Not that I know where they'd come from or what they look like. Men in white jumpsuits maybe?

I close my eyes. Open them. She's still there. My mouth moves ahead of my brain. "I can't help you where you are. You're going to have to crawl closer if you want me to help you."

The response is quietly indignant. "What do you mean you can't help me where I am?"

"I can't get to you. I need you to come closer."

"Why? I'm right here. Please help me." She's crying softly now, the gentle sobs punctuating her words.

There's no crying in baseball. Stop. Please stop. I rub my fingers hard up and down my face, trying to clear the thought. Someone's going to come right now and see that I'm talking to a person. I'm going to be in trouble. "You know what? I don't have time for this. Either crawl closer or stay out in the woods." Making a sweeping gesture along the invisible zone line, I elaborate, "I can't move past here." I push myself up to stand on trembling legs and turn back to the dwelling. I turn away from her, away from someone who needs my help. What am I doing? This isn't me.

"You can't leave me here!" comes the yell from behind me.

"Sure you can. You left me." Mother doesn't sound bitter. More matter-of-fact.

"Wait! Please, wait. Don't leave me here, please don't leave me." Softer, begging now. I've never heard such desperate pleading from anyone. And I've heard a lot of pleading in my life.

The wind chill seeps through my skin, cuts through muscle and bone to my organs.

"Don't leave her," Riley whispers, her voice still childish. "That's not like you, Cel."

I wave my hand near my face like swatting away a fly. Despite the wrongness of the situation, Riley is right. I turn around again, and across the distance, the woman's eyes find mine. For the longest moment, she just stares at me until she pushes herself up, and with agonizing slowness begins to crawl. As I watch her progress, I can't help the sickening dread settling in my stomach. Just *seeing* her is against the rules, not to mention the fact I've talked to her. I didn't mean to, it just happened, I couldn't stop it. Once we get inside, I'll contact the Controllers and explain. Apologize. It is not my fault. I haven't intentionally fucked up the experiment. They are supposed to make sure nobody ever comes near here. This isn't my fault.

The woman stops crawling just over the yellow-green line, which is about twenty-five feet away from the green-white line. Still on the wrong side. Shit.

"Just a little more. Please. You're so close." My voice breaks. "Please."

"I can't," she mumbles. Then she wavers, and crashes to the ground.

Perfect.

"Hey! Hey!" I pace back and forth, clapping my hands. "Get up! Wake up!"

She doesn't. She's motionless. Maddeningly so. Heather, Mother, and Riley have an opinion and they all give them at once.

"You have to go get her, Celeste. It's the right thing and you always do the right thing."

"Fuck 'er. Shouldn't be here."

"Could drag her out, Cel. 'Member when you carried me all the way home from the park after that shithead kid threw a rock at my face and broke my tooth?"

I close my eyes, hoping it'll get rid of the skittering sensation creeping down my arms. What to do, what to do? The stranger lets out a low, choked groan before pushing herself unsteadily to her elbows. She looks up, head wobbling and eyes staring in my general direction, but as unfocused as any drunk's. The woman makes another attempt to crawl and I can hear the moan every time she moves. It's clear she's not going to be able to move into the safe zone. I need to help her.

Godfuckingdammit.

Run as fast as you can, you can't catch the gingerbread woman. Spewing curses, I sprint over the invisible line. The jolt comes instantaneously, throwing me forward until I land on my shoulder, tumbling over the rough ground. Sticks jam themselves into my skin, scratching and scraping. The cold air burns my lungs as I scramble, hands and feet slipping on the snow and loose matter underneath it.

I grab the straps of the woman's hiking pack and pull as hard as I can, back to the safety of the white zone. My muscles twitch, from effort and the fear that another shock is coming. I don't care if I'm hurting her. I don't care if it's not polite. All I care about is what I know is about to happen.

Fifteen feet.

Even though I knew it was coming, the second shock still startles me. It ravages muscles already seized and cramping from the first and I trip, falling backward onto my ass. My tailbone complains and I can't help myself, I drop her. The woman exhales sharply but I can't do anything but gurgle at the back of my throat as my muscles contract involuntarily. Need to move. Need to move.

Frozen, snowy ground burns the bare skin on my hands and spurs me on. Thirty seconds? I roll over, fumbling for her backpack again. Fingers close around something. Get up. Bend over. Heels dig into the ground. Pull and pull and pull. Toward the white zone. She's silent. I'm not. I'm huffing and grunting, my breath coming out in dense white clouds.

Ten seconds.

Almost there.

I'm so close but the next shock is a deadline I'm in danger of missing and the thought terrifies me. With every ounce of willpower I possess, I grit my teeth, strain as hard as I can and pull...pull...pull, letting out a guttural, "Raaaaaaargh!"

Nothing.

No shock, no jolt, no pain. The relief is immediate, my tension unfurling like a flag. I let go of the woman and lower myself to the ground. Adrenaline floods my cells. Trembling. Nauseated. Shit, what have I just done?

The right thing. I've done the right thing. Surely I can make a case in my defense. I draw my knees to my chest, wrap my arms around my legs and look at her while I wait for my body to recover enough for me to move. She's lying on her side, propped up by her pack, breathing but apparently unconscious. Her leg is bleeding, but it's a trickle rather than blood spurting in an arc like you see in movies. I guess that's something.

I put my hand on the wound and lean over, studying the woman's face. Olive skin. Full lower lip. Strong jaw and slightly curved nose. Her eyes are closed under dark, well-groomed eyebrows. She has a freckle or a small mole under her left cheekbone. Not actress-or-model-beautiful but an interesting, attractive face nonetheless. Though I can't help myself, I'm still ashamed for judging the level of her beauty.

I sit and stare, drinking her features in as though they're water and I'm in a desert. But no matter how much I look at her, I'm still parched. Tentatively, I reach out and run fingertips over her jaw. Her skin is smooth and warm. When she doesn't move, I repeat the motion, goose bumps running up my arms at the feel of another person's skin against my fingers. The woman shudders, her eyelids flutter open and a pair of large eyes gaze up at me. They are light brown, flecked with dark. The color makes me think of the jars of real maple syrup my adoptive mom Joanne used to keep on the windowsill. These eyes are beautiful. Unconventional. And surprisingly without fear.

I lean back a little, suddenly aware of how close I am to this stranger. "Name?" Social conventions feel foreign, and I'm surprised at the gruff uncertainty in my voice. Clearing my throat, I try again, making the effort to be softer this time. "What's your name?"

"Olivia," she whispers. The word catches and she coughs a few times, her hand moving too late to cover her mouth. "Sorry."

"Olivia," I repeat. The word feels like caramel fudge in my mouth. Comforting, warm, and soft. I swallow, like I could be nourished by her name. "We can't stay here." Glancing up toward the dwelling, I add, "The house is about a hundred yards away, just up that slope."

"I don't think I can walk that far."

"And I don't think I can carry you," I finish. "But…I have a cart and a four-wheeler I could use to move you?"

"Okay, thank you." She slides a shaking hand underneath mine, placing it against her wound. With her other trembling hand, she's trying to unfasten the straps on her pack.

I crouch, my own trembling hands hovering useless in the air. "Can I help?"

"Please," she says, and I unclip the harness so she can wriggle out of it. She shifts slightly and is unburdened. Her delicate, arched eyebrows arch further. "I'm freezing, do you mind if we move?"

I've been staring. "Oh, yes. Sorry."

Olivia nods, her eyes falling closed. I allow myself another moment to study her features while she can't see me, then I get up and jog on wobbly legs to the equipment shed. Adrenaline and fear make my hands shake even more, and it takes a minute to hitch the cart to the ATV. The four-wheeler bumps and side-skids over the rough, snow-muddied ground as I race back. Worried about accidentally running her over, I slow down to a crawl and roll the ATV back and forth to get it onto a flat part as close as I can to her before I cut the ignition. "How's your leg?"

"Hurts." She opens her eyes and glances down. "But I think the bleeding is slowing."

"Good," I say because I can't think of anything else. Bleeding. I'm suddenly aware that I have her blood on one of my hands, tacky and uncomfortable. I pick up a handful of snow to clean it off.

Olivia grimaces when I help her stand, wrapping her arm around my shoulder for support. She doesn't complain when my arm automatically slides around her waist. She's about my height but curved and more solidly muscular than me. I feel the tensing of that muscle underneath her red soft-shell jacket and for a moment I imagine the sensation under my hands or how she would feel on top of my sinewy runner's body.

A flash of arousal stuns but doesn't surprise me. This isn't the time for that, Celeste. My body pays no attention to the inappropriate timing and my arousal blooms, smoothly winding its way through my body. I feel it everywhere, heating hidden recesses long abandoned, a contrast to the wind chill outside my body. But I can't do anything about it, about the cause. Not now. Not here. Maybe not ever.

With some tricky maneuvering we manage to get her settled safely into the cart, and aside from the sharp gasps that rise over the engine sound with every jolt, she's mostly silent for the journey. Riding as slowly as I can to keep her comfortable, I mentally trawl through the wording of my contract, trying to remember if there's anything about this…scenario. I read every single word of that contract and know they can adjust my payment as they see fit, but only under certain clauses and by reasonable and appropriate amounts which are clearly laid out. There was a list of reasons to extract me or short-pay me, including illness requiring hospitalization, natural disaster, outbreak of disease or nuclear warfare, but I don't recall any clause saying: *If you shoot someone who is trespassing and then help said person we can reduce your payment.*

Even though I didn't do this intentionally, they could reduce my compensation because I did something I shouldn't have, and ruined their data as a consequence. No matter. I think I would give some of that money up if it meant I could spend just one week talking to this real person. Even for just one day. But I can't have that.

None of what I feel or want matters because I have to tell them, and not just as an afterthought in a log because she isn't a false thing that I have to record. Is she? I see her. I feel her. I hear her. She's real. She has to be, because if she isn't real then I've lost all traces of sanity.

CHAPTER FIVE

I deposit the person—no, she's a woman and her name is Olivia—on the couch and run back outside to put the ATV away and collect her backpack and my rifle that I'd completely forgotten about. Her pack weighs maybe thirty-five pounds and has snowshoes, a foam sleeping mat, and a tent strapped to the outside. Serious business. It takes me a few attempts to lift and then swing it up onto my shoulders, and I keep expecting the cameras to swivel in my direction and catch me in the act. The thought makes the back of my neck shudder like bugs are crawling over it. I kick snow over the blood and rush as fast as I can with my load back to the dwelling, where I dump the pack just inside the door. Rifle placed in the safe, locked for the first time.

She's still where I left her, but now slumped to the side with her head tilted to rest against the back of the couch. Her eyes open slowly, like those creepy dolls with creepy sliding eyelids. Though watchful, she seems calm, and I wonder what sort of person trusts a stranger so willingly. Especially a stranger who shot them.

Olivia straightens when I come closer. "Is everything okay out there?"

"Mhmm. I got your pack."

"Great, thanks." She peers at her thigh. Peers at me. "I, uh…I need you to help me with my leg. If the bullet is in there it will need to come out, and the wound cleaned and dressed. There's a first aid kit in the top compartment of my pack." Her voice is low and surprisingly clear, that slight accent skirting the edges of her words. Melodic. Mesmerizing. "It may be best if we go to your bathroom, it's going to be messy. Then I'll need to borrow your phone too, please."

She's not crying anymore. *There's no crying in*—stop. I blink hard to dispel the refrain rattling though my head. "Sure. I have a first aid kit you can use. Give me a moment." I say nothing in response to her comment about needing a phone. Nor to her saying I might need to help her extract the piece of metal I put in her.

On my way down the hall, I yank the door to the computer room closed. Nothing amiss, nobody here, carry on. In the cool basement, I paw through the container of medical equipment, pull out my first aid kit. *There's no cry*—stop, shut up. I jump up and down, shaking my arms out. Out, out, out! Three strikes and you're outta here!

"You're a terrible ten-pin bowler, Celeste," Heather reminds me. "I don't think you've ever bowled above a hundred-fifty game."

"Thanks, I know. Wrong kind of strikes though."

There's a box in my medical supplies with ANTIBIOTICS written on the lid in permanent ink, and opening it reveals stacks of smaller red and green boxes. Olivia will be here for at least a day until they can organize her extraction, and starting a course of these pills is a good idea. I flick through my first aid manual and find the entry marked *Antibiotics*. I've never had cause to use any of these and everything in the manual is simplified for non-doctors like me. Red for sore throats, earaches and the like. Green for open wounds, deep cuts, abscesses or boils. I set a green box on top of the first aid kit and carry my loot upstairs.

I leave the first aid things in the bathroom, then rush back to the lounge area. I've only been gone five minutes, but my nerves are sparking like I want to jolt and twitch and yell. I keep waiting for someone to jump from the shadows and accuse me of doing something bad. Olivia's stripped off her jacket and tossed it over one of the kitchen chairs. We stare at each other in silent appraisal. She pulls off her beanie, setting loose dark, curly hair that falls around her shoulders.

I break first. "Come on, the bathroom's this way."

She's wobbling as I half-support, half-carry her up the hallway. My body tingles, maybe just a leftover symptom of the implant shocks. No, I don't think so. It's her touching me. Olivia hops over to rest her butt against my sink and begins to unfasten her pants, pushing them down carefully. I look away, but I don't want to.

My hands and eyes are suddenly very busy with the first aid kit. The thought of having to clean an open wound makes me shudder and a touch of queasiness churns in my stomach.

"You can do it, Cel. And this is nowhere near as bad as that glass cut," Riley reminds me.

Teeth clenched to stop myself from replying to my sister, I close the first aid box then shuffle over and open the cabinet beside the mirror. "I have Motrin and Tylenol to help with the pain. I'm sorry, nothing stronger."

"Thank you. I'll take a couple of Tylenol."

Still turned at an angle away from her and her gory leg, I pass her the box and she swallows the gels without water before passing the packet back. Fabric rustles. "Hungh, I think the bullet just grazed me."

Without thinking, I glance over, starting at her face and moving down until I come to black panties. Panicked, I shift my gaze from her underwear. But I go in the wrong direction, looking down to her blood-smeared thigh. Suppressing a gag, I turn my eyes from the gore. "That's something then, I guess," I say hoarsely to the floor. "So, what's the plan?"

"I think I'll wash it out in the shower first. Is there any antiseptic liquid or wipes in that kit?" She leans heavily against the sink.

"Uh, I've got…hydrogen peroxide and saline?"

"Saline will do. Could you please take off my boots?"

Nodding, I crouch down and untie the laces of her leather hiking boots. Sometime earlier today she put on her shoes and double knotted them. For some reason this simple, normal act makes me want to cry. The right boot slips off easily but the left is harder because I have to try and angle it off her foot while she's hopping to keep weight from her injured leg. Sharp inhalations. Muscle tight and trembling with strain. Under the blood, the skin on her thigh is goose-pimpled.

Burning shame fills my chest. I'm sorry. I'm so sorry. I could have killed her.

"It's okay," Olivia murmurs. "Not your fault. Obviously I went somewhere I shouldn't have. And it's just a minor wound, really. Should heal just fine."

"Pardon?"

"It'll be okay. You don't need to keep apologizing."

But I didn't. Did I?

I stand up again as Olivia wriggles the rest of the way out of her ruined pants. She pulls her long-sleeved button-up and the thermal underneath over her head. Quickly, I turn around but not before catching sight of a plain white sports bra along with her curves and bare skin. She's toned, but not hard. The heat spreads from my chest to my stomach. "Do you need any help?" I manage to ask.

"No, I think I'm good. But could you maybe hang around in case I pass out?" The sound of her gasping and cursing rises above the shower.

"Mhmm."

An hour ago I was totally alone, as I have been for over three years, and now there's a woman almost naked in my shower. I feel differently about it than I would have expected. I should be excited or pleased, but instead I feel anxious and frightened. It's not my fault. Over and over I repeat those words in my head, hoping they'll stick.

The water shuts off. "May I please have a towel?"

"Mhmm." I sidestep over and pass her one through the open glass door. "How is it?" My eyes pay no attention to my loathing of blood, fixating on the now-clean wound. It does look more like a rough graze than a hole—a ragged tract almost four inches long and a quarter-inch deep, as though the bullet skipped across her skin like a stone over water. The proverbial *just a flesh wound* of old westerns.

There's a slight tremor in her legs as she pats her thigh, then dries the water that's splashed up onto her torso. "Stings like hell but I imagine it's going to feel a whole lot worse when you put that on it." She gestures to the bottle of saline in my hand.

My voice squeaks up when I force out, "Me?"

"Yes. I can't get the angle right to clean it thoroughly *and* keep my balance on only one leg." She reaches up and hooks her fingers over the top of the shower screen, the muscles in her arms taut.

My words won't come out. I swallow hard, working my jaw back and forth a few times to shake them loose. "Just so you know, I…uh, I'm not great with gory stuff."

"It's not that gory." She smiles. "Just squirt that saline into it and make sure you get it everywhere. Can you put on some gloves please?" She's direct, but not obnoxious or forceful— simply a woman who knows what she needs and wants, and knows how to communicate that to people. "You'll be fine, trust me."

The woman that *I* shot is soothing *me*. I make a noncommittal gurgling sound, wash my hands and pull on the gloves from the kit. My curiosity is overwhelmed by my aversion and I gag when she tells me to pull the edges of the wound apart to get the saline solution everywhere. Unsurprisingly, her directions are now pushed through clenched teeth and I feel another flash of shame. This is me. I did this.

"Not everything is about you, Cel," Riley tells me.

"This is," I mutter.

"What was that?" Olivia asks, her voice tight.

"Nothing." I squeeze the bottle to get the last of the liquid into the wound.

"Liar," Riley singsongs.

"Good," Olivia whispers over the top of my sister. "Can you help me sit down on the toilet please?"

I set a folded towel on the closed lid and stand stiffly, uncertain as to how to help her best. Olivia takes charge, grabbing my biceps hard and using me for balance while she steps out of the shower and drops heavily onto the toilet. "Thank you. Now, can you use some gauze swabs to dry the skin around it?"

I do, and the whole time her hands hang by her sides, clenched into fists. "Good, that's good. Now, the uh…" She swallows convulsively. "The uh, Neosporin and a dressing."

I clamp my molars together as I whack a whole heap of antiseptic cream along the bullet tract. Blargh. I'm as gentle as I can be but Olivia's leg is tense and her breathing short and shallow, almost panting. She looks pale. I feel paler.

"You know," she pushes out around breaths. "You haven't told me your name." Classic distraction technique. Clever.

I glance up. "Haven't I? It's Celeste."

"Celeste." Saying my name seems to relax her. "That's really pretty. It suits you."

"Mother used to like looking at the night sky when she was fucked up. Sometimes, she'd call me *Celestial*." Shit, why did I just say that? I may as well have just told her my entire stupid life story.

The look Olivia gives me is so incongruously gentle that my eyes prickle. I blink and clear my throat, trying to get rid of the lump that's suddenly formed there. When I stick the dressing on her thigh, wrapping it firmly in place with a crepe bandage, my hands are still shaking. "I think this is done."

"Thanks. Looks great. I just need a moment before I can stand up." She's inhaling deeply and noisily, her eyes half-closed.

I stand to the side, not knowing if I should offer to assist or if she even wants me to. Everything in my head feels wrong and it takes me a few moments to think of the right wording. "What do you need?"

"I think I should lie down." She sounds woozy, almost intoxicated.

I stare until the thought pops into my head that I've missed the social cue. She *does* want your help, Celeste. "Oh!" I hold out my hands and when she takes them, I pull her up from the toilet.

As gently as I can, I wedge myself under her arm and together we shuffle to my bedroom, so close and in sync we could be competing in a three-legged race. Still only in underwear, her bare skin is against my body, warm and enticing. I'm grateful for my clothes and the barrier they keep between us, but at the same time I hate them for keeping her skin from mine.

Olivia twists sideways to look at me. "I'm going to mess up your nice neat bed."

"Doesn't matter." I help her to the other side, not my side, and when I try to get her down onto the mattress it ends up an uncoordinated juggling act where we're face-to-face and I'm almost hugging her. My breath catches and I drop her onto the bed. "Shit, sorry."

Her face is contorted. "It's okay." She lies still on top of the covers for half a minute, then worms her way under my duvet, the movement slow and clumsy.

"Are you comfortable?"

Olivia nods weakly as I tug the covers up over her bare stomach. "I've got something for you," I tell her. "I'll be right back."

Safely out of sight outside the room, I cover my face with my hands, leaning back against the wall. What am I doing? This isn't candy I'm hiding in my bedside table. This is a *person*. This is something I'm not allowed. This is something that could get me in trouble and has probably fucked up a long and very expensive scientific study. It only takes another few seconds for me to hit full panic mode. I yank the front door open and stumble outside.

Mother follows me. "Jesus Christ. Chill. You're always so fuckin' dramatic." She drags on a cigarette, the inhalation sounding obnoxious in my ears. Mother coughs wetly. "Gonna calm the fuck down, or do I need to give you some time locked up in the cupboard?"

"No! Please don't. Don't do that. I'll be good, I promise. I'll be quiet." Anything but that. Noisily, I suck gulps of air down into my lungs. It's so cold it almost hurts, and I imagine bits of my lungs turning to ice. Though I'm shaking without my jacket, I bend down to take a handful of snow and scrub it over my face.

The temperature shock has the intended effect, disrupting my panic so I can think. I wait a little while longer until my fear has been pushed down enough for me to jam a lid on it. Okay, what was I doing? Why did I leave Olivia again? She needs something. It's, uh…the antibiotics. I rush back inside and slam the door on Mother.

I take a banana, a glass of water, and the small green box into my room. "Here's a banana. Delivered fresh this morning." Trying to sound cheerful and enthusiastic comes off as a little deranged, like *I shot you but here, have some fruit to make it better!* "I've also got some antibiotics. I just thought it was a good idea, to get started as soon as possible. Because, um, infections… suck." So suave, so great at social interactions.

"It's a very good idea. If you can spare them, I'd be grateful." Olivia peels the banana and takes a small bite.

"Sure. Of course I can. Shit, I'm the one who shot you."

"Accidentally," Olivia clarifies softly.

"Yes. Accidentally." I break two pills from the blister pack into her hand. She palms them into her mouth, and I help her lean forward to sip water so she can swallow the pills. Her skin is so soft and warm that I want to touch her forever.

Olivia wipes her mouth and pauses, seeming to weigh what she wants to say. "So, what is all this? You living off the grid or something?"

I hedge. "Um. It's complicated."

"Are you one of those preppers waiting for the zombie apocalypse?" She smiles, just a little.

"No, nothing like that." Unconsciously, I shift my weight back and forth like I'm readying myself to run away from her questions. But I don't really want to run. I want to listen to her talk all day, absorbing the sound of her voice and that accent I can't quite place but makes everything she says sound wonderful.

Olivia makes a soft musing hum and sinks down against the pillow. She doesn't push any more about my strange circumstances, almost as though she's accepted my reticence. "I might try to sleep if that's all right?" Her face is expectant, as though she's asking my permission.

"Mhmm. Sure."

"Could you leave the door open a little in case I need you?" She coughs into the back of her hand. "Sorry, I don't mean to be so intrusive, but I don't think I could make it to the bathroom on my own."

"Of course." Needs me. Someone needs me. "Sure. Okay, that's fine." I nod, yank the curtains across the windows to block out the late afternoon sun, pull the door mostly closed and leave her to rest. After a couple of minutes, I have a thought. I bound down the stairs to the basement, grab a bucket then sneak back in to leave it beside the bed in case she gets sick. She's already asleep.

The dusky light outside barely penetrates my curtains, leaving me with too little light to see her features. I stand a few feet away with my eyes closed and listen to the sound of her steady breathing. For a moment, I contemplate lying on the floor just listening to the sound of another human. Just as quickly, I dismiss my idea. Creepy. Super creepy. I sneak out of my room.

I move around the dwelling, trying to be quiet when all I want to do is stand in the doorway of my bedroom and look at her. I reheat leftover pasta from last night and try to eat it around the nervous lump taking up most of the space in my stomach. I should tell the Controllers, but it's too late...too early to make a log. Don't make excuses. Technically, I can log whenever I want to, but I just don't want to. Why am I stalling? I have to tell them.

I open the romance novel I started reading two days ago and give up after a couple of pages of intrusive thoughts pushing in when I try to concentrate. Thoughts of Olivia, of her face and her voice. Our conversations. She's a real person. I trudge into the basement and put her clothes in a bucket to soak. Maybe I can get the blood out of her pants. Sew up the hole I made. Somebody is here. I'm talking to a real person. I want to tell someone. I can't. *Yankee doo*—stop.

Heather makes a helpful suggestion. "You can talk to me, Celeste. Or maybe write it down."

I use the inside of my elbow to push hair out of my eyes. "Write it down? Yeah, maybe."

Pen and paper. Where are they? I don't remember the last time I wrote something down. I've got coloring books, those stupid intricate patterned ones that drive me nuts after half an hour, and colored pencils. That could work. Where are they, where? I need to move, sitting here thinking is making me crazy. Crazier.

I stalk around, opening drawers and cupboards and trying not to slam them closed in annoyance. After twenty minutes of searching, I find the pencils stashed in the basement with a box of puzzles and books I've read too many times to be able to stand the look of them. I settle with my stuff and a glass of wine at the kitchen table. What color to start my written confession? I've been arrested and am writing my statement. I promise to tell the truth and nothing but the truth.

"I love *Law and Order*," Heather reminds me. "The actress who plays the ADA in *SVU* is so fucking hot."

"Which one? There's been a couple and they're all gorgeous." I pick up a black pencil, carefully tear the first, half-finished coloring page from the book and flip it over to the blank side. The pencil feels odd in my hand, like I'm back in kindergarten. I write the date and then:

Today I shot someone.

CHAPTER SIX

The sound of coughing startles me. I never stir during the night but I'm wide awake now and it takes me a few moments to remember why I'm on the couch, and why there's coughing. I'm not alone. How exciting. How terrifying. In one motion, I push back the blanket and swing my legs off the couch. Still dark out. No idea what time it is.

I'm outside the bedroom door and she's still coughing. Not gagging. She's not sick but sounds more like she's got a dry throat. I knock lightly. "Olivia? Are you okay?"

The words are pushed out quickly between coughs. "Yes thank you."

Resting my hand on the door, I peer through the gap. She's sitting up, hunched over in my bed with her sound leg cocked up, her foot flat on the mattress. The bed covers have slipped, leaving her torso bare except for her bra. She coughs again, kind of coughing and throat clearing simultaneously. I slip into the kitchen, fill a glass with water and take it back to her.

To give her time to pull the bedsheet up, I knock again and pause for a few seconds before I step into my bedroom. "Here. Sorry, I should have thought to leave you a glass of water. I'm not…used to having someone else to think about here." I glance at the clock beside the bed. Just past two a.m.

"Thank you." She takes the glass from me and swallows half the water in one long gulp. A thumb slides over her lower lip to wipe away lingering droplets.

I lean over and turn on the bedside lamp. Under the warm glow, she's a strange color. Sallow instead of olive-skinned, with shadows under her eyes. I fold my arms under my breasts. "Can I help? Do you need something for the pain? Is it time for more antibiotics?" I've slipped into my new role as caretaker like I was born to it, though I guess technically I was—if you count how often I cared for Riley and both our bumps and cuts and breaks and scrapes and bruises.

"No, it's fine thank you. I'll wait until the morning." She leans back against the pillow, and after a few deep breaths she adds, "I'll need to try and get someone to collect me, but I don't have any phone reception here. Can I use your Internet or do you have a satellite phone or something?"

I swallow, the movement uncomfortable and forced with my dry mouth. "I don't. I mean, I can't."

She leans forward. "I'll pay, if that's the issue."

"No, it's not that." I'm so embarrassed. It feels like I have a guest and I'm telling them there's no bathroom in my house and they'll have to go out to pee in the garden. "I don't have a phone and there's no Internet."

"I don't follow," she says with exaggerated slowness.

Surely telling her couldn't hurt? There's no protocol for this situation and I hadn't been told the fact they are running an experiment like this is secret. Just the nitty-gritty details, which I won't tell her about. "I can't contact anyone. I'm here because, well…" Settling on the end of the bed, I take a deep breath and start from the beginning.

* * *

"Wait. Wait. So it's really voluntary?" Her forehead furrows, eyebrows scrunched. She nods, tiny short ones as though each thought is a stepping-stone she's touching on her way to a revelation.

"Mhmm. I guess it's kind of like a job." Though I told her why I was here, I was very careful not to divulge too much of the study, giving Olivia only the bare-bones facts in case I let some confidential details slip.

"And you can't just ask these...Controllers to come and get me?"

"I don't know," I say sharply, fear burning through my veins on the back of adrenaline. Fear. Am I afraid of getting into trouble, or losing her? It's both, but I'm not sure which is the stronger fear. No, you can't *lose* her because she's not yours. I try to rationalize that another day or two of human contact while she heals won't do any harm, because the experiment was ruined the moment I saw her. "I can't think right now, I mean, I don't even know what the protocol for this is. I don't know what to say to them, I just—" My out-of-control thought train runs out of steam.

Olivia raises both hands. "Okay, okay. Calm down, Celeste. I don't want to upset you, but I need to make a plan. How am I supposed to get out of here? I can't hike out." She peers down at her leg, touches it lightly. "Maybe in a week or two but not now."

"I know, but it's the best I can do."

"Where's the nearest hospital?"

"I don't know."

Olivia's brows dip again. "What do you mean, you don't know? How can you not know?"

"I don't know exactly where I am," I tell her softly, that embarrassment creeping up on me again.

She pauses and I cringe, waiting for her to say something incredulous about my stupidity, but instead Olivia says, "Honestly, I'm not a hundred percent sure either, just that it's basically the middle of nowhere." The crease between her eyes deepens. "My GPS died a few hours before you, uh, found me, and I couldn't get a fix on my compass. I lost the trail and was wandering around trying to find it. Stupid mistake and I should know better. I saw your roof and figured someone might be able to help me get back on track."

I run an unsteady hand through my hair. "Look, I *think* they can collect you." Surely they won't say no. Even once her leg is healed, the thought of just kicking her out the door and leaving her to find her way home fills me with sickening dread.

Olivia stretches forward to pat my hand once. "Relax. If it comes to it, I've got a PLB."

"PLB?"

She smiles. "Personal Locator Beacon. If I activate it, an—"

"No!" I'm tied in knots, my stomach twisting and turning more with every passing minute. I can't risk the Controllers picking up on some outgoing signal until I tell them my new secret. But deeper than that, I just don't want her to go, not yet. It's so against the rules, but having her here has opened something I had shut away. A box I won't be able to put the lid back on. Talking to her for the past hour has made the last shred of resolve I had to report this to the Controllers during my morning check-in float away on a breeze.

"You slut," Mother snarls. "Want her to stay so you can fuck her."

I clamp my molars together, almost trembling from the effort of not responding to the voice.

Olivia leans forward. "Are you all right?"

"Mhmm." It's not entirely truthful. I'm sweating. It beads at my temples, my collarbones, slides down between my breasts.

"No, Celeste. You're not. Are you ill?" A warm hand finds its way to my forehead, sliding down to my cheeks. Something a mom would do. Does she have children? We've only known each other for about thirteen hours but she seems totally comfortable with me. She's awfully trusting.

I know she's not in any danger from me but I can't understand how she's just accepted that I'm not some loner psycho in the woods. I close my eyes and try to focus on the feeling of her hand against my skin, on the barely perceptible ridge of calluses at the base and first joint of her fingers. What are they from? Gardening, weights, tennis, general activities, who knows? Inhale. Exhale.

The hand withdraws. "What's wrong? You can tell me."

I open my eyes, force a tight smile and tell her the first lie I can think of. "It's nothing. Really. Think I'm just feeling a little weird about talking to someone again." Actually, that's not so much of a lie.

"Well, that's understandable. How long has it been exactly?"

I know I looked at the calendar when I woke up this morning. No, technically it was yesterday when she arrived. What did the calendar say? I avert my gaze from her distracting face, imagining my handwritten numbers counting the days I've been alone. "One thousand…two hundred and twenty-nine days."

Her mouth works open then closed again. She's staring at me like I've morphed into something inhuman and I can't help but squirm under her scrutiny. It's not that weird, is it? I'm not a hermit, not a freak, just a person doing a thing.

"One thousand, two hundred and twenty-nine days," she repeats. "That's almost three and a half years!"

"Yes."

"No human contact at all?"

"No. Well, actually kind of but not really. I send the Controllers requisitions forms and daily logs, and we instant message. But no voices and no faces."

She looks horrified. "Oh my goodness. Seriously?"

"Mhmm." In my desperation to prove that I'm really not weird or creepy, the rest of my words come out in a rush. "Like I said, it's just like a job. It's not that bad, really and it's helping science and stuff. And besides, I've always preferred my own company." Not entirely true, but the truth of my loneliness is too frightening for our fledgling acquaintance.

"Well, I guess it's a good thing that you've had nothing but your own company." Olivia grins. Her teeth are bright, white and even, except for one of her overlarge canines which is slightly out of line in front of its friends. I wonder what it would feel like under my tongue. Or scraping over my skin.

I push down my inappropriate thought and return her smile. "That's true. Are you hungry? You skipped dinner."

"No, but thank you."

"Sure. Do you need anything else?"

"No, I'm okay."

Her assurance appeases my discomfort slightly but being in here is starting to make my skin crawl. If I stay, I'm going to say something really stupid or inappropriate. I start edging toward the door. "Okay well, good night."

"Good night, Celeste." A pause. A soft laugh. "Or good morning, rather." She reaches for the lamp. Darkness. I can't see her and I'm surprised to realize it hurts. I'm empty inside again. I slip through to the living room and lie back down on the couch.

Groggy and stiff from my restless night, my neck is cricked when I rise to start my morning routine. Down the hall, my bedroom door is ajar. A quick peek inside tells me she's still asleep. Or pretending to be. I sneak in to collect my running shoes and some clothes, stealing glances at her the whole time. But she doesn't wake.

I rush out into the fresh morning and begin my run. It's starting to get too cold, too snowy and windy, too dangerous to run outside and I probably have only another week or so before I'll be forced inside and onto the treadmill. I make my way around the grounds, keeping a steady pace past the spot where I shot her. The spot where I dragged her in. Where I helped her onto the cart and brought her inside. Last night's snowfall has covered all evidence. It never happened.

By the time I'm done it's almost seven a.m. and she's still asleep. A kid waiting for their parents to wake up on Christmas morning has more patience than I do right now. A small part of me wants to make a whole lot of noise and *accidentally* wake her up. Of course I can't do that. That would be rude. I peek again on my way to the shower. I make and eat breakfast as quietly as I can, check on the still-sleeping Olivia then settle in the computer room with the door closed for my daily session with a Controller.

Cont D: We registered two shocks from your implant yesterday between 1537 and 1540. Is everything okay?

Shit shit shit. I don't want to lie, but...I don't know how to tell them what happened. Not yet. I work hard to keep my face neutral, and hope whoever might be watching me from the other side of the camera thinks nothing of my expression.

SE9311: Yep everything's fine. I tripped and fell out of the white into the green. I winded myself pretty badly and couldn't get up.

I fake a self-deprecating smile for good measure.

Cont D: I see. In future, perhaps exercise a little more caution?

Yeah, no shit.

SE9311: Good plan. Will do. Thanks.

Cont D: Do you have anything to report?

Yes.

SE9311: Nope. All good.

My body feels like it's trying to turn itself inside out. Though it hasn't even been twenty-four hours, the near-constant anxiety about Olivia being here is exhausting, that real bone-weary dread. It's been so long since I felt anything like it that I'm not entirely sure how to make it go away. I could make it go away by making her go away. Is that trade worth it?

I wait for Controller D to say something like they saw me and they saw her and they saw us. But they say nothing of the sort. Surely if they'd seen her, if I was in trouble, they'd say something? My stomach flutters uneasily. What if they didn't see her because...she's not real? I force the thought out. She's too real to be not real.

Once Controller D asks a few more perfunctory questions I'm left alone. I write a quick log—excluding an important detail—and leave the room. Door closed.

Another quick peek into my bedroom. Olivia has woken and moved into a semi-seated position resting against the pillows. She's pale but otherwise seems all right. She smiles. "Good morning. For real this time."

It's easy to pretend her smile is because she's pleased to see me. "Hey, morning." I lean against the doorway and spill questions. "How are you? How's the leg? How did you sleep?" The floodgate on my voice has been opened and I cannot push it shut again.

"Quite well thank you, for how I am and how I slept." Olivia stretches, face scrunched up as she reaches for the ceiling. "And my leg feels stiff, and a little sore and swollen but otherwise okay. It doesn't seem to have bled through the dressing."

"That's good." Seeing her in my bed stirs strange feelings, more intense than those I'd have had in my other life, outside of this place.

She's awake when I push backward through the just-open door with a takeaway coffee in each hand. I have the opposite of morning-after regrets. Illuminated by the sun streaming through my windows, she's better looking than she was last night in the artificial light of the club. The woman studies me, eyes wary until I hold up my offering.

"Hey, you're up. Here, I got coffee."

She rolls over, stretching cat-like and the blanket falls away. "Thank you. I need a little something to help me wake up."

I settle on the edge of the bed, my eyes roaming unashamedly over her exposed body. She's absolutely lovely. My voice is a seductive purr. "I can think of something else to help wake you up."

I remember what came after. The hungry kisses, coffee forgotten on the bedside table. She left while I was in the shower and I never found out her name. This memory doesn't stir anything in me, no arousal or warmth. Rather, I feel a blankness where there should be an emotion.

Olivia brings me back to the present and *this* bedroom, and that blankness colors into something that almost feels like pleasure. "Celeste?"

"Yes?"

"Are you all right?"

"Yes." I plaster a smile on my lips. "Just thinking. Are you hungry?"

Blankets are pushed aside, exposing her panties-and-bra-only body. "Actually, yes I am. I also really need to use the bathroom. Can you help me? I'm not sure how well I can walk."

"Of course." I rush over, like I think she might piss the bed if I don't get there immediately.

"Sorry, Cel. I didn't mean to. They're all still here and I was too scared to get up to pee," Riley mumbles.

I tilt my head, away from my sister's voice and the memory of what happened when Mother realized what'd happened during the night.

Olivia grabs the top of my shoulders to pull herself up. "Thanks."

I put my hands on her waist to steady her and immediately feel like I've done something wrong. This isn't the first time I've grabbed someone I barely know, but neither of us is drunk nor are we in a club. We're so close that her breasts brush mine. Everything feels wrong and strange but I don't want to let go. My fingers dig in. Hold on. Let go. Hold on. "Sorry," I mutter.

"It's okay. It's good, actually. I'm a little unsteady."

I maneuver beside her and we begin our shuffle to the bathroom. Olivia lingers at the doorway, fingers curled around the frame. "I think I can manage from here."

"Yeah sure, of course. I'll stay outside until you're done."

I leave her but stand a few feet away from the bathroom door, leaning against the wall. There's a loud thud, presumably her crashing down onto the toilet. "You okay?" I call.

"Fine. Thanks."

"She doesn't need you, kid," Mother informs me airily. "Nobody does. You're useless."

"That's not true," I shoot back.

"What was that, Celeste?" Olivia asks from behind the closed door.

Shit. I run my tongue around my mouth, desperate for some saliva so I can talk. "Nothing," I manage to push out. "Just talking to myself."

"Oh." The toilet flushes. Water runs. "I'm finished. You can come in if you'd like."

I open the door cautiously and glue my eyes to her face. She's leaning against the sink again, keeping weight off her right leg. "I think I'd like to take a real shower, if I could? I feel disgusting." She looks down at herself and her eyes widen as though she's only just realized she's dressed in nothing more than her underwear.

"Uh, sure." I have to consciously clench my teeth to stop my mouth from staying open at the sight of her.

"I can manage the showering by myself if I'm quick, but I think I'll need assistance getting dressed again."

All the options run through my brain at half speed and loop back around to one thought. Naked woman. I slide past her without touching and turn on the shower, checking the temperature as I would for a child. As I did for my sister more times than I can recall. "Um, everything's there, soap and stuff. I'll fetch you a clean towel."

"Thank you, Celeste." Olivia reaches around behind herself and I turn around so quickly I almost stumble. From behind me there's a soft laugh before her bra lands on the floor by my feet. I'm not looking, not looking.

I leave the door ajar so I can hear if she needs anything, then rush around the habitat. She needs clothes, I know that much. In my room, sorting through what I think will be comfortable, I choose sweats and a tee, then hurry down to the basement laundry for a fresh towel. The shower is still running when I come back up.

Closing my eyes just in case, I speak through the gap. "Everything okay in there? I have some of my clothes for you."

"Thanks. Would you mind grabbing me some clean underwear from my pack? Main compartment, near the middle. And my toothbrush and some deodorant too if you wouldn't mind. Sorry, you'll have to ferret around in there."

"Sure, I can do that." I'm helpful, she needs me. I open the door a little more and stretch over to place the towel on the rack.

There's a long pause. "Just so you know, there's also a handgun in there. For protection," she clarifies.

I rest my hand on the doorframe. "Are you saying you want it?" *Many women feel safer hiking alone if they have*—stop.

"No, not at all. I'm just telling you so it's not a surprise."

Her pack is still by the front door where I dumped it yesterday. As well as bear spray in one of the outer compartments, there is indeed a handgun—loaded, safety on. The gun is confusing. That she's had it this whole time spins her behavior into a whole new light. Until now I'd assumed she was staying and cooperating simply because she had no other option. Playing her cards right, ingratiating herself with a stranger to get what she needed until she could leave.

But the gun. She could have used it right at the start, taken what she wanted. Forced me to help her. Crawled out of my bedroom in the middle of the night to collect it. Maybe she's just not the armed-standoff type. I certainly am not. The way she's acting is more trusting or curious, not like someone who is afraid. I set the gun aside and dig through her bag, which is tightly packed with food, a minimum of clothing, and other hiking necessities. It doesn't take long to find what she asked for and I choose a random pair of panties and the other items, then stand outside the bathroom door, hugging the pile to my chest.

Allison laughs. "The Celeste I know would have slipped in there to join her. You love shower sex." Her voice is right near my ear and I feel a hot tongue on my neck. "Have you lost all your game, girl?"

"Not appropriate, Alli," I whisper, wiping at my neck. But there's nothing there.

Water shuts off. I wait and wait until Olivia calls out that she's done. The towel is wrapped around her body and she's breathing hard, face drawn.

I hold up my offering. "I have sweats. Sorry, I put your pants in to soak the uh, blood out."

"Thanks, that's very thoughtful. Would you be able to dry my back?"

My heart stutter-steps. "Mhmm."

She turns around and loosens the towel further so I can rub it over her back. She has a mole on her left shoulder blade, a tiny spot on perfect skin. "I think I can do everything except my underwear and the sweats. Getting underwear *off* was a challenge. I can't bend my leg," she explains. If she's worried about being near me while naked, she's not showing it. The towel drops.

I'm deliberately looking away though every fiber of me wants to look down at her ass. It's like a comedy where I'm some jock caught in the girls' locker room, except at the moment, there's nothing funny about it. She shuffles to face me again. Cover her crotch or breasts first? Pick something, Celeste. Just give her some clothes.

I grab her panties—I'm really not looking at them, I'm not—and crouch down on the bathmat. Olivia's resting her fingertips on my shoulder and I feel the tremor from her exertion as she carefully steps into the underwear. I slide the fabric up tight calves and thighs, tugging the elastic away from the wound.

Without thinking, I glance up to check they haven't snagged and catch sight of dark curls between her legs. The ache in my throat intensifies, and the urge to bury my nose in the patch of hair is almost overwhelming. Olivia leans over, fingers twitching her underwear into place. My gaze moves further upward but she doesn't seem to notice. She's fucking exquisite. Small firm breasts, soft curves, smooth skin. I want to take hours to explore her inch by glorious inch with my tongue.

Riley snorts. "Remember when you first told me you liked girls and I asked if that meant you were going to touch boobs?" She laughs and repeats herself. "Boobs!"

I clench my jaw. Shut up, Riley. Shut up.

Olivia catches my eye, her expression calm and slightly teasing. My ears burn at being caught so blatantly checking her out, and I drop my face to keep my eyes glued firmly on the mat. "Sorry." I fumble for the T-shirt and pass it up to her.

"It's fine," Olivia says. "I think I'm ready for the sweats."

I'm all too aware that under my dark gray tee Olivia's not wearing a bra. "These will be a little long on you, I think," I tell her, more to cover my shyness than out of a real need to explain. They are my favorite pair, the ones with the little rip above the knee. Soft, warm, and comfortable, and probably the closest thing to a meaningful gift I could give her right now.

Olivia makes a soft sound of agreement and we repeat the process of pulling clothing over her injured leg. I roll the cuffs up a few times so she won't trip over them with her shuffling.

Now everything important is covered, I can stand and help her pull up the sweats. My fingers brush her skin. I can't help it. There's no way to dress someone without touching them. My skin is on fire and it takes every ounce of willpower to ignore my urge to keep touching her.

I clear the longing from my throat. "There, all done. Are you hungry now?"

"Starving. And please tell me you have coffee."

"Mhmm."

"Excellent. Things might have gotten ugly if there was no coffee." She gives me the ghost of a smile. "And thanks for the clothes. I think I might even be able to sit at the table like a civilized human now."

The lame joke comes out of my mouth before I can stop it. "Then I'll have to pull out my best silverware and finest china. But the fancy tablecloths and cloth napkins are in a box in my *other* mansion, sorry."

Olivia breaks into a smile. It's luminous. "You're even funnier—" She pauses, the smile wavers then comes back even brighter, if that's possible. "...than I'd thought. I mean, what happened yesterday wouldn't have given you much to joke about, but you're so quiet that I wasn't sure you had a sense of humor."

I don't know what to say to that because I'm *not* the funny gal in the group who's always ready with a joke or something witty. My sense of humor is offbeat and erratic and most of the time only amusing to myself. I pick up her bra and underwear from the floor. "I'll wash these. With your other stuff from yesterday. I think I can fix the hole in your hiking pants."

Olivia takes the change of topic in stride. "That would be great. They're the only ones I have with me." She hops closer, her hand outstretched as though to grab me.

Awkwardness makes my toes curl, and it's made worse by the fact that I'm holding her panties. Being around her makes me a study in contradiction. I want to look at her, to touch and talk. Yet I feel I'm missing a vital connection, something that lets me act like a regular person just having a conversation. She grasps my shoulder for balance and I tense. I'm not a freak. I'm just a person living in a slightly strange circumstance. I'm normal, I swear.

"Celeste? Are you okay?" *Are you okay* seems to have become a standard question during each of our interactions.

I relax my grip on her arm. I don't even remember taking it. "Sorry." Blink, smile, respond. "Yes, thank you. I'm fine. Ready for breakfast?"

Olivia studies my face but it seems she doesn't find what she's looking for, because she glances away again. She slings her arm over my shoulder. "Let's go."

CHAPTER SEVEN

She smells like me, my soap and shampoo, but at the same time she's different. Kind of like when someone else wears your perfume and it somehow changes the scent. On our way past the computer room, I gesture at the closed door. "It's *really* important that you don't go into that room. There's a camera in there," I explain when she lifts a questioning eyebrow.

"Okay. Sure, I'll stay away."

"I'm sorry, I know it's weird," I fret.

"Celeste, don't be sorry. This is your...house and considering the circumstances, you're being very gracious and accommodating." As we continue down the hall toward the kitchen, she leans more heavily on me, her obvious limp clearly painful if her sporadic sharp intake of breath is any indication. And with every one of her halting steps my guilt grows a little more.

"It's the least I could do. After, you know...shooting you." I toss her underwear down the stairs to join her pants and shirt in the laundry.

Her fingers tighten on my shoulder. "You're going to have to let it go eventually and the sooner you do, the sooner we can move on." She lets go of me to grab the back of a kitchen chair and settles herself at the table.

Move on. Move on to what exactly? I run my hand over the back of my neck, massaging tight muscle. "Why are you here, Olivia?"

"Because I can't walk well enough to hike out," she says, like it's the most obvious thing in the world. Which it is.

I shake my head. "No, why are you *staying*? You could have charged up your GPS, worked out where you are, forced me to give you the four-wheeler at gunpoint, and sped the hell out of here. But you didn't. You haven't done any of those things. You're staying."

"I'm not really the Shoot-'Em-Up-Tex type." She smiles like she's enjoying a private thought. "Honestly? Aside from my current physical limitation, that I could no more get on an ATV than fly, I'm curious about all this. Curious about you."

This woman is the most confusing person I've ever met. I've never considered myself an expert at reading people, but usually I can make something from their behavior that gives me a sense of them. But I can't make any sense of her. My right eyebrow dips unconsciously, and I realize it probably looks like an affectation to make me appear clever. I raise it back to its rightful place.

Now that someone is here, I'm hyper aware of everything I do, and I'm questioning everything I say. It's exhausting. And rude because now I'm thinking about my discomfort and not responding. I rest my fingertips on the tabletop. "It's not that interesting. I'm not that interesting."

"How about we let me decide who and what I find interesting," she says lightly. Olivia points at the abandoned Monopoly board still laid out on the kitchen table. "What's that?"

"Oh, uh, just a game I'm playing." My simple life of the past three-plus years is now a giant embarrassment. How can I explain to her what it's like to be completely alone and what I have to do in order to hold on to pieces of myself? I'm trying to hold on now, but it feels like parts of me are leaking out. No, not leaking. Being pulled out by her.

She stares at the board then moves her focus to me. "But…"

"I'm all three players. Celeste One, Two and Three." I straighten the hotels Two has on Boardwalk and Park Place. *That bitch and her luck. When we're adults, let's buy a huge house and live together forever, Cel*—stop. Finally, I glance back at Olivia. "I play a lot of games this way. Scrabble, poker, chess."

The crease between her eyebrows deepens then disappears. "I see."

My earlobes are hot. "It…passes the time."

"Well, maybe we can play a game or two, and pass the time together." She lifts her injured leg to rest flat on the seat beside her. Something I've always found amusing is that they gave me a full-sized table with six chairs. Did they think I was going to have five imaginary friends come over for dinner every night? I could barely even conjure up two imaginary people to play board games with me.

"Okay, I'd like that." It's a truthful answer but also true is that I can't imagine playing games with someone else, not having each player aware of the other players' intentions. I move into the kitchen to start another pot of coffee. "There's no fresh milk, only powdered but I made a new jug this morning. I'm sorry, I ask nearly every month, hoping they'll send me some fresh milk but they never do. They could put it in the dry ice and I could use it right away before it goes sour. But they don't and I really don't know why."

Her smile is patient, almost like she's humoring me while I ramble on about crap. Olivia leans forward with one arm resting on the table. "Powdered milk is totally fine. What else have you asked for but not received?"

"A dirt bike. I know it's more dangerous and not actually useful like the ATV, but still, it'd be fun. A drone, but they probably thought I'd try to fly it somewhere to find a face to look at. Oh, a drum kit! I thought it'd be great for working out frustrations and maybe I could join a band when I get out. Not like there's any neighbors to annoy with my drumming." I smile inwardly.

Olivia interlaces her fingers, studying me intently. "I see you as more of a bass player."

"Noted. I'll ask them for a bass but I don't like my chances if they wouldn't send drums. I've also asked for pet goldfish but I can see how that would be tricky. But they sent me pizza last month, real deep-dish pizza, not that frozen crap from a supermarket. It was incredible." I frown. "Or maybe it was the month before."

"That must have been a very nice treat for you." It sounds genuine enough but at the same time I sense she doesn't quite understand the importance of being given Lou's pizza.

"Yes. It was." My throat feels like it's closing around the words. The coffeemaker dripping is the loudest thing I've ever heard as it marks seconds, then minutes for me. I look everywhere but at her when I ask how she takes her coffee.

"Black with half a sugar, thank you."

I choose a dark blue mug with a white stripe ringing it and fill it with coffee. Half a sugar. Balanced on half the spoon, or half full up the sides of the spoon?

"Celeste? Would you like me to do it?" There's amusement in her question. "You've been staring at that spoon for almost a minute."

Relieved, I exhale. "Yes please. Then you know it's made the way you like it." I set the mug of coffee and the sugar in front of her. "Sorry, I'm not a very good host, making you fix your own coffee."

"You're a wonderful host." Olivia scoops roughly half a teaspoon, balancing a pile of granules on the end of the spoon. Roughly, not exactly. I can do that, next time. The thought of next time makes me smile inside. Olivia sips and makes a small murmur of appreciation. "You make good coffee."

"I used to be a barista," I tell her shyly. As soon as I say it, that embarrassment rises up again. I clear my throat and gesture to the drip-filter coffeemaker. "Not that there's any skill to dumping grounds and water into a machine and pressing the on button." I slosh half milk, half coffee into a mug for myself.

She laughs, a low and genuine chuckle. "I'm sure I could screw even that up."

I make a musing sound as I put the milk away and quickly scan the contents of the fridge. "What would you like for breakfast?"

"Whatever you usually have is fine. I've been living on dehydrated food and protein bars, so anything other than that is gourmet." Her forehead wrinkles. "Actually, there's a bit of food in my pack that I can eat."

"Um, how long are you hiking for?"

"However long it takes really, until I feel like myself again. Maybe a month? I have plans to resupply every five or six days in towns along the way and I just picked up a new batch of stuff the day before yesterday."

I want to ask why she's out hiking alone in winter, why she doesn't feel like herself, but it seems too forward and too personal a question for someone I just met. "Okay, well I have plenty to share and you'll need that food when you leave." My voice cracks on the last few words.

We stare at one another and I wonder if she truly knows what it means for her to be here. I'm still not sure I know myself, but I do know it's wonderful and frightening and about a million other things I can't describe.

"Okay then, if you're sure." Her focus on me is intense but not threatening. She stares like she's really seeing me, almost looking *through* me, and I can't decide if I like it or not.

I do know the scrutiny makes me squirm, and I break eye contact first. "I've eaten already but I have fresh eggs and bacon from yesterday's supply drop. No bread. I don't eat it," I rush to explain. "But I can make some if you want. There's a bread maker and boxes of bread mix. I'll start a loaf if you want." I'm word vomiting again, over-talking, trying to explain things that don't need explaining. I close my eyes briefly then open them to her neutrally attentive face. "Look, I'm sorry, I swear I'm not this awkward and weird in real life."

She grins. "You mean this isn't real life?"

I can't move, and along with the racing of my heart I have the sudden feeling I might pass out. The question comes out a choked whisper. "You're *real*, aren't you?"

Her mouth falls open and she hurriedly says, "Shit, I'm so sorry. I didn't even think. After your being alone and everything for so long and all the…I…that was an incredibly poor attempt at humor." Her expression is earnest. "I'm real, I promise I'm real. You've touched me, haven't you?"

Slowly, I nod, gripping the counter hard to keep myself from tumbling backward. "Yes." I have touched her. And I want to do it again and again.

"Okay, good. I'm sorry, Celeste," she says again. Olivia draws in a slow breath and picks up the conversation. "So, you don't eat bread, but you still have bread mix?"

"No, I don't like bread but I, uh, just keep it in case…I'm forgotten. Then I could eat it if I had to." Even the thought of eating bread makes my already nervous stomach churn so much that for a moment I fear I might puke.

"That makes sense. But like I said, anything is fine. Please don't go to any trouble for me."

"Oh it's not any trouble at all." I need to keep talking to push away the awkwardness. "Or there's cereal and fresh fruit, or uh, I could make oatmeal too. Or if you'd prefer, I could make a non-breakfast meal. There's a lot of food because of the supply drop."

"Celeste." She smiles, her eyes softening at the edges. "Really, anything is fine. Food is food and I'm incredibly grateful that you're sharing. Especially if there's only enough for you."

"It's okay. Like I said, there's more than enough to share. This whole time, I've been keeping some extra stuff aside each month. I mean, I could probably live here for a while without the supply drops. I'd have to figure out how to eat wild meat and what to do about the waste system, but other than that I'd survive."

"Why don't you just take some supplies and hike out?"

The question surprises me. "Honestly, I've never considered it. I'm here because I signed up for this and I have to see it through." I pull out eggs and fruit and set them on the countertop. "But even if I wanted to, I can't leave. Physically, I mean."

She raises an eyebrow. Silently, I walk around the counter toward the table, pulling off my hoodie as I move. Olivia's eyes widen and she straightens up in the chair. Maybe she thinks I'm about to strip for her. Her stunned expression makes me smile, and eases some of that upset feeling in my stomach.

I find the insertion scar in my left bicep and press my thumb and forefinger either side of it. "Because of this," I explain. When I spread my fingers, pushing into the muscle, the outline of the cylinder three-quarters of an inch long and a little thinner than a pencil is visible.

She leans forward to study my arm. "Is that an implant?"

"Mhmm. If I move past a certain point in the compound, it drops me." I snap my fingers. "Just like that. You know like those zapping invisible dog fence collars?" Perhaps a little more extreme than that, but a close enough description.

Olivia looks like she's having a lightbulb moment. "Ah! So, that was what happened when you were running to me? I wondered why you looked like someone had lassoed your feet and yanked them from under you."

"Mhmm. It's not particularly pleasant." Understatement of the year.

"Why not cut that thing out? Then you could leave."

I trace my fingers over the table, following the wood grain. "Cut it out? Well...for starters, I don't have the stomach for it. Plus I couldn't, really. It'd probably ruin their experiment. Though, I think this might have." I gesture between us. I don't *think* it has ruined it, I'm sure it has. Yet I still haven't told them...

Olivia smiles. "And your payment?"

"Oh. Yeah, I guess." Her question makes me realize that aside from my initial freak-out, I've been more worried about screwing up their data than I have been about not being paid. I rest my hip against the chair opposite her and lean down to tidy Three's stash of Monopoly money. She's so messy. "I feel really guilty about you being here. But at the same time, I really like it."

"It's not your fault, Celeste. Even I can see you didn't do it intentionally."

"Logically, I know that. They're supposed to make sure I'm secluded, but I still need to tell them."

"What will happen? Will you be in trouble? Could I vouch for you somehow? Tell them that it was an accident."

"I don't know."

Her caramel eyes find mine. "I don't want you to have issues because of me."

I think it's too late. I'm already having issues. Personal ones. The way she's looking at me warms me, relaxes me, arouses me, soothes me. I want to grind my molars together, to hear the obnoxious squeak of tooth on tooth, just to have something uncomfortable to clear the thoughts and feelings I shouldn't be having. "I think...I think maybe it'll be okay. I'm past the minimum threshold, so technically they have enough data. That's all I am to them, really."

"Data," she says. The word is flat, and without warning the moment becomes unexpectedly charged with some unknown emotion.

I feel like it's all my emotion, filling this space and threatening to smother us. Ruining the moment again. Desperate for some breathing room, I try to make a joke. "At any rate, I guess you being here means I can't walk around naked anymore."

My attempt at levity seems to work, and her eyes make a leisurely trek over my body. "I wouldn't be worried if I saw you naked." The heat rises to my cheeks before I can stop it. She grins, seeming pleased by my reaction, then moves on as though she hadn't said anything suggestive. "Is there anything else I should know, aside from not going near the room with the camera?"

I flail for something to tell her so we can move past the innuendo. "Only drink from the faucets that have the green band around them."

"Why is that?"

"Those are water from the well and have been treated."

"Okay, I'll be sure to do that," she says. "Does it ever run out?"

"Drinking water? It hasn't yet but if it does I can treat the rainwater collected in all the cisterns to make it safe for drinking, and there's another thousand gallons of emergency water stored underground."

"Seems they thought of everything," she says, glancing around the living room.

"Pretty much. The whole compound is one hundred percent eco-friendly and energy-sustainable." I laugh. "Or so the manual tells me."

She swallows another mouthful of coffee. "Is there anything you'd like to know about things that have happened in the outside world over the past few years?"

I bite my lower lip. "Yes. I want to know everything. But please don't tell me. No, wait. Is that awful boy band One Direction still around?"

Her forehead furrows. "Yes? Oh, no…I think they split up? Or someone left? Sorry, I'm not big on that kind of music."

"You just scored a point with me for not liking that shit."

She laughs. Pleasure flits through me. I walk back behind the counter and crack eggs into a bowl.

* * *

After she's eaten, I leave her on the couch with another coffee and head down to the basement to start a load of laundry. I wring her clothes from the bucket where they've been soaking. The water is tinged the faintest pink. Her blood is on my hands again. Diluted this time but it feels the same, like I have the essence of her with me. What a stupid thing to think. When did I start having such deep, existential thoughts?

I stuff things in the washer and pick up her bra and underwear from where I tossed them at the base of the stairs earlier. Her panties are in my hands and I can't help rubbing the fabric between my fingertips. The thought flashes through my head before I can redirect it, and I almost raise her underwear to my nose. My throat tightens when I think about the scent of another woman.

"Pervert," Mother hisses.

Heather laughs. "I bet she smells delicious. Bet she tastes even better…"

"Go away," I tell them both.

I do up the bra, my fingers playing over the fabric, remembering how it feels to remove another woman's bra. To slowly unfasten one hook at a time and carefully lower straps over smooth arms. To wrench the hooks free and yank fabric aside to expose breasts. I close my eyes, imagine standing behind Olivia as I undo the clasp, my lips on her neck as I drag those straps down her arms and—

"Stop it," I whisper to myself.

I toss Olivia's underthings into the machine with everything else and start it up. Sitting on the stairs, I watch clothes tumbling around the washer and listen as a button or zipper clinks against the glass door on each revolution. It's not a regular sound. I can't find any comfort in a rhythm.

My knee cracks when I stand and continues clicking on my way up the stairs, through the hallway and to the lounge. "I'm just going out for a couple of minutes. Are you okay where you are?"

"I'll be fine." Olivia slings an arm over the back of the couch and smiles at me. When she smiles, her whole face joins in. She's not a fake, mouth-only smiler. Or maybe she is but not for me. For me, she smiles like she means it. *Even if you don't feel like it, Celeste, a smile can make you feel bett*—stop.

I pull on my coat and boots, and push outside, hoping some fresh air will clear my head. It's suddenly imperative that I clean the solar panels again. And walk the perimeter. And gather some fresh food. Anything to be away from her, from my confusion.

As I tidy things in the greenhouse and gather vegetables, I think some more about my houseguest. Nearly every waking moment since she arrived has been spent thinking about her. The Controllers need to be told. Despite my desperation to have someone here, the feeling of doing the wrong thing is overwhelming. I can't handle it, I have to do the right thing. Tomorrow, I'll tell them tomorrow. She's still recovering, sleeping a lot through the day. Giving her another day to let her rest after being shot doesn't seem so wrong.

The realization of Olivia not being here anymore sends a sudden sharp pain through my chest. Am I having a heart attack? Relax. Calm down. You can't be having a heart attack. You're young and healthy. It's just panic. So stop panicking. My hands are fists by my side. I leave the greenhouse and rush down to Hug Tree where I wrap my arms around the trunk, forcing myself to breathe deep and slow.

After a while, the pain in my chest abates enough that I can ease my arms from around the tree and walk back to the greenhouse. I'm so frustrated with myself. This person isn't me. I don't despair when people leave me, I don't worry about being left alone. I never have, and I've been left a lot. Yet here I am, losing my shit after barely two days with her. A small voice in the back of my mind—thankfully it's mine this time—tells me that not latching on to her after so much time by myself would be even weirder. I gather the bucket of vegetables and make my way back to the house.

Olivia has moved back to the table, staring at my abandoned game of Monopoly, and she says nothing about my extended absence. No "Honey, you're home" moment. I transfer food from bucket to sink and rinse the greens. I have to remind myself to turn around, to walk closer and speak up so she can hear me because she's a real person and not a thing in my head.

I even ask a question like a real host. "Any requests for lunch and dinner? I'm afraid the variety isn't great."

Cont A: How are you finding the food?
SE9311: Not bad. A little boring, but I'll manage.
Cont A: I'll try to get some more variety to you. Any requests?
SE9311: Real milk, more fresh fruit and some dark chocolate, please.
Cont A: Dark chocolate. Good choice. I'll see what I can do.

"As I said earlier, anything is fine." Olivia turns one of the dice over and over. Six. Four. One. "Perhaps you'll let me help you make a meal sometime?"

"She thinks you're a shit cook," Mother supplies helpfully.

I rub the back of my neck, pushing the voice out of my head. "If you want. You don't need to, though."

"I'd like to. And besides, what kind of Italian would I be if I didn't offer to cook for you? My mamma would kill me," she teases.

Italian, of course that's it. "How long have you been here?" As soon as I say it, I grimace. "I'm sorry, that's a really rude question but…you've got a slight accent." It's not overwhelming, but it's there and it's lovely.

Olivia smiles, shifting on the seat. "It's not rude. My parents and I emigrated when I was eighteen. A little over sixteen years ago." She offers something else, something I didn't ask for. "I didn't want to leave and threw tantrum after tantrum, especially because my sister was twenty-one and already at university, so she got to stay. She's still in Italy, managing a large hotel."

I rush through the math. She's thirty-four or thirty-five. She has an older sister. I add those facts to the short list of things I know about her. "Then I accept your cooking offer. When you're feeling up to it that is."

Because I said I would, I make bread for Olivia, fighting with the machine because I've never used it. As the smell of baking bread fills the house, we start a game of Scrabble. She's good, but not as good as Two. I'm up by eighty-four points when the bread maker beeps to tell me it's done.

The bread looks decent and I feel an odd sense of pride that my first attempt wasn't a complete disaster. Maybe I should be a baker. A butcher. A candlestick maker. Olivia's talking. I turn away from my creation. "Sorry. Pardon?"

"Could I have a slice from the end, please? While it's still hot."

"Sure." Even though I use a dishtowel, the metal insert around the loaf burns my fingertips. I suppress a grimace, tap the loaf from its tin and slice a half-inch slab from the end.

Despite my effort, there's obviously something in my expression that's given away my disgust. Her smile starts slow and turns teasing. "Hot fresh bread with butter, Celeste." The words sound surprisingly seductive. "It's fantastic. You really don't know what you're missing out on."

I do. I know very well. I've eaten nothing but a few slices of days-old bread with cheap spread at every meal for months and months at a time.

"So fuckin' fussy." Mother sounds angrier than usual. "Should have let you go hungry."

Cringing, I draw my shoulders up to my ears. Every time I react to the voices, I see Olivia's expression change. She knows something is weird, that *I'm* weird and possibly unstable. I inhale. Chill out, Celeste. "No, thank you. And I don't have butter or margarine, sorry. There's no point when I don't eat bread." I set the slice of bread on a plate for her.

She picks up the conversation without mentioning my odd reaction. "What about olive oil?"

"Yes, I have that." I fetch the bottle of extra virgin for her, then watch as she makes a small puddle on the plate. Pieces of bread are broken and lightly dipped in oil. The thought of eating that is loathsome. But I sit at the table and watch her anyway, simultaneously fascinated and repulsed.

She chews her snack and watches me watching her. Her upper lip glistens until she wipes her tongue over it to clean the trace of oil away, and I'm surprised by the sudden overreaction of my body to her unconscious action. I'm wet. I cross my legs and try to ignore it. With Olivia here, I can't do anything about my arousal.

"Slut." Mother laughs.

I cross my arms and try to ignore her too. "I need to tell the Controllers you're here. I don't want to."

The bread pauses halfway to her mouth. "I can imagine it's a difficult decision for you."

I shrug, trying desperately to seem like it doesn't matter. Like she doesn't matter. "The longer I leave it, the harder it's going to be. I feel like I'm hiding weed in my bedroom or something."

She hastily swallows so she can laugh. "Thanks for the comparison." Olivia rubs her fingers together over the plate. "When will you tell them?"

I look at her fingertips. There are still some tiny crumbs on them. I hate bread, but I'd put those fingers in my mouth and suck every trace of bread and oil from them. "Tomorrow. I'll tell them tomorrow."

It's only a day aw— Stop.

CHAPTER EIGHT

When I wake with a runny nose and a raw throat, I know I won't be telling the Controllers about Olivia today. I've got a goddamned cold—the first one I've had since I got here. "Ungh," I say to nobody, rolling over and nearly falling off the couch.

The barely-there headache I was ignoring when I went to bed—or to couch, rather—has intensified into a deep pounding through my temples, and I feel so shitty that for a moment I think I might cry. I shuffle to the bathroom to wash my sticky face, scrub at my eyes and supplement my morning vitamin tablets with two Tylenol before I stuff a handful of tissues into the pocket of my sweats and go to check on Olivia. She's sleeping, uncovered to the waist, lying on her left side with an arm under the pillow and the other slung off the bed.

It's light enough to see her face and check the rhythmic rise and fall of her breathing. I watch her for a few moments then close the door as quietly as I can and go back to the lounge.

She'll call me when she wakes and needs my assistance getting up.

My nose and eyes water furiously but a hand to forehead check confirms that I don't have a fever. Then again, I'm not a doctor so who knows, and hands on skin aren't exactly accurate science. I make tea with honey, and lemon juice from a squeeze bottle, then wander down to the basement to search my supplies for some decongestant. There's nothing. Of course not. Viruses are spread by people, and there should have been nobody to make me sick so why would I need that?

I trudge back upstairs, collapse on the couch again and cover myself with the blanket. Huddling under it makes me feel marginally better. Not going outside. Not running. Not doing anything except feeling sorry for myself. How am I going to explain this when the Controllers see me on the camera at check-in time? Hangover? Emotional? I guess I could fake crying. At least it'd be an excuse for constant eye wiping and nose blowing. Sniffing hard, I fumble in my pocket for a tissue.

Joanne, my adoptive mom, reminds me, "Don't sniff, Celeste. Blow your nose like a grown-up. That's a good girl."

This is the first time Joanne's visited me here, and for a moment I wish she was really here to fuss over me and make my favorite pumpkin soup and tuck me in just right. My eyes drift closed again. So tired. Just going to nap for a few minutes until it's time to check in or Olivia needs help.

I have no idea how long I've been asleep for when I wake to Olivia's call of, "Celeste?"

"Yeah?" I rasp.

Her words echo down the hallway. "Can I get a little help please?"

"I'm coming." The words stick in my throat, hoarse and barely audible. I swallow and try again. "Coming."

I trudge into my room. She's already got the covers off and when she sees me, her morning smile dies on her lips. "Is everything okay? Are you ill?" That's the second time she's asked me that question.

I shake my head. No not okay, not no I'm not sick. "I think I've got a cold."

Olivia looks horrified. "Oh shit. That might be my fault. I'm really sorry, I've been half-ignoring a mild one for a week or so." The look of horror turns to one of interest. "I'd have thought I wouldn't be contagious. Maybe your immune system isn't as strong as it should be. Or I was asymptomatic for a while."

Here I was thinking the slight stuffiness in her voice was from secretly crying or something. "Fascinating," I murmur, offering her a weak hand. "You wouldn't happen to have any leftover decongestant or something I could use, please?"

She takes my hand and pulls herself up. "Sure. In my pack, front pocket. Why don't you grab them while I'm in the bathroom?" Her hands are on my shoulders. I'm sick, gross and I don't want her to touch me. Olivia either doesn't notice or doesn't care that I'm clammy and snotty.

While she's in the bathroom, I grab the pills from her pack. Here I am in her things again, trying hard not to look. But I want to. I want to paw through her bag and stare at what she thought important enough to bring on her hiking trip. Sometime last week, she stopped at a Walgreens and bought something for her cold. Walgreens. *The corner of happy and healthy.* What a weird slogan for someone who's sick. With a handful of water from the kitchen sink I swallow pills and make my way back to the bathroom.

"Did you find them?"

"I did. Thanks." I gesture at the shower. "Did you want…?" Before I finish the question, my hand flops to my side. You're pathetic, Celeste. It's a cold, not Ebola.

"Please."

She showers by herself and dresses with my help. It's easier this time, not to look at her, to pretend that I'm fine with touching her. I make breakfast, though Olivia insists she's perfectly capable of doing it herself. I'm not sure if it's because I don't want her in my kitchen, messing up my things or because I want to show her that I make really good scrambled eggs. Half my eggs are already gone. I can't bring myself to care—there're many boxes of powdered eggs and she's worth it.

For breakfast I pick at cereal and take a shower while she's eating. Last night, before I was sick, I thought I'd masturbate the first chance I got. This is my chance and I don't even feel like it. Typical. I sneak into the computer room for morning check-in, still hiding my secret.

Cont C: Good morning. How are you?

SE9311: Good. It's pretty cold outside. I just came in from a run.

Hopefully they'll accept my preemptive explanation as the reason why my eyes and nose are red. Cold. As in temperature not virus.

Cont C: Do you have anything to report?

SE9311: Nope.

I'm desperate to blow my nose. Instead I sniff, trying to make it look like I'm just drawing a deep breath. Snot clogs the back of my throat, making me nauseated.

Cont C: When are you planning on video logging this week?

Shit. Shit.

SE9311: In a few days when I've got something to talk about other than Scrabble.

Cont C: I've always found your word choices enlightening, SE9311.

SE9311: I'm pleased I can teach you something.

Cont C: If there's nothing else, I'll leave you be.

Damn, I was so close to getting a response to my joke. I wonder if Controller C is smiling.

SE9311: There's nothing else.

Cont C: Have a nice day.

The screen changes back to my regular logging program and I quickly write out a log.

Things I miss:
-Driving cars - speeding a little.
-Standing under streetlights.
-Being in a crowded place.

Last night I dreamed I was home. Not that shitty apartment on Henderson, but home. With Joanne. She kept trying to tell me something about Mother, but I couldn't hear her, like my ears were blocked with cement. It was weird, I was my age now but she'd just adopted me. Haven't dreamt about Joanne in years. Not sure why I would now. Maybe tied to the voices. Riley wasn't there.

Even after all this time, typing my sister's name sends a pang of anguish through my body like a shockwave. I log off and leave the room before the bile sitting at the back of my throat breaks free. Olivia glances up from the book she's reading on the couch. "Everything okay?"

I nod, pour myself a glass of water, drink half of it and carry the rest over to the couch to sit beside her. Her fingers move to the corner of the page like she's going to fold it down. Then she pauses and I can see the cogs turning. It's not her book. It's not really my book either and I don't care if she dog-ears it because I do the same thing. But before I can tell her it's okay, she sets the novel facedown without marking her spot. "Did you tell them about me?"

"No. I meant to, really, and I will in a day or two when I don't feel so miserable." I glance at her, knowing how pathetic I must look. "I'm sorry. I can if you want, I can go in there right now and tell them to come get you."

"No, it's fine, really. I get it. I'm still feeling kind of weak myself and a few more days won't hurt."

"Mmm, and I think I'd just like a little company while I'm sick."

She smiles at that while Riley mutters unhappily in my ear, "You got soft, Cel. You didn't want me around when Ma did those things to your jaw and your arm, but here you are begging for someone to stay when it's just a stupid cold."

Before I can stop myself, my face twists into an annoyed expression at my sister's intrusion. I want to yell that she was so little and there was nothing she could do to help me on either of those occasions. But I don't. I clench my teeth down on the words, rubbing absently at my right forearm which has predictably begun aching.

Olivia's concern is clear. "Celeste? What's going on?"

"What do you mean?" I force myself to stop rubbing my arm.

"You look like you're...not here."

I laugh, which sets off a coughing fit. Turned away from her, I cover my mouth and cough until my lungs hurt. Not here. Not here. I'm here all the time. I can't get away from *here*.

I shuffle sideways until I'm what I deem a polite distance from her. It's still close enough that I feel a connective arc between us. Probably my imagination. She touches my arm and I flinch, until I realize she's checking how hot I am. Her grip is light, moving around my forearm, then her hand comes to my forehead. She smiles. "You're warm. I think you should take that sweater off."

I shake my head. The smile dims a little, and after a moment Olivia makes a concession. "Well, take some Tylenol and drink plenty of fluids." As if I don't know how to deal with a cold.

"I'm doing that."

"Good." She taps her fingers lightly on the back of the couch. "Do you mind if we talk some more?"

I run a fingertip around the rim of my water glass. "Sure, I'd like that." Talking is amazing.

She shifts her injured leg to rest on the coffee table. "What did your family think of you doing this?" Her free arm sweeps, indicating the general space around us. "Can't be easy for you to be away from them."

"I don't have family. My birth mother is a drug addict who I have to assume is still alive somewhere. My sister, or rather the only sibling I know of, is dead. I had various foster families but I've been out of contact with them for years. And my adoptive mom is also dead." I don't mean it to, but everything comes out as a dispassionate statement of facts.

Olivia doesn't falter. "And your father?"

I keep my gaze steady. "Not sure. Mother didn't know. Could be a junkie friend of hers, a dealer, or some guy she fucked in an alley for a couple of bucks to buy a hit of meth." I'm suddenly aware of my words sounding self-pitying when they aren't really. It's just that I've told my story so many times over the years, it's become nothing more than a tedious anecdote.

"Oh, Celeste. That must be hard for you." Though it's only the third day, I've learned the change in her tone when she's upset about something on my behalf. I heard it a lot that first day in the small hours of the morning in my bedroom when I told her about my time here.

"It's fine. Really. It was all so long ago."

"I just, I still can't wrap my head around it. How have you coped being in here by yourself all these years? How is it that you're not totally batshit crazy by now?"

I tuck my legs underneath myself. "Maybe I am but I'm just really good at hiding it." Ha. Ha. No, really.

The words seemed to catch Olivia off guard. I smile and slowly, she returns it.

"You're teasing me," she accuses, though the grin makes it clear she's not bothered.

"Just a little. You're too easy." I let the innuendo stand between us. I'm surprised at how easily flirting has come back to me—natural as breathing. Natural as breathing was before my nose was clogged with mucus, that is.

"Maybe I am. It's not the first time I've been told that." And it's easy for her too, it would seem.

I tap my fingernails against the glass, my thoughts suddenly turning somber. "You know, I think maybe I am a little bit crazy. These past few months, I've been…imagining things." Even as I say it, I'm not sure why I'm telling her.

Realization dawns on her face that I'm not joking or teasing now. "What kind of things?" She leans forward, seemingly unperturbed by my revelation.

"People I know talking to me, touching me. Stuff like that." I set the glass down, turn away from her and quickly blow my nose.

Olivia shifts on the couch. "Seems like a logical thing. In the absence of companionship, your brain makes it up for you. … *where from afar all voices and scenes come back.*"

I can do nothing but stare at her, dumbfounded. When I find my voice, I blurt, "That's part of *Childhood's Retreat* by Robert Duncan! You know it?"

"Yes. It's one of my favorites."

A smile tugs at the corner of my mouth. "Mine too." I cough into the crook of my elbow.

Her smile is cautious. "You don't strike me as a poetry lover."

"Really? I love poetry. It's fluid, engaging…easy. You don't have to understand a poem to enjoy it." My fingers trace a triangle on the arm of the couch. "You don't think I'm crazy or anything do you? Because I'm interacting with stuff I know isn't real?"

"No, I don't. I think you've done what you needed to do in order to survive."

In order to survive. I guess that's the theme of my whole life. There's a long pause where we're just looking at each other until eventually, she asks, "Are you afraid?"

"Of what?"

"The voices."

I answer without pause. "No." It's the truth. "I'm frustrated and upset. But not afraid." I can't be afraid of something that's not real.

* * *

Olivia is right-handed, like me. She's a research scientist, working on cutting-edge chemistry stuff for drug companies. Her last name is Soldano. Her favorite color is purple. She likes to be the thimble in Monopoly, which suits me because Celestes One/Two/Three don't like that piece. There's so much we can talk about, even though we barely know each other. But I have to ration it out or I'm going to get overwhelmed by all this knowing.

I've learned what I'm calling her *guilty-grateful* look, a sheepish kind of smile whenever she takes the antibiotics or pills for pain. She also gets that look whenever she asks me for help moving to and from the bathroom, and when she agrees if I ask her if she wants something to eat. It's as though she feels she's a burden, when the reality is that she's anything but.

I haven't asked if she's married, attached or has kids. I don't know if she's a dog or cat person. I do know that she seems to *really* like coffee—so far I've counted an average of four mugs per day. No tea, thank you, she said when I offered, following up by telling me she's never drunk a cup of tea in her life. She mock-shuddered and I thought about teasing her by tossing a teabag at her. But I didn't because we're not that kind of friends. We've reached polite acquaintance stage, like where you can be left alone with the friend of a friend at a party and no longer feel uncomfortable about it. About the talking that is. I'm still twitchy about touching her, partly because I want to so badly that trying to keep myself from going further has my nerves firing.

After lunch, I help her back into the bedroom to rest more comfortably than on the couch. I can tell her leg is bothering her, though Olivia assures me there's no heat in it to indicate an infection and aside from the stiffness and dull pain she feels good. I know now to leave her with a glass of water. "Call out when you need me. I'm going to nap on the couch until dinner."

She fidgets with the pillows. "Why not sleep in here? I'm sure you've got a fever and sleeping on the couch isn't going to do you any good."

"I...can't." *A sneeze can travel six feet, landing on anyone in—*stop.

"Why not?"

Please don't make me explain it to you. Don't make me tell you I can't stand to be so close to you. It's uncomfortable. I don't trust myself. But Olivia is already shuffling closer to the edge of the bed, pulling the other side of the duvet down for me. That side is my side where I always start my night of sleep before I end up sprawled in the middle of the mattress. She looks expectantly at me, her hand smoothing the sheets.

I cover my mouth and cough, then delicately climb into the bed beside her. I'm a plank of wood. Sleeping on the couch where at least I could stretch and relax would actually be more comfortable. So why did I give in so easily? Olivia reaches over to rest the back of her hand against my forehead. I watch it coming toward me. I'm the earth and she is a meteor about to crash into me. At the last moment I scrunch my eyes closed.

"You *do* have a fever," she says with what sounds almost like a touch of triumph. Whenever she touches me, her voice gets low and calm, and I can't help but be soothed by both touch and words. I nod, because what can I say to a fact like that, then roll onto my side facing away from her and pull the covers up to my ears. I wonder if she can hear my heart pounding.

I wake from what feels like a too-short nap, startled by the warmth beside me. While I slept, I rolled over and moved to nestle against her with my arm wedged between us and my face pressed to her shoulder. She's awake, reading a book and she smiles indulgently down at me. I shuffle back to put distance between us again and sit up. Worse sore throat. Blocked instead of dripping nose. Headache but no other ache. Brilliant.

"You talk in your sleep," Olivia tells me, smiling like she's discovered a secret.

Nobody's ever told me this before. "I do?"

"Mhmm."

"What did I say?" The words crack and break around the grossness in my throat.

"Nothing that made much sense." Her hand makes another trip to my forehead and cheeks. "A little warm but not so bad. I don't suppose you have a thermometer around here?"

The flush I feel isn't from the virus partying in my body. I lean back slightly to disengage from her hand. "Maybe. Probably. I've never looked."

"Why don't you see if you can find one? I'd like to know your exact temperature."

I swallow, gritting my teeth against the razors in my throat, and I can easily picture Riley's eye roll at my babyish behavior. "Do you need to get up?" I do a side roll off the bed to get away from Olivia.

"I'm good for now, thanks."

I pee, then brush my teeth and gargle with mouthwash a couple of times to get the taste of sickness out of my mouth.

After ten minutes of half-asleep and sick-uncoordinated stumbling around the dwelling, I find a thermometer in the first aid kit—one of those weird sensor ones I can't figure out. Whatever happened to good ol' under the tongue? I present her with a coffee as well as the thermometer.

"Ohhh, coffee. You're wonderful, thank you so much." Olivia sets the mug down on the bedside table. "Lean close." When I do, she presses the device to my forehead, sliding it to my temple. "Ninety-nine point seven. I don't think it's bad enough to be the flu, likely just my cold. Now your cold."

"Mhmm."

"You need to take some more Tylenol and rest. And you *must* take that sweater off."

"I don't want to," I mutter like a petulant child.

"I know you feel chilled but that's only the virus. I assure you that it's not real." As soon as those last three words are out, she clamps her mouth shut. After an apologetic and helpless smile, she adds, "I'm sorry, I didn't mean…"

I can't help but smile back. "It's fine. I'm going to get some water and clean up a little. Do you need anything?" Sniffing hard, I manage to stop the sneeze that's threatening to escape. *A sneeze can travel six*—stop.

"Can you please find the chocolate in my pack?"

"I'll see what I can do." I have a bunch of chocolate in the pantry. I'll give her some of that so I don't have to dig through her things again. I need to sleep but I'm worried I might not wake in time if she needs the bathroom. She agrees to get up and I help her to the bathroom then deposit her back in the bed.

I leave a sandwich, snacks, and water for her along with some books. She fluffs pillows behind me and not so subtly takes the duvet off me every time I pull it up. "Wake me if you need me," I slur. There's a hand stroking my forehead, pushing damp strands of hair away from my eyes. The hand moves to my cheek.

Coughing and sweaty. Everything's fuzzy. She's reading a book, her injured leg propped up on cushions stolen from the couch. Her hand is almost to her mouth and is holding a square of dark chocolate that's been bitten in half. "Are you okay?" Olivia asks.

I nod. My throat still feels raw, but is more gunky now than anything. To add to my misery, that awful viral weakness has settled in my body. I struggle to sit up. "What time is it?"

"A little after four." She shifts the chocolate in her mouth so it's nestled against her cheek like a squirrel.

"Morning or afternoon?"

"Afternoon."

Pushing my hand through my hair, I gather it up and fix my ponytail. "Do you need anything? Bathroom?"

"If you don't mind, yes please."

We've got the coordination down and I hardly brush against her at all while she hops to the bathroom. I'm worried I might not wake up for her if she needs to move around, so I leave her on the couch and make my way to the entryway. "Just going to get something outside," I mumble.

I throw my coat on over my inside clothes and scuff around until I spot a branch that looks right. The air hurts my lungs and makes me wheeze so much I have to keep stopping to cough.

"You sound like Mr. Hopper." Riley giggles. "Remember how we had to sit there for ages while he talked about the adoption and he had that huge booger, and we thought it was going to shoot out and hit us?"

"Yeah it was disgusting," I agree hoarsely.

I make a quick stop in the shed for tools and fashion a rough walking stick for Olivia. She's about my height so I guess at the size, smoothing and paring it down until it feels right in my hand. I test it out, fake limping around for a few steps. Seems sturdy enough. It'd be better made if I wasn't so weak and wobbly.

"Useless," Mother reminds me.

I can't even be bothered answering her.

Back inside, I present the stick to Olivia with a clumsy flourish. "A walking stick for you, ma'am."

The stick is the perfect height. She smiles and gently touches my shoulder, then starts to hop around with the stick, making a circle around me. "Thank you. You're incredible, Celeste."

Tightness grabs my throat. I'm in danger of losing my voice. It's the cold. It has to be the cold. I manage a whispered, "You're welcome."

CHAPTER NINE

While dinner simmered on the stovetop, I changed the sheets because I'd sweated in my sleep and I can't stand the thought of Olivia sleeping like that. They're now those navy blue ones instead of the nice purple set the Controllers sent me. After dinner, I showered and was ready to sleep on the couch for the night, but she practically dragged me to the bedroom. Now that she has the stick and can move, she's more insistent, as though made bold by her independence.

For the first time since I've been here, I set an alarm in case I don't wake in time to check in. After a few naps beside her, my body is better disciplined, and I'm still on my side of the bed, not touching her, when I wake before my usual time. Sore, scratchy throat but no sweating or serious congestion. *At the corner of happy and*—stop.

I don't remember timeframes for cold symptoms. A week? I lie in bed without moving, my eyes still closed, listening to Olivia's deep, slow breathing. Stealthily, I turn to look at her.

She's on her side, facing me. When she sleeps, she leaves her hair loose and I can smell my shampoo. I reach to touch her hair, to drag the dark strands through my fingers, but thankfully stop myself at the last moment. As quietly as I can, I turn off the now-unnecessary alarm and slip out of bed. Olivia has never woken in the morning before eight, so I have a little time to do what I need to. I walk around slowly outside and make my checks. No snow last night, everything is in order. When I come back inside, I'm shivering with that deep, bone-chilled shudder that comes of cold air and illness. Hot shower then hot mug of tea.

On my way to the bathroom, I strip to my underwear and toss my clothes down into the laundry. My hand is on the doorknob when Olivia emerges from the bedroom. My first thought is mild panic that she's seeing me practically naked. My second thought is how adorable she looks, all sleep-mussed. My third is that the walking stick seems to work well and maybe she's going to leave me soon.

I know she looked at me in my underwear, and the thought would be exciting if I didn't feel so shitty. I'm shaking with cold and maybe a bit of leftover fever, trying to get the door to open. Eventually I shove through, snatch a towel and wrap myself up.

"Celeste?" She rushes toward me as fast as hobbling will allow her, a slight grimace contorting her lovely features. "What's wrong?"

"I'm just a little cold."

She makes a fever check with her hand. It lingers longer than usual. "You're not warm." The thermometer is taken from the bathroom cabinet where it now lives and I'm declared officially not feverish. But I'm still cold and shaking.

"Get into the shower, come on." Her demand is followed by an apology once I'm in there. She needs to pee. I turn away and don't watch. I can't hear her. The glass on the shower isn't frosted. Is she watching me? Now I'm warm.

Suddenly we're in role reversal where she's caring for me, and I don't know how to take it. Still wrapped in a towel, I brush my teeth, catching sight of her in the mirror where she's behind me, watching me. She leaves clean sweats and a hoodie on the closed toilet, along with bra and underwear. I can dress myself, thank you.

When I'm done with my morning Controller duties, Olivia suggests we look at her leg. "There's no heat in it and I feel fine but I'd like to take a look to be sure, and change the dressing." She can stay standing for longer than when she first arrived almost five days ago, and move around with relative ease, but still prefers to spend most of her time sitting down with her leg elevated.

A shudder slides down my spine. I'm not sure if it's because I have to look at the wound or if it's because I'll see her partly unclothed again. It's probably both. I clear my throat and try not to sniff. "How much longer will you take the antibiotics?"

"The guidelines said five to seven days. So I guess another few days." She's already made a point of letting me know that when the antibiotics are finished, how much she's going to enjoy the wine I'd told her was in the basement. She's made plans of things she wants to do in a week, when the likelihood is that she'll be gone well before then.

Thankfully, Olivia leaves her tee on and only pulls her sweats down, leaving her underwear in place. To my non-medical eye, her leg looks okay—less swollen and the wound isn't angry-looking. I make warm salt water, because I used an entire bottle of saline the first time, and repeat my care from day one. This time I'm less nervous, less twitchy, but not less repulsed. Her hand lingers on my shoulder. My hands want to wander and so does my gaze, but I force myself to keep both my gaze and hands in acceptable places.

"You're disgusting," says Mother. "Can't even clean someone's cut without wanting to feel them up."

My hand clenches around the tube of antiseptic cream.

"Who is it, Celeste?" Olivia asks quietly. Not what, but who. She knows.

"Mother," I grind out through clenched molars.

"What does she want?" The hand on my shoulder tightens, but it's not uncomfortable. It's soothing, inviting me to share. Instead of responding, I shake my head. I can't tell Olivia that Mother thinks I'm a pervert. I quickly finish dressing the wound, help Olivia pull up her sweats and leave her to make her own way out of the bathroom.

She comes into the kitchen as I'm heating canned soup, settling in her usual place at the kitchen table. The silence stretches. I make her some toast then pour all the soup into one bowl and set it, and the toast in front of her. Olivia pounces right away. "Why aren't you eating?"

"Not hungry." I slump into the chair opposite her.

"Bullshit," is her quick response. "You barely ate breakfast and you only picked at dinner last night." Olivia pushes the bowl over to me.

I slide it back just as fast. "I'm really not hungry. It's fine."

A muscle in her jaw quivers. "No it's not. You can't starve, Celeste."

"I'm not starving. You eat it, you're trying to heal, Olivia."

"And you're fighting a cold. I'm not going to let you make yourself sicker." The volume of her voice rises with her indignation. Now I've figured out the cues that go with at least three of her moods—gratitude, interest, and annoyance.

"Won't let me, huh?"

Olivia's expression softens. "No. Here. Please share with me." She offers her spoon.

I shake my head and fetch one of my own. We both palm pills into our mouth. Antibiotics for her, decongestant and Tylenol for me. I slip around to sit to her right at the head of the table, making it easier to share from the same bowl, and with every mouthful the childish thoughts loop around my brain. We're sharing saliva right now via spoons and soup. We're practically kissing.

Riley giggles. "Celeste and Olivia sitting in a tr—"

In my head, I yell at her to shut up. What is she, ten-years-old?

* * *

Late afternoon, I'm lounging on the couch feeling sorry for myself. And annoyed at myself for being so pathetic. I've never worried about my own illness or injuries before, but here I am being a miserable baby. Olivia hobbles over to me with a long-sleeved undershirt in her free hand. "Do you mind if I put some things in the corner here on this chair? I'm sick of digging through my pack every time I want something."

I sit up, staring at the blue woolen garment in her hand. "Of course not. Let me make some space in the closet."

Both of Olivia's eyebrows shoot up. "Oh, no. That's not...I mean, you don't have to." Unspoken words linger in the air. She won't be here long enough to make good use of storage space. I don't care. I'm going to make her some space.

She has her stick but my hand is still drawn to her elbow to help her move around, and she makes no complaints. Olivia sits on the bed while I push hanging clothes to one side of the closet and clear a drawer for her. "Here, that should be enough."

"Thanks. I don't have much." Olivia waves off my offer of help, hopping back and forth from her pack on the bed, to the closet and drawers. I hang around and try not to look too interested in her things. She ejects the magazine from her handgun and clears the chamber before pressing the round back into the magazine. "I assume you've got a gun safe for that rifle of yours." The corner of her mouth curls upward.

"Yes."

SE9311: *Why do I have a rifle?*
Cont C: *Shooting is good for hand-eye coordination, and should a wild animal stray close to the house, you have some protection.*
SE9311: *What if I go crazy from loneliness and shoot myself?*
Cont C: *I would sincerely hope you don't, but it would be an experiment result.*
SE9311: *Failure?*
Cont C: *Not necessarily.*
SE9311: *Wonderful. Thanks so much.*

Not that I've ever thought of doing such a thing. Still, my contract indemnifies them if I were to die in here, by any means. Contract aside, I have no family who could pursue legal action against The Organization in the event of my unfortunate demise. They chose their participant well. I have a nominated charity—a drug rehabilitation clinic—and in case I don't make it out they will pay whatever I earned to that.

Olivia's hand jiggles, trying to catch my attention. "Can you put this away, please?" Why is she giving her gun to me? Why not keep it? My mouth is open but there are no words. Olivia explains for me, almost apologetically, "I don't really like guns, but my dad insisted when I said I was going out hiking by myself. Please. I just want it away where I don't have to worry about it."

"Okay." I take both pistol and magazine, my fingers brushing hers, and leave her in my bedroom while I put her weapon away in the basement safe.

"Awfully trusting of her, Celeste," Allison observes.

I'm getting better at not responding to them out loud. Why should I have all the power, Alli? If Olivia wanted to shoot me then she'd have done it by now.

While I'm away from Olivia, where she can't see or hear me, I blow my nose hard a few times. I've never been good with people watching me blow my nose, or listening to me in the bathroom, which made Mother's preference for *communal* living even more uncomfortable.

When I return, Olivia is sitting on the edge of the bed, with a phone in her hands. I spot telltale white earphones straight away. "Is that a—is there music on there?" I ask.

"Yeah." She's smiling as she watches my likely wide-eyed expression. "Do you want to listen? It's almost dead but I have the charger." She holds the phone out, an offering.

Christ, I want to, so badly. My tongue slides over my lower lip. "I really shouldn't. I'm not supposed to." I laugh dryly. "Though I'm already breaking one rule by keeping you here."

"Only for these few days," she reminds me, an edge of teasing in her voice. The phone is still in her hand, taunting me.

"Could I just see what kind of music you like?" I ask tentatively.

"Sure." Olivia unlocks the phone and passes it to me.

The phone confirms there's no signal here. Slowly, I scroll through the list of artists. It's not extensive, mostly eighties electropop or rock. Depeche Mode...Fleetwood Mac...New Order...Queen. I look up, trying to reconcile the woman in front of me with these music choices. Even in sweatpants or her hiking gear she exudes culture and elegance, not someone I'd associate with that type of music. "How old are you exactly?"

She laughs. "Thirty-five, and yes, I know. My musical tastes are a constant source of teasing from friends."

Five years older than me. "Just not what I expected, that's all."

"What music do you like then?"

"Everything," I answer quickly and honestly.

Olivia stares at me, her forehead creasing. "Eclectic tastes. I'm not surprised."

Nodding, I swallow hard and excuse myself, but not before I give her phone back. Being near her, talking about something as normal as music is too uncomfortable right now. I need to get away from her kind eyes and gentle questioning. I step into my boots and push my arms into my coat as I'm walking out the door. I'm still too weak and congested, still too tight-chested and gross-feeling to go for a run, but I need to check the solar panels and greenhouse. Or just do something, anything to get a little distance.

All the exterior systems are in order. The air burns my lungs but not in that clear, revitalizing way I crave. I hide out in the greenhouse for ten minutes, checking my plants and picking greens for dinner. Still edgy and anxious, I make my way over the snow toward Hug Tree. The bark is cold against my cheek. Eyes closed, I indulge myself and pretend I'm hugging a woman and she's hugging me back. For a few long moments, I can *almost* feel what it would be like to have arms around me again. A warm body. Curves and breasts. I clutch tighter, as though I could pull myself inside the trunk of the tree.

On my way back, I see Olivia at the window where she's watching me shuffle back to the house. The door opens as I approach and she ushers me inside. "All systems working as intended?"

I tug off my beanie and set the bucket of fresh produce on the floor. "Yep."

Closing the door behind me, she asks casually, "What were you doing down there?"

"With what?" Scuffing my boots on the mat, I shrug out of my jacket.

"That tree."

"Oh. Uh, nothing." Just hugging it, you know. Totally normal.

Olivia leans against the wall, keeping weight off her injured leg. She grins, slow and sure of herself. "I saw you. It didn't look like nothing."

The heat starts at my neck and works its way to my ears. Caught me. "I was...hugging it."

"Hugging it." Olivia's raised eyebrow turns the statement to a question.

"Yes. Hugging." I lift both hands in a helpless gesture. "Sometimes I just need to hug and there's nobody here, so something had to substitute for someone."

"When did you start doing that?" she quietly asks.

I kick out of my boots. "About four or five months after I got here. Before that I tried hugging pillows and wrapping my arms around my torso and squeezing hard, but neither felt quite right. So...Hug Tree."

"That's really clever of you." There's a touch of sadness interwoven with what sounds like admiration.

I blush like she's just given me a Nobel Peace Prize, and offer a quiet, "Thanks."

Riley giggles in my ear. "You haven't cured cancer, Cel. You just figured out how to hug a tree trunk." Her voice turns wistful. "You give really good hugs though. I miss them."

My houseguest pushes away from the wall and takes a step toward me. "Well, I have two perfectly good arms and a torso if you'd like something reciprocal."

Unconsciously, I cross both arms across my chest. "You barely know me. Why would you hug me?"

She measures her words carefully. "You're right, but I know if I'd been living the way you have, I'd hug the first person I saw even if they were a hobo on the street."

I smile faintly. "Well you certainly aren't a hobo."

Olivia returns my smile. "No, I'm not."

Taking a deep breath, I relax my arms to my sides. I can't deny the appeal of having someone hold me. Especially when I feel so cruddy from my cold. I imagine warmth nestling against me and arms enfolding my body. A face pressed into my neck. Trying to ignore the trembling in my arms, I agree, "Well, all right then. I mean, if you don't mind."

Her response is barely audible. "I don't mind."

I exhale, long and soft. "I'd really like that." I take a small step forward then pause, giving her a chance to back out if she wants to. Olivia makes no move to step away, but rests the walking stick against the wall, opens her arms and waits for me to close the gap.

My tentative arms sneak around her waist and then I'm stalled, unsure what to do next. But it's Olivia who pulls us closer together and the moment her arms lock around my back, something inside me shakes loose. The tension and loneliness of the past years are released in a single heartbeat.

I hold on like she's a life preserver, registering every sensation—the pressure of her arms around my back, the feeling of breasts against mine, the gentle movement of her body under my fingers, the mix of scents in my nose. I bury my face in Olivia's hair, not caring that it isn't polite to nuzzle someone who's virtually a stranger. But it's not sexual or even sensual. It's just nurturing and it's warm and it's safe and it feels incredible.

Olivia doesn't shy away. If anything, she holds on tighter, her hands tracing meaningless patterns over my back. The pressure isn't frightening, she's not forcing me or constricting me. She's just *holding* me. I burst into tears.

"It's okay," she soothes, her words low in my ear. "You're okay." Her nose is brushing against my neck as I cry.

I don't know how long I cry but when I feel like I can talk again, I pull back and swipe at my eyes with the heels of my hands. Between my cold and my tears I can barely breathe. "God, I'm so sorry. How embarrassing."

But Olivia's face holds no judgment or mocking, only soft understanding and compassion. "No, Celeste, not embarrassing. I think it's a perfectly normal response." She takes a halting, hopping step forward to place a hand on my shoulder. "And I'm more than happy to do it again, but for now I really need to sit down." She smiles and starts hobbling with her stick toward the couch.

"Shit, of course. I'm so sorry." I fish in my pocket for a tissue then wait until she's a little way away before I blow my nose.

She's on the couch with her bad leg angled up on the coffee table. "Don't be sorry, Celeste." She pats the seat beside her, leaving her hand resting on the seat, palm up as though in invitation. "Human contact is such a funny thing. We think we don't need it. Until we realize we do." Her voice is soft, almost contemplative.

I lower myself down beside her and after a moment, take the hand on offer. Running my thumb over her soft skin, I revel in the contact. There's heat under my thumb, drawing itself into my body to warm me. To renew me. I lift my eyes to find Olivia watching me and when I speak, my voice cracks. "I do need it."

CHAPTER TEN

I've had the cold for three days and I'm feeling much better, but still not normal. Or whatever normal is for me. When I tried to move back to sleep permanently on the couch, Olivia became so insistent that I stay in the bed where it's comfortable that I gave in with barely any internal debate. What's the point? I want it. She insisted. I even slept better last night, probably less worried about accidentally touching her in my sleep.

She changed her dressing again this morning and told me the edges were starting to scab over. Then she invited me to take a look. No thank you. Olivia laughed, and then in a quiet voice said, "Everything seems to be healing really well. I might be able to walk out in another week."

I choked on my response, and all I could get out was a strangled, "Mhmm." Please not yet. I'm not ready. The truth hangs over my head like a stone about to drop. It's not a question of if, but when. It's always been inevitable, I've always known that I would have to tell the Controllers and start the process of getting her home. The process of taking her away from me.

I don't want to, but I have to. Whenever I think about telling the Controllers my secret, my guilt becomes so overwhelming I have to make myself stop thinking about it in case I start choking.

"You're a really bad liar, Cel," Riley reminds me. "But it's okay, because I'm good enough for the both of us."

I'm not a bad liar, I rebut indignantly in my head. It's just that I don't like lying about everyday stuff. It's only for important things, remember? Like no, I'm not going to tell the cops, and yes Riley and I are fine so you can go away now please. My arm aches, and I rub my palm along my skin as if I could rub the past away.

I leave Olivia at the kitchen table with her breakfast and coffee and take my own mug into the computer room. The Controller is already there, a message waiting on the screen for me like an accusation.

Cont E: Hello, SE9311. How are you?
Controller E? Who the hell is this?
SE9311: Hi. You're new. Who are you?
Cont E: I'm Controller E.
SE9311: Obviously. Why are you here?
Cont E: There's been some changes in the monitoring department.
SE9311: Changes like what?
Cont E: Staff turnover.
SE9311: Who got turned over?
Cont E: A staff member.
Nice sidestep, E. Clearly I'm not going to get any more from them.
SE9311: I see. I assume it won't affect my daily routine?
Cont E: Not at all. Can we discuss the content of yesterday's logs?
I look to the closed door of the computer room then catch myself. Don't want to give the secret away. I sniff hard which sets off a tickle in my throat that I have to clear by coughing. As soon as I'm done, I snatch my hand from my mouth and type an answer.

SE9311: Sure thing.

Cont E: Are you okay?

SE9311: Yeah, sorry. I got a big whiff of bleach while cleaning the bathroom earlier and I think it's messing with my lungs and sinuses.

Riley is right. I'm bad at lying and I hate it, but I can't tell them about Olivia because I just don't know how.

Cont E: Perhaps open some windows to clear the air? And be sure to let us know if anything out of the ordinary happens with your health as a consequence of the cleaning products.

SE9311: Will do.

After I close down the system it dawns on me that I haven't seen Controller A in a while. A couple of weeks maybe? So I guess it was Controller A who got turned over. I hope they moved on to other things, something better than asking how I'm feeling every day. I hope so. I can't think of anything worse than keeping track of my tedious life.

Maybe they really did have a wife who had a baby and now they are taking some time off. Extended overseas vacation. Maybe Controller E is actually Controller A because they got sick of being A. But Controller E doesn't seem like Controller A, who was always nice and seemed a little more willing to talk to me than the others.

Maybe they had a car accident. Maybe they grew bored with reviewing logs. Maybe they stole pens from The Organization and were fired. Affair with the boss. Fight with a colleague. There're hundreds of possibilities but I'll never know for sure. I'm surprised to find I care. I'm also surprised to find I'm a little annoyed and upset that Controller A never said goodbye to me.

By the time I finish, Olivia has relocated to the couch. She glances up from her book, smiles, but doesn't say anything. I sit at the end of the table, away from the game of Scrabble Olivia's winning. Slowly I add words to my private pages of handwritten logs of all the things I can't tell the Controllers.

The words are for them eventually, but also for my own benefit. I've logged every action and most of my thoughts for so long that not getting them out makes me feel like they're going to grow into something so huge I won't be able to contain it. Somewhere in my time here, my handwriting morphed into a barely legible scrawl and it hasn't become any better this past week. Idly I wonder if I'll keep a journal when I leave.

"Remember that time I read your diary, Cel?" Riley asks, all apologetic.

I nod and make a small sound of agreement under my breath.

"You were so angry. I'm sorry, I shouldn't have done it."

No, she shouldn't have. She shouldn't have done a lot of things, but she did and there's nothing I can do about it now.

I stare at the words, trying to make enough sense of what's in my head to put the rest of it on the page. I stare at Olivia, hoping for inspiration. As though drawn by my gaze, she looks up and out of nowhere says, "I think I'll make soup for dinner."

"Sounds great," I respond, for lack of an articulate response.

She spends the afternoon cooking, hopping from the couch to the kitchen to stir and check and add things. She won't let me help. When I ask her why she's going to so much trouble instead of eating canned soup, she tells me I need to eat something wholesome if I want to get better more quickly.

Olivia promises it will taste wonderful, despite using frozen chicken and a mix of fresh and dried vegetables. It's on the tip of my tongue to tell her exactly what I want to taste. The hum of arousal under my skin that started when I first touched her a week ago is steadily getting worse, and I'm sure the only thing keeping it suppressed is the cold.

"Wish I was there to help, Celeste," Alli teases. "Remember how you like me to—"

Olivia interrupts. "Celeste, could you help me with this soup pot, please? I can't manage it with my stick."

"It's ready?" Dumb question. She wouldn't ask for help unless it was.

"Sure is." She points a stern forefinger at me but she's smiling. "No excuses. You're eating."

Dinner is excellent and I tell her so. My praise seems to please her, even more so when I take another small helping.

Then I salt it liberally, as I do all my food, and the pleased expression turns to a frown. She grumbles, "You eat too much salt."

I almost tell her that it's not really something she should be worrying about, but opt for a neutral response. "Maybe I do."

Emotions play over her face. First there's concern, then an almost defiance like she's going to push her point but knows it's not hers to push because she's not my lover or my friend. Finally she settles on a sort of pleading expression, as though she's genuinely upset by my excessive salt intake. She's adorable. I can't stop staring.

Olivia cants her head to the left. "What? Have I got food on my face?" She wipes her mouth with the back of a hand, and even this quick gesture is graceful. She's elegant, beautiful, and she doesn't deserve to be stuck here, cooped up with me.

"No. Not at all." I bite my lip and make a swift subject change, but it's really not one for the better. "I'm sorry, it's rude of me to stare but I can't help it. I, it's, um…you're just…sweet, and beautiful." As soon as the words are out I want to snatch them back. "Jesus, I'm sorry, I shouldn't have said that. I mean it's true, but I shouldn't have said it."

"Don't worry about it, Celeste, really. It's quite flattering, thank you." She looks like she's trying not to smile but the unmistakable lift in her cheek gives her away. "I'm not opposed to you staring if it helps make up for these years of being alone."

But I want more than staring. I want touching. I want it so much that the need has become constant and overwhelming, and I'm forever censoring my body. She gives me things that I'm sure she doesn't even realize and with every piece I get, I want more. I want to give her pieces of me too. No, scratch that. I want her to *want* pieces of me.

"Bit soon for imagining white picket fences, isn't it, Celeste?" Alli asks.

"Hush up, Allison. You're so old-fashioned with your wanting to wait until it's perfect," Heather grumbles. "Don't listen to her, Celeste. Sometimes when you know, you know."

But I don't know. None of my feelings can be trusted. With my eyes on the placemat, I take a mouthful of soup, daintily the way Joanne taught me. The rest of our meal is eaten in silence. Once I'm done with dinner dishes, I settle on the couch to write down some of what I'm feeling about her. About us. No, Celeste, there is no us. It's her and it's me. We are two separate things.

While I write, she showers. I hear the water running and I think of her in there. Naked. Hands running over her skin. The ever-present pulse gets more insistent. It wouldn't take me long, I could just slip my hand between my legs and take care of it in less than a minute.

"Celeste?"

I sit up, snatching my hand away from where it's almost under the waistband of my pants. "Yes?"

"Would you mind coming in here to have a look at this please?"

That is not going to help my current situation. I hop up and rush to the doorway of the bathroom where she's wrapped in a towel, leaning over to examine her leg. "What do you think?" she asks.

"It...looks okay?" I swallow my revulsion and lingering guilt. "Better than before."

She gently touches the skin at the edge of the wound. "I might leave it without a dressing."

I nod and turn away to drink some water from the bathroom sink to ease my dry mouth. Lifting my shirt to dry my lips I see her watching me in the bathroom mirror. Our eyes meet. "What?" I ask.

"Just you, drinking straight from the faucet. I don't really know anyone who does that."

"Yeah I know, it's gross. Sorry. Old habit I can't seem to break." I glance down at the sink. "We uh, didn't always have cups. Mother thought spending money on that sort of thing was stupid when booze came in its own ready-made drinking vessel."

She doesn't say anything but reaches out to touch my shoulder. Ever since we hugged, she seems to touch me more. A brush against my arm or a squeeze of my hand. Her hand lingers on me longer than it needs to but it's not long enough.

Olivia hobbles out of the bathroom with her stick, and I watch her progress until she reaches the bedroom, closing the door so she can dress. I don't worry so much about staring at her now because she watches me too—while I'm cooking, checking equipment, flossing and brushing my teeth, eating peanut butter from the jar and doing dishes as she dries them. We're existing in a weird gray space of forced but comfortable domesticity. I really need to tell the Controllers about her because we are not housemates, and getting as comfortable as I am is dangerous.

I'm reclining on the couch, leaned against the armrest with my handwritten logs on my lap, trying to think of what to say without sounding like a stalker. I'm so overwhelmed that everything I've written about her makes me sound obsessed. Then she's behind me, a hand resting on the cushion beside my shoulder. Not quite touching. The seconds lengthen. Ever since she arrived, my time is all messed up. It moves from point A to point B in a straight, slow line instead of jumping around everywhere at different speeds. She makes everything slow down, drags out our time together. I think I like this slow time with her.

Olivia asks something and I'm so focused on her closeness it takes me a long moment to decipher what she's asking me. I set the pencil down and crane my neck to look up at her. "Tea would be wonderful, thank you. Let me help."

"Don't get up. I've got it. What are you writing?" Her hand has moved again, now resting on my shoulder, thumb massaging the tense muscle of my neck.

I feel myself relaxing into her touch, body responding with a low exhalation like it's pushing all my tension out. "Just…things about you and me. Things I can't tell them now but that I think they'd be interested in."

Olivia peers over my shoulder, thumb still working her magic on the knots. "Do you really think it matters?"

I can tell she's read some of what I've written and I'm suddenly embarrassed. I turn the paper over. "Mhmm. It's silly but I feel like I should record it." I look up at her again. "It would be relevant, right?"

Olivia shrugs. "I really couldn't say because I don't know the parameters of this experiment, but the scientist in me thinks yes, they'd like to know."

"That's what I thought."

Her hand brushes over the back of my head and then she's moving around my kitchen and making me tea. "Lemon and honey again?"

"Yes please." Between the medicine and endless cups of medicated tea, the cold virus is being smothered.

Olivia offers me a smile. "I'll see what I can do." When she comes back, leaning on the stick with a mug of tea in the other hand, she's inordinately proud of herself. "Only spilled a little."

"Ah, thank you." I take the mug carefully, wrapping my hands around it and capturing her fingers by accident.

She laughs and tries to wiggle her fingers free from under mine. "Have you got it?"

I extricate the mug from our fingers. "Mhmm, thanks."

Olivia gently caresses my cheek with a mug-warmed hand. Her eyes soften, mouth lifting in a small smile. If I turned my head, I could kiss her palm. It would be so easy. Instead, I deliberately move my cheek out of the way of her hand.

The smile turns knowing, and she makes her way around to sit next to me. "You don't seem feverish at all and you sound much better. How are you feeling?"

"Not too bad." I sip the tea. It's good. Hot and strong with a nice balance of honey and lemon. "Almost feel like I can start my daily jogs again."

She stretches her legs, a light hand playing over her right thigh, just below her wound. "I think I might have to join you on one of those morning laps around the perimeter. I miss being outside and I'm so tired of being stuck in here." Olivia glances up. "If you don't mind taking it slowly."

"I don't mind. You like walking and hiking then?" Add one point to the pointless small talk column. She's doing an extended hike, so obviously she does.

"Mhmm. I don't get to do it as much as I'd like but every now and then I just crave the fresh air and solitude, you know?"

I don't know so much about the solitude part but I get the need for fresh air. I ask the question I've been wanting to ask for ages. "So, uh…this finding yourself idea. Can I ask why exactly you're doing that?" I hold my breath, hoping I haven't asked too personal a question.

She exhales noisily. "Needed to get away from my life for a while I guess. Personal stuff that I needed a break from."

Immediately I want to know what personal stuff she's referring to. Family? Job? Relationship? I want to know if she's got a boyfriend or a girlfriend.

"That's really none of your business, Celeste," Heather singsongs.

"I'm sorry to hear that," I say politely to Olivia.

"Mmm. It's not as exciting as it sounds. Feeling a little dissatisfied with my life in general. Had a decade or so of bad romantic relationships. Working too hard. Can't seem to find a balance between the two." Olivia picks at imaginary lint on the leg of my borrowed jeans. "I love my job but it's always tied up in feelings of inadequacy."

"How so?"

"I—" She bites the inside of her lower lip, the edges of her mouth turned down.

"You don't have to tell me," I say hastily. I've pushed too far.

"No, it's fine. Just not sure how to explain it." She's still frowning, but it's not so much a frown of displeasure as a frown of thoughtfulness. "My dad pulled a lot of strings to get me my current position right out of college. I know he only wanted to help and the job is the job I've always wanted. But at the same time it makes me feel like a bit of a failure, you know? Like one of my big tests of adulthood and I failed it. Couldn't even get my dream job without Daddy's help."

I see where she's coming from, but at the same time I'm not quite sure I understand. For me, the idea of being given a boost up like that is incredible. "Does he ever make you feel like you owe him for his help, or like you're not capable?"

"Oh, God no. He's not like that at all. I know he's incredibly proud of my accomplishments." She shrugs. "My whole family is great. Just my own weird sense of expectation I guess."

"Does your family know where you are?" Surely there's someone who misses her, someone who is worried? She hasn't mentioned it and with everything else, I hadn't thought about it.

"Well, I'm through-hiking, and they know I'm away for a while. I've been able to take a month off work as I haven't had a proper vacation in years. I've been keeping in contact with them every time I pass through a town, and they know that unless they don't hear from me for two weeks or more they shouldn't worry. I didn't give an exact timeframe for the entire trip because who knows how long it takes when you're soul-searching." She makes air quotes.

"How long has it been since you were in contact?" I wonder if she's finding her soul here with me.

Her nose wrinkles. "Eight days? I think."

"So we…*you* still have a little time." Not enough. There will never be enough.

"A little bit of time, yes."

The things she's shared have made me brave. I ask another forward question. "And have you found what you were looking for?"

"I think I might have, yes. Some part of it at least." Her smile is secretive and a tiny piece of me hopes the part she's talking about relates to me, that I've somehow helped her *find herself*. I dismiss the idea almost immediately. What a ridiculous, arrogant thought.

Olivia tilts her head, making a low musing sound at the back of her throat. "You know, I still find it really hard to think there's nobody out there missing you."

"I have friends, but aside from that, there's nobody. Like I said, my family is gone." I give her a few more facts, adding to what she already knows. Drug-addict mother. Many other families. Fostered. Adopted.

It's easier to build on what I've told her now that we're not complete strangers. Maybe I have needed to talk to someone after all. I run my thumb along the handle of my mug. "Mother was apparently clean when she was pregnant with me, and on and off after. But by the time she was pregnant with Riley, she was getting fucked up again all the time."

A hand brushes over the back of my neck, lightly stroking. I don't bother suppressing the shiver that builds and travels down my spine to make my back muscles tingle.

"You don't have to talk about it, if you don't want to," Olivia murmurs.

"No, it's fine. Honestly, it feels good to talk." I scrub a hand over my face. "Man, Riley could scream and scream when she was a baby but she was lucky in the end I guess. No permanent… damage." Lucky doesn't seem like the right word for it. "They took her away for a while then gave her back when she was almost one and a half because Mother somehow managed to look like she had her shit together."

"How old were you?"

"Nearly six. I don't really remember much. Just that Riley cried a lot."

And Mother didn't like crying. She didn't like a lot of things—me learning how to hide milk from whoever we lived with at the time and how to mash up food to feed my sister, me learning how to lock doors from the inside, me learning how to use her clothing for diapers, and me learning to talk back. I learned other things too—it's hard to dodge a cast-iron skillet when you're trying to protect your baby sister, and that if you make a game out of eating mashed-up food and milk just like your sister does, it helps you forget the pain of your fractured jaw.

I remember more but I'm not going to talk about that. Those details are too much, too much.

"What about your adoptive mother?"

"Joanne? She was foster mom number five. I was, uh, thirteen when she took us in. She adopted us right before I turned sixteen, got all the worst parts of raising two girls. She taught me about periods and bras and boys." I grin. "Until she realized she had to teach me about girls."

"You're gay?"

"Yes."

This information seems to have no effect on her. She's neither repulsed, nor suggestive. She's just Olivia. "Do you keep in touch with her? Joanne."

"She died when I was twenty-three. Cancer. It was horrible." More than horrible. Joanne did everything for Riley and me. She taught me how to care about things again, made sure we went to school and helped whenever I felt dumb. She showed me what it felt like to belong somewhere. What it felt like to belong to someone. The memory makes my throat tighten and clearing it turns into a short coughing fit.

Olivia waits until I'm under control again, then asks, "What about your birth mother? Have you seen her since you entered the foster care system?" Her questions are probing, but I don't feel bristly about them the way I have in the past. Talking about myself and my history usually arouses pity, and pity sucks. But Olivia seems to attach no such emotion to my story. The only thing she seems is interested.

"No, not seen or heard. Mother didn't contest the adoptions. I don't think she even contacted them when they notified her."

The hand stroking the back of my neck moves to my arm. Boldly, I move my hand to take hers, which is warm and dry. Mine feels clammy. I draw in a slow, steadying breath. "When Joanne got sick I was in college, studying to be a lawyer. I wanted to work in family law, helping people with their adoptions and stuff. The way I was helped." It feels idealistic now, and so far removed from my life that I don't see that person anymore when I look for her.

"Wanted to be a lawyer? What about now?"

"Now...I really don't know. When Joanne died, it was like the start of the end for Riley. She just let it all go after that, even more than usual. She spent the small inheritance Joanne had left her then came to me, pleading and begging me to help her. Promising she was done and wanted to be clean. I dropped out of law school and used the money I had for tuition to try and get her some help." But it didn't work, nothing worked. "Joanne and I had both tried over the years, but it wasn't enough. She always went back to it. And it finally killed her." I can't help the bitterness in my tone. I *am* bitter and I hate myself for it. I hate myself for wanting my sister to be stronger. I hate myself for not being able to keep her alive.

"God, Celeste. I'm so sorry."

"Mmm, thank you." I look up. "She was already cold when they found her. Nothing they could do." Once upon a time I would have choked on those words but the soft, empathetic way Olivia is looking at me makes it easier to get them out. It hurts so badly that sometimes I feel like I can't breathe, but at the same time, my sister is dead and I am not, and I have to live.

Strangely enough, Riley doesn't pop up with an indignant rebuttal the way she usually does when I think about this part of our life together. Frowning, I tilt my head, waiting for her. Nothing.

Olivia interlaces our fingers. Her face is barely inches from mine, and her expression still tender. I could lean forward and kiss her, and she'd probably allow it because who wouldn't when someone's told you such a horrible snippet from their life? But I don't want it to be like that. I want it to be real. And I don't want to have the tail end of a cold.

The silence between us is long and comfortable. Olivia's the one to break it. "I don't see you as a lawyer." She isn't the first person to say that. In college I was constantly mistaken for arts or literature. I actually did start out in arts because it seemed like an easy degree but decided fairly early on that it wasn't for me and it wasn't going to pay the bills.

The decision was made easier by the fact I'm not an arts person. I'm science and logic. Logic. Logic is why I struggle in this place because nothing I think or feel makes sense.

I smile my best self-deprecating smile. "I'm not smart, but I worked hard. Actually, I only just passed the LSAT to get into law school. But I passed."

Someone shakes me awake. "Hey."

I look down at the table and the books I fell asleep on, then twist to stare up at the person who woke me. I know her—she and I have a bunch of classes together. She's fair-skinned, clear blue eyes, and light brunette hair pulled into a messy bun.

"Celeste, right?"

Swiping my hand over my mouth, I trawl through lectures, and group activities until I recall her name. "Yes. And you're Heather."

"Yup." Heather leans against the heavy wooden desk. "What are you doing in the common room at this hour?"

I shrug, still fighting the lingering effects of sleep. "Same thing you are, I guess."

Heather grins, transforming someone aloof into someone I suddenly feel like I want to get to know. "Well, I wasn't sleeping on my books like you. I have a bed for that." She pulls out the chair beside me and settles into it. "Are you always here in the small hours?"

I nod.

Heather opens a book. "Need a study partner?"

I push the memory away. "That's all in the past now." But everything is merging—past and present and future. I can't separate out the strands of my life.

Olivia strokes my hand tentatively. "Can I ask why you went into the foster system?"

"Mhmm, of course. Mother was a meth addict. It was mostly neglect, lack of food and clothing and cleanliness and adequate healthcare. We always slept indoors somewhere so that was something I guess, and the other abuse stuff was so infrequent that sometimes I think I don't remember how bad it was."

Most of the time.

My forearm starts up with a dull ache the way it always does when I think about Mother breaking my arm. Even now, after all this time, standing at the top of long flights of stairs sends a shudder of alarm through my body and I have to pause and make sure I'm safe. That nobody is going to grab my hair. That nobody is going to shake me until I feel like I can't breathe, and then throw me down the steps for daring to tell her that her kids were hungry.

"Thank you for telling me," Olivia whispers.

"You're welcome. It's okay, really. I think I've finally moved past it." I frown. "Or I had, before this."

"You seem well-adjusted, all things considered." Her eyes widen. "I'm sorry, I didn't mean to sound judgmental."

"No, it's fine, honestly. I had my phase of loathing and anger, and…uh, a bit of self-harm and stuff like that when I was about fifteen, but I realized it didn't help. None of those things got me anywhere. Joanne stuck us in a ton of therapy and I kind of realized there's no point in hanging on to it." I laugh dryly. "Well, any more than I have to. I carry it with me because you can't *not* with something like that but…I don't want to use it as an excuse to be a bad person, you know?"

"That's really impressive." Olivia smiles, taking the opportunity to touch me again. This time it's a gentle stroke of fingertips over my cheek. "I think that's one of the bravest things I've ever heard. You're perhaps the bravest person I've ever met, Celeste."

"You give me too much credit." She doesn't know about all the times I've been cowardly. About all the times I've taken the easy way out or run away from something. Or someone. I shift slightly away from her, and she doesn't chase.

After dinner it's time for more Monopoly because Olivia likes it better than the other games. It's not my favorite, but I don't care. I'd play anything, do anything to make her happy. I don't know who should play. One, Two or Three. After a brief internal back-and-forth, I decide that I'm going to play as myself. Just plain old Celeste.

Olivia settles opposite me and reaches for the dice. "Is everything all right? You seem pensive."

I shuffle my fake money and count it. "I just…really don't want you to leave. That's all." Looking up, I catch her eye then glance away again. Staring out the window into the darkness, I mumble, "I'm going to tell them in the morning."

Tomorrow, tomorrow, it's only—

Stop.

CHAPTER ELEVEN

When I wake curled around her with my face buried in her neck, I decide I'm going to keep her here forever and never tell the Controllers. I scrunch my eyes closed and push the idea out of my head. Aside from being one of the creepiest thoughts I've ever had—like she's a pet or a toy with no say in how she lives her life—I'm not actually going to be here forever. Dim morning light through the window accentuates the fine hair along her jaw and I want to rub my knuckles gently over the spot and feel the soft down against my skin.

But I can't. I can't touch her that way and I can't keep her here. It's not right, it's not fair and the longer she stays, the harder it is for me. Eyes burning with tears that want to escape, I slip out from behind her and then leave the bed without waking her. Olivia rolls over, sliding an arm underneath the pillow, the other stretching out to the bare space I just vacated. Her fingers curl against the sheet, then go still.

It's easier to be strong and convinced about my decision to let her go when I'm away from her. When she's not grasping my arm as she sleeps, or her feet aren't tucked between mine for warmth. When she's not looking at me. When she's not embracing me.

Easier, but not easy.

She's been here for eight days. Over a week of holding on to a secret that both nourishes me and eats away at me. It's time to tell them, but God I do not want to tell them. I want everything but this. I want to spend months getting to know her, learning her secrets, having her tease things from me until we're so comfortable with one another we're like a favorite pair of jeans. I just need more time. Time to fill in the gaps of my physical longing with an emotional and intellectual knowledge of her.

But what I want doesn't matter. It never does. My whole life, all my thoughts and desires have always been pushed aside in whatever circumstance comes along. I'm nothing more than a paper boat cast into the rapids, tossed and turned in turbulent waters until I become pulpy and break apart.

I settle in the chair in front of the computer but don't log anything, just sit and wait and feel the trembling in my legs. I tap my fingers against the keyboard, not hard enough to actually make letters form on the screen. There's no rhythm, I'm only listening to the soft clicking. It's Controller B this morning. B for Bad. Bitter. Broken. Bastards.

Cont B: Good morning, SE9311. How are you?

No point delaying, I launch right in.

SE9311: I'm fine but something's happened.

Cont B: Are you injured?

SE9311: No but there's been an incident.

Cont B: What kind of incident? Is any equipment or vital system damaged?

SE9311: No, nothing like that. I

The cursor blinks and blinks and blinks.

Cont B: You what, SE9311? Please respond.

SE9311: Someone is here. A real person.

Cont B: Tell me what happened.

* * *

Twenty minutes later when I exit the computer room, Olivia is on the couch with her head leaned against the back and her eyes closed. She starts and sits up, wiping her mouth with the side of her thumb. "Did you tell them?" she asks quietly.

"Yes."

"How did it go?"

I shrug, forcing nonchalance when I feel anything but. Inside, where I can let my emotions run rampant, I'm churning with anger and sadness and fear. "Okay. I guess." *Okay* is a lie. How can I be okay when all I can think about is her leaving, about being alone again and about how much I want her to hold me?

Most of the session with Controller B was filled with the logistics of getting Olivia home, her health after I shot her, checking my mental well-being and ensuring I have enough supplies to support an extra person until she can be extracted. Extract. To remove or take out, especially by effort or force.

I lost track of how many times I apologized and said that I hoped the experiment wasn't ruined, but it wasn't my fault, really and I'm sorry. Each time, Controller B assured me that they know it wasn't intentional, and apparently everything is fine. Whatever their version of *fine* is. The Controller wasn't angry, or surprised, or emotional in any way. I hadn't expected them to be, because words on a screen can't be emotional, but I'd expected more of a response than:

Cont B: I understand. We can arrange for her to be collected from the compound and taken to the nearest hospital if required. We will need to coordinate with weather patterns but I imagine it will be within a few days to a week. And yes, we can call or forward a message to her family if she desires, she will just need to provide us with details.

Maybe they are angry but are pretending not to be so they don't upset me. I didn't tell Controller B how long Olivia has been here. It's a lie of omission rather than an outright lie.

"A lie is still a lie, Celeste," Joanne reminds me. "I want you to think about what you've done and then we're going to talk about why that's unacceptable, and what your punishment will be."

My punishment is that I'm going to be alone again. It's a suitable punishment, because right now I can't think of anything worse. I rub my temples and slump onto the couch a safe distance away from Olivia. "If you're still here, they'll pick you up when they deliver my next supplies."

"Oh? Okay then. How long is it until your next drop?"

"A week or so, maybe more or less, depending on what the weather is doing. Or you can hike out whenever you want to leave. It's up to you." It doesn't matter how she goes. She's going and that's what matters. Stop. This constant stupid self-pitying monologue is a new, generally themed earworm instead of a specific one. It's tedious and it needs to go away.

"I'll see how I feel." She reaches across the gap to place a comforting hand on my thigh, the pressure firm and warm. "What about your, uh…pay and the experiment? Will you leave when I do?"

I turn to her, drawing my leg up so my foot is resting on the couch. "They said they have enough data so it's not a catastrophe. I didn't ask about the other."

"Why not?"

The concept of leaving at the same time as her had never occurred to me until this moment. Psychological experiment aside, I'm still needed to check energy, waste, and food systems. "I didn't even think of it because of all the tech that's still here. And the money…" I throw my hands up. "It doesn't really matter, Olivia. It's just a little extra cash, so what? I'd forfeit it all if it meant you'd stay."

As soon as it's out, I regret saying it and I can't look at her, because I'm too afraid that what I'll see is a woman put off by my desperation. As if it were that simple anyway, bartering money for a companion. I'm sickened by my thoughts, as though what she wants means nothing and it's all about what I want. It's just lust, I barely know her, I only feel this way because I've been alone for so long.

I sigh. "I'm sorry. I shouldn't say that." I chance a quick look at her.

Her thoughts flicker across her face in quick succession. Confusion. Pleasure. Concern. Nothing to indicate she finds me repulsive or creepy. Her expressions are clear and I'm struck by this sudden ability I have to read each one. Starved for so long, I think I've become an expert at realizing how important the nuance of an eyebrow lift or a tongue flicking over a lower lip are. She tilts her head to study me. Her smile is shy. Mine is bold and strangely excited.

"What is it?" she asks.

I tell her about my newly acquired skill, trying to make it sound not weird. I'm not sure I'm successful.

Olivia nods thoughtfully, still with that slight smile. "Remind me not to play poker with you if you're that good at reading me." She takes my hand, interlacing our fingers. The smile turns puzzled. "You bite your nails."

"Yes?"

"I hadn't noticed until just now."

I turn our joined hands to get a better look. "I never used to but it started a year or so ago." The same thing Riley used to do, mostly just chewing the edges rather than biting the nails down to stubs.

Staring at her palm pressed to mine, I can't help the imaginary scenario from unfolding in my head. Remnants of other thoughts or even a dream, where I'm walking down the street holding hands with my girlfriend and our connection is both emotional and physical and I'm complete. Yes, it's just a dream but it's all I can think about now—holding Olivia's hand as we stroll along a sidewalk. Such a normal thing, but I'll never have it with her.

Olivia squeezes my hand. "Celeste? What is it?"

I drag my eyes from our intertwined fingers. "Nothing important." I draw in a shallow breath, force myself to look at her face. "They said you can contact your family or whoever if you need to. You can record a video message and they'll email it."

"Great, thank you. I'll email my father. That will keep my parents from worrying unnecessarily. When?"

"Tomorrow morning I guess, when I do my next log." Video message. Extraction. Alone. "Excuse me," I choke out.

Olivia says nothing when I pull my hand from hers as gently as I can and walk away. She doesn't call after me as I leave the house. I'm dressing on the move, pushing my arms into my jacket sleeves as I jog, then run to the farthest corner of the compound. Facing outward, I draw a deep breath and scream, "Fuck!" into the trees.

Bent almost in half I draw that one word out for as long as I can into a fifteen-second expletive until I have to breathe again. I suck in noisy gasps of air, replacing what I just let out in that childish scream, then straighten my jacket, run my hands through my hair and turn back to the house.

Riley falls into step, her footsteps light on the snow beside me. "Feel better, Cel?"

"No," I mumble, pushing back into the house. I hang my jacket and slip out of my boots as quietly as I can.

Olivia glances up at me, but says nothing to imply anything's amiss, that I look deranged or that she heard my scream. But she must have. "Are you hungry?" she asks.

"Not really, no."

"I'll make us dinner tonight," she says as though I hadn't answered, and then almost in the same breath asks, "Do you want to talk about it?"

Yes, no, maybe. "I don't think there's anything to be said. And I'm not sure you'd understand." I don't say it to be cruel, but she'll never understand how I feel. She can't know how I'm going to fall apart when she leaves. I want to slap my palm against an ear, as though I could push these thoughts out the other where they'll fall to the ground and I can stomp on them.

"I might."

There's no way she can know, no way she'll understand. The longing cuts so deeply it feels like I'm about to come apart, and the fear is so overwhelming that I feel physically sick thinking of being by myself again. I can't tell her. Instead I say, "I...what are you thinking for dinner?"

She holds eye contact with me. "Whatever you want, Celeste."

The rest of the day is stilted and awful, with all the discomfort mine. I've known from the first moment that this was the only way our time together could end, and I should have prepared better for this day. I should have told them that first day and had them collect her right then. I should never have helped her and definitely shouldn't have shot her.

Despite my wooden, outwardly emotionless behavior, at every opportunity Olivia touches me or pulls me in for a hug. It's like she knows I need this, that I need to store up this physical contact to carry me through until the end. Eight more months or so. Not so long in the scheme of things. But still long enough.

I'm riding a constant up and down, like a damned amusement ride I can't get off. All day I go from the despair of knowing she's leaving, to calm whenever she holds me. We don't speak. Just hug. She hugs me like she wants to envelop me completely, her body relaxed and comforting. Then she lets me go, smiles at me, and my relaxation dissipates like smoke until I'm back to where I was—fighting myself, the inevitable.

We don't talk about the past. We exist only in the present. The present is full of quiet time, stolen glances, cooking together, and playing games. The future, probably only another few days of it, is going to be the same and I need to enjoy what I have with her. I will not ruin this precious time by being a sad, grumpy bitch.

"Buck up, Cel." Riley's shoulder punch is softer than usual. "Get over it."

After dinner—cheese and vegetable-filled pasta she made along with an incredibly rich tomato-pasta sauce—we clean up and I pour us each another glass of wine. As she promised, she is indeed enjoying sampling the contents of my wine cellar. She prefers reds and when she found a bottle of twelve-year Barolo yesterday, she was both awestruck and excited. The awe was that I have this bottle and haven't drunk it yet, and the excitement was because her grandparents are from that region of Italy.

Instead of settling on the couch with her to read or talk as I normally would, I tuck a half-empty bottle of white under my arm and hold a wineglass between my fingers. When I move toward the door Olivia regards me, an eyebrow reaching for her hairline.

"It's bonfire night," I explain, standing in the open doorway as I maneuver into my jacket.

"Bonfire night," she repeats, drawing the words out. "What's that exactly?"

"Big fire, party with all my friends, get drunk, pass out outside."

Her smile is slight, not bright. Apparently not a good joke.

I try again. "Burning all my rubbish. I'll be outside for a while until it dies down so I can keep an eye on the fire." Burning the place down wouldn't go over well with The Organization. "Do you need anything before I go?"

"No thank you. I'm good. And I have my stick."

"Okay, back in a bit. Holler if you need me." I close the door, put a barrier between us. Distance is good. It will help me get used to being alone again.

The night sky is clear, the air crisp. By any standards it's a beautiful evening, but no matter how I try, I can't find a shred of appreciation for it. I tug my beanie down over my ears and make my way over toward the fire pit. I toss a couple of lit matches into the mound of garbage. It doesn't take long to catch—the gasoline I poured over the pile helps.

The fire is overly large tonight. I sip my wine, close my eyes against the radiating heat and listen to the sound of the fire. Every now and then I add wood to the flames to make it even bigger and better. Without the sound of wood crackling and popping, bonfire night is just a hot smelly letdown.

My head is quiet for once. Nobody's talking at me. I poke at the fire, ignore the rank fumes and make up my own conversation. Did you know Greer's dating Linda? Oh, really? Shit, I always thought Linda was a fuck-'em-and-forget-'em gal. Nuh-uh, it's getting serious, I think she might pop the question. I sip my wine, hold it in my mouth, swallow. Well, damn, *another* engagement gift I have to buy. I throw the stick into the fire. You're cracked, Celeste.

Unsteady footsteps over snow. "Celeste?"

I spin my ass on the log so I can face her. "Hey. What are you doing? It's freezing out here. And it smells pretty gross."

"Bored and lonely in there without you." Olivia lowers herself down to sit with her right leg outstretched. Her walking stick rests against the log. Then she's leaning into me. I tense. An arm slides around my waist. I relax. She's only doing it for warmth. But how can she be cold in her thick down jacket? The glass of red rests on her knee and when I look down, the firelight through it makes it look like the end of a sunset.

When the sun sets, it finishes things. This thing we have, whatever it is, is almost finished. What an unfortunately timely metaphor I've just discovered. If I think about it anymore, I'm going to cry.

I glance around for something to talk about, and with my own wineglass, gesture to the limb she has stretched toward the fire. "How is your leg?" She hasn't mentioned any issues, and I've assumed that means it's fine. But now I have some desperate need to make sure she's not going to leave here permanently damaged in some way.

"Fine. I actually think it's better than I'm giving it credit for, but I don't want to push it."

"Mmm," I murmur around another mouthful of wine. After swallowing, I add, "You'll see a doctor when you go home, right? Just to be sure?"

"Of course."

We sit quietly together, her still leaning into me. The silence lengthens. I don't want silence, I want the sound of her voice. "What's your middle name?" I ask. I already know her last name, Soldano, but I want all the parts of her. When she's gone, I just want to walk around saying her name. I want to walk around remembering what she looked and sounded and felt like.

"Maria," she answers. Olivia Maria Soldano. Such a beautiful name. After a sip of wine Olivia asks, "What about yours?"

"I don't have one. Neither did Riley." Smiling, I stare into the flames. "I think finding just one name for us stretched Mother's capabilities to the limit."

"Bitch," Mother spits.

I jump at the intrusion. She hasn't been around for a while. Olivia's gloved hand tightens on my hip. "Who is it, Celeste?"

"Mother," I muse. "But it's okay. She's not *that* angry."

If Olivia thinks I'm strange or even a touch insane, she doesn't say it. Every time I've had a false visitor, she treats it as though it is nothing of consequence. Maybe she has a friend with that disorder, the one where you're ten people all at once. She sits up a little straighter. "What does she say when she's angry? What does she sound like?"

I can't answer that. Mother's vitriol isn't the kind of thing I can explain in casual conversation, or even serious conversation. It's too awful, too embarrassing. I shake my head and gurgle out an, "Uh-uh." The urge to get up and walk away is almost overwhelming. But there's nowhere to go that Olivia can't follow. I turn my attention to the bonfire, jamming a poking stick into the fire to shove a scrap of rubbish back where it belongs.

Olivia's hand shifts from my hip to my back, her touch steadying me. "It's okay, Celeste." Is she saying that it's okay for me to tell her, or that it's okay for me *not* to tell her?

I realize then that I want her to know. I want to give her this little, disgusting piece from my childhood. Maybe she can do something with it, help me figure out where to place it in the jigsaw puzzle of my life. I shift uncomfortably on the log. "She uh, she sounds like me. Same voice. Or maybe I sound like her. Except…whenever she spoke, she always sounded apathetic and angry. I don't know if it was the drugs, or just her." I let the stick fall to the ground. "If I've got her voice, does that mean I got other parts of her too?"

"I don't think I've ever heard your voice show traces of either of those things, Celeste. I think you're less like her than you imagine you are."

The observation stops my thoughts in their tracks. Another sip of wine helps to start them up again and after a long ponderous pause, I think I know what she's saying. I'm trapped in this prison that I constructed for myself. Eventually I'm going to have to use the key that's been in my pocket the whole time to set myself free. But it's down so deep that despite a lifetime of fumbling, I haven't been able to grab it yet.

I search for something to say, something to take me away from my thoughts. "Can I ask you a question?" I half expect her to respond the way Riley always used to, with *you just did.*

"Of course."

"Your decade of bad relationships, is that true? You don't seem like the kind of person who'd have difficulties dating or being in a relationship." As I say it, I'm imagining her and me dating, being in a relationship, living together outside of this.

Her eyebrows lift until they hit the wool knit of her beanie. "No? Thank you. And yes, it is true. I've had three long-term relationships in the past ten years, two of whom cheated on me and basically gave the same reasons—I was distant, secretive, emotionally unavailable."

"Really? How so? What did they mean?"

She frowns, considers. "My job requires discretion. Most of it is highly confidential, industrial espionage et cetera. I can't run home to tell my partner what I've been doing all day and I guess that sort of carried over into everyday stuff as well. I think when you have to keep secrets, they become your new normal. You get used to not sharing things and people don't like that, especially not in a romantic relationship." Olivia sips her wine, holding it in her mouth for a few seconds before she swallows.

Secretive. I don't really see it. Sure, she's not constantly throwing out snippets about her life, but that's to be expected in our situation. Every time we've talked, she's shared something with me. "I suppose not. But from what I know of you, you have other qualities that balance that out. And everyone has secrets."

"Maybe. Maybe not. Sometimes I think I'm too difficult to be with. Too set in my ways." The skin around her mouth is taut with tension. "Every relationship breakup, it's been my fault."

"You can't think that," I rebut immediately.

Her laugh is dry, humorless. "Yes I can. I'm the common denominator."

I can't imagine how that's true, can't imagine why she would think that. I take a few moments to think about it. "Are you the same out there as you are in here?"

"Yes," she says. "Or, I think I am. This is me. Out there I just have my job, I play tennis once a week, love movies and music,

aahhh, hiking and being outdoors but I'm still the same person."
She studies me, the glow of the fire illuminating the side of her
face. "Aren't you?"

"I think this place magnifies everything, so in here I'm me…
amplified." I top up my wineglass, check that she still has some
red left in hers. "If you're the same person out there as you are
here then I *really* don't understand what you're saying."

Her mouth works as though it wants to say something and
she's trying to stop it. When she speaks, her voice is hoarse, as
though the words grate against her throat. "About four years
ago, my girlfriend committed suicide and her note basically
blamed me. Said everything all the others had been saying—I
was unavailable, cold, distant, secretive…among other things.
She said if I'd been around more, given more of myself to her
then she'd have felt *needed*. I knew she had mental health issues,
so did her family, but none of us thought she would…do that."
Olivia glances at me, her expression so wounded that I wonder
how something like that could ever heal.

I move closer, rest a tentative hand on her leg. She grabs my
hand, squeezes and doesn't let go. It would be easy for me to
offer a comforting word, a platitude or even a lie to try to make
her feel better. But those things aren't fair. So I say nothing, just
keep silently holding her hand until she speaks again.

"It was the anniversary of her death a few weeks ago, and I
just felt suffocated all of a sudden, like I had to get out and try
to set it behind me for good. I *know* it wasn't my fault, that it was
way bigger than just me, but still…" She inhales a shuddering
breath. "And getting away from it has helped, but I can't help
wondering if when I go back, everything will just be the same.
If I'll be the same and destined to fail the same way over and
over again."

"I'm sorry," I murmur, staring down at our hands. There's
really nothing else I can say.

"Thank you." Her thumb strokes the back of my hand. "And
I'm sorry, this is so self-pitying."

"No it's not. Thank you for telling me."

"You're welcome," she says tightly.

The tension in her is a living thing, and I want to soothe her, to bring her back to the easy conversations we've had. "Can I call you Liv instead of Olivia?" I turn to her, study her profile. It's smooth and strong and mysterious, yet at the same time sweet and kind and thoughtful.

Olivia goes along with my subject change, shoulders dropping as if relieved. "If you'd like. But I think I'll just keep calling you Celeste. It's such a beautiful name."

If Mother is pleased, she doesn't say. I don't think she's used to anyone telling her that she did something right in her miserable, pathetic, toxic life.

CHAPTER TWELVE

I take a few moments, as I have every morning since she arrived, to watch her sleep. Liv sleeps like someone who has no cares or stress, like someone who feels safe. She lies on her side, a hand slung under the pillow and hair loose and curling over it. She snores a little. If I could, I'd burrow under the covers with her for the rest of the week, snuggle the way lovers do on rainy days.

But we aren't lovers. I don't even know what we are. When I leave her and quietly close the door of the bedroom, my limbs are heavy with reluctance. She'll likely still be asleep by the time I come back inside, and I envy her this ability to sleep in. I wander once around the edge of the compound to stretch my limbs and check that everything is as it should be. Not much snow overnight. The weather should hold for a transport within the next few days.

I say the word a few times. "Transport. Transport." She's going to leave me. I stand in the white zone with arms limp by my sides, staring out at the world. The world she's going into while I stay here like an animal at the zoo. But I'll be out eventually. My cage is not permanent. This small shred of optimism makes me feel marginally better, but I still don't feel good about it.

Back inside, shower, a mug of tea, a woman still asleep in my bed. Coffee brews, ready for when she wakes, and I've left her mug and the sugar set out ready in case I'm still in the computer room. I place all my handwritten pages of notes, numbered and dated, in the drawer of the desk. When I leave, someone will find them and can put that data with all my other data. Assuming it's even relevant, which I'm not entirely sure it is. I'm not going to tell them that the notes are there. If I tell them I've been handwriting things for a week then they will know that Liv has been here for longer than I implied.

I mime playing a piano on the keyboard until I can think of things I want to say. There's so much but none of it feels appropriate to log. It all feels too personal, too deep, too precious. Eventually I just spill some words to satisfy the Controllers.

I didn't sleep well last night, possibly because of the news I told Controller B yesterday. For the first time since I came here, I didn't dream. My dreams are usually so vivid, like in my sleep I'm living the life I can't in here. Aside from those things everything else in here is normal. I'm afraid someone on the other side of the screen is angry with me because of what happened but it really wasn't my fault, and I did what was right. I'm sorry if not leaving a bleeding person in the woods ruins the study. And I'm sorry that what I just said sounds passive-aggressive.

I've been thinking about college, about maybe going back. It's the first time in a few years that I've actually thought I could, and that it would be a good idea. When I came here, I was sure I would start back when I had the money, and then I didn't want to, and now I do. Does everything always go around in circles like that?

Things I miss:

-The sound of seatbelts clicking. I feel like I want to just keep pushing one in and releasing it to listen to that sound over and over.

-Barstools.

-Shadows of buildings in the city.

-Hot dogs, extra mustard.

The log I'm typing fades away, replaced by the messaging system.

Cont D: Good morning, SE9311. How are you?

SE9311: Hello. I'm fine thanks.

Cont D: Do you have anything you need to report?

Yes, I do. I need to report that I want Olivia to stay. I need to report that I don't like being here anymore, now I know what's coming. I need to...I don't even know what I need to do.

SE9311: Nope. All fine.

Cont D: How is Ms. Soldano?

Perfect. Wonderful. Sweet. Kind.

SE9311: She seems OK.

Cont D: I see you've already completed a log this morning. Can you please ask Ms. Soldano to come in so we can start the process of getting her home?

I want to scream *no*, to throw the keyboard against the wall and cut the power cord so there's no way for them to talk to her. Every time I think these things, I want to slap myself. I have no claim on her, I have no right to ask her to stay. Even if I did, she couldn't or wouldn't, and the sooner I jam the truth into the dense matter between my ears the sooner I can move on with what I need to do and then move on with my life.

Cont D: SE9311?

SE9311: She might still be asleep.

Stalling.

Cont D: That's fine. I'll wait until she comes in.

SE9311: Sure. Then I guess I'll see you next time I see you.

Cont D: Indeed. Have an enjoyable day.

Unlikely.

My hands are deep in the pockets of my jeans and as I walk up the hallway, I scratch my thighs through the fabric. Hard and rough. It's uncomfortable but I need something on the outside to match the bad feeling that's inside. Olivia is awake and on the couch, both feet propped up on the arm. She's not reading or drinking her coffee. She's just staring absently at the wall, twisting a strand of hair around and around two fingers.

"Liv? You can go in and talk to them and record that thing for your family. And they'll discuss how to get you home." All the words came out in a rush, like my mouth was making sure my brain wouldn't intercept what I had to say.

"Oh. Thanks." Liv hops up, grabs her stick and follows me back to the computer. She looks strange in the computer room chair. Suddenly she sits straighter, seems more serious and even a touch arrogant.

I can almost picture her in another life chairing a meeting of science brains. *Doctor Smith, the Bunsen burner in your lab is broken, please don't use it unless you want to blow up the lab. Doctor Jones, we need more calcium dioxate.* Or something. I show her how the messaging system works—it's not complicated but I want to make sure she's totally clear. "You good?"

"Yes, I've got it, thank you." She squeezes my hand and all I can think is that from the camera up in the corner they are watching us touching. And I don't want that because her touching me is my thing, not theirs.

I close the door so I don't have to listen to her making plans to leave.

"Not fuckin' surprising she can't wait to get the hell away from you." Mother's fetid breath is on my neck. "Nobody wants to stick around, even your sister died just to get away from you."

Wow, ouch. "That's not very nice."

"Truth hurts, kid." Mother's laugh sounds like the Wicked Witch of the West. It echoes through the dwelling then stops as suddenly as it started.

I have no idea how long Liv will be in the computer room doing the thing I don't want to think about. If I sit and let myself think about being left here while she goes back to her life I'm going to scream. Almost on autopilot, I pull out ingredients for fresh pasta and get to work. It'll take up an hour of my day, an hour of not thinking about the inevitable.

Making pasta is quick and mindless work and by the time the dough has had its first trip through the rollers, I hear the computer room door closing. The moment Olivia sees what I'm doing, her expression changes from thoughtful to interested. "You make your own pasta?"

"Mhmm, sometimes when I need to switch my brain off. I shared a house with a chef years ago, and she taught me."

She laughs quietly. "You never said anything when I made *mezzelune* the other night." It's a sweet and teasing accusation that I don't know how to respond to, and the way she pronounces that Italian word makes my knees rubbery. Liv breaks a small piece of dough from the end of the sheet, squeezes it between her fingertips, rubs them together gently and then pops the dough in her mouth.

I can't move past the fact that she just ate raw pasta. I've eaten dried uncooked pasta, the cheap stuff you get in a packet, crunching the macaroni down quickly because I was so hungry and so afraid Mother would snatch the handful from me. But something about the raw egg in the dough Liv's eating turns my stomach. I stare at the pinch mark left by her fingertips.

"I like cake batter, remember?" Riley says. "Who cares about raw egg? Food's food, Cel."

Olivia nods thoughtfully, her lips curving into a smile. "She taught you well. That is as good as Nonna's, which is the highest praise I can give anyone."

"Really?"

Olivia dusts flour from her fingertips back to the granite bench top. "Really." She slips around to my side of the bench and wraps an arm around my waist. "What sauce should we make to put with it?"

"I don't know." I don't know anything. I can't make a decision beyond just breathing in and out and existing in this moment where she's got her arm around me. I feed the dough through the rollers again and in a matter of seconds that tiny imperfection she made has been erased.

* * *

We don't talk about her extraction beyond confirming that they will collect her in the middle of the night on an as-yet-unspecified day. They're going to make Olivia wake up at some ungodly hour just to make sure I don't see how they get here. Despite the fact the whole psych part of the study has gone to shit, the testing of the secret tech is still secret.

I need to plant some seedlings I've been cultivating in small pots on a greenhouse shelf, and late in the day we make our way to the greenhouse to do just that. It's a wonderful afternoon, my favorite kind where the sky is a dense and uniform gray that promises snow. Olivia digs beside me, sitting on a straw mat with her injured leg stretched out and the other leg bent to rest her foot against knee. When I asked if her leg hurt, she shook her head, telling me the skin just pulls a little when she bends her knee. She smiled, adding assurances that it only feels tight but not sore. "What are we planting again?"

I turn to her. "Peppers and zucchini."

"I make fantastic stuffed peppers." A muscle in her jaw jumps. She doesn't need to say it. She won't be here when the peppers have grown to their full size ready for her fantastic stuffing. "Maybe I'll write down the recipe for you?" she adds, her voice calm and even.

I nod, scooping dirt back around a seedling. When I place the little stake that says ZUCCHINI in the ground beside it, Liv speaks again. "They said they'll be here in two days to collect me, and to give you a small delivery to replace what I've used."

"Okay," I say, because what else can I say?

"Celeste, I—" Her trowel hits something, the sound a muted *tik* that cuts off whatever she was about to tell me. I glance at her face then down to her hands, which are now scrabbling in the dirt. She holds up a pair of sunglasses, shakes dirt from the frames and passes them to me. "Are you trying to grow a sunglasses plant?"

I laugh because despite the somberness of our mood it *is* funny. "Thanks. I lost these...months ago, and I looked *everywhere* for them." I hold the glasses up to the clear roof panels, trying to catch some diffuse light. "That arm is all bent now. Useless I guess."

She regards me thoughtfully. "Not everything that's damaged should be discarded. Some things are worth keeping even if it doesn't seem like it."

The way she's studying me makes me unsure exactly what she's talking about. It feels like a metaphor but at the same time, it can't apply to me. She barely knows me. I've only told her the tip of the iceberg, the things that are polite enough to share. Underneath the surface is... No, I don't want to think about that. In the short time she's been here, she's already made me think too much about those things I try to forget. Carefully, I bend the metal arm of the sunglasses straight again.

Together we finish planting until we have two perfect rows of seedlings. I help her stand again and bend to brush dirt from the legs of her pants. Liv swipes her hands over her butt and I turn away, not wanting to watch even this simple, non-sexual thing.

I only have two more days to absorb enough of her to last me for the rest of my time here, and despite what I promised myself, I'm wasting it being sullen and melancholy. This sort of mood sits at odds with me, because I've never been one to dwell on the sadness and injustices of a situation. Things are what they are and that's that. I'm used to disappointment and not getting what I want, but she makes it hard to just let things be and to accept it this time.

Olivia licks her thumb then smilingly rubs the side of my jaw with it. "What's wrong?"

Everything is wrong but I can't say that. "I just..."

Her touch lightens, thumb sliding down to my chin. "Tell me, Celeste," she says gently.

Closing my eyes, I push the words out in a rushed breath. "I don't think I'm strong enough to stay here without you. I don't know how to be alone again."

"Open your eyes. Look at me," she says quietly.

Reluctantly I comply, expecting to see a mocking expression. Her lovely face is anything but. It's sweet yet burns with fierce intensity. "That's where you're wrong, but it's not for me to tell you that you can do it." She's creeping closer. "You have to find it out for yourself, and I know you will." Olivia reaches for me and I step into the circle of her arms. She hugs me hard then releases her grip slightly without letting me go.

This hug feels different, more intimate somehow though it's the same press of body to body as always. I let out a long breath, then inhale again, imagining I'm breathing some of her in to keep with me. "Maybe you're right. I don't know."

She leans back slightly, putting some space between us. "What's going to happen when you're finished with the experiment?"

"I guess I'll find somewhere to live, get a job and try to forget about you." Saying it out loud actually eases some of the tension in my throat. I've known all along that it couldn't go anywhere. Aside from the fact she's leaving and I'm staying, she has a job and a house and a life. A life I can't fit in to. Nor can she fit in the life I had out there.

"You want to forget I was here?" she whispers. Though the words are quiet, they're laced with an intensity that is both strange and exciting.

"No," I choke out. "But I can't trust what I'm feeling because it's all mixed up in this." I wave my arm vaguely, as if that gesture could encompass everything that's tied into this place.

"This is one of the realest things I've ever known, Celeste." Her tongue flashes out to sweep along her upper lip. "Tell me, what are you feeling?"

"I'm not sure. This feels special somehow and it's just hard for me right now, Liv…to think that this place is all I'm ever going to have of you." I make myself look at her, to keep eye contact. "I'm sorry, I don't mean to whine."

"It doesn't have to be all there is, Celeste." Her fingers tighten on my biceps. "You're not going to be here forever. Perhaps when this is over, we can meet up again and see what happens."

"I don't even know where you live." It seems laughable to think that we've never spoken about something as basic as where we're from.

"Just outside of Seattle." She releases me and moves to the door of the greenhouse. "You?"

"Chicago. Or at least, that's where I was living before." I shrug. "I've never really felt like anywhere was home."

"Well, when you're finished with this, let's just see, okay? We don't need to etch anything in stone right now, but I would like to see you again when you get out. I know that for certain." She loops her arm through mine, leaning into me as we make our way back over the uneven ground toward the house.

"A lot can change in seven months. Feelings change." Not mine, I'm certain of that. But hers probably will.

Her chin lifts, and her gaze is sure and steady. "True, but sometimes feelings only get stronger."

CHAPTER THIRTEEN

After dinner, she showers while I do the dishes. Then we swap and she dries them while I shower. This back-and-forth, the way we cook and do chores together, is seamless and organic. Would Liv and I be the same out *there*, if we'd met in a bar or been introduced by friends? If I'd bumped into her on the street, scattering her groceries to the sidewalk? An awkward first meeting after matching on a dating app? I'll never know.

Liv shakes her head when I offer another glass of wine, and suddenly I don't want any more either. I drain the last mouthful of mine and hold out my hand for her empty glass. She smiles her thanks and passes it up to me. Her forefinger strokes mine, the touch sending a light burn over my skin. Suddenly it's very important that I wash the wineglasses right now instead of leaving them for the morning the way we usually do. I leave Liv on the couch with a vague statement letting her know I'll be back in just a minute.

"What're you running 'way from?" Heather wonders idly. She sounds like she's been drinking. What day is it? Thursday

138 E. J. Noyes

and three-dollar cocktails at Mary's. I've never known anyone who could slam four mojitos in her first hour and still be standing—and talking—the way Heather can. "You like her. Big deal. Insta-love is totally a thing, Celeste. Or insta-lust, at least."

"Celeste?" Olivia's behind me, her hand on my shoulder a lead weight I can't shake off.

"Yes?"

"You've been staring at the sink for three minutes."

"Oh."

"Turn around," she says softly.

Reluctantly, I comply, but move away from her to stand next to the refrigerator. I can't meet her eyes. I'm too afraid of what I might see in them—the soft understanding that makes something inside me twist and break and mend itself all at once.

"Look at me. Please." She keeps telling me to look at her. Doesn't she know how hard it is when I always feel so off-balance around her?

I raise my eyes to hers, and they are absent of any pity or even that knowing expression I'd expected. Instead, they are bright. Almost feverish. Her hand cups my cheek. "I'm leaving the morning after tomorrow."

"I know," I mutter. Why does she have to bring it up? Why is she reminding me of the worst thing in my life right now? I press myself against the refrigerator door, my hands behind me flat against the cool stainless surface. She follows me and she's so close there's no room to move or think or breathe.

"Not even two full days. There's not enough time," she says hoarsely, desperately. Liv's thumb brushes softly over my upper lip, then traces the curve of my mouth. Her soft exhalation seems almost reverential. "You're so beautiful, Celeste. Can I kiss you?"

The question lingers between us like a wisp of smoke. I let it solidify into something real then pluck it from the air and draw it close where I can examine it. I didn't know this was what she really wanted. I'd hoped and dreamed but I didn't know she wants it as much I do.

I nod, hardly daring to believe she's asking me. I give her my wordless yes, the desperation for her overriding everything else. Her hands are warm and smooth against my cheeks, holding me in place. Olivia pauses, her gaze moving from my lips back to my eyes as though she's making sure I still want this. I do. I want it. I can't think of anything I've ever wanted more. My hands come up to gently touch her waist. Then she leans forward and kisses me.

Kissing.

I'd forgotten how much I love it. Forgotten the give and take, the testing and teasing. I'd forgotten the first tentative touch of a tongue, shy then growing bolder. Olivia lets me lead, matching me every time I push or retreat. It's sweet and hot and I want more. So much more. I pull her closer until our bodies touch at almost every point. She groans.

Heat spreads from my lips, down my neck and into my belly. Then lower. My arousal is a wildfire and I know I should pull away and let it go out, but I can't. Not with her. But I have to. I yank my hands from her waist and clench my fists, jiggling my arms by my sides. "We should stop," I breathe.

"Do you want to stop?" Her voice is low and husky, her breathing short and shallow, and the naked want in her eyes rekindles my desire.

"No," I manage to choke out. "But...we barely know each other." Despite that, it feels as though we're a few seconds away from falling into bed. People sleep with people they just met all the time. One-night stands are a thing. They were my thing. There's nothing wrong with wanting her.

"You screwed that girl from the bar 'member? The one with that fantastic tattoo," Heather reminds me in her fifth-mojito-of-the-night voice. "You only knew her a coupla hours."

I scrunch my eyes closed.

Fingertips dance on my neck. "Celeste."

I open my eyes again and drag them up to meet hers. Olivia brushes hair from my forehead. "I want this," she says, quietly but firmly. "Wherever it takes us. But we don't have to do anything if you're not comfortable. It's okay if you're scared or just don't want to." The implication of her words reaches deep. She's giving me the choice and all the power to make this decision for us.

"No it's not that. I want to, I really do. I…I'm just worried I might be overwhelmed. If that makes sense? It's been so long, and I don't want to be rough with you."

Liv's mouth twists into a seductive smile, and she lets out a soft chuckle. She steps forward again, placing her hands on my hips, then leans forward and brushes her lips against my ear. I shudder and the tingle slides along my spine and down my legs. Her tongue flicks lightly over my earlobe. "Oh, sweetheart. I want you rough, and hard. I want you soft, and gentle. I want you every way, whatever you give me and I want to give it all back to you." She pauses a moment to let her words sink in, then slowly slides her tongue up my neck, ending with the barest nip just under my ear. "And God help me, I'm so turned on that I want it all right now."

I can't do anything but nod and fumble out a single word. "Okay."

Our frantic relocation from kitchen to bedroom gives way to a slow, sensual undressing. Olivia is languid as she pulls my shirt over my head and bends to bury her face in my breasts. She makes a quiet sound of appreciation, kissing my nipples through my bra before she unfastens and pulls the fabric off. My jeans are unbuttoned, my skin explored and worshipped with lips and hands, and I can do nothing but stand there and allow her to do what she wants. She tugs my jeans and underwear down until I'm standing in front of her naked, and uncharacteristically uncertain.

Olivia lowers herself to sit on the bed. Her hands glide lightly over my torso, leaving gooseflesh in their wake. She looks up, eyes hooded with desire and utters a single, simple sentence. "Oh, my…wow."

She exhales, leaning forward to press kisses to my thighs. So close. I hold my breath while she skirts around my sex teasingly, maddeningly. I lower my gaze to watch her make her way back up my belly, all too aware of the feel of my arousal. Hot and thick and desperate. There are no thoughts that make sense, only pure and carnal need. I climb onto the bed and take none of the same care removing her clothes—my frantic fingers are clumsy as I undress her and pull her back down on top of me. Our kisses grow hungry, the desire almost burning but when I reach for her, she grabs my hand and pulls it away.

She holds my hand, fingers curling around mine. "Not yet, sweetheart, just wait…" Olivia slides her thigh between mine, giving me pressure where I need it, but it's not entirely selfless. She's grinding herself against me, slick against my skin, a low panting moan accompanying her movements. Excitement builds in my stomach until it's a tight knot taking up almost every bit of space, leaving room only for the anticipation, which spreads downward in a low, constant throb.

Liv props herself up, tracing her fingertips over my face, leaving nothing untouched. Lips, eyelashes, nose. Her fingers run over my eyebrow, back and forth along the sensitive skin of the scar that bisects it. She kisses me lightly. "I want you to fuck me so badly, but first…" She brushes my jaw with soft lips. "… let me make love to you."

"You slut. Whore," Mother spits into my ear. I slam my eyes closed on her, the effort of trying to force her out making me tremble.

"Celeste? Hey, hey." Hands are in my hair, warm against my face, lightly touching my mouth to bring me back to myself. I open my eyes again to find Olivia's, dark and guileless and full of lust. "What is it, darling?" she asks.

"Nothing," I whisper.

"There's no need to hide that from me." She brings her head close so our foreheads are touching. "There's nobody else here, Celeste. It's just you and me. Okay?"

I clench my teeth, begging myself to forget about everything else except what's happening right now in my bed, in my body. "Mhmm."

"It's you. It's me. And it's this." Her fingers slip over my wetness. "It's only this, sweetheart."

I capture her lips again, my hunger rising as she makes slow, lazy circles over my clit. Anticipation and excitement flutter in my stomach, mixing with the deep pulse of arousal until I can barely stand it, arching into the pressure. I'd forgotten how something in my legs twitches when lips and tongue touch my nipples to suck them into hard peaks. I'd forgotten what it feels like to have hands on my body. I cry out, feeling the imminent threat of climax. I want it, fuck I want it, but it's going to be over far too quickly and I'm afraid this is all I'm going to have.

Lifting my head, I can't help my desperate, choked, "Oh God, no, I'm going to come."

Liv's expert guidance holds me right on the precipice without letting me fall over and then the touch withdraws. "No you're not, not like this." A sexy, throaty growl.

I groan, bucking my hips to find something to keep that exquisite pressure, lest my climax slip away and be lost. But there's nothing. Liv takes my chin in her hand, kisses me forcefully then makes her way down my body. I'm explored and worshipped again, her tongue finding every spot that makes me pant and gasp and beg. Lips close around me, unbearably sweet but not enough to send me over the edge. When she reaches up to thumb my nipples as her tongue works me toward release, I can't help but gasp. Desperate to hold something back, I bite the side of my hand to keep from crying out but a moan escapes anyway.

My teeth are locked hard in my skin. I have a fistful of blanket to keep me grounded but I'm still being carried away. Her hand gropes blindly over my torso, searching for me, and I pull my hand from my mouth to grasp hers, our fingers intertwining instinctually as she pushes me higher and higher. I crest, and this time she carries me over. I cry out my climax and this touch, her hold, tethers me to the earth even as my body tries to float away.

Time stutters and slows. We lie face-to-face. Not talking. Just being together. I'm no longer here or there. For now, I simply exist and nothing more. Strangely enough, I'm okay with the thought. I follow the curve of her lips with a forefinger, memorizing the landscapes and the textures of her face.

Liv tucks my hair behind my ear. "Are you all right?"

"Mhmm. You?"

"Yes. Perfect." Despite that assurance, she's squirming, and after a few seconds she adds a smiling clarification. "Except for one small issue."

I can't blame her. She hasn't come yet—a situation I need to rectify. I laugh softly. "I'm very sorry." My thigh slips between hers, feeling her heat again.

She pulls me closer, her answering laugh slow and sensual. "I hate to ruin the mood, lying here with you is incredible, but I wonder if you wouldn't mind helping me out?"

Reaching between us, I feel how slick and hard she is. I groan and murmur a helpless, "Oh fuck." Kissing her slowly, I let my tongue sweep over her lower lip before slipping inside to caress hers. A gentle push and I'm on top of her. Liv locks her good leg around my waist, pulling me closer, wanting more. She's trying to grind against my hand but I hook my arm under her knee, stretch her up and spread her apart.

Fingers teasing her clit, dipping gently inside her and then out again. I drag my fingers up to my mouth and suck the taste of her from them. She's sweet and delicious—that thing you'd been without and forgotten you love…until you have it again, and you wonder how you ever went without it. I've been starved and I didn't even know it.

Liv groans. "That's so fucking sexy." She pulls me down for a kiss. Hard and frantic now, her tongue dueling with mine, like she's trying to taste herself on me. I bite the skin of her neck and enter her again, claiming every hidden ridge.

I feel each flutter and clench, amplified by our shared desire. The tightening around my fingers, the tension in her muscles, the low moans and gasps she's making tell me everything I need to know. My teeth graze her neck, her nipples, then I soothe them with long sweeps of my tongue. She tastes of sweat and soap and something that I can't name but that is just *her*.

When I wriggle free and begin my pilgrimage downward, Olivia lifts herself from the bed, propped up on her elbows. We keep eye contact the whole way down and she watches every lick, nip, and suck over her taut belly, curved hips, muscled thighs until I come back up to the junction between her legs.

"Spread for me," I beg. "Can I taste you?"

Liv offers herself to me, whispering, "Please, please." A gentle hand tangles in my hair.

She's magnificent, like a piece of ripe fruit. Her plummy folds glisten with arousal, begging to be tasted. She writhes desperately but I want to look at her first. I need to see her, to commit this to memory so I can think about her when they take her from me. I try out words in my head and then quickly discard them again. There's only one thing I can say, and when I finally manage to utter it, my voice breaks with emotion. "You're so fucking beautiful."

Hands reach for me, fumbling over my arms and shoulders. "Please, Celeste, I need you."

I kiss her clit lightly and with that simple kiss, my tongue and mouth remember what to do. When I make my first tentative sweep, she moans and fills my mouth. I'd forgotten how it feels to have arousal wet against my chin, hands tugging my hair, thighs clamped around me, holding me, supporting me, begging me. She makes me remember everything. She makes me ashamed that I'd forgotten how this can be. I drown in her and I don't care if I never break the surface to take another breath again.

Olivia grows and swells. I feel her heart beating under my tongue, the pulse growing with each sweep I make. I thought I'd forgotten this but with every look and touch, I remember. I remember how I fit between thighs with my shoulders braced and toes curling in the sheets. I remember how my arm is long enough for my hand to trace over breasts and dig nails into skin. I've been here before, in this moment in time. But being with her in the now is entirely new.

"Oh God. Just like that. Fuck me, *please*," she begs. Liv cries out when my tongue flicks under her clitoris and my reward is a renewed flood of her essence. "I'm going to come," she murmurs, then lets loose a long, hoarse string of Italian that I can't decipher. I slip my fingers inside her, and she says something I do understand. "Don't stop, Celeste, right there... there, that's...I'm coming..."

* * *

Awake. Entwined. Indistinguishable. She's pressed to my back, one arm around my waist holding me tight and the other under my neck cupping my breast lightly. Warm, even breaths blow across my cheek. I'm sore in all the good places, muscles tight from hours of lovemaking.

For so long, my body hasn't felt like mine and now it does— the change natural, simple, organic. I close my eyes again and reconnect with myself. I say a silent hello to my breasts, my thighs, my hands. I apologize to myself for my indifference. For my detachment. For my apathy.

The hand on my waist moves to make long and lazy sweeps up my belly before I'm pulled tighter against her. She kisses my neck, nuzzles my skin. "Good morning."

"Morning." I roll over, still enclosed in the cage made by her arms.

She kisses me, her lips warm, soft, and soothing as though she simply wants to spend a lifetime languorously kissing. "How are you?" Liv asks.

"Good." It seems an inadequate description, but to tell her that I feel like I'm suddenly a whole person again feels too deep. Being this close to her now feels strange and a shyness overwhelms me. Gently, I slip from her grasp. "I'm going have a quick workout."

"And I'm going to fall asleep again," she counters.

I use the treadmill, wanting to stay inside where I can be near her. Olivia is still in bed when I finish and take a shower, but she stirs sleepily when I come back to get dressed. I sit on the bed, running my hand over her bare arm. Even without the veil of desperation and lust from last night, I revel in the feeling of skin under my fingers. "I'll start coffee."

"Wonderful." Smiling, she stretches, a little moan escaping as she arches her back. "I'll be out in a few minutes."

Coffee gurgles and drips. My teabag is steeping. Every now and then there's a dull thud outside, likely snow falling from the roof. I'll need to shovel the paths to the greenhouse, shed, and solar panels. Footsteps sound behind me. She's not using the stick I made her, but her gait still has the barest traces of a limp in it.

Then she's molded against my back and sliding her arms around my waist. "Mmm, you smell good." Soft kisses on my neck. I lean back into her, my eyes closed. Lips brush over my ear. "Are you sure you're all right, Celeste? I kind of just sprung that on you last night, and it was probably pretty intense."

When I twist in her loose grip, she lets me go so I can turn right around to face her. "Better than I've been in a while." I pull her close, keeping my hands on her hips. "It was intense but also…incredible."

"Incredible, huh?" She grins, a little cockily. She has every right to be cocky.

"Yes," I say seriously.

"For me too." Olivia takes my face in her hands and kisses me sweetly. My shyness from when I woke beside her evaporates and we spend long moments just kissing. Her nose brushes over mine before she pulls back. "Is that coffee ready?"

I pour some for her, add the right amount of sugar and set her mug on the counter. "I need to check in. I'll be back in a little while and we can have breakfast?"

"Sounds good." Olivia pulls the mug toward herself, a smile teasing her lips. "I'll be here."

Reluctantly, I leave her to go back to the tedium of my life. Logging, reporting, making lists all seems loathsome and pointless now after the wonder that was last night.

Cont E: Hello, SE9311. How are you?

SE9311: Hi, I'm good. Can I ask you a question?

Cont E: You may.

SE9311: She's really here, isn't she? Olivia - you've seen her? Spoken with her? She's not a false thing?

Despite all of it, I still don't quite trust myself, that I haven't just made up an elaborate companion. All in my head. The world's hottest, most amazing wet dream.

Cont E: Yes, she is real. On that matter I need to advise that there's been a weather delay on our end and we can't extract Ms. Soldano tomorrow morning as scheduled.

My heart beats hard against my ribs, knocking around my hopes and anxieties. We're going to have more time.

SE9311: When will you get here?

Cont E: It's hard to say. Could be a few days or might be a week. How are you with provisions? Will you be okay for a while longer?

I can't make my fingers work fast enough to type out just how okay that is, and make a mistake that I have to delete. I type it again slowly, making sure my words are clear and they'll know I'll be okay for as long as necessary.

SE9311: Everything's fine. I can manage for quite a while still.

Cont E: Even with an extra person in the compound?

SE9311: Yes. It's fine, really.

Cont E: Thank you. We'll be in touch when we know more. Could you please advise Ms. Soldano, and pass along our sincerest apologies for the delay? We've emailed her family on her behalf but if she would like to contact them herself again, please let us know.

SE9311: I will. And I'll tell her all of that.

I almost type *thank you*, but stop myself just in time.

And then Controller E is gone. I make a quick report for them, avoiding details of last night. I haven't even said anything about Liv and I touching or hugging, and I'm certainly not going to lay out the intimacies we shared.

Olivia looks up from her nest on the couch where she's curled up with blankets and cushions, coffee on the table and book in her hands. "Is everything all right?"

"Mhmm fine, but there's been a weather delay with tomorrow's pickup. They aren't quite sure when they'll find a window, but it might be another couple of days or perhaps a week."

Her expression is unreadable. "I see. So…no ride home yet?"

"Not yet, no. They've sent an email to the address where they forwarded the video, but if you want to write something or make another video, they said you're welcome to."

She shrugs. "We'll see how it goes. An email to my father on my behalf will suffice for now."

The excitement of possibility has my blood humming. I make myself coffee, taking my time pouring and stirring. When I sit beside her, she stretches over to kiss me. I rub my knuckles softly over her cheek. "I'm sorry. You must be getting sick of being cooped up in here with me."

"I'm nowhere near sick of being here with you." Olivia shuffles so she's behind me, legs on the outside of mine and her hands resting on my shoulders. Her thumbs dig in, finding all my knots and trying to get rid of them. "And I couldn't be less sorry that they can't collect me yet."

I believe her but it still doesn't ease my discomfort. "Mmm."

"Are you okay with it?"

"Absolutely," I say instantly. "But it's just…the longer you stay, the harder it's going to be. For me." My head falls forward, neck relaxing under her touch even though the topic we're discussing is anything but relaxing.

"Celeste, you're going to be just fine. You're so strong, look how long you've been here. It's just a little more time once I'm gone. I know you can do it." She's trying hard to soothe me, to placate me but it isn't working. It's not her fault of course, she can't know what it's really like.

"I'm sure I *can*, I just don't want to." I reach over and set my coffee on the low table. "What happens after, Liv? How am I supposed to just keep going like nothing's happened? Like we never—" The thought just stops, like my brain can't comprehend what comes after this.

Her hands still a moment, then resume their methodical kneading. "I'm not sure."

I can't even think about it, not having her, because I can't even recall what it was like before. No face, no voice, no scent, no touch, no taste. I tilt my head to look back at her and move the subject away from the thing that wants to strangle me. "That feels really good."

"Yeah?"

"Yeah."

Her hands slide over my shoulders, brushing my collarbone before coming to rest on my breasts. She squeezes lightly, thumbs teasing my nipples. "How about that?"

"Feels even better."

I feel her pressing against my ass. Hands are inside my shirt, pinching nipples that are now painfully erect. "And that?" she asks in a low voice. I groan, and she yanks my shirt over my head.

CHAPTER FOURTEEN

Every moment I have to spend in the computer room is a moment I don't get to spend with Olivia. Our time together is already too short, and the irritation of wasting it on telling faceless people how I feel has me rushing to wrap up my morning reports.

SE9311: Nothing you need to talk to me about?

Cont B: No. Thank you for your logs.

SE9311: You're welcome.

I don't even remember what I wrote yesterday.

Cont B: The weather system is still unstable, but as advised, we anticipate the transport will be there within a week. We'll keep you informed as best we can.

One week, or perhaps less. That's all we have. It's nowhere near enough time.

SE9311: Thank you.

Fuck you. My face screws up the moment the thought intrudes. It's not Controller B's fault. It's not anyone's fault. It just *is*. It's something I cannot control, another thing in a long list that is beyond my reach or understanding.

Cont B: Are you all right, SE9311?

I glance at the camera in the corner and nod.

Cont B: How is Ms. Soldano?

It's sweet the way they call her that, as though from the very beginning when I told them her name and how she'd come here they'd applied some measure of respect to her.

SE9311: She seems fine.

Cont B: How are you finding sharing your space?

It's wonderful. It's heartbreaking.

SE9311: The whole thing is a little strange, but I'm getting used to it. She's very easy to get along with.

I hope they aren't paying attention to how much I'm blushing.

Cont B: I'm pleased. Please let us know if anything changes. And you're due to video log for the week.

SE9311: Right, sorry. Things have been all up in the air and I forgot. I'll get on that right away.

Cont B: Thank you. Enjoy your day and we'll be in touch.

Of course they will. Before I can stop myself or think about what I'm going to say I bring up the video logger. The little window that shows me my face also shows me that my hair is a mess. Quickly I pull it back into a ponytail and start the recording.

"So, I guess what you're really interested in is how things have changed now Olivia is here. It was weird and awkward, and a little horrible to start with. I didn't know what to say or do and it was really overwhelming. It's a lot easier now but sometimes I still feel strange, like I'm second-guessing myself every time I say or do something. Also…I feel connected to her which makes me feel even weirder because I barely know her."

I exhale a deep sigh. "Actually, it feels good to say this, to verbalize all my confusion. I don't know what part of my feelings are real and what's just because she's the first person I've seen and spoken to and, uh…touched in over three years. I guess, if nothing else, it's a good thing for your study to see how quickly someone who's been alone will latch on to the first person they see. I'm kind of grateful to have had it happen here, because I'm super embarrassed to think what I'd be like when I get out. Like, I'd probably have fallen in love with the first person I saw, but this is kind of a test run where it's less embarrassing to admit that you think you're in love with someone you only kind of know."

Love.

I open my mouth to take it back, to cover it with some joking slip-of-the-tongue explanation. But there aren't any explanations or jokes that will cover the truth of what just fell from my mouth. I shut off the recording, log off, and leave the room.

Liv's sitting at the table with a board game set up, waiting for me. "No problems?"

"No, everything's fine. Sorry it took a while. I had to do a video log for them."

"That's quite all right." She holds her hand out to me. "Are you ready to start this game?"

I really don't feel like playing Monopoly right now, but she wants to. "Sure." I take her hand and let her pull me closer until I'm standing between her slightly spread knees.

Liv releases my hand and slides an arm around my waist. She pulls me tight, resting her face against my belly as her other arm wraps around my butt. When she exhales, the warm air pushes through my shirt to touch my skin. "I wish we could stay like this," she says. "Just for a little while longer."

"Me too." My hands go to her hair, gently running through her dark waves.

Liv leans back to look up at me. "But we can't, can we?"

It takes every bit of strength I have to agree with her. I shake my head, and my response is surprisingly steady. "No, we can't."

The truth is, what I want doesn't matter. It doesn't matter that I think it's cruel and unfair. It doesn't matter that she might want the same as me, though perhaps with less intensity than I do. We are bound by things beyond our control, and the only thing that matters is that we make the most of the small amount of time we have left.

* * *

I'm living my own personal, reversed Theory of Relativity where all the wonderful time with her is slowed down instead of sped up. When I wake in the morning, naked and warm with her against me it's easy to forget, for just a moment, that we are marching toward our inexorable conclusion. The only thing that's stopping me from breaking down completely is the idea that I might see her again when I finish up with the study. If she hasn't moved on from this strange fling or whatever it is we're doing.

Midafternoon, Liv sets up the board on the dining table for our first chess game, while I pour wine and put out a bowl of chips. I make my opening move, pawn to E4. She stares at the board, teeth worrying her lower lip and after almost two minutes, she answers with pawn to C5.

I smile. "Sicilian defense. One of my favorites." She's clearly not a novice player and I'm simultaneously excited for the challenge, and absolutely certain I'm going to be outmatched.

"Mine and my father's favorite too." Liv reaches for her wine.

I counter with knight to F3 and the game is on. Liv is careful and clever, and I feel like she's always four steps ahead of me. I like chess, I know the theory and strategy—mostly from re-re-reading books in here—but I've never mastered that intuitive foresight of really good players. Liv plays chess like her life depends on it, and with every move she makes I learn a little more about her.

She doesn't do anything without thoroughly examining the board, and then my face, then the board again. I imagine her, in her other life, navigating her work and personal life the same way. Thoughtful, careful. She's not sneaky about her moves, everything is open and clear but intensely competitive. She plays proactive to my reactive. We break here and there to get more snacks, pour more wine and steal kisses in the kitchen. We have a quickie on the couch and she starts a casserole for dinner.

Before we stop to eat, we're still battling for the upper hand but I have to admit she's probably going to win the game. After we've eaten her delicious meal, I gather our dishes, dump them in the sink and run water. She half-rises from her chair. "Leave them, Celeste. I'll take care of it."

"No, you made dinner and I'm already up."

It takes less than ten minutes to wash up, and she's quiet the whole time I'm in the kitchen. I hear footsteps as I'm pulling the dishwashing gloves off and a moment later warm hands cup my breasts, and fingers find my nipples to pinch them into tight points. "Stay there," Olivia breathes, her touch drifting down over my stomach to unfasten my jeans and yank them down.

I jolt at her touch and set the gloves aside, turning my head to find her. "Liv, I—"

But I'm shushed with a firm kiss. She's pressed hard against me, hips pushing into my ass, breasts against my back. She's kissing me, tasting my neck, nuzzling my hair. Her fingers are on my clit, pinning me in place and I can't turn around. Then she's inside me, deep, finding all my hidden places.

While I'm braced against the sink, Olivia takes me hard and fast, with her teeth in my neck and a hand closed over my breast. I gasp with every firm stroke until my climax comes, too quickly, and I ride out the waves, shuddering under their weight. Once I catch my breath, I turn to face her and it's then I realize she's wearing nothing more than a bra and panties—like she started to undress but was overcome with lust. She has her fingers in her mouth, sucking me from them. I grab her hard and kiss her furiously, possessively, pushing her toward the bedroom.

Liv stops and yanks her panties down. "No, right here. God I can't wait. I need you to fuck me." She glances around, eyes wild, then backs up to the table and hops up to sit on it. Legs spread, she reaches for me and I'm on her in seconds, fitting right between her thighs. My jeans are still at half-mast, thighs slick with the aftermath of my climax and now, fresh arousal.

She's so fucking wet, it paints my hip as she grinds on me. I'm in slowed-down time. I feel every single precious moment. My shirt is tugged over my head, bra gone. I take hers as well, dropping it on the floor next to mine. Nails dig into my ass, heels against the back of my thighs pull me closer, urge me harder and faster. I slip inside her heat and thrust. Gently at first, wanting to hold her on the edge of climax for as long as possible, but her panting and writhing soon makes me abandon that idea. So I fuck her. Just like she asked me to.

Nipples are hard against mine. Arm around my shoulders. Mouth against my neck. She begs me to keep fucking her. To make her come. With every thrust, she gasps and asks for more. Heat coats my fingers. I haven't even touched her clit but she's shuddering, deep tremors moving through her body. When I move my thumb to stroke her clit she bucks under my touch and buries her teeth in my shoulder.

I'm so aroused I can barely stand. I pull out and step back, kicking out of my jeans and panties. Liv whimpers, scrabbling and scratching my shoulder to try and get me back to where I was, with my fingers deep inside her. She quiets a little when I push her down to lie on the table and bend over to close my mouth around her nipple.

Licking, sucking, biting, I fumble for a chair and sit heavily. Liv squeaks when I yank her to the edge of the table and dive in, taking her in my mouth. She's lifting her hips again, pushing up against my tongue, trying to force me to go faster and harder. I place a steadying hand on her belly and slow down, making long soft strokes to pull her back a little.

"Please, I need to come. Please let me." *This* begging is one of the sexiest things I've ever heard.

Grazing my teeth over her clitoris makes her moan. I do it again, ever conscious of the fresh flooding arousal between my own thighs. Fuck it. I slide my free hand between my legs and touch myself. The first contact makes me gasp. The second makes me groan.

Liv lifts her head. "Are you...oh, fuck. I'll come if I hear you do that."

"Good," I murmur against her. I remember how that feels, the low vibrato of someone talking against my clit. Seems she likes it too. Her cries reach a high note when my tongue slides inside her. Stomach clenching, my legs tremble with every stroke of my finger against myself and stroke of my tongue against her.

I dig nails into the soft skin of her thigh, trying unsuccessfully to hold off. My climax comes just before hers and the moment I cry out against her sex, she groans and comes in my mouth. Her heels press hard against my back, a hand yanking my hair, every pulse under my tongue strong and glorious and feeding my own release.

I drop my forehead against her thigh, and rest slick and satisfied until Liv slides off the table and onto my lap, straddling me. She's wet with sweat, and she slips a little until I steady her. I hold her tight around the waist, my head on her shoulder. I kiss her neck, tasting the saltiness of her.

"It'll never be enough," she whispers against my ear.

"No," I agree hoarsely. "It won't."

"I never expected this, Celeste. But I don't want to give it up." She sits up straighter, slings her arms around my shoulders. "It's typical, isn't it? Even if there was a way for me to stay, I can't. I'm an unknown and unwanted factor in this experiment. Plus...I have a job and a life out there that I need to return to. And you have a job *in here* for just a little longer. Me being in here means you can't do that job the way you're supposed to."

She's right, but that doesn't make it easier. "I know." I cringe slightly, waiting for Mother to pipe up with her usual about people not wanting to be near me, but she doesn't. A surprised hmmph exits my mouth.

"What's wrong?"

"Nothing. I just realized something is all."

"What?" Her left eyebrow lifts a fraction.

"I think the false things are leaving."

She studies me with her head tilted. "Really?" The hint of a smile teases the edges of her mouth.

I rush back through the past few days. The last time was Mother's intrusion when Olivia and I first—

I nod slowly. "I think so, yes. It's been days since I heard anyone."

Liv's smile becomes fully formed. She takes my face in her warm hands, pulling me close. The kiss lingers, a gentle tongue exploring my mouth until she pulls away with a final soft peck on my lips. "That's incredible."

"I think…" My eyes close briefly. "I think it's you. I think I'm in love with you, but I don't know if it's real or if it's because of this." I fling my arm in a shallow curve.

She's silent, slowly blinking.

"It's okay. You don't need to say anything. I know it's weird and way too fast. And like I said, maybe not even real." I add the last part just in case I've frightened her. Because if it's just my circumstance that's making me feel this way, then there's no need for her to fear the fact I've fallen insanely fast. But…it feels *so* real.

Her mouth opens. It closes. Her tongue slides quickly along her lower lip. "I care about you, Celeste. I know that much." Her words are quiet and without any sort of cruelty and I feel the warmth of them deep in my body.

It's enough. I didn't expect her to respond at all and this admission is more than I'd ever hoped I'd hear. She kisses my nose, then disengages from my lap and bends to collect her underwear from where she hastily dropped it. Liv straightens, stares at the chessboard, wearing her concentration frown. I stare too, but my face is probably more one of surprise that none of the pieces moved while I fucked her hard at the other end of the table.

She leans over to move her knight. "Checkmate," she murmurs.

CHAPTER FIFTEEN

I wake sometime in the night and know right away that what roused me is the absence of her. It's a black hole. An empty well. A missing limb. This is what my life will be like when she goes—I will fall asleep only to wake up all night long, wondering where she is. I'll wander aimlessly around the compound, remembering places she's been, places she touched me, places she made me feel real again. And I will never feel complete again.

When I roll over, a faint light from under the closed bedroom door casts an eerie glow through my room. She must be in the bathroom. I wait for a few minutes but she doesn't come back. Maybe she's sick. Concern rising, I call, "Olivia?" But the word is almost inaudible and unintelligible with sleep hoarseness.

After another minute or so, I swing my feet over the side of the bed to the cool wooden floor and pad naked across the room. When I'm almost at the door I hear typing, fast and fluid. Liv doesn't have a laptop. Is she on my computer? Their computer. I pause, listening for a few moments to be sure what I'm hearing really is the sound of fingers on a keyboard. Yes.

Stealthily, I open the bedroom door and sneak down the hall toward the computer room.

The closer I get, the louder the typing is. It doesn't make any sense. The computer is not an ordinary one and needs log in details, and even if she figured them out there's no Internet or anything useful on it. Maybe Liv is just typing to feel connected to her old life? Maybe I'm having one of those weird, super-realistic dreams. I give my arm a clichéd pinch. It clichéd hurts.

At the partially closed door to the computer room, I realize immediately that all my assumptions are wrong. Liv is typing what looks like a report formatted similarly to the logs I write daily, her forehead furrowed as her beautiful, talented fingers fly over the keyboard. My skin prickles. I'm too hot, too shocked, too afraid to do anything but ask the most basic and obvious question. "What are you doing?"

At the intrusion, Liv hits a key hard and spins the chair around. "Hey," she says smoothly. Her face gives nothing away, but I know what I've just seen.

"What are you doing?" I repeat. "You shouldn't be in here."

"I had some thoughts about a drug formula and wanted to get them down before I forgot." The words are quiet, calm. "Sorry, I should have asked if I could use the computer, but I didn't want to wake you." At that, Liv stands and walks over, reaching to pull me close.

I take a step back, through the doorway of the computer room, away from her lying hands. "How did you get access?"

"It was turned on."

"No. It's never left turned on overnight. That's part of their protocol. And it logs me out automatically after I leave it for more than ten minutes." I know I'm right, that it was turned off because I've followed that protocol to the letter for over three years. Panic sits behind my sternum, and at any moment it's going to bubble up and choke me.

Liv shrugs, seeming unconcerned. "Well it was."

My response grinds out through clenched teeth. "Show me what you were writing."

Olivia laughs, low and melodic. "What? Really? You want to read about chemical formulas and data?"

"Yes."

"Come on, darling, you're being silly." She tries to tug me down the hall, away from the computer room.

"No I'm not. Show me." I grab Olivia's arm to stop her from leaving, my fingers digging into her soft skin. Liv gasps and chastened, I loosen my grip immediately, afraid I've really hurt her. "Shit. I'm sorry. I'm sorry."

Liv rubs her bicep. "It's okay."

I take a few long slow breaths, trying to settle myself and after twenty seconds or so I'm calm enough to talk again. "Show me." This time it's less clenched teeth, and more quietly forceful.

She hesitates, until I move around her to tap the keyboard. Even then, all she says to me is an urgent, "Wait!" When I turn around, an unrecognizable expression—somewhat akin to fear—crosses Liv's face. She exhales. "Okay."

Liv swiftly inputs something, and the screen transforms into a familiar interface. The logging system. Only this time, it's not from me. It's *about* me, logged by a user identified as O.M. SOLDANO.

Olivia. Maria. Soldano.

Oh, God. Oh, no no no.

I can't—

This isn't—

I click and scroll, eyes skimming over the words. Everything is there, laid bare. Details of our interactions, conversations, my demeanor, things we've done since she arrived. Sexual encounters. I can't take it in, can't examine it properly, can't understand. I jab my finger at the screen. "What is this? What the fuck is this?"

To give her some credit, she doesn't even try to be evasive, but responds with a calm, "It's exactly what it looks like, Celeste."

My question comes out unevenly, riding the dips and curves of my emotion. "You're spying on me for them?"

"No, sweetheart, not spying. Just monitoring the same way as always. Onsite as opposed to remotely via the logs and check-ins."

"Monitoring me? You? You've been reporting on me this whole time? Every night?"

"Yes, and this is obviously the first night you've woken. You're an unusually sound sleeper." Olivia is relaxed, almost dispassionate. Like it doesn't matter. Like I don't matter. Now she's been caught, she's not even bothering to skirt around the truth.

I want to vomit. "Oh? Well I'm sorry my circadian rhythms interrupted you *spying* on me."

"Celeste…"

"You knew everything this whole time? You lied?" The tightness in my throat makes it hard to get the words out.

Mother's noxious stench is in my nostrils. "Crybaby." She sounds bored, as though she's got somewhere better to be and torturing me is a chore.

I sniff hard, rubbing my nose as if it would help push that fearsome odor away.

Olivia steps forward, hands outstretched. "Celeste, please."

"Tell me," I insist. My chest is so tight I can barely breathe. You're okay. You're fine. You're running through the woods. At the beach diving under waves. Standing on the sidewalk watching cars rush past. Breathe. In and out. In. Out. I start walking backward. I can't let her catch me.

Olivia lowers her hands, but she's still moving toward me. "All right." She sighs. "Yes, I knew about it this whole time. I'm part of the experiment." Two steps forward.

"Part of it?" My back hits a wall and I scoot sideways along it, up the hallway away from the computer room.

"Celeste. Please, relax." Her voice is low and calm. Too calm. She says something in Italian.

"What?" I stare at her, my hands behind me feeling for obstacles as I move away.

She murmurs again, this time a long hypnotizing stream of Italian. It's not angry or intimidating. It sounds soft. It sounds… loving, and the whole time, she's creeping closer to me with her hands outstretched, palms up. We're playing a slow, horrific version of Keep Away. Neither of us is winning.

I'm totally exposed physically and emotionally and I can't stand it. "Do not come any closer. Are you even real? Are you a person? Don't touch me." I keep backing away, toward the kitchen, afraid to turn away from her. My heart pounds hard against my ribs as I bump into the walls, the table in my desperation to get away. I trip over a chair and stumble, catching myself on the couch.

"Told you. You're so fucking dumb," Mother whispers in my ear. "Nobody wants you."

I swat at her. "Go away."

Olivia implores, "Celeste, *please* relax. Just talk to me."

"Talk?" My voice pitches strangely. "How can I talk to you when I can't even trust you now? Everything's a lie, isn't it? All these things I thought we had in common. It's all a lie, right? You only said those things because you knew what I needed to trust you."

"No! Only a few minor details were false, like why I'm here. Everything else I told you is the truth. They chose me because I profiled as the closest match for you."

Profiled. What an awful, clinical word. "But why, Olivia? You used me. You let me touch you. You touched me. I thought—" I inhale a deep, shuddering breath. "I thought this was real." I duck around the couch and sidestep to the kitchen.

Liv follows, still a couple of feet away from me. She's trying to get close but I'm faster than her. Sneakier. It took me a while to learn, but now I'm very good at staying out of the way of hands that want to hurt me.

"It is real, Celeste, I promise. You and me, this is real."

"That's bullshit! Why? Will you get a performance bonus for *fucking* me, Olivia? Are you even a lesbian, or was every touch and kiss horrible and forced and sickening for you?" My stomach heaves and I clap a hand over my mouth until I can regain control. I can't stop to puke. If I stop, she's got me.

"No, it's not like that," she insists. "I wanted this. I want you. I'm not some random person they pulled from the street. I asked to be assigned into the dwelling." She smiles, a little sadly. "Celeste, we've known one another far longer than you think."

That stops me. Both my hands fumble for the kitchen countertop, for something to hold on to. "What do you mean?" Now her gaze is steady and sure. "I'm Controller A."

I've run out of gas. Someone cut my power cable. I'm dead in the water. I can't move. I can't think. It's all I can do to keep breathing. "What?"

"I'm Controller A."

"You're Controller A?" I repeat dumbly.

"Yes."

Bile rises up the back of my throat and I try desperately to swallow it down, to put a lid on my betrayal but there's no stopping it this time. It keeps coming up until I have no choice but to lean over the kitchen sink and expel it. It's over. She'll catch me now. Liv is by my side in seconds, pushing sweat-wet hair out of my eyes and rubbing my back as I heave and heave.

Vision blurred and dizzy, I want to tell her to stop touching me, but I can't breathe enough to get the words out and when I try, I choke on the vomit in my throat. Still bent over the sink, I shift and squirm under her touch, trying to push her away. But she doesn't move from my side. Her hand is too hot against the back of my neck, burning. I stop retching and finally manage to gasp, "Don't touch me."

Olivia removes her hand to run water in the sink, but she's still right beside me. I twist away and straighten up, away from the stream of water. Cupped hands make a small pond to splash water onto my face, but I'm naked and there's nothing to wipe my face on, no T-shirt or towel. She fetches a dishtowel from a drawer and passes it to me. Despite my body's best efforts to get rid of it, the nameless feeling still sits in my stomach, burning like acid.

I turn around, rotating away from her and lean against the sink. Liv reaches around to shut off the faucet, calm and methodical, going through the motions of someone who cares. She opens the fridge, takes out water and pours me a glassful. I accept with a shaking hand, rinse and spit then drink the rest of her offering.

"Please, Celeste, can we just sit down and talk? Let me explain what I can to you."

I ignore her request, a more immediate need taking my attention. "I'm going to put some clothes on."

She looks like she's going to protest, but at my hard stare she nods and indicates with a gesture that I should go and get dressed. I stop in the bathroom to scrub and gargle the taste of vomit from my mouth, then as quickly as I can, yank on clothes to cover my vulnerability. There's a scream inside me that desperately wants to be heard. I could slip out the front door and run away from her. But I can only go so far. She's always going to follow. Always going to find me. I'm trapped here with her.

I feel a tug on my tee and Riley's urgent whisper of, "Hide in the cellar with me."

"I can't," I murmur absently. "Be quiet and stay behind the boxes. Be a good girl for me and it'll be okay. I promise I'll keep you safe."

I pinch my arm again hard, and it still hurts. I pick up my lambskin rug from the end of the bed, rubbing the worn fleece over my face. I feel it. I smell it. I'm here in this bedroom and this is really happening to me.

Olivia is in the same place I left her, leaning against the kitchen counter. Grateful for the chance to ease off my trembling knees, I walk past her and sink down onto the couch. "Why are you here? I want the truth." *You can't handle the tr—* Stop. No.

Olivia settles on the couch too, a cautious distance from me. "I'm here because I want to be here. It's complicated, and there are many factors at play, but this was always part of the psychological component of this experiment. Cut the subject off for an extended period, monitor them closely so they're safe, then reintroduce them to a human contact. Nature versus nurture would be the best way to describe this portion. See how far the subject would bend the rules for companionship. See how seclusion would change their core ideals and values."

"And did I pass?" I ask sardonically.

"There's no pass or fail, Celeste. But you behaved exactly as I'd anticipated." Liv sighs quietly. "Exactly as I'd *hoped.* The environment and seclusion didn't change your integrity or your compassion. You chose me—" She closes her eyes, inhaling sharply. "You chose the *companion* over compensation."

Why do I suddenly feel like I chose wrongly? "Maybe I just felt obligated because I shot you. Maybe it was just the fact that you were a body to fuck. Maybe it had nothing to do with you specifically." It's not true, but I want to hurt her. To tear away her armor and pierce her somehow. To make her feel as awful as I do right now.

But none of my attacks seem to penetrate.

Olivia ignores the barb and rubs a hand over her wounded thigh. "Perhaps you're right. Please be sure to note that in your log." She's so calm and in control, playing some role I can't begin to imagine.

"You've been working this whole time, haven't you?" I spit at her as I wrap my arms around my torso. What I desperately want is a hug, but I can't stand the thought of her touching me.

"Please believe me when I tell you it wasn't work for me, Celeste. After I read your list a few days before your birthday, I knew." A flush appears on the tips of her ears, the only indication of discomfort she's had during this showdown or whatever it is that's happening between us. She clears her throat. "I was always a candidate for insertion, and of all of the Controllers you'd developed the best rapport with me. I have quite a large amount of sway within the department, so..." Her eyes flick up to meet mine. "It's partly why I kept myself apart at the interview, your first one."

I search frantically through memories from close to four years ago. "I don't remember."

Olivia allows herself a faint smile. "That's because you never saw me. I was behind the glass, but I was there. I sensed something in you. Something that made me curious, among other things."

I wave away her feeble excuses for betrayal. Is betrayal even the right word for what she's done? What *has* she done? Desperate to understand, I drop my guard, just a fraction. "Do you even care about what you've done to me?"

"Yes, of course I care," she snaps, her hands clenching to fists by her sides. It's the first time I've seen her lose any part of her incredible self-control, and I'm equal parts fascinated and frightened. Then as quickly as it happened, the anger is gone again, and her mask is back.

I lean closer, searching for something but I don't know what that something is. "Tell me everything. I deserve it."

I half expect her to tell me I don't deserve to know anything, that it's not a contractual obligation but she raises her chin and explains, "I'm the lead scientist on this study. I've read all your logs and check-in transcripts. Watched every video report." A blush on her cheeks joins the one on her ears. "And as time passed I found myself even more drawn to you." Olivia stares at her hands and it's like she's seeing them for the first time. Like they don't belong to her.

I can't hear this. Not now. I need to believe she's not invested because her doing this if she *feels* something for me is even more heartbreaking. I need facts, not emotions. My voice is barely above a whisper when I ask, "Is this really about colonizing other planets, or is it just some sick joke to mess with someone's head?" Though it's probably completely irrelevant, I have a sudden urge to know if my suffering is actually going to help anyone in the future.

She pauses, stares right into my eyes then says evenly, "There are many factors to this experiment, and yes that is one portion of it. In a colonization situation, a hostile environment, it's important to ensure people will help those in trouble even if they're strangers. Our species won't survive if people won't build communities with unknown persons and eventually procreate."

"Procreate." I snort. "That's a little difficult for you and I, locked up here don't you think?"

"Yes, and your sexuality is why you were chosen. The agency that contracted us to conduct the experiment didn't want the liability or complication of unwanted pregnancy. The basic human ideology is the same regardless of sexual preference, so…"

I'm not sure how I should feel about that. "Is your name really Olivia Soldano?"

"Yes."

"You're not a chemical engineer are you." Statement, not a question.

"No." Olivia slings her arm over the back of the couch, as though she's trying to appear relaxed and non-threatening. Crossing her legs completes the charade. "Technically I'm a psychiatrist, but I also have a neuroscience degree and a PhD." Doctor-Doctor Soldano. Clever.

"Is there a girlfriend waiting for you when you're done with me?"

She raises her eyebrows ever so slightly. "As I've told you, I'm single."

I laugh even though there's no humor in this. "Well I guess that's something. You're a liar but not a cheater."

"That's unfair, Celeste," Olivia counters.

"Is it?" I narrow my eyes, searching for something in her expression. There's nothing. She's a blank slate. "I hardly think you're in a position to comment on what's fair."

"You're entitled to think that."

I have no idea how she's so calm. Like none of this is relevant or even matters to her. "What about those stories you told me? About your relationship issues, your ex-girlfriends cheating and leaving you and…you know. Lies? Something to make me feel sorry for you?"

The look on her face tells me they were anything but. It's the same expression of horror and guilt she had when she told me about her girlfriend's suicide and I know nobody could fake that. Olivia shakes her head. "No, not lies. I wish they were but it's the truth." She stares at me, drawing in a few slow breaths until her face changes back to calm, composed Olivia.

My molars come together hard, the words forced. "What if I hadn't gone for it? For you?"

Olivia shrugs but the nonchalance seemed so affected. I can read her as plainly as a book, but what I'm reading now makes no sense. She's bothered, thinking that I might not have wanted her. For some reason she's not schooling her expression to neutrality. Why?

"It doesn't matter," she says. "There's no right or wrong result. But all your psych tests indicated you would act the way you did. Take in someone who was lost. It's quite exciting actually. The ideal candidate profile I constructed, the one you matched, turned out to be spot-on."

"Well, aren't I the perfect person, a regular Good Samaritan," I grind out. "Except for shooting you, I'm a regular Mary-fucking-Poppins."

"Well, you weren't supposed to shoot me," she says dryly. "My story was to be that I'd just become lost while hiking."

I clamp my lips together. "It was an accident. You know that and you know how sorry I am."

Both her hands come up, palms out. "I know and I apologize. I didn't mean it that way."

My heart refuses to slow down, still beating in response to my rage. "Fuck! All those bullshit lines and questions about what I was doing and my past, pretending you didn't know what was going on when you knew damned well. I'll give you this, you're a good actress. In every way," I add bitterly.

Even as I say it, I feel like I have no right to my feelings. I've got what I deserved because my whole life has been one great betrayal. Mother. Riley dying. Joanne dying. Myself. "Even your cover story about hiking with all your fake gear, everything so carefully constructed, you guys had it all figured out." I think about all the shit she carried in, pretending she'd been out in the wilderness for a few weeks, how pointless it all was. "Why did you need the gun?"

"I told you," she says evenly. "For protection."

What could she need protection from? They probably dropped her just over the ridge, where I couldn't see or hear the delivery, so she'd only have to walk a few hundred yards to reach me. Me. Me. Me. The answer snaps into focus. "Protection from…me, right?"

"Yes. Even monitoring you as closely as we had been, we couldn't be one hundred percent certain about your mental status."

"So you'd shoot me." Like a rabid animal.

"If necessary, yes. As an absolutely last resort." She looks nauseated.

I feel nauseated. "What a wonderful payback that would have been for you."

Her response is surprisingly forceful. "You don't get it, do you? Do you actually think I would have wanted to do that? I've been watching you for over three years, Celeste. I've been talking to you, worrying about you, *loving* you for over three goddamned years! This, us, isn't new. Not for me."

I move swiftly past her admission. I can't take it, can't listen to her lies anymore, can't listen to her manipulate me with words like *love*. "What about leaving? How was that supposed to go down?" I'm surprised at how easily I can discuss this now. Some part of me has shut down or been pushed aside so I can get the facts and the logic I so desperately need.

"That would have been dependent on circumstances and your state of mind. Either with your knowledge or by slipping away for extraction in the middle of the night like I'd just hiked out and left a goodbye note."

Like building blocks, things begin to click into place. I'd noticed Controller A was gone but thought nothing more of it than the line fed to me about staff restructuring. The way that sometimes Olivia would say things that made me think she knew me, and why I've always felt I knew her somehow but dismissed it as wishful thinking. I pushed it all aside as nothing more than distorted thoughts because I was so desperate for a connection.

What she did to me worked because despite everything that's happened in my life to make me more cautious than most, I'm still naïve. Because even with all the shitty things that have been done to me, I can't imagine someone doing that and I needed to know someone wanted me. Wanted to believe that for once, something amazing like this would happen to someone like me. I could cry. "I'm so fucking stupid. God, this worked because I'm dumb, because I wanted to believe it even when it was obvious from the start that it was too good to be true."

"No, Celeste, it *worked* because that's how we designed it to work. Because all but the most suspicious, cynical people would react the way you did. You're anything but dumb. You're extraordinary," she adds softly. "Despite everything that's happened in your life, you're still a good person. Sweet, compassionate, and kind."

She's trying to push down my defenses with flattery. I can't yield. "Please don't," I insist.

"It's true," she says, as though my request hasn't even registered. "It's part of why I feel the way I do about you."

The way she feels about me…is how exactly? Suddenly and inappropriately amused, I snort. "I shouldn't be surprised. I said I missed sex so they dropped some off for me, right? I mean, when I said I missed riding a bike, the next supply package had one." A mountain bike for me to ride around the compound. I'm pretty good at it, jumping over logs and stones and splashing through the shallow parts of the creek.

"I remember," Liv murmurs. "I chose that bike myself. Went to the store and picked one in your favorite color. I argued with my—with one of the Directors for a week about whether you should be *allowed* it. Some things I was able to get for you, other things they wouldn't budge."

I push aside her cute, manipulative story to keep rushing through events of our time together, trying to find a place where it should have clicked. I'm surprised and ashamed to find all the little markers that I should have picked up on are so clear now that I know. I'm such an idiot. "God, my cold. Was that real or did you like…spray some virus up my nose while I was asleep to make me sick so I'd share a bed with you?"

"No, Celeste. You caught that from me organically. They moved my insertion timeline up because I had the cold and the medical department wanted to test your immune response."

"Which was pretty shitty. As was the cold you gave me."

"Mhmm," she agrees. "I'm sorry you were uncomfortable. It was never our intention."

I've heard enough. Enough apologies—real or not. Enough explanations. Enough lies. I'm done. "Get out," I hiss.

Olivia recoils as though she's been struck. "I can't, I have to stay here until I can arrange transport, and I've already delayed it once."

"That was you? You deliberately stopped the supply drop?" Of course it was her. I fucked her, she wanted to keep gathering data, up close and personal. Whatever remains in my stomach threatens to rise and I swallow hard to push it down again.

"Yes."

"Change it. Fix it. Make them come."

"I'm sorry but I can't. My hands are tied."

"Walk out of here then." Just do something, anything to get away from me.

Her face softens, voice incredulous. "You really have no idea where we are, do you?"

For a moment, my resolve wavers before I remember that I can't be soft. I tighten my jaw. "Obviously not. It wasn't part of the orientation brochure."

"We're in a remote area, an eighty-mile drive from the nearest township. The Organization owns this entire area, almost five hundred acres of secluded heavily wooded land. I can't just walk out of here." Everything she says is excuses on top of lies on top of betrayal. "There are protocols that must be followed. I'm as bound by the rules as you are."

Rules. Like those even matter anymore. All I can think of is the way she manipulated me into sleeping with her even after everything I shared with her. After everything I told her about what Mother did. I feel used and so dirty.

"Ugh." Mother's disgusted scoff is loud. "You call it manipulation but I taught you how to survive. And you wanted it just as much as she did, kid."

I crane my neck, moving my head away from the voice. "Please, why can't they just collect you right now?"

Olivia sighs. "I just told you it's not as simple as having someone collect me, darling."

"Don't call me that. You've got no right."

"I'm sorry." She sounds it. "As I said, we can't just come in whenever we want to. It's costly and time-consuming, no frivolity allowed. Every transport has multiple checks and approvals, paperwork to be filed. Your cargo requests are discussed and approved or denied then packed and checked again. Personnel has to be arranged. It takes time, at least two days."

There's only one request that I care about this time. Her gone. I bring my hands to my face, so confused and so defeated by everything that's happened. Eventually I let them drop and admit, "This feels surreal."

She looks incredibly sad and for a moment I forget myself and want to gather her into my arms. "I can imagine," she says. After a long pause, during which she's holding my gaze, she continues, "Do you know what one of the hardest things was for me?"

I shake my head. I don't want to know. I want to stand up and move away from her but my butt is stuck to the couch and my feet are encased in concrete on the floor.

"When you told me you loved me last night, and I couldn't say it back. I wasn't allowed because it would have swayed your thought processes, but I wanted to, badly. So I'm saying it now. I love you, Celeste. I'm in love with you. I have been for quite some time." Olivia manages to capture my hand, and she pulls it to her breast. I feel the fast, strong beat of her heart. "Feel that? Feel how much my heart is racing because I'm so scared I'll lose you."

Her words snap me out of my stillness. "You never had me so you can't lose me." A lie but it's mine this time. I snatch my hand away. "I'm going back to bed. You can sleep on the couch. I want you gone as soon as possible. Make it happen. I don't care how."

CHAPTER SIXTEEN

I smell her beside me and know it's not a false thing. Her scent clings to the linens and permeates my soul, and I want to bury my face in her pillow and do nothing but breathe the scent in. Instead, I roll onto my back, stare up at the ceiling and listen to people talking at me.

"People lie, Celeste," Heather says. "I mean, yeah it's still a fucking shitty thing to do but you should know by now that people are assholes."

"This is more than lying, Heather! This is…" Alli sighs and smacks her lips together. "I don't even think there's a way to describe what this is."

Riley laughs like a hyena. "Being a cu—"

"Riley!" Joanne admonishes my sister. "Do not use that word! It's disgusting."

On the other side of my closed door, Olivia walks around the habitat. I know the sound of her footsteps like I know my own face. The measured cadence broken by that tiny, even pause in her gait. I did that, I gave her that limp. She's pacing. Can't sleep either. I have to stop thinking. If I could just put a label on how I feel, then I might be able to make sense of it. But there's no combination of words that will ever describe this maelstrom inside me.

"I know you're sad, my little moonbeam," Joanne soothes. "But there will be other girls, sweetie. Come on, close your eyes. If you don't sleep, you're not going to be able to concentrate at school, and you have that important exam today."

"Cel?" Tentative, tiny Riley steps make their way across threadbare carpet. "Are you awake? Can I sleep with you? I'm so cold and I can't find any socks."

A door slams. Mother snarls, "Shut the hell up, you two, or he's gonna kick us out. Ungrateful little bitches, I told you he hates kids, so keep your mouths shut or you can get the fuck out and sleep in the yard."

"I'm sorry, Cel," Riley whimpers. "I didn't mean to wet the bed again. Please don't tell her. We can just change the sheets, right?"

I can't stand this any longer. It takes only a few minutes to strip my bed of sheets, pillowcases, and the duvet cover, taking Olivia's scent with them. I carry the bundle down the stairs and stuff it into the washer. Then I remake the bed with fresh linens, ignoring Olivia's call from the couch to ask what I'm doing. Burying my face in my pillow to smell clean laundry detergent doesn't help. She's still here.

I try begging myself to fall sleep. I try meditation. Yoga. Masturbation, no climax. Counting sheep and horses and goats. Reverse psychology. Nothing helps. Toward six a.m. after exactly no sleep, I'm about ready to scream.

When I emerge from the bathroom, Liv—Olivia—is already at the table with her coffee. It's the first time she's ever been awake before me. Unless she was just faking with her eyes closed this whole time when I woke before her. She regards me warily. "Good morning."

"Hello." I walk past her and to the front door where I slip my boots on and shrug into my jacket.

Her voice follows me to the door. "Where are you going?"

I don't answer.

"Celeste? What are you doing? Please answer me."

"You're not the boss of me," I tell her childishly and pull the door closed on her response. Brilliant work. Very mature. Very respectful. It takes me twice as long as usual to clear last night's snow from the solar panels. I'm wading through emotional sludge, dulled by the weight of no sleep sitting on top of what happened last night. I love her and I'm in love with her but I think I might hate her too. Above everything is the overwhelming confusion of not even knowing if any of those emotions are real.

"You're conflicted, Cel. I get it. You felt the same way about Ma," Riley reminds me. "Despite all the shit she did, you loved her and wanted her to love you but hated her just the same."

"Go away, Riles."

"Can't," she says, and I imagine her shrug—the one that had shoulders, eyebrows, and hands reaching skyward.

"Why not? Why don't you ever give me any useful advice?"

"Can't go 'cause you won't let me. Don't have anything useful to say because you don't want to hear it. You want to suffer through it on your own." The unspoken *duh* is clear.

I turn around, foolishly expecting to see my sister behind me. Of course, there's nothing there. Except Olivia in the doorway of the habitat. We stare at one another, not moving, for the longest time. Then I turn away and make my way down the hill. I can hear Olivia loudly saying something but I ignore her and start jogging.

"Like gum on her shoe." Mother is matter-of-fact, but for once, not mocking. "Chewed up and spat out once she didn't want you no more. Don't take it personally, kid."

"Leave me alone," I growl, picking up my pace.

Distantly, I hear Olivia calling my name as I rush toward the edge of the compound. Before I can talk myself out of it, I cross from white into green. Instantly, I'm dropped to my knees by the jolt and I roll hard onto my left shoulder. But I force myself to get up and to run. My legs are trembling from the shock but I keep pumping them as hard as I can, racing toward yellow.

Olivia's yelling now, voice raw and panicked. "Celeste! Stop! Don't be so—"

The shock in the yellow is far worse than the green. I bite my tongue and cry out as I fall, unable to help myself. My whole body twitches on the ground, jerking against my will. I'm not sure I can make it to red, but I have to. I just need to get away from her. I just need to sleep. There's wetness between my thighs but it's not arousal. I peed. The smell is at once familiar and terrifying.

"Get up," Mother seethes. "You want them to catch you with my stuff in your pocket? They'll send you to jail and where will your sister be then? Fucking dead with nobody to take care of her. Get up, you useless piece of shit!"

I'm wobbling but I'm upright. Just. Staggering and stumbling. Groaning and flailing.

"Celeste! Jesus, please stop!" Olivia's close, but not close enough to do anything. She can't stop me. She can't catch me this time.

I see the red signs a few feet away and throw myself forward. I'm a fast runner, I can make it before yellow gets me again. I cross the line and then it's all at once. A shock, worse than any I've had and a burning in my arm where the implant is buried. Floating. Reprieve. Bliss.

* * *

I come to in the shower as I'm being washed, and outrage simmers at her seeing me naked without my permission. But underneath my outrage there's an interest in how tender she is. There's nothing sexual about it. No lingering brushes over my breasts or thighs. She's soft, caring and dare I say it...loving.

Clumsily, I brush her hand away from where it's gently rubbing a washcloth over my thigh. "Stop." My tongue is swollen from where I bit it. I run it along my teeth a few times, feeling the sting when they touch the raw part.

Olivia smoothes wet hair from my face. "How are you feeling?"

Again, I swat her, rolling to face the tiled wall. "Go away."

"Celeste, I need to ensure you're okay."

"You've got no right." Vulnerable. Naked.

She stands and takes a step away. Now her hands are no longer on me, I'm acutely aware of the absence of touch as my skin chills. Olivia sighs. "Actually, I have every right. You're a test subject and therefore I'm responsible for your welfare. I *could* cite a number of contract clauses and remind you that you're to follow all directives given to you by employees of The Organization." The unspoken *but I won't* hangs between us.

Her words sting as much as the cut on my tongue. "Protecting the assets?" I have a lisp, hopefully just temporary and related to said lingual impediment.

"No," she says hoarsely. "Worrying about the woman I'm in love with."

I turn my head toward her but I can't look her in the eyes. I settle on her mouth. Her beautiful mouth that I've kissed so many times. I want to kiss it now and I'm disgusted with myself. I look down, staring at my thighs, at the bruise and graze on my left one. "Please. Just leave me alone. Let me get dressed. I can't do this…not naked. Please."

There's a long pause, and I ready myself to push back at her, but all Olivia does is nod. She leaves me, closing the bathroom door most of the way. I rinse myself, shut off the water and sit on the floor of the shower until I'm shivering.

There's a knock on the door. "Celeste? You've been in there for twenty minutes. Is everything all right?"

"I'm fine." It's the polite response, not the honest one.

"Do you need help?"

"No!" The thought of her coming in and touching me again turns my stomach. I force myself to my feet, dry and dress. Strangely, I feel like the cold she gave me the first week she was here has come back, bringing a cloudy head and weak limbs.

She's right outside the bathroom and pounces the moment I exit. "How are you feeling?"

"Fuzzy," I admit grudgingly.

Her expression softens. "After a red zone, uh…knockout it's not unusual to feel unsteady."

"How'd it do that? Knock me out with a shock?" I walk past her, scooting around so we don't touch, and continue toward the lounge room.

She follows. "It's not just a shock in the red zone. After the initial trigger the implant releases a dose of strong, instantaneous anesthetic."

"Let me guess, a prototype being tested?"

"Of sorts."

"Well it works. Will it malfunction and leak more of that stuff into my arm?" I sniff.

"No. The design prohibits that."

"How'd you get me back inside?" There's no way she would have been able to lift me into the cart.

"I rolled you onto one of the cardboard boxes from the shed and dragged you."

Clever. "I peed myself, you know," I say accusingly. "In the yellow zone."

"Yes, I noticed." She doesn't seem bothered by it.

"Maybe you could talk to someone about that. Tone down the zap a little." I flop onto the couch, tuck my legs up underneath me.

She smiles. The expression is strange and out of place, like there's nothing horrible between us and everything is fine. "The whole point is to discourage people from going there, Celeste."

Good point. "Can I ask you something?"

"Yes, of course." Olivia sits on the couch with me, mercifully at the other end where there's no chance of her touching me.

"It was you who sent Lou's pizza, wasn't it?"

"Yes, that was my idea. I organized it and went online to choose the variety of pizzas myself."

Manners dictate that I should thank her, here and now, but I already thanked *Controller A* when it happened. I don't want to be soft, to let her think I might forgive her. I clear my throat. "Why didn't you ever send me fresh milk? There's plenty of room in the cold boxes." It's been bothering me for some time and while I'm asking pointless questions, I may as well ask that one.

"The team felt it unnecessary given the comparable nutritional value of fresh versus powdered."

"Let me guess. You tried to get them to send some of that too?"

She seems surprised. "As a matter of fact, no. I agreed with them."

I pull the edges of my unzipped hoodie tightly around my midsection and cross my arms on top of the overlap. "So you're not the saint you're trying to make yourself out to be."

"I never said I was a saint, Celeste," she says evenly.

No, she didn't. That was all me, thinking she was perfect. "What if they hadn't let you come here? You would have had to put your feelings aside and watch me with whoever they did send."

"Yes." She looks down, her jaw working back and forth. "It's likely we wouldn't have met in person, unless I found the courage to find you on the outside. I planned for that eventuality because I wanted you so much."

It sounds like such a line that I can't help but scoff. At the sound, Liv looks up, eyes blazing. "You just don't get it, do you? How hard it's been all this time for me to see you and interact with you so *impersonally*. To do that while I had these feelings that I couldn't do anything about."

"No, I don't know, Olivia. Clearly there's a lot I don't know," I reply bitterly. "What about if you'd been allowed to come here but we never fucked? Or if I'd never found out the truth?"

She massages the bridge of her nose. "Then I would have been extracted, resumed my life and spent it missing you, still wanting you and hoping to get over you." She says it as though it's the most obvious thing in the world. "And maybe I would have figured out some way for us to meet up again, the way we talked about."

"And now?"

"I'll resume my life, spend that lifetime missing you, wanting you, and regretting you being hurt." She hasn't said regretting what she did, and I don't know that she does. "Celeste, I wish you could believe me when I say I love you and I'm sorry my actions hurt you. I never meant to get involved the way I did and I'm sorry. I'm weak, and it's as simple as that."

"I want to hurt *you*," I whisper. "And I hate myself for that."

"I know."

"But I want to touch you. I want to hold you and be inside you the way we were. And I hate myself for that too." Finally I look up and meet her eyes. "What's real? Which one of those is the right feeling?"

"All of them, Celeste. Everything is real. Everything is right. You seem to think that everything should have a hard delineating edge, but the reality is it's all fluid. Emotions, feelings, behaviors. They all bleed into one another." Her eyes seem darker. Less caramel and more weak coffee. She sighs. "I understand how you must feel."

"Do you? Do you really? I don't think you do because if you did, then you wouldn't have done it." A tear slides down my cheek, surprising me. I wipe angrily at it. "Why did you do it?"

"Because I *had* to, Celeste. The circumstances don't make how I feel less valid. I don't know how else I can make you see that this is real for me." She slides along the couch toward me. Her hands close around my biceps. "Will you let me show you?"

My muscles flex under her grip. "Don't touch me. Please don't. I can't stand it."

But she does and I have nowhere to go. Her grip is loose, her thumbs stroking my biceps. I'm not afraid. I can move if I want to but I don't know if that's what I really want. She's letting me choose if I should squirm out of her grasp or stay. Before I can make a decision, her lips are on mine. They still feel like my safe place. She's warm and soft and tastes the same as she always does but still, everything is different.

I can't help myself, I kiss her back. She groans softly and holds me tighter, and I'm excited and sick all at once. I'm kissing her and then the sickness is more than the excitement and I don't want this anymore. But I can't stop myself and the only way I can get her to stop is to bite her lip. Not hard enough to draw blood, but hard enough that she recoils. Eyes wide. Hand on her mouth. She pulls it away and stares at her fingers. Her tongue sweeps over her lower lip and she never stops looking into my eyes. I'm drowning in hers, trying desperately to breathe.

Hastily, I stand up and leave her in the lounge room while I hide in the cellar with the door closed. Sitting on the stairs, I stare at the washer cleaning my soiled clothes, and the dryer, and the stacks of boxes, and the racks of wine she was supposed to drink. Above me, she walks around the dwelling—to the bedroom, the computer room, then back to the kitchen. She's cooking something. She's in the lounge. She's making coffee.

I'm alone. Nobody wants to talk to me.

When I finally emerge from the cellar, my body is stiff and cold and doesn't want to cooperate. We move around each other in an uneasy sort of dance that neither of us know the steps to. And the worst thing is how everything contradicts everything else. I can't make sense of my feelings, can't make sense of hers because everything is tied up in this fucking experiment. I think I hate myself too, just a little, for being so naïve.

I've always prided myself on my honesty, especially to myself, and if I'd just stopped to really think about it instead of reacting, I would have realized. If I'd wanted to, I would have seen how wrong it all was. How her being here made no sense, was so convenient. How The Organization seemed so accepting of it all. But I didn't want to. I believed The Lie because it suited me to believe it.

After dinner, Liv goes into the computer room and closes the door. I brush my teeth, go to the bedroom and close that door. We're closing doors to keep each other out when the reality is we're already inside each other, in all those unreachable places that keep things safe. A soft knock startles me and I sit up, pulling the covers tight around myself. "Come in."

The moment she's in the room, she speaks. "I'm leaving in the morning. Early."

This thing I fought so hard against, and then fought so hard for, is here. All I can say is, "Oh." There's so much more I want to say to her, so much I want her to explain to me but now all of it seems pointless. In the dim light with her so far away, I can't quite make out her expression but she seems upset. Her voice is tight, her posture stiff.

Olivia approaches the bed and I tense, but all she does is set a pill and a glass of water on the bedside table. "Please take this sleeping tablet. They can't deploy the sleeping gas they usually use to make sure you don't see the delivery method, because it will affect me too."

"Gas…how ingenious. I always wondered why I never heard anything on supply drop nights." It triggers a thought. "Why did I have to take a sleeping pill then when I got that filling done? Why not use the gas?"

"Because then we would have had to tell you about the gas," she says, as though it's the most obvious thing in the world.

"Oh."

She stares at me and her expression is so blank, it's unnatural. "I'm so sorry, Celeste." It's the only thing she says before she walks out of the bedroom and pulls the door shut.

CHAPTER SEVENTEEN

The sun is almost to the top of the trees when I wake from my drug-assisted slumber. I haven't slept this late in years, but the groggy, sleeping pill hangover means I don't feel better for the extra rest. The habitat systems sound with their usual white noise, but over that there's nothing. Nobody.

My head feels dense and spins a little when I sit up and swing my legs off the side of the bed. I slip my feet into Uggs and leave the bedroom, afraid of what I'll find. I want to call her name, to see if she's really gone, because while I'm disgusted that she was here these past few days, I'm even more afraid that she's not. Halfway up the hallway, I cave and push out a tentative, "Liv? Are you still here?"

No answer. I glance into each room, then the basement and even peer outside into the clear morning. She's really gone. In her place is an envelope with my name on it in bold, beautiful handwriting. The white square is propped against the canister holding my tea bags. She knows that's the first place in the kitchen I go each morning.

Hands rest on my shoulders from behind, the softest kisses are placed on my neck. "I don't understand your tea first thing in the morning. Tea doesn't wake you up, Celeste."

"It's not about being woken up. It's about starting the day with something pleasurable."

"Yes. Hot, strong coffee." A low, throaty laugh.

I tilt my head back to look at her. "Or something else equally as pleasurable…"

Of course my brain jumps straight to what happened after that. I try pacing to push the thoughts away, jumping, singing, even gripping and twisting the skin on my left wrist until it burns. But nothing stops the very real memory of her straddling me, rocking back and forth as she took her pleasure on my fingers. Goddamn you, Olivia.

I toss the envelope aside. It skids over the counter and stops against the microwave. As I follow its progress, I notice the mug she always used, the blue with the white ring around the top, is gone. How dare she take my mug. Their mug…her mug? I fill the kettle. Ignore the letter. Make tea. Ignore the letter. Drink some of my tea. I'm already so late for check-in that my procrastination isn't going to make any difference.

Ignoring the letter works for about ten minutes, then it becomes as overwhelming as everything else in my life. I slide a knife under the envelope flap to slice it open, almost amused that she sealed it—it's not like anyone else is here to read it. Her writing is smooth and flowing with long tails and large loops.

Celeste,

There are no words that will ever sufficiently convey how truly sorry I am that this experience ended this way. It wasn't how I wanted things to be between us. I don't believe I'll ever be able to find a way to express to you how much our time together meant to me.

Please, if you take one thing from all of this, I would hope that you could find a sliver of trust to believe me when I say I love you.

Take care of yourself.
Olivia.

I trace the lines and curves of her beautiful writing with my forefinger. Now she's gone and I wish she wasn't. The confusion that's been present ever since I found out about The Lie morphs into something so big I don't think I can hold on to it. What kind of sickness is it to want her when she hurt me this way? All my thoughts spin around and around but won't stick. She lied and manipulated me. She said she didn't want to, but she had to because of the study. She betrayed me, she used me. She said it was all real. She said she loves me.

Love.

No matter how hard I try to push past it, I can't stop dwelling on that one word. The concept of her loving me is a massive speed bump I'm getting stuck on. No, I'm *letting* myself get stuck on. I'm stuck on it so I can keep this little bit of hope, because if I don't then I'm left with the thing that's been with me my whole life—that niggling doubt and the ever-present fear that nobody wants me.

I close my eyes, straining to hear Mother's voice. I wait and wait for her to say it but she never does. So I say it myself, flat and emotionless the way she used to. "You're not worth anything. I wish I'd never had you."

I scrunch up Olivia's letter, walk out to the burn pit and set a lighter to the paper. When the flame is almost licking at my fingers, I drop the burning ball. Only when I'm completely satisfied that nothing but ash remains do I go back inside. I really should check in. It's hours past my usual time but that's their fault, the fault of whatever pill she gave me last night. Not mine. Just like her being here was not my fault.

Mug of coffee. Still groggy. What shall I say to them today? I start with the basics.

SE9311: Hello.

Cont A: Good morning, SE9311.

My heart stutters when I see that designation. My knees are shaking under the desk. My hands are shaking on top of it. I think I might hurl. I can barely type a response.

SE9311: What are you doing here?

Cont A: I'm working. How are you? You're quite a bit later than usual. Is everything all right?

SE9311: Really? You're asking me how I am?

Cont A: Yes.

Well, Olivia…I'm angry, hurt, devastated, betrayed, and so fucking confused I can barely tell what's really happening and what's in my head.

Cont A: SE9311, do you have anything to report? Are you okay?

SE9311: Not to you, no. I don't want to see you here ever again. I won't talk to you. Get someone else. I'll be back in 10 minutes.

I stand up and leave the room as quickly as I can. I stuff my feet into the boots waiting by the door and run outside. I didn't even take the time to put a jacket on, I'm shuddering and I don't care. I run, stumbling in unlaced boots along uneven ground, down the hill to Hug Tree. There's something inside me, something rage-filled that wants to come out, and for a brief and terrifying moment I consider punching the tree trunk. But I don't.

I am many things—gullible, sad, loving, broken. But I am not violent. I have never been violent. "I am not like Mother," I whisper to myself. "I'm not, I'm not. I'm a good person. I deserve to be loved."

I wrap my arms around the tree and squeeze it as hard as I can, my arms and ribs protesting against the force. The pressure doesn't ease any tension from my body. My cheek is pressed to the slightly smoother section of tree where it always rests, and I clutch the trunk harder as though I could somehow transfer feelings from under my skin to under the bark. Then I would be okay.

From above I hear a faint grinding whirr and when I look up I see one of the surveillance cameras swiveling in my direction. It's *her*, undoubtedly, checking on me. Those cameras have never moved in all the years I've been here. I imagine her, wherever she is, wearing makeup and dressed in a nice business suit and heels calmly instructing a security person to spy on me. I raise a childish middle finger at the camera and turn back to the dwelling.

Controller Take Two is Controller E, the newbie who replaced Olivia—sorry, *Controller A*—when she first came here. And now it seems they are tasked with picking up the slack for her again.

Cont E: Are you there, SE9311?

SE9311: Yes.

Cont E: How are you?

SE9311: Fine. Thank you.

Such a stupid societal convention. Clearly, I'm not fine. I count to twenty, trying to slow the racing of my pulse with some deep breathing. It doesn't really work.

Cont E: Would you like to discuss it?

SE9311: Yes I would. But not with you.

Not with anyone in that place. Not with anyone connected to her.

Cont E: May I remind you of your contractual obligations? I'm willing to be a sounding board, or you can log your feelings by either text or video.

Fuck the contract, and there's no way I'm going to video log myself talking about how broken I am. She shouldn't be allowed to see those things, to listen to me say those words. I draw another deep breath.

SE9311: Is she gone? Is she watching this?

Cont E: Dr. Soldano is not in this room.

I don't have the tools to know if Controller E is lying or not and regardless, what they've said doesn't really answer my question. Not in the room doesn't mean she's not watching me or tracking what's happening between me and Controller E. She'll see this log, because she told me herself that she's read every text transcript and watched every video. I'm caught in a triangle of obligation, my need to talk to someone about it, and my loathing for what's happened. The words fall off my fingertips.

SE9311: I'm confused. I don't know if what I felt was even real. I feel like I have no right to be as devastated as I am. I feel like I don't know if I'm even in love with her or not. And if I'm not then I have no right to my feelings. But I don't know because I've been warped by what happened before she came here. I feel like everything she said was a lie, manufactured to suck me in and make me feel something for her that wasn't real.

Real. Real. Real. It's been the buzzword of the past few years and the most terrifying thing of all is that nothing has ever felt as real as my connection to her. But if the false things feel real, then will real things feel false?

Cont E: I can understand your confusion and the emotions you're experiencing.

SE9311: I'm sure you can't. But anyway, whatever. Tell me, E – was it real? Was it really real for her?

The cursor blinks. Blinks. Blinks. Come on. They owe me. *She* owes me. She probably is there, standing over Controller E's shoulder. Watching me. Telling them what to say to me. I turn toward the camera in the corner, then immediately realize my mistake. You just broke rule number one, you stupid fucking idiot. Never let her see that you need her and how she can hurt you. Ashamed, I turn back to the monitor, watching letters then words appear.

Cont E: I can't discuss details of the experiment and I certainly wouldn't presume to speak for Dr. Soldano.

S9311: Of course. Thanks for the party line. Is that all?

Cont E: If that's all you wish to say, then yes.

S9311: Yes it's all I wish to say.

Cont E: Okay then. Enjoy your day.

What a ridiculous thing to say. I turn off the screen without logging anything and stagger from the room.

Hours, minutes, a day later, I come back to the computer room. Slowly, I drag the chair close to the desk. I remember the way she sat in this exact spot, so poised and almost elegant even though she was wearing sweats with a hole above the knee and a hoodie with the sleeves pushed up. Olivia will read these chat logs, my personal logs and watch any videos I make. She gets to keep watching me while I'm left here with nothing. The time away from this room has hardened my resolve. Screw her, if she doesn't like what I have to say then she shouldn't have done this to me. The monitor flickers before the password prompt stabilizes. With one finger I enter my password and navigate to the logging program. I don't think, I just type.

I need to talk about what happened because if I don't I think I might lose it. I'm sure she'll fill you in on everything I told her, but this is my stuff and the stuff I couldn't say, or didn't think to say while we were talking about what she did to me. The truth of what being here has done to me.

I want to tell you guys about time. Fast time and slow time. Since I came here I've lived with this weird time thing, where nothing seemed to move the way it should. Every day kind of rushed past and I'd lose massive chunks of time, like days and then weeks that just seemed to never actually happen. But they had obviously, I just hadn't noticed. And I liked it, because otherwise I'd have to sit here by myself and examine every single second of every day. And that would really fucking suck.

When Olivia came, all that time-speed weirdness left and I felt every moment with her as if someone had hit the slow-mo button on the remote. And I felt like I could actually see things for the first time in forever. Now she's gone and everything's rushing past so fast I can't grab hold of it.

And I hate it and it's her fault that everything is awful again. But it's mine too because what kind of idiot am I to believe someone would really come to me in those circumstances? I believed it because I wanted it to be real. This whole thing is a million emotions all caught up in one big ball of string and I can't separate each one out. I guess all I can say is…well done, you guys got me really good.

I just want my slow time back, Olivia. That's all. But I don't
think I want it with you.

I hit submit and turn off the monitor.

My guts are a tight knot of anxiety and every time I try to
eat something, it sits like thick mud in my stomach. After two
attempts at lunch, I give up and instead set up the chessboard
and start a game. But after White's opener to D4, Black can't
think of how to counter. My mind is completely blank. I stare at
the board, willing a thought to come to me.

"Is your fever back? Let me feel," Olivia murmurs.

I swipe my hand in front of my face, pushing away an
imagined forehead check. "I'm fine."

"You don't seem it, darling."

"Why do you think that is, Liv?"

She doesn't answer.

"This isn't fair, you can't be here like this. Please don't come
again." Gently, I sweep all the chess pieces back into the box and
put it down in the basement.

I sleepwalk through the rest of my day, following the routine
of checks and balances. I medicate myself with half a sleeping
pill, afraid I might wake during the night and be empty again.
Afraid to stay awake listening to all my people telling me things
I don't want to hear.

The bed shifts, weight on my body, the tickle of hair on my
stomach. "Celeste? Tell me what you want me to do." A hot
mouth closes around my nipple.

"Lick me," I beg her, fumbling for a hand I can't find.

But I wake before anything else happens. It's three in the
morning, the habitat dark and still. I clutch the duvet where
it's bunched around my breasts and try to calm down. My body
still hums from the dream I had about her and I can feel how
aroused I am, but when I touch myself there's no follow through.
It's blank space. I reject her and everything she did as though it
was meaningless.

"I'm sorry, Celeste." She sounds so sad.

"What do you want?" I ask the empty room.
"You." Olivia exhales, long and loud. "Just you."

When I wake again just after dawn, it's raining lightly but steadily, the soft thrumming on the roof promising slushy snow and chilled bones. Perfect moping weather. After breakfast, logs, and check-in, I bundle myself up in a fluorescent rain slicker and make my way carefully along the path to the greenhouse. The rain has pushed any overnight snow from the solar panels, not that they'll be much use in the gloom, so there's little for me to do but be in the greenhouse. I still have work to do here and I'll be damned if I let her stop me from seeing this thing through until the end.

My pepper seedlings are almost four inches high and the zucchinis are starting to reach out tentatively. She planted those seedlings, hands gently piling dirt around the base of each one. She smoothed everything down so lovingly as though she wanted to be sure what she was doing would last.

"Do you remember when I found those sunglasses, Celeste?" Olivia laughs. "That was so funny."

"Go away. Please leave me alone." I look around the greenhouse, knowing even as I do it that I'm not going to see her. My voice shakes when I ask, "Riley? Heather? Alli? Are you there? Anybody? Please." Even Mother would be preferable to *her* right now.

The sound of rain on the greenhouse roof is the only answer. Why won't anyone else talk to me? I drop to my knees and pull up everything Olivia and I planted together. Then I hurl them at the glass wall. The glass doesn't shatter, or even crack. I am a person in a glass house. I really shouldn't be throwing stones.

* * *

I stumble through my days, each one a mirror of the one before. The Controllers—aside from Controller A who remains mercifully absent—pick at my carcass like vultures. I don't protest. They're allowed to do whatever they want, ask whatever they want. It's what I signed up for. I tell myself that over and over—I asked for this, it's my choice, I still have some control.

Mother and Riley won't talk to me. Alli and Heather are disapprovingly silent. Joanne is sad and doesn't know what to say, so she says nothing. I need them all to come back, even if it's only to admonish me for being so stupid. So blind and trusting. I need someone to sympathize with me and agree that what they did to me, what *she* did to me is awful. I wait and wait for someone to talk to me. Anyone. Nobody does. During the day I'm as alone as I've ever been.

When Olivia's voice comes to me each night I'm back in slow time where I can finally just…breathe. It's a sick irony, that the thing I don't want, the thing that hurts so badly is the thing that helps me. Then she leaves again and everything is moving up and down and sideways, leaving me even more hollow than I was before.

Twenty-one days after she left, I break. I can't take it any longer. I can't handle having her in my head. I can't handle having everything here reminding me of her. Everywhere I am and everywhere I look absolutely *reeks* of her.

Each of these things on their own would be fine. The solitude. The voices. What Olivia did. My own self-loathing at my idiocy. But cumulatively, they've conspired to overwhelm me. And I've broken. She's broken me. The only person who ever has.

The moment a Controller appears on the screen I tell them what I want.

SE9311: I'd like to go home now please.

Cont B: Please repeat, SE9311.

SE9311: I'm done. With this.

Cont B: I require confirmation. Please input your exit passcode.

I open the desk drawer to my right and pull out an envelope. Inside is a single piece of paper with a phrase on it, as if I might forget the thing that would get me out of here. I type my termination code which I chose right before I came in here.

SE9311: Childhood's Retreat. Robert Duncan. EXIT.
I'm suddenly yanked back to Olivia quoting from that, my favorite poem. Knowing how she used those words makes me nauseated. Every step of her being here was portentous, too neat, too perfect, too coincidental. For the millionth time since I discovered The Lie, I remind myself of what a fucking idiot I am.
Cont B: Code verified. A transport will be there for you at 9 a.m. tomorrow. Please refer to the manual for your exit guidelines.
What I really want to say is *Fuck all of you*. Instead, I use one finger to type my final message.
SE9311: Thanks. It's been...interesting.
I shut down the computer and close the door of the computer room for the last time. Didn't Olivia say it took time to organize transports? That procedures and checks had to be followed? Another lie. She said and did whatever suited her own purposes.

For the rest of the day I follow the steps on the checklist, readying everything for the crew who will come in just hours after I leave to prepare things for the next person. Even though it's not listed, I do a thorough cleaning of the habitat, because I'm not a slob. I entertain wild thoughts of making an extravagant final dinner, but in the end I heat a canned meal and eat it while sitting cross-legged on the couch.

I've pictured this moment of leaving so many times, and in all those fantasies it was a wonderful catharsis. I would walk around the habitat, touching things, saying quiet and overly sentimental goodbyes. In the fantasy, I would feel sad but at the same time, I would also be relieved to be going back to my old life.

The reality is stark and boring and I can't help but wonder why I was so excited about this mystical old life that I'm about to return to. Is it even worth going back to now? Everyone will have moved on while I've been stuck in this time warp.

Olivia doesn't visit me during the night.

I wake well before dawn and lie in bed until the sun rises. When it's finally light enough outside, I take a walk around in the early morning chill, looking at everything I'll never see again. I skip breakfast and coffee. I check and double-check that I've packed my lambskin, and stuff toiletries and the few clothes I brought with me into my backpack. The books I carried in at the beginning are left in the shelves along with all the books they delivered to me over the years. I've read and re-re-re-read them so many times that if I never see another J. R. R. Tolkien or George R. R. Martin book again it'll be too soon.

At precisely nine a.m. a helicopter lands on the concrete slab, the heavy whump-whump-whump of the rotors making the habitat shake. I shoulder my backpack, close the door and walk away from my life without looking back.

One thousand, two hundred and sixty-five days. A little more than six months short of my four-year goal.

I tried. I really did.

CHAPTER EIGHTEEN

I nap on the helicopter, waking at the sound of my name and with the realization that we're on the ground again. A sweet woman in a figure-hugging houndstooth-patterned dress leans over me, and the hint of exasperation in her voice makes me feel like she's been trying to wake me for a while. When I ask why she didn't just shake me awake, she smiles and tells me she thought I might not like being touched unexpectedly and without permission. That's kind of them.

A fancy black car is waiting to take me to the place where I will be officially set free. I click the seat belt in, undo it, click it in again. The sound is incredible, exactly as I recall. Being driven feels odd—rough and coarse, all the jolting and bouncing around not quite as I recall. My forehead is practically stuck to the window, watching the constant passing of new scenery. The barrier of glass and plastic and metal keeps me safe, allowing me to get used to this change without *being* in it.

Fifteen minutes later when we arrive at the facility, I know I'm in a different place from my initial interviews, but I don't know exactly where I am. They tell me calmly that there will be no more than two people with me at any given time, to help my transition. They don't want me to be *overwhelmed*. Too late. I'm already stuck on faces, expressions, and the sound of different voices. I'm not overwhelmed, but I'm definitely in awe. People. Plural. They gently bring me back to the present every time I zone out listening to and watching someone speak.

They give me lunch—medium rare steak with fries and a fancy salad. A beer in a frosty glass sits on the table and to the side is a gooey triple chocolate brownie. The meal looks and smells fantastic.

"If you could have anything to eat, what would it be?" Olivia's finger-walking her way up and down my leg.

I don't even have to think. "Oh shit, that's easy. Ice-cold beer and a steak. Thick filet mignon, char-grilled and still bleeding inside. Like a really good grass-fed aged steak, not the frozen vacuum-sealed stuff they send me here. A mountain of fries. And a salad for balance." I laugh and add, "Then something rich and chocolatey to finish."

It's exactly what I would normally love. Exactly what I said I wanted. But I only manage a couple of bites, then have to leave the rest because I can't stomach something she had a hand in offering. I'm taken to a sterile white room. Comfortable examination bed. Barefoot, paper gown. I lie on my back and pretend I'm sunbathing on the beach, while my blood is drawn and other annoying but not uncomfortable or invasive tests are performed. I move as requested, and answer questions with the minimum of words.

Maybe they think I'm overly affected by the experience and currently having some sort of traumatic breakdown. I'm not. I'm out of sorts the way I always am during checkups, but not anxious. I do feel weird when I have to look between two people to talk, and have to remind myself to move my head, to make eye contact with both of them.

Being here brings all my feelings to the forefront. More than anything else, above the weirdness and hurt and sadness and loss, I'm kind of...angry. Angry at them but it's a nonspecific *them*. Mostly I'm still angry at myself for being so stupid. Angry at Olivia. No, no I'm not. I try to dredge up some anger for her, something to make me hate her but no matter how hard I try, I cannot. I hate what she did to me but at the same time it was my fault for not seeing what was right in front of me. Blaming myself has always been such a comforting and familiar fallback.

Someone's talking.

"I'm sorry, what was that?"

The woman speaks again, slowly, as though my issue is a lack of understanding rather than a wandering mind. The implant will stay in for the next six months—as dictated in my contract, she is quick to remind me—in order to keep track of my whereabouts in case I forget to notify them. Accidentally forget, of course. I'm not bothered. Actually, I'm more distressed by the thought of its extraction. The small tube under my skin has become a comfort. Perhaps they'll let me keep it after all this is done.

"Ms. Thorne?"

I speak to the ceiling. "Yes?"

"We're finished here if you could please get dressed, and someone will escort you to your psychological debriefing."

I go where I'm told and sit at a plain wooden table with a cup of coffee handed to me by a smiling blond woman. It's nice strong coffee, but there's not enough milk in it for my liking. I drink it anyway. She sits in a corner making notes while an older gentleman with perfectly slicked hair and Clark Kent glasses asks the questions.

The debriefing is long and tedious. How did I feel when... did I find it hard...can I tell him about...? It's different from what the Controllers wanted—now it's broad queries, rather than specific to days or events or thoughts.

I'm forthcoming, answering honestly and patiently, but when they ask me about Olivia the words stick to my throat. I can't swallow them back down and I can't get them out. My mouth works open and closed until finally, a sound escapes. Very gently, I'm prompted and reminded that I'm contractually obligated to answer truthfully and with as much detail as I can.

Smiling Woman leaves the room for a minute then comes back with a glass of ice water. She passes it to me, and both she and Older Gentleman wait patiently until enough time ticks past for me to put form to my thoughts. I choke out the words, nauseated the whole time, reaffirming that yes it was stressful and uncomfortable and hard when Olivia arrived, and yes I had *feelings* for her.

Older Gentleman asks me to elaborate on those feelings and I can't help but think this whole thing is some sick, twisted joke. He's not cruel or threatening but what he's doing is incredibly discomforting. I try to be evasive, brushing it aside with, "I was hallucinating voices and smells and touches, so who knows if what I thought I felt about her was even real. Can't you just use my logs? I already told you everything there." My eyes beg him to just leave it alone, to not make me say it out loud. If I say it, then it's out in the world and floating around where anyone could take it and use it against me.

He tilts his head, wordlessly acceding to my request, then picks up his tablet and resumes questioning me. Mercifully it's no longer about Olivia. Is she watching me somehow? On a screen in a cozy office, separated from the damage she's done? Laughing at me? Pitying me? Wondering how and why she ever touched someone who can barely even articulate something that matters so much?

Eventually I'm told, "Thank you, Ms. Thorne. I believe that's all we need." Older Gentleman smiles like a kind father. "You've done very well."

And I wonder what exactly it is that I've done very well with.

I go to another room where I talk for an hour to Classic Nerd who wants to know all about the operation of various systems within the compound. Were they easy to use, did they work as intended, was there anything that I found difficult about operating them, could I repair them easily with the supplied manuals and tools? I gather what they're really trying to figure out is "Can we sell this tech to Everyday Joe?" or "Will this work on Not-Earth without breaking down every day?"

When I'm done, Suit waits outside the door for me. He's tall and well built, plain-looking but his dark brown eyes are sweet and kind. "Hello, Ms. Thorne." The man's voice is a high tenor, his accent upper-class somewhere I can't place. "I have instructions to take you to the Assistant Director's office for your final interview and then you'll be driven to the airport for your flight home."

Home. No place is home and everywhere could be home. I nod and Suit escorts me along the hallway to the elevator and up to the top floor. I can't tell if he's a security guy or just an assistant. By the time the elevator stops, I've decided he's both. The elevator door opens, and he moves aside so I can step out into a beautiful atrium which leads to what appears to be an office with floor-to-ceiling windows looking out over the city. I wonder what city it is.

"When you're finished, I'll meet you downstairs in the lobby," Suit says from behind me.

I have to remind myself to stop, to turn back to him so I can say, "Great, thank you." The elevator dings softly and then I'm alone.

I take bold strides across the marble floor, slowing for a few moments to look at the healthy greenery growing in the raised indoor garden beds either side of me. Warm late afternoon sunlight streams through the ceiling of the glass atrium to cast long shadows over the plants. I softly touch one of the broad leaves. Waxy. Spongy. I lean in and smell that unmistakable smell plants get when they've been watered recently, like moist soil and clean air.

When I step from marble to the thick cream-colored carpet of the office, the plush weave sinks underfoot, and I have the uncomfortable sensation of going to a job interview when I'm completely underdressed and have no chance at all of landing the position. To my left are two russet-brown leather couches laid out in an L-shape around a dark wooden coffee table, which holds an in-progress chess game. Photographs of cliffs overhanging sapphire seas adorn one wall, and on another is a series of small paintings—female nudes, tasteful and elegant. Startlingly blue eyes stare at me from the painting on the far right.

There's a bookshelf stacked with board games, and a half-finished Lego spaceship sits on the floor, with pieces separated by color in neat piles around it. This office has a strange mixed vibe of understated opulence and childish frivolity, which throws me even further off balance. Someone clears their throat and I do a one-eighty turn to my right to face a large antique desk. Stunned, I falter for a step before recovering my balance.

The Assistant Director watches me approach her desk.

I'd know her anywhere, even though here she is just a beautiful stranger. Well-fitted and expensive skirt suit. Hair up and held by a silver clasp. Lipstick on lips made for kissing. Mascara on long eyelashes—those same eyelashes where with her forehead pressed to my skin, she'd blink and tickle me with them, then laugh when I squirmed. Butterfly kisses. Riley used to do the same. Did I ever tell anyone about that? Is it another thing she used against me? The swell of her breasts under the jacket makes me think of the taste of her and how she feels under my fingers. Lazy mornings in bed. Conversations about everything and nothing.

All false.

I haven't seen her in twenty-two days. She's the same, but so different. When I stop on the other side of her desk, Olivia sets her pen down. Her smile is cautious but still the one I know, and I beg my heart to slow, my brain to behave. When she comes around from behind the desk, she's now taller than me and I glance down to confirm my suspicion about her footwear. Damn, her legs in those heels are out of this world. I allow myself a long look at the curve of her calf, the same curve where I'd rest my hand while she had her feet propped in my lap, and my attempt to slow my heart rate is immediately thwarted.

Her hand is outstretched. "Good afternoon, Ms. Thorne."

Ms. Thorne. Ouch. I've heard it all day but it stings coming from *her* mouth. I take her hand, shaking it lightly. I do not linger. I do not let on that the mere contact of her skin on mine sets me aflame. "Hello, Doctor Soldano." Two can play that game, but there's no pleasure in putting myself on equal footing with her. Nor will there be any sort of victory.

Dr. Sol—no, I can't do it—*Olivia* gestures to the leather seat in front of the desk. "Please, sit. There are a few more things we have to go through and then you can be on your way." She's not dispassionate but I recognize that she's removed herself from what she's telling me. Clinical detachment is a skill I've yet to master. She wields it like a weapon.

I sit where indicated and fold my hands in my lap. Once I'm settled, she moves back around to sit behind her desk, her hands resting lightly atop the blotter. Since leaving the habitat I've run through the gamut of emotions, and now I'm here in front of her, I'm settling on resigned. Resigned isn't an unpleasant emotion. It's simple. I just have to sit here and talk to her and pretend like it's not killing me one slow inch at a time.

She wears makeup and one of the nicest perfumes I've ever smelled, and though the scent is lovely, it throws me even further off balance because it's not her. Or maybe it is her and the scent I knew all that time was the wrong one. Maybe the Liv I knew was the wrong one. Olivia turns a pen over in her delicate fingers. Fingers that have explored my entire body. "You look well," she observes. "Though you seem a little tired."

"I am well, thank you. As I can be that is, all things considered," I can't help but add. After she left, I was sure everything I felt for her was false, just my brain warped by the experiment. Now I'm here, I'm not so sure. *Now*, I think my feelings were real but hers were not. Hers were simply in line with whatever she needed to say and do to keep me compliant.

She says nothing in response to my gentle dig and passes me a thin document folder. "Before we continue, you'll need to sign another nondisclosure agreement."

"Why? I already signed one before I went in."

"Yes, that was pertinent to the lead-up to the study. This one encompasses the duration of your stay. The program will continue, as will our associations with the agency, other corporations and their technology, and we need to ensure that

202 E. J. Noyes

you will share no information about the tech and systems. It's for the protection of all involved, and also to ensure that future candidates are untainted." The pen she's holding is offered to me.

"Will you fuck the future candidates too?" I ask before I can stop myself and am immediately ashamed of my cruelty.

A muscle flickers in her cheek but other than that her face is blank, her gaze unwavering. She doesn't answer. And she doesn't look away. I suck in air and push it out with a mumbled, "Sorry." She deserves my apology because despite everything, I've been unnecessarily rude.

The fear that's been simmering is now edging toward panic as it surges through my body, and I try desperately to keep it down out of her sight. I take the pen, skim the document and scrawl my name at every flag sticking out from the pages.

I wonder how Olivia could still be so neutral, as though what happened between us never occurred. Obviously it was just a job. She lied to me. Clearly it wasn't real for her. The thought is sickening, but at the same time I remember what it felt like to be with her and the feeling slowly abates. Nobody is that good an actress. She had to feel *something*, even if it was nothing more than lust. Deep down inside where I hide my emotions, I wonder if she still feels it.

I hold up the pen. It's a very nice pen—inky and feels like it was made for my fingers. "Can I please keep this?"

Olivia's expression is like I just asked her if I can pee on her carpet. "Yes, of course. Take it."

"Thank you." I clench my fist around my prize and push my just-signed papers forward. On her desk, off to one side, is a mug. Blue with a white stripe and a chipped handle. She chipped the handle when she was washing up one morning. Black, half a sugar, doesn't have to be exactly half. Surely she's taunting me.

"And here's the electronic bank transfer receipt for your payment, and our paperwork confirming the same. The money will be cleared by tomorrow." With a steady hand, Olivia offers me an envelope. She swallows, visibly. "I'm sure you remember your contract clause that states compensation can be adjusted as we see fit in line with certain clauses or due to certain occurrences."

Adjusted. I take the envelope from her, jam my forefinger under the flap and tear it open. Paper cut. $500,000.00. The full amount as if I'd stayed for the whole four years. I put my finger in my mouth, tasting blood. Metallic. Earthy. Not unpleasant. I think of the time I cut my finger because Mother was talking to me while I was cutting vegetables in the greenhouse. Everything comes full circle. How can I be the same but so different?

I recognize Olivia's name in the flowing loops and curves of one of the two signatures approving my payment. Her signature is as beautiful as everything else about her. I really wish I could hate her. Things would be so much easier if I did, but I don't. I can't.

"Thank you," I murmur. All this money, and for what? Was it even worth it in the end? How can I measure the worth of my mental anguish and emotional distress in dollars? So much of my life for this money and right now, it really does feel pointless.

"The Board agreed to pay you for the full four-year period, including the bonus. It was agreed—" Olivia clears her throat. "It was decided that you would have stayed if it wasn't for the unfortunate set of circumstances."

I look at the two pieces of paper in my hand. "Is that what you're calling *us*, Olivia?" I shift my focus back to her. "An unfortunate set of circumstances?"

She opens her mouth then closes it again. I desperately wish that she could remove herself from the job, from the research and whatever else that's in the way of her telling me the truth. It's right there, she wants to let it out. I just saw it. I push her with a question, something to remind her of our past but also because I genuinely want to know. "How is your leg?"

The edge of her mouth tightens then releases. "It's fine, like it never happened."

Like *we* never happened. What can I even say to that? I put the papers back into the envelope.

Olivia inhales deeply as though the breath will give her strength to say whatever she has to. "As stated in your contract, a representative of The Organization will contact you in one, three and then six months for follow up. Please be sure to keep us updated with your address and contact details."

"Sure," I mutter.

She gathers the papers I signed, flicks through to check each signature then places the document in a tray. Olivia looks up and the fine tension lines around her eyes smooth out. Memories rush through my head like a DVD on fast-forward. Olivia hugging me for the first time. Holding my shoulder as I dressed her wound. Cooking with me. Our first kiss. Laughing at my silly stories. The sound as she climaxes. Lying in my arms. The exquisite touch of her hands and mouth.

"Celeste? Is there anything else you needed?" She reaches blindly into the handbag on the shelves behind her and pulls out a soft leather purse. "Do you have enough cash for tonight?"

Celeste. Not Ms. Thorne. A frightening hope swells, but it's not enough to overcome the fear. I know now that there is so much I need from her but I also know that I will never get any of it. But I'm going to try to get one final thing. "I don't need *your* money, thank you. May I ask you something?"

"Yes, of course."

Yet another thing trips in my memory. Me asking Controller A—Olivia—if I could ask a question, while I was wondering how crazy I was. I didn't expect an answer then and I don't expect one now. "Did they force you to sleep with me?"

Her eyebrow gives the barest twitch but other than that her expression doesn't change. "I'm not at liberty to discuss the finer details of the study," she says smoothly.

There's nothing I can say to that dismissal. Olivia leans down and when she straightens again she's holding a duffel. "Here are all your personal belongings, including mail we collected for you while you were away."

My whole life reduced to a single bag of miscellaneous stuff I left with them before locking myself away. "Thank you." I dig through the bag. Laptop. Phone, probably at least two models out of date. Wallet with about a hundred bucks in cash and my credit cards—some expired. Driver license and other ID. A small diary notebook filled with phone numbers and various account details. Keys to my storage space and post office box. No house keys. I live nowhere. Officially vagrant just like Mother. Not for long. I'm leaving here and I'm buying a house. I just don't know where yet.

She passes me another envelope. I'm acquiring quite a collection. "Here's a plane ticket, and accommodation for this week to help you with the transition. All hotel charges will be covered for food, beverages, massage, movies." She smiles. "Whatever you want."

"Thank you."

She points at the envelope. "There's also a card in there with a number you can call any time, day or night while you're at the hotel, if you need assistance. Assistance with *anything*—anxiety, can't make the hotel TV work, nightmares, wondering what the best item on the room service menu is. Someone will be there within ten minutes to help."

"Thanks." I look at the ticket. O'Hare, Chicago. First class. There's also a booking confirmation for one week at the Sofitel. A decent hotel. It's a nice gesture from them to give me a roof over my head until I find a place to live.

She seems to read my mind. "When you're settled, we'll forward your clothing from the habitat." Olivia clarifies, "They won't be needed for the next candidate."

"Donate them to Goodwill or something, please. I don't want anything from that house." Except you. The thought springs into my head without my permission. I don't want it there, but it is, and won't leave, because it's the truth.

Riley was right. This is exactly like Mother. Even though I know Olivia doesn't want me, that it's pointless trying to make her love me, I just can't let it go. I am destined to spend my life chasing after people who have left me without even sparing me the tiniest backward glance.

Olivia nods. "All right then." Her gaze is measured, so piercing and so penetrating that I want to look away.

But I don't. I won't give her that. I make myself look into her eyes. "Well, I guess that's it. Thanks for everything." There's nothing more to say. I pick up my bag and my envelopes and leave her office.

The Suit escorts me through the downstairs lobby and pauses outside the revolving door to wish me luck. There's a hired car and driver in the lot, engine running. He gestures to it. I smile a tight-lipped smile of thanks, hoist my duffel onto my shoulder and walk away from this place.

Running footsteps, high heels loud on the asphalt. "Celeste, wait!"

At her call, I turn around. "What?" My single word comes out less-than-politely. I'm too tired, too overwhelmed to even try to mask my emotion.

Olivia slows to a walk and steps close, right into my personal space. Out here, her perfume blends into the scent of mown grass. I want to throw myself at her, to pull her into my arms and make her remember us. To remember everything we had. Even if it wasn't real, it was so damned good.

Her voice is low and sincere. "They didn't force me to sleep with you. It was completely voluntary, and one hundred percent optional. I didn't have to do it but I wanted to, Celeste. I wanted you, desperately, and I couldn't help myself." Her eyes glisten with tears, and she shrugs helplessly. "You make me so weak."

Again, I just don't know what to say.

A warm hand closes around my bicep. "Take care of yourself." Her tear-filled gaze is intense and she holds my eyes for what feels like an eternity. "I miss you so much," she murmurs, then she lets me go and rushes away. Before she disappears into the building, Liv pauses, turns back and stares at me for a long moment before she steps through the revolving door and is gone.

CHAPTER NINETEEN

At the airport I discover I'm in Seattle. Obviously she must live in Seattle if she works at that place. Mentally, I move another point from the lies column to the truths column. The truths outweigh the lies, but the lies are so big that I can't help but weight them more heavily. I wait for my flight with those last words of Olivia's echoing inside my head.

I miss you so much.

I want to believe her, because there's no reason for her to have said it unless there was a sliver of truth within it. But I can't separate it from everything else. I can't know if all she's doing is trying to curry favor with me for my future dealings with The Organization, or smooth things over to give herself closure. Before I can decide, my flight's called.

Her voice is lazy, dulled by the past few hours we've spent in bed. "Do you like to travel?"

"Honestly, I've never really had the chance. I don't even have a passport...and I don't like flying much, so even if I could I probably wouldn't."

"Why don't you like flying?"

I turn to her. "Not being able to see outside makes me feel claustrophobic."

"Sit next to the window then." She grins and rolls onto her side, head propped on her elbow.

"You have to pay more to choose, and the ticket person always puts me in the middle bit between strangers." The two times I've flown that is.

"Hmm. Maybe one day you'll get a window seat."

"Maybe. But I think it's also not being in control, or not knowing how the plane actually works, like how does it stay up?"

"Planes work because they're designed to work." Her fingers are softly sliding up the inside of my thigh. "When you get back you could research the mechanics of flight so you're less afraid."

"Mmm, it seems so complicated."

"Simple physics. Lift and thrust." Her smile is seductive.

I raise my hips to give her better access. "I know a lot about thrust."

The hand moves higher. "Yes. You do…"

The flight attendant shows me to my first-class window seat. *I miss you so much.*

When we land, I shove to the front of the line and rush up the gangway. Too many people. Too close. Too loud. I'm bumped and jostled through the terminal, my panic rising with every touch and sound. I push into the nearest bathroom and lock myself in a stall until I've calmed down enough to make my legs work again so I can leave. It takes a while. I'd expected it would be hard to be back out in the world, but I didn't expect it to be this overwhelming.

I rush out of the airport and into a cab to the hotel. Four walls and a ceiling to keep me safe inside. I call room service, ask for a glass of ice-cold milk and drink it down in two long gulps. I've waited three and a half years to drink a real glass of milk and it's upsettingly unsatisfying. I have the uneasy feeling that a lot of the things I've been looking forward to will be the same.

I learn we have a new president, the notion awful and unbelievable. Some musicians and actors I liked have died. Celebrities have divorced. Others have married or had kids. So much has changed and the idea is both thrilling and terrifying. At the same time, other things haven't changed—global warming, pollution, people doing horrible things to other people. I think I'm a little indignant to realize that life really did keep on going without me, and that the world does not need me in order to keep spinning.

I find Heather's number in my notebook, hoping it hasn't changed, and remind myself that The Organization will pay for all calls I make during my stay at the hotel. Her voice mail kicks in and my anxiety eases a little at not having to talk to her. I stare at the wall. "Heather-Bear? It's me. I'm, uh, I'm back. I'll be in town for a few more days then I'm heading out. Not sure where I'll go. You can reach me on this hotel number until Thursday. Bye." I check my notebook for email passwords, delete a million spam emails then log on to Facebook to let everyone know I'm still alive, and back from my "extended social media break."

I close the curtains, turn off the lights and crawl into the huge, very comfortable bed.

"Celeste? Are you awake?"

"I am now." I groan and roll over, fumbling for the light.

"Leave it off," Olivia insists. In the dark, she slides the sheet down and presses herself to me. A warm mouth covers mine. Hands are on my breasts, then cupping between my legs.

I groan. "Liv, please…"

"Please what, darling? What do you want me to do?"

"Fill me," I urge her. "Love me."

I come abruptly awake as she enters me. The dream is a lie. My pulse pounds between my legs and when I reach down, I can feel how aroused I am. The brush of fingers over my clit sends a warning but I pull my hand away. It'd be so easy to make myself come. But I don't want it that way. I don't want to come by myself with just the memory of her. I want her all over me and inside of me. Nothing and nobody but her.

And the thought makes me want to cry so badly, but I can't even do that.

After a morning spent at the window eating a fantastic room service breakfast and watching the street with my nose pressed to the glass, I graduate to the balcony. For the rest of the day I sit at the table outside doing nothing but ordering room service and staring down at those who live their lives on the street. They can't touch me up here. I'm still apart from them.

"Like an angel above, Celeste," Olivia says, almost reverently.

"Don't say that."

Heather phones me while I'm eating nachos before it's dinnertime and watching a reality television show I've never heard of. She lives in Texas now, working in taxation law and married to an accountant. She tells me I met her now-wife at a party before I left, but I don't remember the woman she describes in great detail. Alli scored her dream job working as a film producer and moved to LA, and she calls or emails Heather sporadically. The rest of our circle of friends stayed in Chicago and Heather suggests I contact them. I tell her I might, but know I won't. I've been away for so long. What will I say to them?

I think Heather's pleased to hear from me but she mostly sounds confused, as though I'm someone so far in her past she doesn't remember how close we were. Maybe I'll visit, but not any time soon. My old life feels wrong, something I want to leave in a packing box and never open.

Near midnight, I get around to opening the few dozen letters in my duffel. Bank statements mostly, new credit and debit cards to replace those that have expired. Three letters from a lawyer in Arkansas, all postmarked a few months apart and the most recent one from four months ago. I open the oldest letter first.

RE: Estate Nathalie Lynette Thorne; DOB 3/18/1966, DOD 12/6/2016

Dear Ms. Thorne,

It is with deepest regret that I must inform you that your biological mother, Nathalie Lynette Thorne passed away...

Regret? Why does this lawyer who probably barely knew Mother regret her dying? I don't.

I skim the rest of it, trying to make sense of the words. A few legal terms jump out at me, and I'm reminded of my time in college when I thought I'd make something of myself. There's a brief mention of an estate. What estate? Mother had nothing to leave anyone except fistfuls of heartbreak and meanness. The next two letters are more of the same—where are you, please contact us urgently blah blah blah.

I call their office at a polite hour in the morning and lie that I've been out of the country and therefore out of contact. Still not knowing where I'm going to settle, I tell the lawyer I'll come to Arkansas and sign some paperwork in a couple of weeks. I'm surprised Mother had a lawyer and even more surprised to hear that she had a small amount of money and some non-trashed belongings left to me. Seems she got clean somewhere along the way. Somewhere between her breaking my jaw and my arm and having her kids taken from her, and the recent past.

My jaw aches. I unclench my molars, open my mouth and stretch it to ease the tension. "Mother?"

She doesn't answer but I tell her anyway, "Just so you know, I still hate you. But...at least you fucked things up so badly that I could get away from all your shit and have a sort of normal life." I fold the lawyer's letters back into their envelopes and stuff them in the bottom of my bag.

I call to activate my new bank cards then take a cab downtown so I can buy some clothes and credit for my old cell phone. I almost buy a new phone, but the thought of having an extended conversation with a salesperson about phone models and plans dissuades me. I'd forgotten how the city sounded and smelled. Lights. Noise. Crowds. There's a sudden rush of a cop car, ambulance, and fire engine speeding past. I stare dumbly at the blur of light and sound and feel a familiar tension in my body. It's too loud, too bright, someone's in trouble, someone's hurt.

Staring down the street, I notice a familiar man standing fifty feet away. The same guy who took me up to Olivia's office. The Suit. Only now he's casual in jeans, sneakers, and a tee. I stare. He smiles, then looks away, but he doesn't leave. Flustered, I end up ducking into the first store I see and buying a bunch of clothes without trying them on.

I wait in line at McDonald's and the pharmacy and then sit and wait some more at the post office so I can cancel my post office box lease. I'm jiggling my legs, tapping anxious feet against the floor and trying to tell myself that it's normal to be surrounded by people. I remind myself that this used to be my life, hours waiting. For meals, coffee, movies and concerts to start, and for friends to arrive. The whole time I'm aware that Suit is following me. At a respectful distance, and unobtrusively. But he's still there. Monitoring me. Making sure I'm all right?

I fish the card with that number on it from my purse and watch him unclip the phone from his belt to answer on the second ring. "Hello, Ms. Thorne. Do you need help with something?"

"No, just, um...checking."

He chuckles. "Very well then. I'm here if you need me."

"Okay. Thanks." I hang up without saying goodbye.

Midway through my transition week I buy a secondhand pickup because I like the idea of throwing my stuff in the back and just getting the hell out of wherever whenever I want. I almost call Suit and ask if he knows anything about mechanical stuff. I take boxes of belongings—clothes and books mostly—from my storage locker and toss them into the tray, and it's as satisfying as I'd imagined.

After my week in the five-star hotel I leave Chicago to begin my drive around the country, wondering where to live. I think I'll probably settle *somewhere* in the mid-north west, but it's a big country and I have all the time in the world to decide. I am going to give myself until my one month follow-up with The Organization to mope and feel whatever I need to feel about what happened with Olivia. Then I'm going to set it aside the way I always have and move on. After thirty years of pretending I don't care, I'm pretty good at it.

My life rushes by in days of fast time. Different cities and states while I search for something I'll never be able to name.

I'm in mourning and I find nothing that comes close to the feeling I had when I was with her. I don't even dream about her now. She doesn't come to me at all. She left for good when I left the hotel. I struggle to remember her voice. But I remember the way she felt. And I remember the way she made me feel. Like I was worth something. Like she understood me.

I remember, even as I'm trying to forget everything that happened between us. I'm trying to forget every look and all of our touches, gentle and loving but also hard and sensual. The sound of her words and soft assurances. The way she begged and praised and directed.

I miss you so much.

I make my way down to Arkansas and sign papers for Mother's lawyers. They have a cardboard box and a check for a small amount of money. Less their fees, of course, they are quick to tell me. I put the envelope in my bag without looking at it and toss the unopened box into the back of the truck.

I don't visit Heather in Texas. I couldn't bear for her to look at my face and know, as she always does, that something is wrong. We talk on the phone a couple of times, and she sounds genuine when she tells me she wants to see me and to stay in touch. I promise, and I mean it, that I will come and see her later. Later, when all my emotions are in their right place and I can be a friend again.

My one-month follow-up check-in is done in a motel just outside of Kansas City. I have to hang around longer than I'd intended, because I am still technically homeless. The scientist introduces himself as Edward, then tells me that he is in fact Controller E. He's an older guy with close-cropped graying hair and a strange lilting cadence to his speech. He's calm and polite but sitting in front of him without the barrier of the messaging system has my discomfort levels reaching for the moon.

Controller E-for-Edward asks if he can record the interview, but it's not really a question because this part of my life is still technically under their control. I stare at the blinking red light on the small recorder between us, and all I can think is that Olivia will probably listen to whatever I say and there's nothing

I can do about it. Edward tells me that I seem to be acclimating well. I smile politely and answer every one of The Organization's invasive questions.

After he leaves, I climb under the motel's thin blankets and cry. And the temptation to drive to Seattle to see Olivia is so overwhelming that even though it's 2:26 a.m. I almost pack my things and leave to do just that.

I'm sick of fighting with what I want and wondering if she wants the same. Tired of feeling this way. Tired of pretending I don't miss her and that I don't want some sort of closure. Then I remind myself that I've had my closure—the money is in the bank, and she's made no attempt to get in contact with me. Close of business. Most importantly of all, my one-month self-imposed deadline is up and it's time to move on.

I'm done.

Goodbye, Olivia Soldano.

I miss you so much.

Colorado. Utah. Wyoming. Montana. All fast time. A little way outside of Butte, a *For Sale* sign on a beautiful twenty-acre piece of land with a small three-bedroom farmhouse catches my eye. I turn around and drive straight to the realtor's office in the small town a few miles back. The property is a deceased estate, well-priced, and just begging for someone to move in. I have no other house to sell or things to organize, so after an inspection I pay cash and settle in after three weeks living in the motel and getting to know the locals.

It's a small town with a cute touristy vibe. I'm certain that my romantic prospects will be limited here, but I'm strangely okay with that. If I want sex, I can drive into one of the big cities and pick up a woman in a bar. We can fuck all night, then I can leave her in the morning and pretend that it's filled the hole Olivia left.

Don't think about it. Don't think about her. You're moving on.

But I miss her so much.

With my truck, I sort of blend in with the rest of the community. I still can't get into the habit of hanging my elbow out the window without feeling like an imposter, but I'm trying. I wave at people, make small talk at the supermarket and a few nights a week eat a meal at the diner. Enlisting locals to fix things around the property helps to cement my place in the town. I manage minor repairs, paint walls with swatches of color as I try to decide which one suits, and move furniture around until I'm happy with how the space looks.

I own a house bought with money I earned fair and square. I'm a grownup, a success. I so wish I could show Riley and Joanne my farmhouse, which is light and airy with an open plan layout. It's small and comfortable, quiet and peaceful and totally not what I thought I wanted. I even have a small balcony off my upstairs bedroom.

All those years alone in the habitat, I thought what I wanted was to be surrounded by people and noise, and never be alone again. But after traveling around, looking for whatever it was I was trying to find, I've made peace with my aloneness. Now I can recognize the way it lets me just *be*. How if I sit still for long enough, and stop thinking, then I can breathe again. My solitude has become my safe place.

* * *

Three or four weeks after I move into my farmhouse, I spot a *Help Wanted* sign taped up in the lawyer's window on the main street. The door has an old-fashioned bell over it, which rings loudly when I push inside. I smile, faking enthusiasm, while my stomach twists at having to converse with someone at length instead of just small talk in the store or ordering a meal.

Glenna the receptionist's smile is large and genuine. "Ms. Thorne! Nice to see you again, honey. How's the new place working out?" Her boss, Archie had handled the conveyancing for my property, and Glenna had made me cup after cup of weak coffee while I sat in this very office going through paperwork.

"Oh, it's great." I jerk my thumb toward the door as though I'm indicating my house is right outside, and immediately feel awkward about the gesture. Still not quite back into the swing of normal interaction. "I saw the sign out the front. I'm looking for a job."

"Oh! Well, it's just a general office clerk position." The way she stares at the sign is like she'd forgotten it was there. "The girl just up and left the day before yesterday. Quit town too."

"That's a shame," I say politely. "I studied law for almost three years before…well, life got in the way. I'm good with computers and filing, and I'm hardworking and punctual. Could I drop off my résumé for you?"

"I'm sure you'll do just fine." Glenna gives me a knowing smile. "Why don't you come in first thing tomorrow and we'll see how you do. Anything you don't know, you can learn." In this small town, it's as easy as that.

Monday to Thursday I work from nine to four, then on Friday we finish at one p.m. so Archie can play golf and Glenna can have her weekly salon gossip session. Each day after work, I go home, work on the house and then slump on the couch. Sometimes with water, sometimes with a glass of wine. I wonder if I should get a rescue dog. Someone to keep me company. One weekend, I drive two hours to the shelter, and last less than ten minutes looking at caged animals before I can't breathe and have to leave.

It's the little moments like this that catch me out, remind me of my time in the habitat. I can truthfully say I no longer mourn my loss, if Olivia can even be called that, and I'm not bitter anymore but I do think about her every now and then. Mostly in the still, quiet darkness when it feels like the nights back there with her. Eventually, if I try really hard, I might be able to convince myself that I don't care at all about Olivia Soldano.

One Friday after work, my glass of wine somehow turns to three before it's even four p.m. As usual when I'm home, a random Spotify list is playing in the background. When I come back from the bathroom, I hear the start of a Fleetwood Mac song I haven't heard in years. Olivia loves Fleetwood Mac. I'm left standing completely dumb as the lyrics of "Gold Dust Woman" sink in.

It's not a sign, it's not an omen, it's just a random coincidence. An algorithm picking music for me. When the song asks me if she shattered my illusions of love, I snatch my phone from the speaker dock and close the app. My thumb goes unconsciously to my contacts, makes a selection and calls. It's answered after only two rings. Nothing to say who I've called.

"Hi, this is Celeste Thorne." I almost give my ID number of SE9311. "Is Olivia...Doctor Soldano there?"

The kind woman tells me, "I'm afraid not, Ms. Thorne. She left this department two months ago. Would you like me to pass along a message? Or if you'd like to hold, I can make some calls and inquire if she's onsite?"

The sharp pang in my chest is like I've fallen out of a tree and landed on my back to be left winded and helpless. I lose my nerve. "No, it's fine. Thank you very much." I hang up the phone, and gulp down the rest of my glass of wine. I don't pour another.

CHAPTER TWENTY

Two months into my Montana life, I buy seven goats—four girls and three neutered boys. After carefully considering my new pets, I name the goats after the Seven Dwarfs from Snow White, gender be damned. Someone has cattle they want to board so their pasture can rest, so thirty friendly steers move into the acres beyond my yard fence. I acquire four chickens that lay too many eggs for just me, so I end up baking every weekend and still have to give Archie and Glenna leftover eggs.

I visit with the animals every day, taking treats for them and leaning on the fence patting goats and cattle until it gets dark. I think about the zen retreat Heather said I should open, but the thought of people invading my zen to find their zen makes me lose a little of my zen.

My three-month check-in is set for Sunday afternoon, and I'd already decided it will be on my back porch because I don't want to let the scientist into my house. She arrives right on time, smiling widely and extending her hand as she walks toward me along my newly laid sandstone pavers. Right away, she tells me her name is Siobhan and that she's Controller C. She's younger than me, with flaming red hair and skin so pale I'm surprised she's not combusting right now in the sun.

Unlike Controller E, she doesn't ask if she can record our conversation, just starts the device and begins chattering. The interview doesn't take long and she seems almost excited to see that I'm acclimating better now, settling into a location with a firm address, and interacting with the locals. She asks me if I think the study has had any lasting negative effects. I lie when I tell her no, it has not.

After my checkup, we talk a little about Scrabble and an app that lets you play with friends. I would have to make friends for it to be useful. I send Controller C away with some of the triple chocolate brownies I made this morning, and directions to the place in the next town over that has the best chili dogs.

Two down, one more to go. Then I'm completely free of that life. Free of *her*.

* * *

A small girl sits on the side of the road under a beach umbrella, next to a handwritten sign proclaiming KITTENS 10$. The cardboard waves in the light breeze. I pull over and walk back to her. I know this girl—her mom works in the diner and I've seen her there a few times doing homework at a booth in the corner while she waits for her mom to finish a shift.

I don't know if she'll remember me, but I offer a friendly, "Heya, Billie."

She lifts a hand to shield her eyes. Her squinting smile is missing two teeth. "Hello, Miss Celeste. How're you?"

I stuff my hands into the front pockets of my cargo shorts and rock back on my heels. "Good thanks." Kids always make me feel weird because I feel like I should be an adult, but most of the time I just want to get down on the ground and hang out with them. A therapist once told me it was part of my strange childhood. Because I wasn't allowed to be a child when I was a child, I found my childishness when I became an adult and it was safe to let myself go.

"Do you have children?" I ask Olivia as she tucks the bed cover around my waist. "You're very…nurturing."

She laughs softly and passes me a glass of water and some more decongestant pills. "No. But I've always thought someday I might. I love kids. You?"

"I like kids, and sometimes I think about it. Maybe I would if I thought I could offer a child something." I shrug. "Plus…uncertain genetics."

"It's not all about what's in your cells, Celeste." Her hand rests gently above my left breast. "It's what is in here. And you've got so much heart."

As I stare down at this child with her missing teeth and neat high ponytail, I wonder if Olivia really wanted kids. She said she didn't lie, not about the important stuff. So, after everything else, it stands to reason that her statements in this case were true. My fingers curl as if they want to make a fist, and I pull my hands out of my pockets to tap fingers against my thigh instead.

I ask Billie the world's most obvious question. "You're selling kittens?"

Billie nods solemnly, ponytail bouncing. "Yup. Got two boys left." She gestures to the box beside her.

"How old are they?"

"'Bout ten weeks. It's a real good mousing family, their momma catches everything." She sighs, tugging at a loose thread on her sleeve. "But nobody wants the boys for mousing."

I crouch down to peek inside the box. Two black and white kittens are playing, tumbling over one another, rabbit kicking and pouncing on imaginary things. I dip my hand inside and scoop them up. One bites my finger with his tiny needle teeth. The other climbs up my arm to my shoulder, and I grab him before he can jump down onto the grass and run away. "I'll take both."

Billie brightens considerably. "Yeah?"

I wonder if she's been told she has to stay out here until all the kittens are gone. "Yeah." I carefully deposit the balls of fluff back into their cardboard pen, and fold the flaps of the box over to close them in. A small shudder runs down my spine, and I tug the flaps apart a little to create a gap where the four corners intersect. Air. Light.

I fish into my pocket for some cash, which she stuffs into a pencil case. On a whim I pass her another five dollars. "Here you go. Why not buy yourself an ice cream?" Or a toy, or a candy bar, or save it up, or whatever kids do.

She turns the note over in her hand. "You sure?"

I pick up the cardboard box. "Yes I am. Have a great day."

"I will." This grin is lopsided and adorable. "Thank you, Miss Celeste."

"You're welcome."

Now I have two kittens, nothing to feed them and no idea what kittens need. Real smart of me. I pull over on the main road and carry the box into the shop with the freshly painted Veterinary Surgery sign hanging above it. In the waiting area there's a flannel-clad guy with a large, dopey-looking mongrel sleeping between his feet and an older woman, with a cat in a cage, sitting as far away from the dog as she can. I head straight for the receptionist. "Hi, just wondering if you have any appointments available this afternoon?"

"Is it an emergency?"

"No." Unless a lack of knowledge counts as an emergency.

She taps a few keys. "Doctor Chapman has an opening in forty minutes."

"Great, thanks. I'll take that one." I give her my name, then settle in a corner with the box on my lap, peeking through the gap at my new pets. One is sleeping, the other scrabbling at the cardboard. They are so different. Jekyll and Hyde. Jekyll has a white top lip like he fell into a bowl of milk. Hyde has two long white socks on his back legs. Jekyll stretches to grab some of my hair that's brushing the box around the peephole.

"Celeste Thorne?"

I look up and spot a tall woman with dirty-blond hair lingering at the entrance to the waiting room. I stand and throw a quick glance at the wall clock. Forty-five minutes gone without me noticing, just watching kittens play. "Yes, that's me."

She smiles and gestures for me to follow her. The door of the small exam room closes behind us. My armpits sweat despite the fact the veterinarian has a sweet smile and a soothing voice when she introduces herself. "I'm Doctor Samantha Chapman."

Wrong kind of doctor. Veterinarian, not like Doctor-Doctor Soldano, psychiatrist and PhD.

"Hi, nice to meet you." I juggle the box to offer my hand but the kittens are moving around, making the box wobble. I have to grab the box again with both hands before it tips out of my arms. One of the kittens squeaks.

She grins but says nothing about my slapstick antics. Her eyes are light brown and when she smiles like that, they seem to sparkle. "Great to meet you too. What have we got here?"

"Kittens. An impulse purchase."

Dr. Chapman laughs. It's an infectious, appealing laugh, one I imagine her friends joining in with after she's told a funny anecdote. "Baby animals often are. May I?"

"Of course." I set the box down on the examination table. My stomach hums with strange anxiety about letting go of the kittens I've owned for exactly seventy-eight minutes.

She peels back the cardboard flaps. "So, what can I help you with, Celeste?" Her voice is soft and cultured. Nothing like the slow drawl of the people here. She's an outsider like me and I wonder why she's here. Maybe she's hiding too.

"Well, I just wanted to have them checked out and start vaccinations. Find out what I need to do. And I need to get some food and stuff for them. And uh, I'd like to have them neutered."

"How old are they?" She scoops up both kittens, one in each hand.

"I was told ten weeks."

She gently bounces the boys up and down as though weighing them. They squirm and shadow box. "Usually we'd do that around four months, so why don't we make an appointment after they've had their final vaccinations."

"It's safe? I mean, they'll be okay? It won't hurt, will it?"

Her smile is indulgent, as though she's asked this every day. "The risk is very low. It's a routine procedure, short anesthesia and we give them pain relief to ensure that discomfort afterward is minimal."

"Sure, okay." I watch her checking my kittens out, her touch gentle and sure, like she really likes animals. Probably why she's a veterinarian then. I hold Jekyll and Hyde for their injections, my thumb caressing soft kitten fur as they squeak and mewl. The vet smiles at me when I murmur what good, brave kitties they are.

"All done. Clean bill of health." Dr. Chapman holds out her hands for my kittens and I pass them to her, thinking she needs to do one final test or check. Instead, she brings them both up to her face and kisses each one right between their ears, rubbing her nose in their soft fur. "They are very good boys." She looks at me, her face partially hidden by kittens. "You're new around here, aren't you?"

"Mhmm, yes I am. Well, newish."

"Me too. How'd you like to grab a drink or coffee sometime?" She passes me Hyde.

I deposit him back in the box. Why is she asking me, a person she just met, out for a social thing? I'm trying to think of all the reasons when she speaks again. "I just thought, you know, if you don't know many people. I've only been here six months and I know what it's like to be new in town."

I hold my hand out for Jekyll and before I can stop myself, I agree, "I'd like that."

"Great." Her smile seems like an exhalation. She's relieved. I'm not. I already know how it will go. This veterinarian is nice enough, but she is fast time. She isn't what I want. Or need. I left my slow time thousands of miles away. I left her in another lifetime.

When I leave the clinic I have a whole bunch of litter and trays, kitten toys, and food, as well a phone number, an email address and plans for drinks after Dr. Samantha Chapman closes up her clinic on Friday afternoon. My kittens settle in right away, rushing off to explore the house then passing out asleep whenever and wherever they get tired. I lie on the floor on my belly to watch them playing, and when I carry them upstairs to go to bed, they settle against my neck, their low kitten purr thrumming against my skin.

Jekyll curls up between my neck and shoulder, and almost immediately lies still. Hyde bats at my hair, before settling in to chew it. His tiny claws scrape my cheek. I close my eyes and feel my life stretch out again. Slow time. Never thought I'd have it again. I could cry at the unfairness of it all, that moments like this will be the only time I'm ever going to be able to pause and really live my life.

Friday night, Samantha and I head to the bar at the south end of town. We settle in a corner booth to eat greasy food, drink cheap beer and then later, bourbon. My time with Samantha is…nice. Enjoyable, not earth-shattering, just comfortable. She doesn't like to be called Sam because her asshole, family-deserting father used to call her that. She's originally from Maine but came here because she wanted to get away from her family and her ex, and she likes the climate. She's sweet and smart and funny and very heterosexual. There is no chance of anything between us, and I'm grateful that I don't have to worry about anything beyond what feels like the tentative start of friendship.

Samantha skims over details of her ex-fiancée and her ex-best friend who are now together and expecting a baby. I give her the sanitized version of my past and I don't talk about *my* ex, if I can even call Olivia that. Samantha and I toast to the past and the future, but instead of excitement for what might come, the hollow inside me deepens. I don't look forward to the future. All it holds for me is more time alone. I still can't bring myself to go out and find a meaningless pickup. My life has had so many meaningless things that I don't want any more.

I leave my car at the bar and we catch a cab home. After I walk her to her doorstep she gives me an impromptu, slightly tipsy hug then tells me she hopes we can be friends. I hesitate a few moments before returning the embrace. "I'd like that," I tell her truthfully. Friendship is okay. Friendship I can handle.

A spark of hope flares that maybe I *can* move on after all and live a normal life with a job and my cats and a circle of friends. Nobody dead or absent is talking at me and the people in this town are sweet and kind.

I work. I fix up my house. I play with my cats. I bribe my goats with grain, bananas, and carrots so they'll stand still long enough for me to brush them. Samantha and I have dinner or lunch a couple of times a week. On weekends we go hiking, or swim in the creek that flows through my property, or we watch movies and talk about starting a board game club for us and a few of the other singletons in town. The plan is to spend nights with drinks and food and games—no Monopoly—and enjoy each other's company the way friends do.

Samantha loves coming to my house in the morning because I have a café-style coffee machine and beans shipped from California. She says my coffee is better than any in town and suggests I open a coffee shop or café to fill in for the one that closed three months before I moved here. She thinks I'd make a killing, catering to the tourists who move steadily through the town and are directed to the push-button coffee machine at Al's Gas Station. Not to mention the horde of stay-at-home parents who are just waiting for a place to congregate for gossiping.

I almost snort at the thought of opening what Heather and I used to call a "Hot Mom Trap" in this small town. Masses of moms, perpetually dressed in their gym gear, are always keen to meet up with friends for coffee and lunch after dropping their kids at school. It's an interesting thought. I liked being a barista, spending my days talking to people. But that was then and I don't know if I could do it now. I place my grand idea of owning a business on the shelf with all my other dreams, right in between Lawyer and Olivia.

One Saturday in late June, Samantha tries to give veterinary attention to Sneezy, one of my goats who is lame. I forget to latch the head bale on my new vet crush properly, and Sneezy escapes to run around the barn, gleefully thwarting our attempts to catch her. Samantha is butted and knocked down, and I just manage to get my hands on the goat for a few seconds. She drags me along until I trip over a water bucket. The Three Stooges would be proud.

Finally we manage to stop our hysterical laughter to agree that Samantha is better sticking with small animals and leaving the farm animal stuff to Dr. Bennett in the next town over, and I should have read the directions for my new farm equipment in order to be a better vet assistant. We drink another beer, wait for Sneezy to get tired of cavorting then bribe her with grain and pumpkin, and restrain her properly so Samantha can drain the abscess and dress the hoof. We laugh the whole time, and when we're done, we wash grossness off our hands, switch to wine and move inside for Chinese food and movie night.

She's a really good friend and I'm glad for her. But it's all rushing by so quickly that I wonder if I'm really living my life or just watching it go by. I try so hard to make it slow down, to be present in my new reality but it's so slippery that I cannot grasp it. Some days I think I almost have it and then it falls from my fingertips and out of reach.

Midway through dinner and our second bottle of wine, her phone chimes a text. She chokes out a laugh, then tells me, "They had the baby."

It takes me a few moments to remember her ex-friend and ex-fiancée. "Oh?" is all I manage around a mouthful of sweet and sour pork.

She turns the phone around so I can see pictures of a newborn human. "My sister Facebook stalked them, because my ex-bestie is so dumb she doesn't set any of her shit to private." Then she says exactly what I'm thinking. "That is one fucking ugly baby. I think I dodged a genetic bullet with him."

I make a musing sound of agreement, pushing food around the container with my fork. "Do you want kids?"

"I used to think I did, but now I'm not sure. I have an endless supply of kittens and puppies to keep my ovaries happy." She chases down her mouthful of food with an even larger mouthful of pinot grigio. "You?"

"Yeah, I do." After a beat, my brain steps in and I can't stop myself from saying, "My ex did too."

"So what's the problem then?" Samantha studies me, one eye half-closed. "Usually the kids thing is a huge break-up point. So is, you know…cheating."

I smile. "She never cheated." I know that for certain. "It was just a bunch of other stuff. I guess you could say the way we met was a setup, but not like the cool way when friends set you up. It's kind of weird and I can't really explain it, but she knew me for longer than I knew her. And I didn't know that initially. And when I did, it all felt like a big, fat lie."

Samantha's nod is repetitive, like she started it and forgot to stop. "You love her?"

"I think I did, yeah. Actually, I think I still do. At the same time I also feel…felt betrayed by her, but I've kinda come to the conclusion that she never lied about who she really is." There's only the smallest amount of pain now, thinking about Olivia. I guess I'm making progress. "I think…being with her was hard, but not being with her kind of feels so much harder. The whole thing is just fucking confusing." I reach for a fortune cookie.

"Heavy shit," says all the beer and wine Samantha has consumed.

"Mmm." I crack open the fortune cookie, half expecting it to have something that will provide an answer to all my problems.

How much deeper would the ocean be without sponges?
Lucky numbers: 11, 5, 39, 87, 18, 6

Great, thanks. Very helpful.

CHAPTER TWENTY-ONE

My little piece of Montana is coming along nicely, turning into a haven where I imagine I will eventually be made whole again. This place is *mine*, somewhere I don't have to hide or pretend, and its simplicity soothes and revitalizes. As does the physical labor I've put into its restoration. All the floors have been sanded back and varnished which gives it a slightly more modern feel. The exterior repainting is complete and now my farmhouse and barn are decked out in a palette of slate blue with charcoal and white trim. The newly repainted interior is full of furniture I've picked up at yard sales or the antique store I found one Saturday morning while driving aimlessly around the county.

One weekend when I'm moving some things out of the spare room that Samantha sleeps in after movie nights, I find the box of Mother's stuff in the closet. Still unopened. I banked the check from her estate months ago, donated the entire thing to a center for drug addiction, and wondered what Mother would think about her last $2,243.87 being used in this way. Maybe the only reason she had the money was because a center like that helped her out.

My first impulse is to burn the box unopened but as I'm carrying it downstairs, something stops me. I don't know why I sit on the couch and pull the lid off, and I sure as hell don't know what I'm expecting to find. It smells musty but otherwise inoffensive. I think I expected it to smell like her and I'm almost disappointed that it doesn't.

Inside are loose sheets of paper, newspaper clippings, some photographs and two plastic dolls with tattered dresses and scraggly hair that I have to put on the floor behind the couch where I can't see them. I feel like they are looking at me, boring holes in my back with the blue eyes I colored back on them each time they wore off.

There are two sealed envelopes, one with my name and the other with Riley's. I can't open that one—it's not for me to see what Mother wanted my sister to know. I even consider not opening my letter, because what could she have possibly written that would explain the past thirty years? But in the end, that old pathetic hope flares. Maybe she finally realized everything she did that was wrong and cruel, and will apologize for being such a shitty, abusive mother. There's the barest tremor in my hand when I slide the letter opener under the flap of the envelope marked for me.

Her handwriting is blocky and rough, almost robotic, and she leaves overlarge spaces between each word as though she's thinking long and hard on what to write next.

Celeste,
I don't even know what to say but I've had this feeling like I should leave something behind, something of mine for you, before I die.

I just want you to know that I'm sorry and I don't even have any reasons or excuses. That's all I can really say. And I want you to know that I tried the best I could. I know it didn't seem like it but I really did. It really was better for you this way.

I hope you're doing okay.
Nathalie.

I read it again, and then a third time. Such a plain, ordinary, shitty note with her vague and broad not-quite-apology. Nothing in it to indicate she showed any real remorse or even the faintest shred of caring about me or Riley. Caring would stretch her emotion to the limit—I gave up trying to apply words like *love* to Mother a long time ago. The more I stare at the letter, the more convinced I become that the only reason she wrote it was because she was afraid of what would happen after she died, and wanted to put a little more weight on her side of the scales in case there really is something after this life.

But I don't see the titan I've always pictured when I think of Mother. In every image I have of her, she's a dark, powerful, and imposing figure towering over me. The malevolent, bitter force who shaped my entire life. But I see none of that in her simple words. All I see is someone at the end of her pathetic life, someone who is afraid.

And the thought bothers me.

For my whole life I've kept her as the monster under the bed when really she's nothing, a nobody. I've given her all this power, power she didn't deserve. Does this mean that everything she said to me in the habitat wasn't true? That I spent all that time torturing *myself*?

I'd thought I was okay, that I had made peace and come to terms with what she'd done to my sister and me. But now I have the sickening feeling that I've spent my whole life lying to myself, expanding incidents into something bigger or even something they weren't. I close my eyes. Inhale. Exhale. No, Mother *did* do some really appalling, abusive things, and treated my sister and me like we meant nothing to her. She hurt us—emotionally, physically, psychologically.

But from where I sit now, so far removed from it, I see the uncomfortable truth—that my perspective of those who hurt me is warped. Olivia did a shitty thing, one shitty thing, wrapped up in the huge thing she calls love. Then when I learned about it, it was me who let the shitty thing overtake everything else, me who ignored all the good things, the way I felt about her, the things I now know were real. I rub my temples. It's all right to be upset with her for her lie and the way she manipulated me for the experiment. I'm entitled to that feeling.

But at the same time she played by the rules I agreed to when I went into that place—that I was up for pretty much anything they chose to do as long as it didn't physically harm me. And I still overturned the board and stalked away like a sore loser. I grew angry with her, afraid of her, pushed her away when what she did to me was the barest fraction of what Mother did to me. I wasted years of my life wanting to forgive and understand Mother who was truly a bad person, and I didn't bother trying to forgive or understand Olivia who I know is a good person. And now I know all of this and there's nothing I can do about it.

I fold the letter back into the envelope and drop it on the floor beside the box. The newspaper clippings are of Riley in the eleventh grade when one of her art assignments was chosen to appear in a local gallery. The other is of me when I made captain of the state soccer team. I shuffle through the loose photographs, noting that every one of them is of Riley and me, both together and separate. There are none of Mother and for a painful instant I wish there was, just so I could look at her one last time and try to understand.

There's one photo in particular to which I pay close attention. I know I'm nine and Riley five. She's holding an empty ice cream cone and crying, chocolate smeared all over her face. I'm looking down at her, my own full strawberry cone clutched tightly in my hand, which is partially encased in the plaster that continues all the way up my arm to mid-bicep.

Mother's voice is an echo in my head, not a whisper in my ear. "It was an accident, I'm sorry, okay? It's this fucking detox again, okay? We're going to have an ice cream and forget about it, okay?"

My voice, weak and groggy from the pain medication. "I don't want an ice cream. I want to go back and get my shoes." Her apology tripped me up, but even through the fogginess I remembered what had happened and knew it wasn't an *accident*.

Mother, surprisingly gentle as she tried to persuade me to take what amounted to a bribe. "What about Riley? Bet you she wants one."

That was all it took for me to nod my agreement—the mere hint that my selfishness would keep something from my sister. After Riley dropped her scoop of ice cream on the grass, I passed her my cone and helped her hold it while she finished the treat. The whole time, I watched Mother sit on the bench, the disposable camera beside her as she smoked nervous cigarette after nervous cigarette. She stared at my cast, and probably wondered if someone from the hospital was coming after her for sneaking me out without paying.

CHAPTER TWENTY-TWO

In my calendar for today, Friday, is an appointment at four p.m. for my last interview. Six months gone. My feelings are mixed, but the most prevalent is the certainty that I'm ready to put the final piece of that portion of my life into place and move on.

Even though I've come to terms with my actions, I still catch myself thinking about Olivia. Mostly wishing I could apologize for my rudeness or explain what I did and why I did it or wondering if she's thinking about me. That thought disappears quickly when reason kicks in—why would she be thinking about me?

I make my way back to work after waiting at the post office for fifteen minutes because Kevin Loman has lost a parcel. The problem is he lost this parcel in his house somewhere, not in the mail system, and he can't accept that there's nothing the USPS can do about it. I love my small town and all the people in it. My umbrella is ineffectual against the rain as I hurry back along the wet sidewalk. It's the day we finish work just after lunch, and

I want to get home to make sure the house is completely tidy before my appointment.

Glenna looks up when I push back into the office. "Looks awful out," she says, but her tone is her usual cheerful one, not annoyed or sad the way most people are when the weather sucks.

"It is," I agree. It's cold and windy and I'm told this much rain is unusual for September. It's the kind of weather where you just want to be curled up inside with hot tea and a book. My favorite kind of weather aside from snow. I hang my coat, brushing perfectly round droplets of water from it.

"Oh, while I remember, someone came in looking for you while you were out."

"For me? Who was it?"

"She didn't give a name. I let her know that sort of thing, creeping around, wasn't how we do things around here." Then it's not Samantha or any of our small circle of game-night friends, because Glenna knows them. *She* is a stranger, likely the person from The Organization invading my personal life instead of waiting until this afternoon as scheduled. Her audacity flashes a streak of annoyance through my body.

I look outside as though the person might be right there staring back at me, and an uncomfortable sensation skitters down my spine. None of the Controllers would have any need to come to my place of employment. None of them except for one who had no issues inserting herself into my life. I try to sound casual when I ask, "What did she look like?"

"Pretty brunette. Dressed real nice. Little bit of an accent. Looked like she was from the gov'ment or something, all official and driving a new rental. Polite as heck, even when I told her to go away."

Pretty. Accent. Well-dressed. My mouth goes dry. "Oh?" I pass Glenna the postal receipts. Moments ago they were fine. Now they are slightly crumpled from my fist tightening around them.

Glenna studies me, a thinly plucked eyebrow arched. "Is everything all right? You're not in any kind of trouble are ya?" A slow grin forms. "You know Archie's not real good with the criminal stuff."

My heart double-times. "No, nothing like that." I force myself to smile. "Sounds like a friend I had a falling out with last year." I emphasize *friend*, not ex-lover slash maybe betrayer slash person I still think about nearly every day. My town is a small town, most people don't know I'm gay and I don't want to make waves. Not when I'm still an oddball newcomer.

It's not that I'm worried about being victimized or ostracized. It seems kind of surprising for around these parts, but everyone talks fondly of Graham and Victor, the sixty-something farmers who've lived together up on Old Mill Road for as long as most of the town remembers. And the same of Diane and Zara, the women who run a flower stall at the farmers markets, who live with their pack of rescue dogs and eat at the diner every Wednesday night.

It's just not quite the right time to share that part of myself. Obviously Samantha knows and she keeps dropping hints about her cousin who plays in the WNBA. Maybe one day I'll just stroll into town hand-in-hand with a girlfriend. One day. If I ever get the nerve to put myself out there again.

The moment I get home, I tidy up the mess made by the boys while I've been at work, dust furniture, and run the vacuum and mop over the already-clean floors. She's going to be here in less than three hours, and everything feels like it's messy and out of place.

The doorbell echoes through my house as I'm pulling on jeans after my shower. I don't check my reflection and on my way down the stairs, I drag my wet hair into a ponytail. I'm surprised to see my hand shaking when I grab the handle to open my front door.

Even though I've known all afternoon that the person coming to see me was most likely Olivia, seeing her on my doorstep sparks a whole mess of emotions. Nervous. Excited. Scared. And an unexpected flash of arousal. *That* feeling is deep down, somewhere I thought I'd never feel anything again.

Her hair is longer and lighter. She's wearing makeup again, and is dressed in a tailored charcoal pantsuit, pale pink silk shirt and low-heeled boots. These images combine to make her the same attractive, poised woman from my exit interview. Beautiful.

But she's always beautiful, even when rumpled and rough and sleep-mussed.

This elegant Olivia doesn't feel like my Olivia. But she was never my Olivia, was she?

My fingers tighten on the door handle. "What are you doing here?"

"I'm here for your final interview," Olivia replies, with the slightest tremor in her voice.

"Why? They've sent a lackey for the last two." The moment the words come out of my mouth, I'm aware of a change—time lengthening, drawing every moment with her out. Slow time. If I ever needed confirmation that she's the right thing for me, the proof is right here in my changed existence. It's a sick joke that this thing I can't have is the thing I need to make me feel like I'm living again.

Her shoulders drop. "Because I asked to. Because I needed to see you. I thought if you knew it was me who was doing the interview it'd be harder for you, having to think about it before it happened."

"Why did you come to my work today?"

"I just…wanted to see that you were doing okay, that you'd found something normal I guess. That you had good people around you." She graces me with a faint smile. "I tried to be sneaky, but your coworker came out demanding to know what I was doing."

Even though I'm annoyed at her invasion into a sphere of my life she has no right invading, the overwhelming thing sitting on top of it all is that she cares about me. She cares, but she still did that thing to me, back in that other place. This is the thing I'm finding so hard to let go of. All my emotions are fighting with one another but I have no choice, I've got to let her in. "I thought you left this project. I called—" I'm painfully aware of giving away too much of myself. "Um, come in."

Her right eyebrow lifts a fraction, then settles again. "No, I was made Head of Research so I'm working in a different department, that's all. Still Assistant Director, though. And still qualified for the task of interviewing you. Perhaps over-qualified." Now her smile is a little self-deprecating. Olivia closes her umbrella, shakes it off outside the door and leaves it resting against the exterior wall. She brushes past me and into the house.

"Congratulations on your promotion." I lock the door, then am suddenly conscious of the fact it means that yet again, I'm basically giving her no choice as to whether she wants to be with me or not. I unlock the door. My skin crawls as though it senses her watching me, and when I turn around my suspicions are confirmed.

"Thank you." Olivia's eyes run up and down my body, eventually settling on my face. "You look well."

"Thanks." I'm conscious that I should respond in kind. "You too." It's not a lie, but it feels hollow. Because while her outside is pleasurable, it's what lives inside her beautiful body and mind that I love.

Love. There's that word again.

I gesture toward the couch, and she walks ahead of me, her gait smooth and not the one I recognize. Silly to expect that she'd still have something left from our time together. That she'd be carrying us around the way I have been since she left me in that house in the middle of nowhere. The kittens sprint past, struggling for traction on the smooth wooden flooring. Olivia laughs then bends down and scoops up Hyde while Jekyll leaps around her feet.

"What are their names?" She sits gracefully on the couch, knees together, ankles crossed.

I point my introductions. "Hyde and Jekyll."

"Those are great names." She scratches under Hyde's chin then behind his ears, all the while scuffing her booted foot on the floor to play with Jekyll. I didn't know she liked cats, something that escaped our countless hours of conversation.

"May I offer you a drink? Water or coffee?" The formality of my words makes me cringe.

She looks up as though just remembering I'm there. Still absently stroking Hyde, she nods. "Thank you. Coffee would be wonderful. This weather really gets inside your bones." A slow smile. My breath hitches.

Olivia settles on the couch to play with the boys while I take my time making coffee. When I do so for Samantha or myself I'm less fussy, but now I pay careful attention to the way I grind and tamp the beans. For Olivia, a *caffé crema*, because she once told me that she would drink this type of coffee with her grandparents when visiting them in northern Italy. I know it's true because the Liv I know would never lie about coffee. Fancy cup and saucer. No plain mugs for her.

From the kitchen I can hear her chuckling and the sound of toys being batted across the floor. Playing with someone's pets is such a normal thing for a visitor to do. That's all she is. A visitor. When I start to pull her coffee, she looks up at the sound of the machine. Confusion, then interest flickers across her face before she turns back to the cats.

I baked cookies last night ready for my final interview, but I know she doesn't really like cookies. There's chocolate in the pantry. Dark. Expensive. Swiss. The kind we both like. I break off a few pieces, set them on the saucer and store the rest in the fridge away from the rain-hiding ants I can't bear to kill with spray, even as they invade my house.

I remember Liv in the afternoon, drinking coffee and eating dark chocolate while she read a book. Chocolate and caffeine together is good for your mood, she'd assure me, smiling playfully as she popped another piece in her mouth. She liked to let it melt, stored between her cheek and teeth as she sipped coffee. "A fancy kind of mocha," I'd said and she laughed her agreement. I blink the past away and measure half a teaspoon of sugar, balanced on the front of the spoon. It doesn't need to be exact.

When I set the cup and saucer in front of her, she stares at it like it's something she's never seen before. Olivia clears her throat and utters a soft, "Thank you." She bites a thin piece of chocolate in half. I see that out-of-line canine and imagine it biting into my shoulder as she rides me with my fingers deep inside her. Gooseflesh tightens my skin and nipples. Oh God, why now? It's not fair.

Olivia raises her coffee cup halfway to her mouth. "I have a set of questions I need to ask, just like your other two interviews, and then you're all done." There's a small bulge in her cheek, the chocolate squirreled in there as always.

"Sure thing. I know how it goes." I sound appropriately nonchalant. Thankfully there's no physical aspect to these checkups. If she touched me, I would totally lose it.

After a sip of coffee, she makes a noise I remember well—an unconscious sound of pleasure. Smiling, she drinks another mouthful. "My goodness, that's fantastic. The coffee I had this morning from someplace called Al's was beyond dreadful."

"Mmm, yeah you should stay away from there. I think the rumor is that Al's coffee is actually leftover nuclear wastewater from the seventies."

She laughs, raising the cup slightly. "Well, thank you for this."

"You're welcome."

Olivia steals one more sip and sets it down with what seems like reluctance. Cup is exchanged for tablet and the now-familiar recorder, which she sets on the coffee table. Liv taps the tablet screen and inputs something. She studies me. "How are you feeling in general? Any physical complaints or illnesses that you think are worth noting?"

"I had a stomach flu last month, but I don't think it had anything to do with…this. Other than that, I'm fine."

"You seem a little thinner. Are you sure you're well?"

"I hadn't noticed." It's not an evasion or false modesty, simply something I don't pay attention to. "And yes, I'm okay."

She eyes me for a long moment before lowering her eyes to concentrate on typing something on the tablet. "Have you noticed a change in appetite? Increase in alcohol consumption? Any drugs?" The questions are asked without looking at me.

A muscle in my jaw flickers and I have to unclench my teeth. She knows how I feel about substance abuse. "No drugs. And no changes. I'm exactly the same as when you left me." Still broken. Still confused. Still wanting you.

"I didn't leave. You told me to get out." She tells this quietly to the screen.

"Can you blame me?" I snap back. "What did you expect after everything that happened? That we'd have a happily ever after?"

Her nostrils flare ever so slightly, just enough to telegraph her emotion. "This isn't relevant," she says smoothly. And there it is, she's gone again. So much for needing to see me. I've never known anyone who can wall herself off as quickly and as well as Olivia. It must be exhausting for her, like having two people inside one body constantly fighting each other.

"No, you're right," I concede. "It's not relevant."

Olivia lets out a long breath. The second half of her chocolate. More coffee. "What about your auditory hallucinations? Have they returned?" She won't look at me.

But I'm looking at her. "No. Still gone."

"Olfactory?"

"Also gone." I do not smell Mother anymore, haven't for quite some time. Right now, I smell Olivia who wears the same perfume as the last time I was in her presence. I'm still not sure how I feel about it. It's nice and it suits her, but it makes her even more different.

"I'm really pleased to hear that." She sounds genuine enough.

"Thank you," I say on an exhalation.

This time, she looks at me when she asks her question. "How are you finding relationships with others?"

"Fine."

Olivia watches me, clearly waiting for me to give her more. I don't. She pushes a little. "Are you struggling to meet or connect with people?"

"Not that I've noticed, not anymore that is. I have a good friend here, and a small circle of other friends I hang out with." It feels like I'm trying to prove something to her, something pointless and inane. I'm trying to prove that I don't need her, that I've moved on.

Her voice is suddenly quiet. "What about, uh, romantic interactions?" For the first time during the actual official interview, a smile tugs at her lips. She turns the tablet around for me to see the question listed. "I'm not being nosy. It's right here as always." Still, she looks very interested.

I lift my chin and meet her eyes. There's a curiosity in them that goes beyond professional, but there's also sadness. My answer is truthful and the same as the previous interviews. "No. None. Not since you."

She places the tablet on her lap, her fingers curling over the edge. "Why do you think that is, Celeste?"

I've missed the way she says my name, the musical way it falls from her lips. I close my eyes against the sudden pain in my chest. "You've got no right to ask that."

"I know," she says softly. "But I'm asking it anyway."

Opening my eyes again, I search her face for some sign she really wants me, knowing even as I do it that I won't find what I'm looking for. I blow out a long, noisy breath. "If I had to guess, I'd say probably because I don't think anyone would be as physically and emotionally satisfying as my last lover. I'd also say it's because she broke my fucking heart. And maybe, just maybe, it's because I can't even think about anyone except you that way." I want to say more, but there's no point. No point in telling her that when I imagine kissing someone or having someone else's hands on me I want to scream. That when I think about her with someone else, I feel sick.

"I'm sorry. I shouldn't have asked," she says quickly as she lifts the tablet again. Barely audibly she adds, "I shouldn't have come here…I don't know what I expected."

We engage in a little more back-and-forth about my feelings and interactions and thoughts. I set the remnants of my sarcasm and hurt aside and answer each question for her. My coffee sits untouched on the table. She finished hers, and the chocolate, twenty minutes ago. Liv could never let coffee go without drinking it all.

After the most uncomfortable forty-five minutes of my life, she says, "I think that's all. Thank you for your time."

"You're welcome." I clear my throat. "So, we're done for good now?"

Olivia stands. "Yes." She holds the tablet and stylus out to me. "If you could just sign here to confirm you've had your final interview, I'll leave you alone."

Alone. What if I don't want to be left alone? Wordlessly, I scribble where indicated. Over. Done. Finished. I pass the tablet back, carefully, so I don't touch her.

She drops it into her satchel without looking at my signature. "I have a list of physicians who can remove the implant for you under our medical plan. Or I can do it now, I have local anesthetic and instruments. It will be quick and will only require three or four stitches." Her expression is intense, like she wants to say more but doesn't dare.

"Can I leave it in?" I know the implications of keeping it in my arm. If I do that, she will always be able to find me.

"If that's what you'd prefer." She drops an envelope on the coffee table. "If you change your mind later, there's the list."

"Thank you." I stuff my hands into my pockets, bunching my fingers up. "Well. Thanks for everything, I guess." For showing me what I wanted and what I can't have. For teaching me how to find the truth of what I needed all this time.

"Yes, and thank you for your participation. Your input has been invaluable. The agency who contracted us was very pleased with the results." Olivia pulls a large manila folder, the papers inside about an inch thick, from her leather satchel and sets it on the table in front of me.

"What's that?" I ask, suspicious.

She hesitates. "These…are my personal logs, from our time together and also from after. Every time I thought about you, I recorded it." She looks unusually embarrassed. "I didn't submit them, but I'm hardwired to record everything I think. So I did."

I don't want to read them, but fuck, I want to read them. "Why? Why would you want me to have this?"

"Because I need you to see the truth and I can't pretend that my feelings for you don't exist." Liv brushes cat hair from her expensive wool pants. "I read all those handwritten logs of yours from our time together. Did you mean what you wrote?" She's watching Jekyll chase a plastic ball around the floor.

"At the time, yes."

Slowly, her focus moves to me. "And now?"

"I'm not sure." I think I do still mean it, but there's so much more layered over the top that I can't separate it out to find the truth.

Her expression is unreadable. "If you think of anything else you want to add to your answers from this interview, or if you just...want to talk, I'm staying at the motel in town until my flight leaves tomorrow afternoon. Room twelve," she tells me as she walks to the entryway. "Take care of yourself, Celeste."

Numbly, I follow her. She pauses, staring at a series of framed photographs hanging in the entryway. Some are mine, some are the ones Mother left for me. They run sequentially— starting with childhood and teen years with Riley, right through to the last pictures I have of us together. Olivia points at one of the frames close to the door, a series of black and whites taken in one of those photo booths you find in malls. I'm twenty-two and Riley's eighteen. She wanted to do this silly, retro thing to celebrate finishing school and I protested that it was dumb. But now I'm so glad I relented.

In the first three we're smiling stupidly or pulling faces, then for the last one she slung her arm around my neck, pulled me close and whispered *Love you* in my ear. The photo was taken right as her mouth formed the 'L' sound for love, and I've got the beginnings of a smile lifting the edges of my mouth.

Olivia runs a forefinger along the edge of that frame. "This is Riley?"

"Yes."

"You two have the same eyes."

"Yes."

"She looks like she loved you very much." It's all Olivia says before she opens the front door and steps outside.

The rain stopped sometime during our conversation and now it's gray and dreary to match my mood. It's getting dark, and I worry about her driving on slippery roads through a town she doesn't know. I almost tell her to be careful, but it's not my place to worry about her now, if it ever was my place. There's a moment as she's fastening the strap around her umbrella when she looks at me and all her emotion is bare. She's stripped herself naked and laid herself out as though she's asking something from me.

I wait for her to speak but she doesn't and neither do I. Olivia nods quickly, as though my silence has strengthened her resolve, and then she walks away. When she's halfway to her rental car, some part of my brain realizes this could be the last time I see her. Words spill from my lips, all in a rushed breath. "I heard you, you know. After you left."

Olivia pauses on the path, still facing the road. After a long moment, she turns and strides back, stopping a foot away from me. Her eyes beg me to tell her the truth. "What do you mean?"

I close the front door to keep the cats inside and push my hands deep into my back pockets to stop them shaking. "I didn't tell them, but once your *body* left everyone else did too. Nobody would talk to me. But you did. Constantly."

She covers her mouth with one of her delicate hands but it doesn't stop the sound of her shocked sob. After a shaky breath, she lowers her hand. "Why didn't you say anything?"

I really don't know the exact combination of reasons, but I do know one. "Because I didn't want you to have the power to hurt me more than you already had. I'd already given you so much, Olivia, and I didn't want you to have all of me. There wouldn't have been anything left to keep me together."

Her hand drops to her side. The umbrella falls to the ground.

I lift my chin, look into her caramel eyes and tell her, "I lasted all that time by myself in that place and I never broke. Not once. Not through every hateful thing Mother kept saying. Not with all the guilt from my sister and my friends looping in my head. But you made me break in less than a month, Olivia. After you left, I couldn't stand being there. You broke me," I repeat tearfully.

Olivia sucks in a breath, her eyes wide. Her expression is a strange mix of fear, worry, and relief. She closes the gap between us and light fingers trace along my jaw to my chin. "Funny," she murmurs, her eyes on my lips. "I think you put me back together again."

My skin burns under her touch, and I feel the shudder at

the back of my neck run down my spine. Before I can think, Olivia's hands are on my waist and she's pulling me to her for a kiss. When I realize what she's about to do, I know I'll push her away the moment she does it. But when her lips touch mine, my conviction flees. In that single instant, everything slots into place and I feel like I can finally breathe again. Instead of drawing back, I pull her closer. I clutch her hips, my fingers clenched around her suit jacket to hold her in place.

She fits against me the way she always did. Her hands wind through my hair and when her tongue parts my lips, my blood hums. Time slows again and then again as we kiss. It's hours and minutes and years. It's past and present and future. It's everything.

It's everything, until without warning Olivia wrenches herself away, snatches up her umbrella from the path and rushes to her car. I stand on faltering legs, a clump of my shirt gripped in one hand and the other against my lips as though I could hold on to the lingering touch of her kiss.

She drives away without a backward glance.

CHAPTER TWENTY-THREE

The folder she left is like a lighthouse in the fog—a beam that hits me in the face and demands my attention. No matter what I do, how I try to distract myself, I keep finding my eyes drawn back. A few times during the evening, I get as far as brushing my fingers over the thin cream cardboard, determined that I'm going to open it and delve into Olivia's secrets. Then my fingers retract and hover above the folder, as though they are sentient and know better than I do that it's not a good idea.

Jekyll starts to gnaw on the edge of the cardboard. I snatch him up, kiss between his ears and rescue Olivia's notes. Now both hands are on the folder and I can't help myself. My fingers move with a casualness that I don't feel as I flick through the pages. The notes are filed chronologically and look like screenshot printouts from the reporting system I used every day. Each one has a date and a time—always between one and three a.m. I close the folder again, set it up high where the cats can't get at it, and walk away.

I put up some shelves in the guest room as I'd planned earlier in the week. Luckily there are no neighbors nearby to complain about the noise of power tools at this time of night. Her words still break through the noise.

I miss you so much.

You put me back together again.

I last for maybe an hour more before I slink back downstairs to the folder, my resolve shattered. A glass of wine would make what I'm about to do easier, but at the same time I don't want to dull any of this experience. I owe it to myself, and to her, to see what she wanted me to see without being impaired.

I set a glass of iced tea on the coffee table, curl my legs underneath myself and rest the folder on my lap. The thin cardboard strains around the stack of papers that are bound to the seam. I suppose if I'd written down every thought I'd had about her, my folder would be just as thick. Possibly thicker. I'm surprised by the slight tremble in my hands as I begin to read the material Olivia left for me. Things about me. Things about her. About us.

She spared no detail, and in some instances that detail makes me uncomfortable. Seeing myself laid out this way is strange. Some events in her logs stand out in stark relief while others seem like nothing more than fleeting glimpses in my memories. Sometimes I see myself in her words, other times I feel like I'm reading a private investigator's notes about a stranger.

In most cases the wording is formal and clinical—Olivia's professional detachment. Perhaps that detachment is the only way she could do what she had to do.

She's incredibly squeamish but still treated my leg. I didn't realize how badly being shot hurts, and it wasn't even a penetrating wound. It was lucky that it wasn't more serious or my insertion would have been completely invalidated, and I don't know what I would have done then. Or rather, what my team would have done.

Her voice gives me shivers. In person it's even more gorgeous than the video recordings and raspier than I remembered from her interview too. She's jumpy around me, likely because she doesn't trust me yet. This disconnect between what I know and what she knows is maddening.

Her eyelashes are the longest I've ever seen. Beautiful. Her eyes are so blue, so bright they seem unreal. Whenever she looks at me, her gaze is so intense that I feel naked.

Celeste has a great sense of humor. I don't think I realized it before but now, actually being with her, it's obvious. She talks a hundred miles a minute, like her brain is ten steps ahead of her mouth and she's constantly trying to catch up.

She sleeps so soundly that it's easy to sneak out to fill in my reports and logs. I'm glad, because I don't want to have to medicate her to keep her asleep for that time. It wouldn't be right, nor would it be fair. I just don't want to do that to her, to secretly break her trust more than I already have to.

Celeste is not a good patient, she doesn't seem to know what to do with kindnesses and I can tell she's discomforted by sharing her bed with me. My feelings aside, she needs to rest so she can eliminate the virus. It doesn't seem to have affected her greatly, which is a relief. It feels good to care for her, even if it's tricky, still hobbling as I am with this leg injury.

When she concentrates, she nibbles on her upper lip and suddenly seems like an innocent child. Her concentration is fierce and hard to break, and it makes me wonder what exactly she's thinking. Sometimes she says something and it's nothing like what I thought she'd say. She constantly surprises me.

I initiated physical contact in the form of a hug. She accepted. She's about three-quarters of an inch taller than me, but I fit perfectly. Close up that way, she smells even better. It's more than the soap and shampoo and skin lotion I choose for her. It's something more. It's Celeste. She felt so good in my arms that it was hard to make myself let go.

Being able to put my own feelings into physical form brought such relief. I didn't know I'd been holding so tightly to my want of her. Love, lust, infatuation…I'm not even sure what I would call it. But it's been there for so long, that I'm scared I might not be able to hold it in for much longer.

Papà warned me about this, the possibility that my personal bias might compromise the results. Privately I agree, but for the first time in my life, I can say honestly that I don't even care. She's passed the minimum threshold and anything from here on is just extra product testing and data. I hate that word. She's not data and she shouldn't be in here. She should be out in the world, seeing and touching and tasting. She should be <u>living</u>. And I would so love to be witnessing her doing just that.

She asked questions and I had to answer. Actually, I didn't <u>have</u> to answer but I wanted to. I told her about Camilla's death, and my failures with Tracy and Lindsey before that. Told her the awful truths about why I'm alone. And she kept saying she couldn't see it, how it would be my shortcomings that caused my relationships to fail. Probably because what she sees in here is the woman she wants to see. A fantasy. Fantasy sums it up fairly well—my thoughts about her, about what comes after this, are nothing more than fantasy because when I leave, even if by some miracle we met up again, I would be the same person. I would still have to keep my work a secret from her and I don't want that. Celeste is the first woman I've ever wanted to share everything with, the first woman I've ever wanted to fully give myself to. Knowing that and knowing it'll probably never happen makes me want to weep.

I offered a kiss and she accepted. She was nervous but I could tell she wanted to be intimate. I was nervous too but more than that, I'm afraid of how badly I wanted it. When we made love, it was unbelievably incredible. I can't find any clinical sort of breakdown or way to explain how I feel, other than <u>whole</u>. I feel whole. I need to stop being so emotionally involved with her but I can't. Not when she touches me and looks at me that way.

We debated our points of view on different topics. Politics, religion, science, movies. She's not pushy about her ideals — she seemed to just want to talk rationally, to be heard by someone. And she listens like a person absorbing new ideas and trying to see how she could fit them alongside her own viewpoint. I expected to have to push back at her in order to get her to see my side. I could picture us, years from now arguing about small things and then making up. Falling into bed to reaffirm our bond. I want that. I want her.

She talks in her sleep, frightened murmurs about nothing that makes sense but when I hold her, she settles and goes quiet again. I want to talk to her about her childhood, to soothe her but I don't know how to bring it up. What I knew before was awful. What she's told me in here is even more awful. I don't know how she's such an incredibly compassionate, gentle person after all that. And I'm certain there's so much more that I'll never know about her past...

So beautiful. She makes me want to write poetry, which is ridiculous and emotional, but I still feel it — the beauty in our shared existence. It's not even about the sex, though the sex is incredible. It's everything else, all the small ways she makes me feel needed and vice-versa.

She told me the voices are gone. Scientifically, I can postulate that it's because she now has company and the stimulus to fill that deep need for connection. Emotionally, I want to believe I chased them away. That I'm enough for her and that I can make her feel safe. My emotions are getting in the way of the study. I need to find a way to separate myself. I don't think I can.

She told me she loves me, but I could tell she's embarrassed at how quickly she found these feelings. She thinks it's because of what I represent rather than what we share. I can't soothe her by telling her that I felt something for her the moment I saw her. Or that I fell in love with her when I watched her talking about playing an imaginary tennis match with herself the 46th day she video logged. She told me she won 6-4, 6-3 and I laughed so much I was nearly crying. I'm not sure how many more times I can push back my extraction.

N.B. Log abandoned as 'interrupted by subject,' marked as incomplete entry. OMS authorization.

She knows. I don't know what to do. I told her the truth, kept to the facts. The hardest thing I've ever done was to act as though I don't care and it was all about the science. It's so much more for me. It always was. I shouldn't have come. I knew I'd become too involved but I thought I could compartmentalize it all. I couldn't. I can't. I will never be able to.

I wonder if deep down, I wanted her to catch me so I could let the truth out.

I'm not sure what I expected would happen when she found out. She can't understand my reasoning because she feels like she's only known me, really known me for a month where I've been watching her, wanting her for years. We're in different stages of this and can't find somewhere in the middle to meet. I've been so selfish. Greedy. And it's hurt her. I wish it hadn't. Wish I hadn't. But I couldn't help myself.

Then there are just pages and pages of text with manually entered dates and times. The first date is the day she left, and the last one is yesterday's. There's an entry most days, sometimes every few days. I flip through the pages, reading snippets of her life and thoughts. With every new line I skim, a feeling builds inside of me. It's like I'm standing at the bottom of a well, and a person up top is slowly inching a ladder down to me. That dangerous feeling again. Hope.

I can't sleep. I'm inappetant. I can't stop watching all those years' worth of her video logs.

This afternoon I saw a woman who looked like her and I felt my heart racing, my palms growing sweaty. I'm still not sure what I thought would ever come of me being there. That fantasy again. Did I really think we'd have a romantic relationship once she left, even if she never found out? How would I have ever hidden that part of myself from her? I could not have a relationship built on half-truths, especially when I already lied to her when I arrived.

I need to know, I have to make sure she's fine. Edward assures me she's okay. I've listened to the interview recording so many times, hoping to hear something that tells me she's not completely forgotten me. Then I just end up listening to her voice, ignoring all the words, closing my eyes and remembering her.

She called the old department, asking for me but didn't leave a message. She wanted to talk to me, but then she didn't? I choose to take the first part of that, to believe that maybe she doesn't hate me.

Siobhan says Celeste looks well, and that she has a house, a small farm with some animals. I'm pleased, imagining her in this space, living freely. I listened to this interview as well, hoping again that Celeste might have said something about me. Something more than a quick answer brushing me aside. She didn't.

With every line, my suspicion as to why she gave me these log entries is strengthened. Olivia wants to show me that I mean something to her, that our relationship—whatever it was— means something. She wants me to see it was real. And I do see it. I see it in these pages of notes, confirming what I'd hoped all along. She's taken off her armor and put herself out there for me to see. Now it's up to me what I do with her trust.

I miss our conversations, the ones where we talked about everything and nothing at all. Our few precious weeks weren't long enough. I just...miss her. The absence of her feels physical, like there's an emptiness inside of me, which I know sounds ridiculous. Those few dates with Nicola were nothing more than pointless and hollow experiences, and I had to tell her honestly that I'm just not available emotionally for a relationship or even meaningless dating. I wonder if I ever will be...I wonder if I even want to be. Some part of me feels like it's a penance of sorts for what I did. I shouldn't have lied to Celeste, used the experiment to put myself in front of her that way, knowing that she would likely comply because of the circumstances. But I was scared. Scared she might choose someone else, or worse...that she wouldn't even want me without the desperation born of being alone.

Another dream about her. Sweet and soft and turned erotic. I woke up aroused but couldn't do anything about it. When I touch myself there's nothing. That part of myself is empty as well. I want to regret what I did but I can't, not all of it. I regret hurting her but I don't regret being with her. How could I? Not when it made me <u>feel</u>.

I've been selfish, and even as I did it I knew I was being selfish and that selfishness hurt her. Hurts me. And here I am, about to put myself in front of her again. I'm so scared. Scared she'll send me away when I turn up on her doorstep. Scared she might not feel the same way. Scared of how I deeply I feel, and mostly I think I'm scared that I'll never be able to move past this without her. I don't know how to let go of how I feel so I can live my life again. But I don't think I want to let this feeling go.

That's it. I can't read any more. I leave some kibble for the boys, grab my coat and rush out to the garage.

CHAPTER TWENTY-FOUR

The rain is back and has brought more howling wind with it. Fat raindrops batter my windscreen as I drive at a crawl and park outside the only motel in town. Pulling my coat over my head, I rush across the lot and duck under the covered walkway running along the inside of the horseshoe-shaped complex. There's light showing through the drawn curtains of room twelve. She's still awake even though it's...shit, almost half-past one. Seems her nocturnal habits haven't changed.

I knock softly on the door and listen for footsteps. A pause. Chain dragging. The door opens. The raw relief on her face is evident. "You came."

"Yes. Sorry it's late."

Without hesitation, Olivia pulls the door back to let me inside and we're in one another's space again. I shrug out of my jacket and hang it on the wooden hook beside the door. I don't know if I should touch her or not. Do we hug? Does she want that? Less than nine hours ago, she kissed me then ran away. There's an awkward beat, before she takes a half step backward.

I don't know if it's because she doesn't want to be near me, or if she doesn't trust me…or herself.

She's wearing a pair of sweatpants that I immediately recognize from the habitat, the pair with the small tear above the knee. I gave her those sweatpants to wear the morning after we first met. "Aren't those mine?" Well, technically not *mine* but they were mine when I lived in that place.

"They are." She averts her gaze for a moment. "We gave everything to charity as you requested but I wanted these. I… needed them." Her hands smooth over the front of her thighs.

Needed a piece of clothing. My brain skips. Needed me?

Desperate for a distraction from the anxiety taking over my body, I look around the worn room. One queen bed, a table with two chairs, and a television bolted to the wall. Strewn over the table are papers and folders, a laptop and her tablet. Olivia makes a vague sweeping gesture as she walks across the room to the kitchenette. "Take a seat wherever you want. Do you want coffee?"

Guess that takes care of my indecision about touching her. "Sure, thanks." I settle onto a chair, running my fingers over the chipped Formica tabletop.

"They've only got instant." She grins and for a moment she's the woman I remember from our time together. "What kind of establishment expects a guest to drink instant coffee? Though I guess it's better than Al's sludge. Just."

Her grin is contagious, but my answering smile is still shy. "This place isn't exactly the height of sophistication."

"No," she agrees, that grin still turning her lips up. "But I like this town. It's got a good feeling and I think these people would actually stop for you if you were stranded on the side of the road. You chose a great place to settle, Celeste."

I stare at her tearing open a small packet of coffee and suddenly she's my Liv again, the woman who loves few things more than lingering over coffee. I think of mornings by her side as we sipped from steaming mugs. Curled together on the couch, talking, laughing. I think of her favorite mug, the blue one with a white stripe ringing it and the chipped handle. The one she took from the dwelling and had on her desk in that fancy place.

"Celeste?"

I startle. "Yes?"

"Would you prefer tea instead?" asks Liv, who claimed she'd never drunk tea in her life. I believed her, as I now believe everything else she told me before I knew about The Lie.

"No thanks. Coffee's fine." I know I won't sleep if I drink coffee this late. But then again, I was never going to sleep, even if I hadn't opened that folder and read everything she's written about us.

There are no words between us now, just the sound of her making coffee with a plastic spoon and an old kettle. My fingers feel too long for my hands, like they're going to fumble everything I touch. I peek at them. They are the same as always. I'm unchanged, yet I feel so different. Olivia sets a mug in front of me and I can tell it's made just the way I like it—a mug that's half cold milk and half coffee. I glance up. "You remember."

"I remember everything," she responds, her voice a husky whisper.

"Thank you." I swallow a tepid mouthful. Instant aside, it's perfect. "Why did you kiss me before and then run away from me?"

Her lips part, as though the question surprises her. She only pauses a moment before answering, "I kissed you because I wanted to, because I'd wanted to from the moment I saw you." She shrugs, her smile rueful. "And…I ran away because I panicked. I couldn't stand that I'd done that to you again, sprung it on you and exposed you to my weakness. I guess I was just a bit freaked out."

"Okay. That makes sense." I drink another mouthful then set the mug down. "I read those things you left me."

Olivia lowers herself heavily to the chair, like she started to sit but then gave up and let herself fall. "Oh. And?"

"Was it the truth?"

"Every word."

I'd suspected as much because what reason would she have to lie to herself in months of journaling? Slowly, I nod. "Olivia, I just don't know how I feel. Even after all this time I can't label it. I miss you, I miss the time we had but I still hate what you did and I hate myself for being such an idiot."

"Celeste—"

I lift my hand. "Please let me talk. I hate what you did, even though I understand why you did it." Deep breath. Relax. "I need to know something, away from your job. I just need you to answer me, truthfully with real spoken words. I need you to tell me, not you the Assistant Director of Whatever Corp USA, not you the scientist, but *you*. I think I deserve it."

"I can do that," she says evenly.

"If you felt that way about me then why did you do it? Everyone would have known that even if I hadn't found out, coming in and being with me...that way, would make me fall apart after you'd left. If you love me, how could you do that to me?"

Olivia blows out a breath, is silent for long moments. "Because I *had* to. Me, the woman who'd fallen in love with you. Not me the scientist." She swallows hard, fingers tightening on the mug. "I regret the circumstances, deeply regret that I hurt you, but I can't regret what we shared because it was one of the most incredibly intimate and fulfilling things I've ever experienced. I already told you, Celeste, you make me weak. But aside from that, I suppose I thought I could help you from the outside after I'd left, make it easier for you to deal with the absence."

"Nothing would have made it easier," I insist hoarsely. "Because it felt so right and so real that the moment you left everything became colorless, empty, like someone had sucked everything good out of my world."

"I'm so sorry," she says, the words taut with emotion. "It was all real for me too."

Slowly, I turn the mug in circles on the table. The grating of ceramic on Formica is oddly comforting. I glance at her. "At the start I thought what I felt was just because of the situation, like my thoughts had been warped so much that I only latched on to you because you were there."

"I know."

"But it's not true. When you left, I knew it wasn't false. It's the truest, purest feeling I've ever had. I love you, Olivia." My voice cracks, breaking up awkwardly. "I can't help myself. I've thought about you pretty much every day since you left, and until I saw you, I thought I was doing okay, you know? I'd grieved for us, for what happened and I'd moved on. Really I had. But I know now that I was just *existing*. Everything was rushing past me so fast I couldn't grab any of it."

"I know what you mean," she whispers.

"My biological mother died," I tell her. Olivia doesn't respond but she reaches out to take my hand, squeezing it reassuringly. I stare at my fingers curled around hers and am suddenly overwhelmingly calm. "She had some things she left for me, useless stuff mostly but there was a letter."

"Do you want to talk about it?"

"No. Not about the specifics but...I do want to talk about what it made me realize."

"What's that, darling?"

Darling. I've missed that word so much. "I realize that for my whole life, I've held Mother up as an ogre, a monstrosity. I felt like she overshadowed and undermined everything, influenced everything in my life. Always there chipping away at my foundations. And I think I've built her up to be more than what she was. I mean, she was awful and she did awful things but *I'm* the one who gave her all the power to hold me back."

Slowly, she nods. "What you felt and experienced during your childhood was valid, Celeste. *Is* valid. The same is true of your feelings about what happened in the habitat, about...what I did. Don't discount that."

"I won't. I'm not. I mean I *know* I'm allowed to feel these things. But it's like I can't even trust my own memories about Mother anymore. Some of it I know is true but I wonder how much of it I've forgotten, maybe the not-so-bad stuff she did? It can't have all been bad right? I feel like I've weighted my scales so that I can blame every bad or uncomfortable or upsetting thing I've ever experienced, everything that has ever gone wrong for me, on her. But now I think that's not fair. Not fair to her, and not fair to me."

Using just her forefinger, Olivia pushes her mug aside. "Can I offer an opinion?"

"Yes, of course."

"I think you've done what you needed to in order to live and move forward. You've lived in *your* reality, the same way your mother and sister lived theirs. What was true for you may not have been for them, but that doesn't make it any less real. It just makes it yours."

I can't help smiling. "When did you get so smart?"

"I've always been this smart." She laughs. Then the laughter fades, and she grows quiet and contemplative. "I just wasn't allowed to let you see it."

The somberness of the second statement reminds me of everything that was in the way of us. "Mmmm." My fingers tighten on hers. "Liv, I'm sorry."

"For what?"

"I behaved badly. I let this thing expand until it took up every piece of me when I should have dealt with it and moved on. Hanging on to things like this causes nothing but upset. It eats away at you until there's nothing left but misery. I thought I'd already learned that lesson but apparently not well enough. I should have let it go."

Liv's eyebrows rise but she lets me keep talking. "What you did was cruel and it was underhanded, but it was also within the boundary of what was allowed. I signed up for the experiment and you stuck to the rules. I took all the anger I should have directed at myself for being so naïve, gullible, and ignorant out on you." I draw a deep breath around tears that want to be free. "But you coming here is still unfair. It's unfair to come back and then leave again. You can't expect me to give you everything only to have it snatched away again. I can't spend my life putting myself back together over and over again."

"I don't expect that from you, Celeste. I don't expect anything. I hope and I dream, but I have no expectations." She doesn't attempt to stop her own tears. They slide slowly down her cheeks, over her chin. "And I would never take anything away from you. Not even myself," she adds hoarsely.

"Don't cry. Please don't cry." Even as I say it I know that telling someone not to cry is the stupidest thing.

Her mouth twists in a helpless kind of expression. "I just don't know what to do. What to say to you," she admits. "I tried not to come here, but it was the same as trying not to come to you in the compound. I can't stay away."

"I'm glad you came. Maybe it's too late, but I know now that being apart and not having you is infinitely harder than being upset with you. I can't do it anymore, Liv. I'm so exhausted."

"It's not too late." Olivia slides off the chair and moves to me. She gently pushes my knees apart and crouches between them. Her cheeks are wet with tears, her voice choked when she says again, "I'm sorry, Celeste."

"I know. I am too." Now I'm about three seconds away from crying as well.

Arms slide around my waist and she drops her face into my lap. "I'm sorry," she repeats, almost panicked now. "I love you."

"Come here." I tug at her, trying to get her to stretch up where I can kiss her. "Please. Come here."

She pushes herself up and launches herself at me, almost toppling my chair over backward. Her arms loop around my neck and her body presses hard against mine. Our kiss is hungry, needy, almost consuming me with its ferocity. I pull back, trying to catch my breath. "Slow time," I whisper.

She tilts her head, blinking rapidly but the fresh tears spill anyway. "With me?"

I nod and pull her onto my lap, kissing her again until the unnamed thing rises within me—the thing that's more than arousal or desire. It's stronger than lust or even love. It's a deep need, the deepest I've ever had, to be loved, to be known, to be needed and understood. And she gives me all those things without even seeming to realize it.

I'm content to just kiss her, to feel her hands against my face and the familiar press of her breasts to mine. Content that is, until she makes that groaning sound at the back of her throat I remember so well. When I hear it, I don't care about anything except being naked with her. It doesn't matter if we don't make love, I just need to feel her bare skin against me. "Please, Liv," I choke out.

Her eyes swing back and forth, searching my face. "What, darling?"

"Let me touch you, all of you, please." My words tremble with urgency.

She yanks me up and to the bed, where we frantically undress. I need to kiss and touch every millimeter of her until my lips and tongue and hands remember. My fingers move of their own accord, seeking and soothing. I trace the scar on her thigh. My scar.

"You were always with me, Celeste," she murmurs. "Even when you weren't." Her hand closes around mine and she pulls my fingers into her mouth. She sucks them like a piece of candy, her tongue sliding languorously over my skin.

The movement of her tongue reminds me of other times and other places. Her eyes are dark and watchful with that look I know so well. She wants this as much as I do. We come together again, but we don't fight for the upper hand. We move together and with every brush of lips and tongue, I know this is real.

Looking down at her I have a sudden, unexpected feeling that I could bury my face in her neck and just cry. Cry for what I almost lost. Cry for the hurt and the wasted time we let come between us. Liv soothes me with soft words and caresses and when she reaches up and pulls me down for another kiss it's sweet and gentle, as though all our urgency from earlier has evaporated.

She rolls me over to reverse our positions. Her hands find my breasts, a thigh between my legs gives pressure and her tongue tastes the sweat sheening my skin. I know I'm saying things, but I can't quite make sense of them with all the sensations she's evoking clouding my thoughts. But Liv understands and she settles between my legs. She slides her tongue through my wetness before taking my heat in her mouth to gently lick and suck me.

I can't breathe, I can't find words except endless yeses and I can't think about anything, except how good it feels and how much I want to come in her mouth. Liv's hand clasps mine as she flicks her tongue over the underside of my clit. A low moan slips from my throat and she does it again and again until I come on a strangled cry, soaring above pure physical pleasure to some plane far above what I'd ever known.

She stays with me, hot breath on the inside of my thigh until I float back to solidify in my body again. "I've missed that so much," she murmurs against my skin.

I want to say something deep and meaningful, something that will convey just how empty I've been without her but the only words that come to mind are, "Me too."

Wet, open-mouth kisses make a pilgrimage over my belly and breasts. The weight of her on me is comforting, like a blanket in the winter. I wrap my arms around her waist and roll us onto our sides to face one another. Our bodies slip together, the sweat left from our reacquaintance removing all traces of friction. I stroke her leg, up the inside of her thigh to brush light fingers over damp curls.

"I haven't been able to come," she confesses. "Not since you…"

"I know, sweetheart. You told me."

An eyebrow scrunches down for a moment and then she smiles with surprising shyness. "I told you keeping logs was a good idea."

"Mmm." I brush hair away from her eyes. In this light they are less caramel and more maple syrup. "I haven't either, not until just now."

She swallows thickly. "What if I can't?"

Some gross cocky part of me wants to strut and swagger, because she hasn't been able to climax since the last one I gave her, so of course it's me who will be able to make her come. But she doesn't need that. She needs sweetness and reassurance. She needs the words that she once gave to me. I kiss her softly and press my forehead to hers. "It doesn't matter, Liv. It's not about that. It's about you and me, and it's about this." My hand finds her heat. "It's about us."

Her eyes close partway and she pushes into my hand, begging me with her body. My fingers slip and glide through her folds and my own body clenches with fresh arousal when I feel how much she wants this. Wants me. "You're so wet." I kiss her neck, lingering as I murmur, "Is this for me, baby?"

"Yes," she gasps as my fingers brush her clit. Then in the next heartbeat she tenses, her voice tremulous. "Celeste, I'm… what if I can't—"

Gently, I shush her. Kiss her. Soothe her. "No more *can't*, baby, and no more talking. Except to tell me what you want me to do to you."

Olivia groans at the light touch of my fingers to her entrance, her hands loosely fisted in my hair. "Oh, God. Just make love to me."

Love.

Not fuck.

She wants me to love her.

I do love her, I never stopped loving her. Every part of me loves every part of her and now I need to show her. I need to make her remember us. And if she doesn't, I'll remember enough for both of us until she catches up to me. I want to be on top of her, to cover the length of her body with mine. I want to be inside her, to feel those muscles pulse and flutter around my fingers. I want to leave no part of her untouched, unkissed, or unworshipped.

"Inside me, please," she breathes, and when I glide into her, she groans.

My thrusts are gentle and shallow, fingers curling to find the spot that makes her breathing hitch and her toes press against my calf. When I kiss my way down her body, lingering on her breasts to suck her firm nipples into my mouth, she urges me on with increasingly incoherent encouragement.

I feel her desperation with every tense and release of her muscles, in the clench around my fingers and the way she begs me. When I settle between her thighs and spread her apart, Liv's breathing grows even shorter and more erratic. I draw in a slow breath at the sight of her puffed and shining with desire.

I kiss her gently, my nose against her curls and I taste that desire. Liv moans, an unabashed sound of surrender and a small part of me takes pleasure in it because the sound is all for me. It's *me* she wants, and it's me that's going to give her exactly what she needs.

There is time enough for teasing later, right now I just have to feel her glorious climax. I make long firm strokes with my tongue to bring her to the edge, exactly the way she likes. Then when she begins to crest, she will want a light touch, circles around her clit, and gentle lips to carry her over. Nails dig into my shoulders. Hips lift to meet me.

She's so vocal now, a long keening cry of, "Ohmygodpleaseplease...*please*." Her ass muscles clench, pushing her even more forcefully up into my mouth. She's so close all it would take is a light swirl of my tongue around her clit. I pinch a nipple between thumb and forefinger, rolling it gently back and forth, loving every miniscule tremble and twitch of her body.

This coordinated dance of hands and fingers and body and tongue is something I thought I'd lost. With a final, breathy whisper of my name, she begs me to finish her, to make her come. I suck her between my lips and do exactly what she wants, and when I run the flat of my tongue around her clit she explodes and floods my mouth. I can't help my groan of pleasure as *her* pleasure covers my tongue.

Liv squirms and shudders, her hand stroking my hair. She whispers something that I think sounds like *thank you* but I can't be sure because my blood is thrumming so loudly in my ears. I make my way back up the bed to lie beside her and she pulls our bodies together so we're face-to-face. Our kisses are sweet and slow.

Time stretches. It gives me every millisecond like a precious gift. I close my eyes and snuggle into her. Liv pulls the covers up and she's saying something, but I'm already drifting away, thinking of having endless slow time with her.

Light passes through the curtains and the sound of cars outside on the main street startles me awake. It's stopped raining. She's still with me in this motel bed, our limbs twined together like vine and tree. I touch her chin. Her cheek. Her nose. She smiles and reaches up to grab my hand. "That tickles."

I replace my fingertips with my lips and after a thorough good morning kiss, she sighs. It's a smiling, contented kind of sigh. "Are you okay?" she asks me.

After a moment's pause, I answer, "Yes."

"But?"

I capture her hand and kiss her palm. "But…I'm confused about where we go from here. I don't know what this means." Are we together now, dating? And if we are, can I bear to see her only at weekends or whenever she can make time for me during the week between her job? I can't leave Jekyll and Hyde from Friday to Sunday night while I go visit her.

"I want to keep seeing you."

"Me too. But I'm just not sure what that looks like."

She barely takes a breath before she says, "I told you, I like this town, it has a nice feel to it." She hitches my leg over her thigh and draws patterns on my skin with her nails. "I'm growing tired of big cities and daily commutes."

I pause, trying to decipher the words. "Are you implying what I think you are? If you are, then you have to say it, Liv. I don't want any uncertainty. Not after all our other half-truths and confusion."

Her hand moves to my cheek, her gaze unwavering. "I want to move here, or somewhere nearby. I want to live close to you because I want us to try dating or being a couple or whatever you want to call it. I want that because I love you and the thought of being away from you makes me feel like I can't breathe. And I promise, no more secrets." She laughs. "You already know what I do, so I don't have to hide it from you."

"Okay, but what about that research, and your job? How can you do that from here?" I don't even know why I'm asking, as though some part of me still wants to sabotage this gift she's offering me.

"I can easily work remotely. Once a month or so I will need to go back to Seattle for a few days for meetings and planning sessions but other than that…" She shrugs, leaving all that's unsaid linger between us. She wants to be here with me and will do what she can to make it work. "I mean, it will take a few months to get everything set up for me to work offsite so we might have to have a breaking-in trial period. If you don't mind having me as a weekend houseguest until I can move?"

"I don't mind," I say immediately. "They'd really let you do that?"

"Yes, I can do pretty much whatever I want, Celeste. My father is one of the Directors of The Organization. He didn't just get me a job, he created a department for me to run. Why do you think I'm still working there after what I did? I mean, I'm very good at what I do but there's a little bit of nepotism at work here." She grins cheekily.

"Ah, lucky."

The smile dims. "Yes, very. When I came home, Papà put on his Director's hat for about three minutes to give me a dressing down for potentially compromising the study. Then he hugged me until I stopped crying and told me it'd be all right in the end."

I swallow this piece of information. She cried over me. I roll onto my back, pulling her on top of me. "You'd leave everything to live in Nowhere, USA with me?"

"I've already lived in Nowhere, USA with you, Celeste." She laughs. "And I loved every second of it. I don't want to be apart from you anymore, it's too hard." Liv steals a kiss then rests her forehead against my cheek. When she blinks, her eyelashes tickle me.

I grunt, then pull slightly away. "Butterfly kisses." After a pause I add, "Riley used to do that."

Liv's response is quiet, almost gentle. "She did?"

"Mhmm. I never told you that, did I? I never told anyone while I was in that place?"

"No, darling. You never did," she says earnestly. Her eyes widen, willing me to believe her.

And I do.

Olivia is the thing that keeps air in my lungs, blood moving through my veins. If she leaves me again, or I her, I don't think I would survive it. Everything is already there, right under the surface, just waiting for me to be brave enough to give her my yeses again. I swallow my uncertainty and my worry and give her my truth. "Liv, I just…love you and I need you. It's as simple as that."

"I need you too, darling. I'm going to stay with you for as long as you'll keep me."

"You promise? You won't leave me again?" It sounds so needy and childish but losing her again is now my deepest fear.

Olivia's smile is soft, her eyes gentle, and when she speaks I know she's telling me the truth. "No, Celeste. I love you. I promise I'm not going to leave."

EPILOGUE

Samantha, wearing blood-spattered scrubs and paying no attention to the fact I turned the sign from *Open* to *Closed* ten minutes ago, breezes through the door. "Tell me you haven't cleaned that machine yet." She makes good use of the thirty-dollar-per-week coffee subscription I offer for locals, coming by twice every day for a takeaway and a chat between clients. Then she sneaks a pastry and waves goodbye as she walks out with it already in her mouth. But my good friend gives me free vet consults, and flea and worm treatments for the boys and my Seven Dwarfs goats. Everything works out in the end.

"Another minute and I would have told you to go away." I start on her usual tall extra-shot skim latte.

"You're a goddess disguised as a mortal."

I huff a dramatic sigh and fake a hair flip. "I know."

Samantha leans on the counter, watching the progress of her coffee like a parent watching the birth of a child. She raps her knuckles on the counter made of polished wood I sourced from old railroad ties. "Oh! Shit, also sorry but not really sorry. I have to cancel girls' night tonight. Brad wants to take me out again."

I whistle through my teeth. "Well well well, lucky you. I suppose I'll just have to drink wine and have a rom-com marathon all on my own." Liv isn't due back from Seattle until late tomorrow, and as is customary for the nights my girlfriend is away, Samantha and I hang out with wine and takeout and movies, and talk shit until we fall asleep on the couch.

"I hate thinking of you all alone, and I was totally going to turn him down but he wants to show me his prize-winning bull." She scrunches up her shoulders. "Isn't that the cutest thing?"

"Is it a euphemism?" Instead of the usual animal I make in Samantha's latte foam, I do a decidedly lewd interpretation of *Brad's Prize Winning Bull*.

Samantha's eyes widen. "Actually, I don't know." Her lips curve into a cheeky grin. "But now that I think about it, lord help me I hope it is."

"I don't even want to know." I leave the lid off the takeaway, slide the cup over to her and wait until she has had a good hard look at what I've drawn in the foam.

Samantha bursts into laughter when she notices, both eyebrows bouncing up and down as she raises the cup to her mouth. "Come by once you've closed up, I did a cesarean this afternoon and I swear these are the cutest kittens I've ever seen."

Every kitten is the cutest kitten she's ever seen. "How about I drop by tomorrow before I open, and you can also tell me about this...bull."

"Oh I will," she says airily. Samantha leans over the counter to hug me and swans out of the store as brightly as she came in.

"Have fun," I call at her departing back.

I double-check the sign really does say *Closed* and get to work finishing up. Breaking down and cleaning the coffee machine is mindless second-nature work, the kind I love, the kind that lets me think about Liv. This work trip is slightly longer than usual, with an extra meeting to go through a new client contract. She'll call me late tonight to let me know how it went, and if Samantha was there, I would have hidden in the bathroom for ten minutes while my girlfriend said dirty things to me and made me listen to her pleasuring herself.

Even though our time apart isn't long by any stretch, the absence of Olivia is everywhere and not just at home. Since I opened this place four months ago, she's come by every day for lunch and her second coffee of the day, then driven back home to work for the afternoon and to wait for me. Our domesticity is the target of good-natured teasing from our friends in town but I barely even remember what it was like before. Without her.

It didn't take me long to get used to the differences between that time living together and this time. The smell of her perfume and her wearing makeup when she leaves the house. Her working until late and sliding into bed to slip into my arms and pillow her head on my breasts. The odd way she folds laundry and doesn't care if she leaves books and papers strewn over the table. Now our shared space is my haven. Olivia is my safe place.

My day's totals balance and I send a silent thanks to the accounting gods who have smiled favorably on me. Everything is locked away and I'm just doing one last wipe down of the counters when the door opens. "Sorry, we're closed," I say as I turn around.

Liv smiles, unbuttoning her long cashmere coat. "Well, that's a pity. I have a craving for something tasty."

I drop the cloth and spray bottle on the counter and cross the floor in three long strides to pull her into a hug. In the nine months since she moved here, Liv's flown back to Seattle eight times, mostly only for two or three days. But when she comes back and I hug her again, I feel like I've been holding my breath the entire time she's been away.

"You're home early. Thank you." I frame her face gently with my hands and kiss her. She responds as she always does when we kiss, with a gentle sigh as if all her worries have suddenly left her. "Missed you," I murmur.

"Missed you too." She kisses me again. "Sorry to barge in on girls' night."

"Not that it matters, but you didn't. She canceled on me because of Brad's bull." At Liv's slow eyebrow raise, I laugh and tell her, "You probably don't want to know."

"No, sounds like I don't," she drawls.

"I'm almost done here if you can wait a minute?"

"Darling, I'll wait longer than a minute for you." Olivia shoos me back to the counter.

She watches from the other side as I get to work rushing through my final cleaning. "How'd the meetings go?"

"Good. We got the contract."

"Congratulations, honey. You worked so hard on it." I set my cloth and bottle under the counter. "What about the figure? Did they agree?"

"Celeste..." Liv reaches for me, pulling me close. "I don't want to talk about work."

"What do you want to talk about then?" I kiss her neck.

"I want to talk about the dinner we're going to make, the bottle of wine I'm going to open, the long hot bath we'll take... and then the hours I'm going to spend showing you exactly how much I missed you." She slips her hands under my shirt, nails carefully scratching my skin.

I close my eyes. "If you keep doing that, we're not going to make it home."

She laughs lightly, and withdraws her teasing hands. "You don't let me have any fun."

"I let you have plenty." I make a deft subject change, knowing if I don't then I'm going to drag her in back and let her have all the fun she wants with me and then we'll never get home for her hot bath and wine. "How're your parents?" I shrug into my coat and guide her toward the door.

"They're both well. Papà wants you to know he bought a new Scrabble board, and I have a letter from Mamma to give to you."

"A letter?"

"Mmm, if I had to guess the contents, I'd say it's thanking you for the lovely book and then a passive-aggressive paragraph about why you haven't visited for two months."

"Noted. You told her we'd both be there next month for your birthday, right?"

"I did, yes." Her eye roll tells me that her mom still thinks that's too far away. "Oh...and I received *another* underhanded dig about the grandchildren thing." She exaggerates her accent, gesturing expansively. "Oof! It is getting so late, Olivia, and you are getting so old. If you and your Celeste wish to start a family then you need to do it soon!"

My tummy drops and lifts like I'm riding a rollercoaster. "Oh. Did you say anything?"

"Aside from mentioning that we've talked about it? No, I thought we'd wait until it was certain." She doesn't even bother disguising her joy.

We've done more than talk about it. She's had checks and tests, and next month, we're going to try. When I think about her with our child in her belly then later nurturing it at her breast, me raising a child with her, my heart grows so full I think it could actually burst if any more love were to be put into it. "I love you."

"Love you even more."

Arms around her waist, I keep her close. "Good. Looks like we figured out a way to procreate after all, habitat or no habitat."

"Yes, we did." Her low chuckle echoes through the café. "If we're going to have a baby, we should probably get married then, right?"

"Probably," I agree. The words sink in, and my heart flutters like it wants to leap from my chest and run a victory lap. "Did you just propose?"

Both eyebrows lift in surprise. "Actually, I think I might have. Did you just accept?"

"Yes," I blurt.

"Good." She kisses me fiercely, possessively. "Come on, let's go. I want to see if sex with your fiancée is as incredible as sex with your girlfriend."

I laugh and usher her out of the café. When I turn around to lock the doors, her loving hand finds its way under my coat to stroke my back. Liv says hello to someone across the street, and brief conversation about the weather is called back and forth. I can't help smiling at how perfectly pedestrian it all is.

"I'm parked just over there beside you," she says.

The air is cool, hinting at frost in the early hours, the crispness bringing clarity. I lift my face to the late afternoon sky as her hand snakes into mine. A memory teases at the edge of my thoughts—a log entry from that time, of things I missed— walking down the street holding hands with someone. She's holding my hand and we're walking down the street. I lean into her, squeezing her fingers.

Liv's voice is quiet and curious. "What are you thinking about?"

There are so many things in my head that I could never find words for, but I focus on one important thing. "Just…how I finally feel like I'm where I should be, but it's even better than I imagined."

"It is?" she asks teasingly.

"Mhmm, because I have all these things plus the things I never even knew I wanted." The words spill out in an emotional, nonsensical jumble. "And now I have them, or I'm going to have them, and I can't help but wonder how I never knew what I needed. Until you came along and showed me what I could have and what things could be like."

She raises our joined hands and kisses the back of mine. "I always knew, Celeste. Even before you told me you loved me, I knew this is what I wanted. And I can never tell you how much it means to me that I'm sharing it with you."

Smiling, I let out a little huff as everything hits me at once, all those hopes and dreams come true. A world of possibility stretched out in front of me.

Liv nudges me gently. "What?"

"Still just thinking, is all."

"About what now?"

"My friends. Starting a family." Sliding an arm around her waist, I pull her to a stop, bringing her close for a soft kiss. "*You.*" I have to blink away tears, and when I finally manage to speak again, it's choked and hoarse. "I'm not alone."

"No, darling," she agrees softly. "You're not. I'm here, and you'll never be alone."

Bella Books, Inc.

Women. Books. Even Better Together.

P.O. Box 10543
Tallahassee, FL 32302

Phone: 800-729-4992
www.bellabooks.com